W9-BFV-561

LOCKDOWN

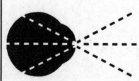

This Large Print Book carries the
Seal of Approval of N.A.V.H.

LOCKDOWN

A NOVEL OF SUSPENSE

LAURIE R. KING

THORNDIKE PRESS
A part of Gale, Cengage Learning

MAURICE M. PINE
FREE PUBLIC LIBRARY
10-01 FAIR LAWN AVE.
FAIR LAWN, NJ 07410

GALE
CENGAGE Learning·

Farmington Hills, Mich • San Francisco • New York • Waterville, Maine
Meriden, Conn • Mason, Ohio • Chicago

GALE
CENGAGE Learning®

LIBRARY OF CONGRESS CATALOGING-IN-PUBLICATION DATA

Names: King, Laurie R., author.
Title: Lockdown / by Laurie R. King.
Description: Large print edition. | Waterville, Maine : Thorndike Press, a part of Gale, a Cengage Company, 2017. | Series: Thorndike Press large print mystery
Identifiers: LCCN 2017021436 | ISBN 9781410499103 (hardcover) | ISBN 1410499103 (hardcover)
Subjects: LCSH: Psychological fiction. | Large type books. | BISAC: FICTION / Mystery & Detective / Historical. | FICTION / Mystery & Detective / Traditional British. | FICTION / Mystery & Detective / Women Sleuths. | GSAFD: Suspense fiction.
Classification: LCC PS3561.I4813 L64 2017b | DDC 813/.54—dc23
LC record available at https://lccn.loc.gov/2017021436

Published in 2017 by arrangement with Bantam Books, an imprint of Penguin Random House, a division of Penguin Random House LLC

Printed in the United States of America
1 2 3 4 5 6 7 21 20 19 18 17

*For all the children who came here
from somewhere else*

From the notes of Dr. Cassandra Henry, school psychologist, turned over to the San Felipe Police Department following the Guadalupe Middle School incident.

LIVES COMING TOGETHER

SUM OF ITS PARTS

A COMMUNITY BUILT OF PIECES

GUADALUPE STAFF:
Linda McDonald — principal, caring, smart. Listens.
(Gordon Kendrick, Linda's husband — school volunteer. British, 70s.)
"Tío" (Jaime Rivera Cruz) — school janitor, hired October. What was he before??
"Coach" (Joseph) Gilbert — Nick Clarkson's granddad, coach & math teacher. Retired — temp position since January.

STUDENTS:
Nick Clarkson (6th grade) — client.
Brendan Atcheson (8th grade) — basketball, v. good-looking. Chip on his shoulder?
"Mina" (Yasmina) Santos (8th grade) — friend of many esp. Sofia. Not Mexican-American.
Sofia Rivas (8th grade) — basketball <u>last</u> year, not since sister <u>Gloria Rivas</u> was killed.

"Chaco" (Santiago) Cabrera (7th grade) — cousin to Taco Alvarez. Tries hard to live up to it.

(Bee Cuomo — was 6th-grader. Friends: Nick, others??)

CAREER DAY GUEST SPEAKERS:

Thomas Atcheson — Brendan's father, biggest Name in San Felipe: problem for B?

CAREER DAY

GUADALUPE MIDDLE SCHOOL
The Dark Hours

■ ■ ■ ■

BRENDAN

Brendan dropped to one knee in the dim alley, watching for motion at the far end. He'd already been hit once. Plus that, he was low on ammo — but his pulse was racing so fast his finger wanted to jerk down on the trigger, spraying the filthy bricks and Dumpsters with his last bullets. (And that would be the end of *everything*.)

The Enemy darted from left to right, bringing a compulsive twitch that wasted a couple of rounds, but Brendan forced his finger to pull back. The guy'd have to come out to fire, and when he did, crimson splatter would fill the —

"Brendan? Brendan James Atcheson, if you're still playing that *goddamn* game . . ."

The alley vanished into black screen as Brendan leapt in the direction of bed. But as he moved, his foot brushed the basketball sitting on the floor. He nearly went back for it — the thing was rolling directly toward

11

the door — but he couldn't risk it, just dove under the covers and jerked them to his ear like a child. As if blankets could be armor against the approaching threat.

He forced his face to go slack, struggled to control his breathing. When the light from the doorway spilled against his eyelids, his heart beat faster than when he'd been facing death in the alleyway. He waited: for Sir to step inside, lay his hand on the warm game console, spot the basketball in motion. For Sir to . . .

THOMAS

Tom closed his son's door quietly. He knew perfectly well Brendan wasn't asleep. He probably should have gone in and forced a confrontation, in spite of the hour. But if Tom had to deal with the boy's attitude on top of everything else — well, even a reasonable man had his limits. And that "goddamn" he'd let slip just now . . .

Only the desperate swore.

Yes, a confrontation with Brendan was necessary — and soon: the boy was getting way too full of himself. Just not tonight.

Tonight he simply needed Brendan to go the *hell* to sleep, so he could focus on tomorrow. Conquering adversity was what Thomas Atcheson did, the thing that had carved him a place at the top of a cutthroat industry. Give him a locked door, he'd find another way. Show him a dead end, he'd chisel a path through it. Present him with strikes, incompetence, and a Byzantine

13

permit process, and he'd still manage to build a campus that won awards.

His competitors had learned that, to their detriment; his former partner, even his ex-wife. The current situation was no different, no matter how high the stakes. There was sure to be a loose end in this maddening tangle of emergencies, threats, and frustrations. Absolutely *had* to be. All he needed was to find the end of that thread, and it would lead him to the solution.

The boy didn't know how good he had it, being able to sleep.

12:31 A.M.
LINDA

Sleep was proving every bit as elusive as Linda had feared. She'd thought about the pills — but the previous three months had taught her that on a day like tomorrow, chemical grogginess would be worse than mere fatigue. At least there was a mix of lacerations keeping her awake tonight, in place of the usual haunting regrets. It was almost a relief to stare at the dim ceiling and anticipate the things that *could* go wrong, letting her thoughts toss and turn instead of her body.

Paper cups will be fine, right? Nobody expects proper cups and glasses — and lunch itself will be off real plates. Wait: did I warn the speakers against wearing gang colors? Like that substitute who'd turned up in a blouse made of red bandanas and — oh, yes: that made it into the letter, after talking to Mrs. Hopkins about the Taco Alvarez trial.

What about the typo in the flyer — had

she corrected that? Her leg twitched with the impulse to get up and check — but no. Mrs. Hopkins had caught it, too.

Praise the heavens for school secretaries! And for the teachers (most of them) and the volunteers that Señora Rodriguez (*I do wish I could like that woman more*) had commandeered to help with Career Day. And the Social Studies department for the grant they'd got, and the old hippie who'd finished restoring the mural just in time — and not to forget "Tío" (was he actually anyone's "uncle"?) because, oh, what a difference a good janitor made in a school's life. (Ridiculous to be suspicious of the man: he lived to keep Guadalupe running smoothl—)

Dear God, had she been about to use the word *smoothly* about Guadalupe Middle School? A school bubbling with hormones and suppressed rage, with threats all around it and a huge, suppurating wound at its —

Linda snatched desperately at the downward spiral of her thoughts before the name Bee Cuomo could surface, and forced her mind back onto minutiae.

That loose button on her blouse! The blessed thing was *sure* to pop off at the worst possible moment. Like during school assembly, fifty minutes that was already fill-ing her with dread — and not only because she'd have to give a speech. The gym would be packed to the rafters with seven hundred–plus adolescents on the brink of boiling over, into impatience, mockery, even the violence that was never far away. A pressure cooker waiting for a perceived insult or a slip of the tongue . . . or a display of their principal's bra.

Do not *forget to wear the* blue *blouse tomorrow*!

Linda would bet that Olivia Mendez never went to work with a loose button. Ever-competent Sergeant Mendez of the San Felipe Police Department, watching Gordon walk across the distant playing field the other day, that too-intelligent, endlessly speculative gaze of hers . . .

As if she'd said it aloud, Gordon shifted on his pillow. "You're not sleeping."

"Oh hon, sorry, I didn't mean to wake you. I'll go make myself some tea."

"Worried about tomorrow?"

"You could say that. I can't help thinking I've set us all up for a . . . a catastrophe." She didn't even like to say the word aloud. "There must be something I'm overlooking."

"Linda, I cannot imagine you've overlooked *anything*."

17

Her laugh was forced. "Compulsive, right? When I was small, I'd lie awake and invent horrible scenarios. My parents dying, the neighbor's dog biting me. I must've heard someone say it's always the unexpected that creeps up on you, and figured if I could *imagine* a thing . . ." Her voice faded away.

"Dear heart, you have it all under control. You're prepared to the hilt, with good help, competent volunteers, a responsible team of guests. There's nothing to worry about. Tomorrow will go fine."

His calm voice almost made Linda . . . believe. *There's no restlessness in him, is there? You've been imagining problems, like you always do. This is Gordon, the most trustworthy man you know. There's no reason whatsoever to think —*

His arm came out then, to stroke warm fingers up and down her arm. Up, and down. Wordless, and hypnotic. Before long, her nerves ceased their rattling. Paper cups and loose buttons, vanished children and gang rivalries, bulldog police sergeants and too-efficient janitors and all the rest gathered together in a narrow stream, circled around a hole, and poured away into the darkness.

SOFIA

This little time between taking the pill and falling into it was the best. A melting time, warm and dark and comforting.

At school, Sofia stuck to half pills. They softened the edges without making her groggy. But at night, after everyone went to bed, she could let go. Here, in these slow minutes as the pill worked its way into her, there was no murdered sister, no Alvarez brothers looking hate at her, no pressures for grades or looks from Mina or missing sixth-graders or boys or . . . nothing.

Just the melting, rich and warm and delicious, tingling along the ends of your nerves, making the world soft and deep.

Some nights — not always — she was aware of a last, juddering breath, sucked into her chest just before she tipped into the dreams. Like a relieved infant settling into its mother's arms.

2:21 A.M.
BRENDAN

The fingers on Brendan's hand twitch when he dreams of guns.

One gun in particular: the Smith & Wesson 380 Bodyguard. There are loads of bigger ones, but Brendan suspects that big handguns are a sign of insecurity. (As in, *big gun, small dick* — something he'd *never* say to Sir, whose weapon of choice is a monster Glock 40.) And anyway, the Bodyguard speaks to Brendan. The way it looks, with the ruggedness of a revolver folded into the sleekness of an automatic. And a laser sight, which is just plain slick.

More than looks, he loves how it feels. The very first time he held it, the Bodyguard's twelve ounces of polymer and steel nestled into his palm like a puppy's head. Its sights seemed precisely engineered for his eyes alone, for the exact length of his arm, the trigger waiting for the touch of his finger to send the rounds, *powpowpow* — dead center

20

into the man's outline at the far end of the range. Perfect as dropping one in from the three-point line.

But now the dream is turning, as Brendan's dreams so often do. The weapon in his hand shifts, all on its own. The laser dot jerks away from the paper silhouette to track along the wall, forcing his elbow out, fighting his wrist into an impossible angle. The red spark travels across the other people in the gun range, people with no right to be there — Principal McDonald, Mina Santos, Jock. All of them oblivious to the danger. And still the sharp red light crawls, to the floor, up Brendan's body, touching his neck, his face.

Until he is looking straight at the Bodyguard's perfect mouth (knowing that there is one round still in the chamber). The red dazzles his eye. In the dream, his forefinger twitches —

And Brendan jerks upright in the sweaty sheets, throat raw with the fading cry.

THOMAS

Tom Atcheson looked up at the ceiling. Brendan?

He should have gone in and dragged the boy out of bed when he went to check on him two hours ago. Control was a tenuous thing, whether with a company in turmoil or a rebellious son. At least the boy was set for the academy next September: a real school would straighten him out.

Depending on others to solve the problem wasn't a sign of weakness or cowardice. Was it?

No: a man *had* to prioritize. He'd been right to shut the door and walk away.

This time.

True control — with work, with family — sometimes required an *appearance* of weakness. Vulnerability could be the leaves covering a trap.

Tom picked up his pen again.

He wasn't entirely happy with his plan for

22

the 9:00 a.m. board meeting, but he had to admit there wasn't much more he could do about it now — other than fire the entire board, of course, which according to his useless lawyers he was no longer in a position to do. And no *way* would he be maneuvered into surrender! What, turn over his business — to say nothing of that gorgeous campus he'd put his heart and soul into building — and take "early retirement"? He'd rather shoot himself.

Sleep might help, but he could tell that wasn't going to happen. Instead, he turned to his notes for the talk at Brendan's school. "Career Day." What an exercise in futility! Urging ill-trained children to become entrepreneurs was like telling finger-painters to aim for the Sistine Chapel: those with drive required no encouragement.

But the boy's principal had asked, and when Thomas Atcheson made a commitment, he kept it, no matter how pressed his day had become or how pointless the exercise might be.

Advice for young people? Obviously he had advice — for people of any age.

Don't trust your partners.

Don't marry a harpy with lawyers in her family.

Don't have a son who fights you at every turn.

And never, ever let people screw you into a corner.

2:45 A.M.
CHACO

Chaco put his head around the dark corner of A Wing, filled with . . . what was the word? *Foreboding.* Yeah, so the janitor made him nervous. Gave Chaco *misgivings.*

Scared the shit out of him.

Far as Chaco knew, *Tío* wasn't nobody's *uncle,* wasn't even from Mexico like everybody Chaco knew. Sure, he talked Spanish, but his accent was, like, *exotic* — from somewhere else. Nicaragua, maybe? El Salvador? Tío was just the limpiador, walking up and down in his dirt-colored uniform and cleaning the floors. Big thrill for the old guy was the day he got to shut off the water in the girls' baño, stop it running all over the floor. Real hero, man.

Maybe the reason Tío made him nervous was 'cause the dude was so pinche quiet. Tío talked quiet, he didn't turn on a radio the minute the bell rang — even his cart with all the mops and brooms, the same one

25

the last janitor used, didn't rattle and squeak so much. And, like, the other day when one of the substitutes shouted some question down the breezeway at him? Tío didn't just shout back an answer. Instead, he put away his broom and walked over, all polite, to see what the guy wanted.

Funny thing was, the teacher looked a little . . . Not *embarrassed.* More like he thought maybe Tío coming at him so quiet (*like Angel*) meant the old guy had a knife. *Edgy,* maybe? Wanting to *edge* away?

Anyway, yeah, Chaco felt a little *edgy* tonight himself, crouching in back of A Wing, away from the all-night floods, a can of spray paint in his hand. He really, *really* didn't want to turn around and find Tío there, looking at him.

Which was stupid. Or — what was that word he'd found the other day? — *ludicrous.* (Chaco had a private collection of perfect words — words he'd never, ever use out loud.) Tío didn't spend the night at school, and no way could he just guess who'd done a tag. Chaco knew all about crime labs and *forensic science* and stuff, so he was wearing a set of his uncle's overalls he'd fished out of the trash, and his most beat-up pair of shoes, and he'd dump it all on his way home. He'd take a shower in the morning

26

so he didn't smell like paint. How would Tío know?

Besides, there wasn't really much choice. He was almost thirteen — and he was family to Taco Alvarez.

So now, at near to three in the morning, Chaco the Tagger crept down the A Wing breezeway, the old rubber on his shoes making a kissing sound against the smooth concrete. Nothing moved, no cars went by. Under the main breezeway, into the entrance arch — and there it was, all shiny and new-looking, hundreds of little chips and tiles with pictures of school things and people on them. He hesitated, just a little, 'cause really, it was kind of dope. *Intricate,* like. And a man didn't tag someone else's art unless it was enemy action. But this was a school, and in the end he had to prove himself to Taco (*and Angel*) and yeah, to Sofia Rivas. Though she'd probably just give him one of her looks, all *arrogant,* or maybe *condescending.*

Chaco's arm went up to shake the can, making the little ball inside *ting* back and forth five, six times. He chose his spot with care, right there on the face of the school secretary for his first letter, and —

And as if the pressure of his finger had triggered a lot more than paint, the universe exploded into a blinding glare of flood-light, outlining every tile, giving texture to the grout, showing the cheerful expressions on a crowd of pieced-together figures.

The can bounced and skittered across the walkway as Chaco fled into the night.

GORDON

Gordon ran beneath the waning moon, fighting the need to circle the park.

The fight lay not in the running, but the circling back — although granted, three and a half years ago when he'd first made this circuit, he thought his lungs would explode. He'd been old, then: washed-up, worn-out, ready for the knacker's gun. Not *put out to pasture,* though. Men like Gordon Hugh-Kendrick were not generally granted a placid retirement. Men like him ran until they were brought down.

To his astonishment, it turned out he'd merely been tired: bloody tired and older than his years, so wretched he'd made one last mad, whimsical, despairing lunge for shelter — only to hit pure gold. Instead of a farewell tour, he'd found haven, and comfort, and a degree of purpose. The affection of a good woman.

Forty-four months later, Gordon was . . .

29

if not at the top of his form, certainly better than he could have dreamed. And surely the low cunning of age counted for more than the dumb muscle-mass of youth?

Which would be fine (he reflected, dodging a fallen crate on the road) but for two problems. One was specific: he'd got sloppy, back in September, and let his name appear where it should not. He couldn't even blame Linda, not entirely. Despite thirty years of rigid habit, he'd failed to check a list he knew was headed for the police department. And though five months on, he seemed to have dodged that particular bullet, he couldn't risk a second mistake.

The other problem was more general. With a fit body and faint return of optimism had come restlessness. The familiar itch of being in one place for too long; the inborn need for challenge — his kind of challenge, which was thin on the ground in a sleepy farm community of California's Central Coast. Hence the hard joy of running a little too fast through a hazard-strewn dark, and the temptation to keep going.

But not today.

He'd been honest with Linda from the beginning — well, more honest than he'd been with anyone for many a year. And not only had she lived up to his terms (apart from that one slip), she'd only just begun to sleep through the night again, fifteen weeks after the disappearance of Bee Cuomo. Gordon would cut his own throat before letting her down. Not forever — maybe not even for much longer — but today? Today was important to her.

So this morning he would circle the park and turn back. He would polish his shoes, shave his face, and don the appearance of an ordinary man, to spend the day walking amongst the unsuspecting.

OLIVIA

The early morning air had just taken on the oddly rich smell of celery when the figure dashed across the road at the limits of Olivia's headlights. Her hand snapped out to trigger the cruiser's lights and siren — then her front-brain caught up, canceling the cop's chase-impulse. No pre-dawn burglar, this, but the same gray-haired Englishman in khaki shorts she saw pretty much every time she was out this early. Linda's husband, Gordon . . . something. Not McDonald. Olivia had met the man a handful of times, but she'd seen him all over: Safeway, the library, coming out of a martial arts dojo, mowing his front lawn. Once, weirdly enough, up at the homeless encampment near the levee, squatting beneath the drifting smoke of their illegal cook-fire like some gung-ho anthropologist with a primitive tribe.

So what's your story, Gordon-not-

McDonald?

Back in September, she'd had the excuse to run a background check on him — a legitimate excuse, since his name was right there on Linda's list of volunteers. His hyphenated name . . . ah: Hugh-Kendrick, that was it, although he went by just Kendrick. Gordon Hugh-Kendrick, and could you get any more English than that?

He and Linda made for an unlikely couple — the twenty-odd-year difference in their ages; his thin/gray/British and her round/blond/Midwest — but they fit like pieces in a jigsaw puzzle. (Even if Olivia suspected that Gordon's piece belonged to an entirely different picture.)

Still, everyone was entitled to their privacy, and although Gordon Hugh-Kendrick might rouse Olivia's nosiness (honestly, was there anything that *didn't*?), his record was clean as can be, and as a cop she had no right to pry further. Even if she'd wondered, back in September, just what a wider background search might reveal. Wider as in, international. And then in October when the Department was turning the city inside-out for some clue about what could have happened to Bee Cuomo, she'd nearly given in to the urge . . .

Until she'd looked at what Bee's disappearance was doing to his wife, and thus to the man himself, and knew that Gordon Hugh-Kendrick had nothing to do with it. And if he didn't, then running a background check bore a big red stamp of NOT YOUR BUSINESS.

Because even if she wasn't caught doing a personal search and fired — or best case, officially reprimanded — whatever she learned from it would stand between her and Linda, forever and ever. And Linda McDonald, embattled principal of a perpetually sinking ship, was on her way to becoming a friend — a rare enough thing for a cop to have.

So: no snooping beyond that of any normally inquisitive civilian.

Although perhaps she'd get a chance for one of those normally inquisitive conversations later today. Linda had said Gordon would be there for Career Day, and Olivia was scheduled to be one of the speakers: The Joys of Being a Cop. Unless she'd been buried under an avalanche of paperwork, or summoned to an urgent felony, or (God forbid) dragged back to the Taco Alvarez trial.

She'd already wasted a full day listening to the two lawyers squabble over her right to testify against a man she'd been arresting since he was fourteen. And then yesterday . . . that gesture Taco made. Should she tell the judge? No one else noticed. Taco's attorney would claim she was trying to sway the jury. But there it was, a message from Mr. Taco Alvarez: the hand on the table shaping a gun, thumb coming down like the hammer.

Threat, pure and clear.

If her boss were around, Olivia would ask his advice, but the Chief was back East, leaving Olivia Mendez to wear not only her usual two hats — uniformed Sergeant and plainclothes Detective — but also that of Acting Chief.

Didn't matter. Plenty of time. Taco Alvarez wasn't going anywhere.

The celery aroma faded, replaced by the vinegary smell from the apple-juice plant, and Olivia slowed to take the pulse of San Felipe. The Kwik Mart was doing its usual early morning business, men in suits ordering pricey coffee drinks for the pleasure of an insult from its tattooed barista. (And talk about stories: that pierced and well-muscled ex–gang member was married to a nerdly accountant, with two little girls she dressed in pink.) Olivia braked for a glance down the adjoining alley (a place she knew a little too well, for a girl who grew up to be a cop)

35

but that light the city got the owner to install remained unbroken, and the space was empty.

She crossed Main Street at the signal, looping around for a survey of the industrial area near the tracks. All quiet here, the air smelling of fresh sawdust from the lumberyard. The sandwich place hadn't fixed their dangling sign yet, and Olivia made a mental note to have one of the men go by with a deadline. A glance down the street beside the lumberyard — and her foot stamped on the brake, her hand slapping the cruiser's gearshift into Reverse.

But it was only Señora Rodriguez, self-proclaimed community activist and widely-recognized pain in the ass. One of the Señora's designated Causes must live down here. Olivia put the cruiser back in Drive, and continued on.

It being February, spring planting was just starting up, and work was slack at the cannery. The guy who ran her favorite burrito truck hadn't got back from Mexico City yet, and the paleta man — the old guy who went everywhere, saw everything, and who she suspected of sending a couple anonymous tips that led to arrests — wouldn't sell much ice cream until later in the year.

But wait: old Tío had a real job now, janitor at — yes, Guadalupe, the school that had so dominated Olivia's life this year. She wondered if he'd show up here in June, selling the kids frozen goodies from his pushcart, or if that shifty fellow with the blaring ice-cream truck would move into Tío's territory.

She waved to the manager of the sprinkler supply and turned up Main Street. Past the burnt-toast smell from the coffee roaster and the sad windows of the Goodwill and the line forming outside the church's soup kitchen. She doubled back around the anonymous Women's Shelter, went by the second-hand furniture shop, the barber, the theater — then again, up at the limits of the cruiser's headlights, a lean figure in khaki shorts flashed across the street.

For an old guy, Linda's husband sure could run.

5:45 A.M.
LINDA

Linda's clock was so old-fashioned, it gave a little wheeze before its alarm went off. As usual, she hit the button before the ring started — although this morning she was nowhere near sleep when it wheezed. She had managed a few hours of unconsciousness after Gordon's soothing, but when he got up for his run, the whirring of her mind (which, equally old-fashioned, seemed to have gears instead of silicon chips) started up again.

Career Day? What was she *thinking*? Just a year ago, her life had been so easy! Sure, the elementary school had its problems, but at least she had an experienced staff, community support, and children that memory tinted as sweetly innocent.

And then the city's Busybody-in-Chief, Señora Rodriguez, had walked through the principal's door and pronounced the words *Guadalupe Middle School,* causing Linda to cower behind her desk. As if wood or metal or anything short of a loaded gun might be an effective defense against Señora Rodriguez.

Guadalupe was the Señora's most recent Good Cause, a school in desperate need of . . . everything, really, but beginning with a principal. Seven hundred and twelve students, ages eleven to fourteen. Half child, half adult, all hormones and passion — an age group Linda found problematic as individuals and a nightmare en masse. Even the best of middle schools were cages for the dangerously adolescent. And the bad ones, those that suffered an indifferent staff, poor choices, and school board neglect?

Schools like Guadalupe had been — even before this past grim year?

Better to bulldoze it and turn it into apple orchard.

But no one Linda knew had ever managed to put off Señora Rodriguez when she had the bit in her teeth. So Linda had sighed, and let the woman drag her off to a school with a history of bad grades, truancy, and fistfights, a school with an alarming turnover of newly-fledged teachers, a school whose buildings were a mix of the rundown (library, cafeteria, most of the classrooms) and the ridiculously elaborate (the gym). A school splintered into gangs and cliques, whose corridors would be filled with the hunched shoulders of the beaten, most of whose teachers would have prescriptions for mood suppressants. A school that drove its last principal to suicide.

A school that sidled up and murmured sweet nothings in Linda's astonished ear.

She'd held herself aloof during the Señora's tour of Guadalupe, nodding and asking few questions, until the Señora stepped away and left her alone in the arched entranceway.

Its tiled walls had once been a mosaic. Under the years of filth, felt pens, and chewing gum lay a mural somebody had spent a lot of time on. Up at the top (beyond the reach of student arms) was a row of surprisingly ornate hand-painted tiles — a sort of picture frame, wrapped around a sky as blue as the afternoon beyond the archway.

Linda studied the brutalized surface, trying to pick out the design. The tiles themselves were a mix of tidy rectangles and anarchic shards: a long rectangle evoked the school's façade; in the blue sky, a spatter of chips made for an Impressionistic, breeze-stirred flag; ten thin triangles shaped the circle of a wheelchair. Some of the tiles were painted, rather than pieced: a woman's face

40

here, obscured by felt pen beard and horns; a cluster of high-top shoes there; a brown hand sinking a basketball.

Linda stepped closer, her attention caught by that face: a woman with an expression of authority, captured in a few deft lines. Wasn't that the school secretary?

Bemused, Linda let the Señora drive her back to the elementary school, all the while composing a refusal, polite but firm.

The job would be thankless. If Guadalupe's new principal managed to get test scores up five points, the school board would demand to know why it wasn't ten. If absenteeism and violence fell a notch, why not two? Playground bloodshed, drugs, and student pregnancy would be daily concerns. It would be terrifying and exhilarating and the mere thought of it made Linda want to take to her bed.

But that night, she had a dream of using her thumb-nail to scrape the felt pen from that tile face. The next morning, Gordon asked why her sleep had been so restless. As the day wore on, her thoughts kept going back to that mosaic. And when the final bell had rung, Linda picked up the phone and called the district office with a list of demands — a very long list.

Over the summer break, Guadalupe was

turned inside-out: classrooms to teachers; sports equipment to art lab; math curriculum to wall maps; with new policies on cellphones, parent communication, sex ed, and bullying.

The school year started the third Wednesday in August. By the Friday night, Linda was exhausted, overwhelmed, and — yes — exhilarated. By Tuesday, she loved Guadalupe Middle School as ferociously as an elderly cat-lady with 712 runt kittens. She spent the next two months tracking their growth, worrying and obsessing and celebrating their every tiny victory — only to have the winds of winter sweep across her charges when pigtailed sixth-grader Bee Cuomo failed to reach school one morning.

Linda had lost children before, as a teacher and as a principal: leukemia, a gun accident, and one horrible weekend, three children from one family to a drunk driver. She well knew the shudders and cracks that ran through a school community, the fear and sense of abandonment and vulnerability that took time and attention to heal.

But she'd never before had a child simply . . . disappear. How the hell did one comfort and reassure children when no one knew what the threat even was? November dragged on, days and then weeks in limbo:

no body, no ransom demand, no hint of sexual predator in the girl's online life or family history. Nothing but a blankness that had swallowed a child.

The uncertainty was toxic and all pervasive, touching even those who'd never so much as met Bee Cuomo. Kids began acting up; parents fell off the wagon; playtime recklessness edged into self-destruction. As Linda watched her school cringe away from the media scrutiny on the one hand and the grinding fear of the unknown on the other, she knew it was tearing itself to shreds.

But for some reason, it stopped short. Somehow, her school full of damaged, recalcitrant, and neglected children had done the exact opposite of what the entire district expected: they hadn't melted down. Instead, the kids seemed to feel the gaping absence of Bee Cuomo as a chasm yawning at their own feet, and slowly, by tiny, hard-fought increments, seemed to be clawing their way back from the edge.

The moment she'd realized this, Linda had furiously pushed everyone else away: outside experts, district overseers, trauma counselors, all the police other than Olivia Mendez. In recent weeks, she'd found herself holding her breath, trying not to look at things too closely, and doing nothing that might disturb this fragile equilibrium. She'd put off making a decision about what kind of memorial service to hold. She'd let the district know that the testing schedule could go on as planned. She'd refused to cancel events like Career Day.

Any one of those decisions might prove disastrous, but . . .

"Today will go fine," she said aloud into the dark bedroom. Once upon a time, it would have been a prayer. Today, all Linda felt entitled to ask of the universe was that Gordon had left some coffee in the pot.

CHACO

Chaco woke up to the smell of coffee and the sound of his mother's shoes, scuffling across the old floor. *Weariness,* his mind offered. *Retribution.*

He'd got, what? Two hours of sleep? He'd been awake till he went out the kitchen door at 2:15, and got back maybe an hour later. Then just when his feet were starting to warm up, a little voice sneered, *Hey stupid, you think that light mighta been hooked up to a camera?* His heart pounded so loud he thought it would wake up his little brother — until he forced himself to *think,* like cousin Taco. *The light was at your back, right? And you didn't turn to look, did you?* So what if a camera took his picture? All it would show was some kid wearing too-big overalls and dirty shoes. Just a kid.

Still, it took Chaco a while to feel warm again, and what seemed like five minutes later Mamá came in with the cup of mostly-

45

milk coffee and the gentle shake on his shoulder. The coffee was her way of saying he was doing a man's work. The shake told him it had to be now.

He threw back the covers and put his bare feet on the floor — harder to fall asleep if you were sitting up. *Vigilant,* that was him. When his mother looked in a few minutes later he wasn't exactly awake, but the mug was still in his hands. She crossed the room to give him a kiss, and to whisper that there were some eggs if he wanted to cook those, but not to put cheese in his sister's until they found out what was causing her stomach problems. When he didn't answer, she asked if he was all right.

He grumbled he was fine and stood up to prove it. They both heard the car door slam, two doors down, which meant her ride would be outside in a minute. He made a little wave toward the hallway, then followed her along the icy linoleum to the kitchen, the only room they kept warm in the winter.

She looked up from buttoning her coat. "I nearly forgot. They called last night and asked if I could work Saturday. I said yes."

"Oh, Ma."

"I know, I told you I wouldn't, but it's time and a half, and I thought I could ask Angel to —"

"No!"

"He can borrow a car seat for your sister, and —"

"No, Mamá, promise me you won't ask him. Angel is . . ." Angel is what? Crazy? Dangerous? *Malignant?* "Angel's got things to do. The little ones like the swings in the park. We can walk down there."

"He said he didn't mind. That maybe he'd meet some of your friends there. Oh, *mijo,* you're shivering — go stand near the heater!"

It wasn't the temperature that made Chaco shudder, it was the idea of Angel around his friends. "We don't need Angel! We'll be fine."

Headlights flared across the window, and Chaco's mother picked up her lunch bag. "I have to go. If you're sure, about Saturday? I'll take the little ones in with me Saturday night so Sunday you can sleep late. You have a good day, *mijo.*"

"You too, Mamá."

"Make sure your brother wears his coat."

"I will, Mamá."

She rested her lips against his forehead. "My big man," she murmured. "I'm sorry I have to work so much."

"It's okay, I don't mind. You better go."

Cold air reached through the doorway,

then she was gone. Chaco warmed his shins in front of the heater's red bars for a minute, drinking the last of his coffee-milk, before turning down the expensive electricity.

Maybe he'd meet some of your friends there. Yeah, right. Angel was sending him a message. *Friends* could only mean Sofia Rivas. *Meet* meant delivering a threat. If Chaco didn't want Angel to confront Sofia directly, then Chaco'd have to do it himself. Tell Sofia what would happen if she and the kid Danny testified against Cousin Taco.

The idea of Angel 'fronting Sofia made Chaco's worry about the paint can feel pretty stupid. Though it was a good thing nobody'd seen him running away like some . . . some *invertebrate.*

Any chance of getting respect from Taco or Angel after that would've gone right out the door.

5:52 A.M.
TÍO

Jaime Ygnacio Rivera Cruz — *Tío* to the residents of San Felipe and the students of Guadalupe Middle School — watched yesterday's coffee rise up the woven threads of his clean rag. He squeezed it, then slid his left hand into the shoe and began to rub the damp cloth around and around, his father's trick to bring up a gleam on aged leather.

Perhaps it was time to buy a new pair. He had money now, more than he could have anticipated just a short time ago . . .

But discarding these would feel like an admission of defeat. And Señora Rodriguez had told him of a reliable shoe repair shop, at the other end of the county. He had doubts: this was not a generation of repairers. Still, he had bought these shoes for his wedding. They were on his feet the proud day he was hired for his first real job, and on the Sunday morning his son was bap-

49

tized. He had worn them on the rainy afternoon that son was lowered into a hastily dug grave, and again two weeks later when his wife was buried at the boy's side. The shoes had gone with Tío across the border and through the desert to America, many years ago. Old comrades, who deserved preservation.

When the shine was to his satisfaction, he set them aside, washed his hands, and finished dressing. The rest of his clothing was equally respectable: the brown janitor's shirt was freshly ironed, as were the trousers, every button and fold in place. No necktie, though. Tío still did not feel properly dressed without a necktie, but appearance was all, especially when it came to the fragile sensibilities of adolescents.

His first day at Guadalupe, he had worn a tie and the students had mocked it. The second day, he had let his collar go bare for the sake of invisibility. The tie would remain in the drawer until such a time as he could reclaim his dignity.

He studied his reflection in the cracked mirror. Of the many faces he had worn in his life, this one might be the most deceptive. And to think how terrified he had been of the uniform — of the very idea of setting foot onto school grounds. How close he had come to turning the job down untried.

Little did he anticipate the doors that would open to a lowly school custodian. *Limpiador* simply meant one who cleaned, but his old English dictionary told him that *janitor* had to do with doors. The janitor was a doorkeeper. And the word *custodian*? In either tongue, that had to do with custody, with possession. With guarding.

The word made him the possessor of Guadalupe Middle School and all its persons. To guard the place as he saw fit. Children might disappear, boys might shoot each other over drugs, but not while they were at *his* school.

And surely the triangle of crisp white undershirt at the neck bore the same function as a necktie?

Yes: on such a day as this, it was better to show the uniform than the man inside.

Perhaps, however, not when it came to young Mr. Santiago Cabrera — who called himself "Chaco" as an emulation of his dangerous cousin, the man with dreams of drug cartels in his heart. Chaco Cabrera needed to see past the surface of his school's janitor, just a little.

Because Tío had plans for Chaco. Plans that did not include permitting the boy to

51

follow his gangbanger cousin "Taco" into a courtroom on a charge of murder.

6:02 A.M.
#SPEAKFORBEE

Bylines beat coffee any day. Bylines beat pills and powders (not that she used the hard stuff) and even most of the sex she'd had.

Not that a *Clarion* byline meant much, but a girl had to start somewhere, and if they wouldn't let her cover the Taco Alvarez trial, she'd dig up her own damn stories. Like the one whose folder she held in her hand.

There was potential in this school. Something big under the surface, she could just smell it. What had started as a page-three human-interest piece — Career Day? Give me a break! — ended up setting her reporter's nose to twitching.

The picture she was looking at was the latest in a series linked to the hashtag #speakforbee. Most of them were based on a photograph of local Ford dealer Charles Cuomo that he'd used in an incredibly tacky ad campaign starting barely a month after

53

his daughter disappeared. In this one, Cuomo's cheerful features were overlaid with Hannibal Lechter's leather mask — an effect so disturbing, any potential customer would think twice about a Ford.

Half the old farts working for the *Clarion* didn't know what a hashtag was. For them, #speakforbee would be one of those things the kids got up to. Like *viral* meant disease, not an idea that infects minds.

An idea such as the local Ford dealer turned into a monster.

She closed the folder on the image and started to drop it into the desk drawer, then paused to glance at the one that was already there.

This folder was related, but different. Several inches thick, it held an unruly collection of printouts, clippings, official reports, and her own notes, dating back to the late October day when the Ford dealer's daughter failed to show up at school. From the first sketchy police report to the *Clarion*'s front-page follow-up, three months later, the file included flyers with Bee's face, maps used by community search teams, reports from the sniffer-dog handlers, and a lot of stuff she shouldn't have had (such as camera records of cars in the vicinity that day). The file traced the story's arc, from the initial sharp fear of a community toward the empty, chronic ache of not knowing.

The flyer, Bee's school photo, showed a child who hadn't caught up with middle school yet: old-fashioned braids, clunky glasses, and metal braces. Years from makeup and fashion tips. The possibility of never figuring out what happened to Bee Cuomo troubled her as a person, but it outraged her as a reporter.

It also made her determined to dig more deeply into Guadalupe Middle School than anyone else seemed to have done.

She dropped the slim #SPEAKFORBEE file on top of BEE CUOMO and shoved the drawer closed, then went to see if the *Clarion* had a long-lensed camera that actually worked.

GUADALUPE MIDDLE SCHOOL

TO HOLD CAREER DAY

Guadalupe Middle School will hold its annual Career Day today, with a stellar list of guests. The school's principal, Linda McDonald, has invited local residents from a variety of backgrounds to speak to the students about jobs ranging from law enforcement to weaving. She has also given this year's Career Day a theme: "Unexpected Threads."

As Ms. McDonald says, "Many of us come to our careers by an indirect route: we train for archaeology and end up in computer science, or plan to teach and become actors instead. This school, in this California farm community, is linked to the wider world by a million unexpected threads, any of which can be grasped by a Guadalupe student. School is a time to learn, but it is also a time to explore.

"This Career Day celebrates the discoveries our speakers made in their own lives. By telling us their stories, letting us see how they came to be here, I'm hoping that these members of our Guadalupe community not only encourage our students to dream large, but show them the cold, hard tools they'll need to succeed."

Shortly after Ms. McDonald was hired last May, the school board discussed canceling the event. During last year's Guadalupe School Career Day, one of the key speakers, District Attorney Raymond Crosby, was assaulted by an alleged fellow gang member of Thomas "Taco" Alvarez, after charges were filed against Alvarez for the shooting death of sixteen-year-old Gloria Rivas (a former Guadalupe student) and the attempted murder of Sergeant Olivia Mendez. The Alvarez trial is currently under way. This year, Principal McDonald says, the presence of Sergeant Mendez among the guests should help quiet any unrest.

Other Career Day speakers include the aptly-named Suze Weaver, an internationally famous fiber artist; local family therapist Dr. Cassandra Henry; Allison Kitagawa, professor of Japanese history and aunt of sixth-grader Beatrice Cuomo, the Guadalupe Middle School student whose disappearance in late October remains unsolved; and high-tech entrepreneur Thomas Atcheson, whose son, Brendan, is a star player on the Guadalupe basketball team.

GUADALUPE MIDDLE SCHOOL

Dawn, and sunlight finds the low spots in the hills to the east of San Felipe.

Half a mile overhead in a cloudless sky, a businessman on descent to San Jose International rests his bleary eyes on the fingers of light across a multicolored tapestry: rich brown soil readied for planting, dark maroon lettuce seedlings, myriad shades of green from celery to kale. An east–west curve of river dips under a north–south stream of highway. Near that crossroads, the sun touches a sprawl of low buildings, the sorts of huge rooftops and industrial-sized lots that suggest raw materials rather than finished products. Traffic builds on the freeway's asphalt tributaries.

To the north, where suburban rooftops give way to plowed fields, sunlight flares against glass: the clerestory windows atop the cafeteria of Guadalupe Middle School. Grades six through eight: 712 adolescents between the ages of eleven and fourteen; forty-eight teachers, full- and part-time; and twenty-one administrators and staff, principal to janitor, part-time nurse to the three lunch ladies. Today, the number of souls at Guadalupe will hit 820, although beyond those threads (as Principal McDonald has so colorfully told the local paper) lie a million others that weave the students into the fabric of their community: the warp of teachers and staff, the weft of visitors and volunteers, binding experiences, passions, and ideas into a tapestry of life, both light and dark.

A part of today's population are twenty-three outsiders, bearing with them twenty-three stories of childhood, training, decisions, and work — all the events that brought these adults out of Indiana and India, Australia and Austin, England and New England, and set them down at a California middle school's Career Day.

The growing dawn finds a few cars already in the staff lot. Lights go on in the cafeteria, where low-income students will soon gather for government-subsidized breakfasts. The jet-lagged passenger overhead hears the flight attendant's recitation, and pulls his gaze from the placid landscape to search for his shoes. He does not see the long, white-

59

topped buses emerging from the district lot. In forty minutes, the first of them will deliver its load of noisy adolescents to Guadalupe Middle School.

The morning will pass, devoted to dreams. The Visitor's lot will fill, guests will be welcomed and introduced, then escorted to their respective classrooms.

By the time lunch hour comes, the school will be exploding with energy as young hearts whirl around the sheer *possibilities* of the lifetime stretching out before them. More prosaically, the guests will be fed, then their stories will resume.

The firefighter will speak not only of heroism, but of injuries and insurance premiums. The forensic technician will balance the satisfaction of figuring things out and locking bad guys away against the boredom of testimony, the paperwork, and the sense of being a small part of a large team. The game designer will describe how difficult it is to make a profit out of those thrilling red splashes on a screen. The weaver will make no effort to conceal her dependence on luck, and the propensity of artists to starve. Students will be given the raw material for their life's plan, and shown the means to turn it into their life's tapestry.

All that is, at least, the plan.

But today, the weaving of dreams will unravel long before the final bell.

A long white van will drive onto the school grounds. A dark figure will get out. Carrying a heavy nylon bag, he will walk calmly into the school from the side road. The door to classroom B18 will open, and not quite shut again.

Two minutes later, the first *pop-pop* will echo across the quads and fields.

Adult voices will stutter into silence; adolescent heads will snap up; farm workers in the field across the road will straighten, looking at each other in wide-eyed disbelief. At the next *pop-pop-pop,* a wave of fear will crash across the school. A woman walking through the playing fields will drop her bag and break into a run; another woman in the school office will scramble from her chair. Before the two come together, the midday sun will be sparkling off a thread of blood oozing down the center of the concrete quad.

Career Day, at Guadalupe Middle School.

■ ■ ■ ■

CAREER DAY

Before the Beginning

■ ■ ■ ■

When the call came in, Olivia thought it was just another Halloween prank.

Olivia hated Halloween — and had long before she became a cop. Maybe it wouldn't be so bad if she'd lived in a more white-bread town, but having the Anglo holiday of candy and costumes smack up against *Día de Muertos* made for an orgy of sugar and disguises and trouble.

When she was a kid, white makeup scared her and she was allergic to the pungent marigolds that were traditional to the holiday. As a teenager, she'd had some bad experiences at parties. As an adult, she hid in her darkened house as the neighborhood dogs worked themselves into a frenzy. And as a cop . . .

As a cop, she'd seen too much. The mix of manic kids and whimsical death — *Día de Muertos* has a particular focus on the death of children — made her stomach knot as October wore on.

Her first season in the Department, eleven years ago, an old-timer had warned her that worst of all was when October 31 fell on a Monday. She'd laughed, thinking this was like Friday the 13th or craziness under a full moon, but she wasn't laughing long: a Monday Halloween followed by the two days of *Día de Muertos* meant the lunacy began at dusk Friday and didn't let up until Thursday morning.

This year was her third Monday Halloween on the police force. The Department's overtime budget for the month was already blown, with two drunken crashes, a house fire caused by a jack-o'-lantern, a shoot-out, and eleven brawls: four in bars, one in the bowling alley, two in grocery stores (the bloodiest one over the last package of bargain candy), and the rest in neighborhoods over smashed pumpkins. The movie theater shut when its late-night horror film sparked a little too much audience participation.

She'd told herself all day that by the time darkness fell everyone would be sick of it all — sick, or under arrest — but she didn't believe it. Once dusk gave way to darkness, the adolescents would come out and gang rivalries would mix with the wildness in the air. If only it would rain! If only Thursday would come. She was tired and cranky and she'd eaten two of the three sugar skulls the desk guy had brought in.

That's why, when the phone rang Halloween evening, she thought it was a joke.

There'd been a recent rediscovery of prank calls, a thing of the past due to caller ID, when local kids found that they could use disposable phones, stolen ones, or the surviving public box behind the thrift store. The fad would die after a couple of arrests, but because the Department was too pushed to hunt down the perpetrators, any call the 911 dispatcher suspected of being a prank — anything short of a blood-on-the-ground emergency — was being diverted to the Department for triage.

The call came in on the dedicated line at 6:40, that dividing line between innocent dusk and troublesome darkness. With a sigh, Olivia put down her case notes from the Gloria Rivas murder and picked up the receiver: would this be a report from the Russian gangster Yuri Nator, or a giggling bomb threat?

"Sergeant Mendez, San Felipe Police Department, how may I —"

A man's voice cut her off. "My daughter's

not home."

He sounded irritated rather than worried, as if Sergeant Olivia Mendez were personally to blame for this disruption of his evening. "How old is your daughter, sir?"

"Ten — eleven, I guess."

Olivia carried on a silent conversation with the remaining decorated skull on her desk. The slur of his words suggested the man was drunk — she hoped to hell he hadn't just arrived home. Would it be worse if he'd been home for several drinks and just discovered his child wasn't there? In either case, she wasn't keen on pulling a car off the streets for a guy who'd forgotten what day it was.

"It's Halloween, sir. Could your wife have taken her trick-or-treating?"

"I don't have a wife."

"Well, someone else, then?"

"Why would she go trick-or-treating? She doesn't like candy."

Then she's like no other kid I've ever met, Olivia did not say aloud. She reached for her pad. "Okay, sir, I'll send someone by, but it'll be a while — we've got some troubles in town. Could I have your name and address?"

"This is Chuck Cuomo," he said impatiently — and before Olivia could hunt down why she ought to know his name, he provided it. "I run the car dealership. It's my daughter, Bee."

She wrote down *Bee Cuomo — father Chuck* — and the address, sketching a martini glass on the pad as she asked if he'd phoned any of Bee's friends, and listened to his bluster that the girl had no friends, and in any case he didn't have their phone numbers.

She was about to interrupt — who the hell didn't know his daughter's friends? — when he said the words that made all the difference, the words that were to define the coming months in San Felipe, the words that pushed aside the Gloria Rivas murder and the Taco Alvarez paperwork and the follow-ups to house fires and bar fights.

"There was a call from her school on the machine when I got home. Why the hell they didn't use my cell number I couldn't tell you. Maybe they didn't have it? I don't know. Anyway, they called to say she wasn't there, like that weird kid and his mother said."

Olivia Mendez sat up in her chair. "Sir? Bee wasn't where?"

"She wasn't at school today. Jesus, don't you speak English?" He made a noise under his breath, and continued with an exaggerated enunciation. "The secretary at Guadalupe phoned and left a message to say Bee Cuomo was not in school today and was this an excused absence? Of course it wasn't, but there's nobody answering the phone there at this time of night, so I —"

This time she did cut him off. "Sir, I'll be right out. Don't disturb anything in her room, but see if you can remember the names of her friends. And, Mr. Cuomo? Maybe you should make yourself a pot of coffee."

She hung up and yanked open the drawer where she kept her holstered gun.

Día de Muertos.

Olivia looked at the sugar skull on her desk, and shuddered.

■ ■ ■ ■

CAREER DAY

Dawn to First Bell

■ ■ ■ ■

LINDA

Linda McDonald glared at the mirror in disgust. Why on earth had she thought this was a good week for a new hairstyle?

Her exercise in self-loathing was interrupted by an English drawl from the next room. "Have you ever considered how odd it is that the word *career* as a noun refers to the methodical choices of a person's professional life, while as a verb it means to veer wildly out of control?"

"Thanks, Gordon, that's *just* what I need to hear on this particular morning." Linda bent over the bathroom drawer, crossly flinging around the contents as if a choice of eye shadow might improve matters. When she straightened again, he had moved with his usual disconcerting silence and was standing right behind her. His arms reached out, and Linda caught back her immediate impulse to pull away and exclaim *You're all sweaty — we don't have time — oh my blouse!*

Beyond that initial twitch, she did not resist. Gordon was rarely demonstrative (he was English, after all) but he had a way of knowing when nothing but physical communication would do.

In any event, exclamations over clean blouses — and, below that, the mistrust of touch that she had worked so hard to kill and bury deep — belonged to the surface Linda, the woman she should have been, and still looked like.

Besides which, she'd idiotically put on the white blouse with the dangerously loose button. If Gordon hadn't forced her to look at herself, she might have raised her arms in the assembly and . . .

Smiling for the first time that morning, Linda closed her eyes and leaned back against this man who was her husband. He tucked his unshaven face into the soft skin under her ear, and she stood, breathing in his smells: male sweat, shoe polish, fresh coffee. The odd suggestion of hut-smoke that always seemed to cling to his person. All the pheromones that were Gordon. Her thoughts ceased to throw themselves against the cage of her mind as she leaned, and breathed. After a while, she let her eyes come open, gazing at their two-headed reflection in the mirror. His irises today were more gold than green.

His voice rumbled in her ear. "You will do just fine. Your talk is perfect."

"They'll be too busy gawking at my hair to notice what I'm saying."

"You look lovely."

"I look scalped."

His stubble made a sound against the blouse fabric as he shook his head. "No, I've seen scalped people. You look nothing like them."

She frowned at the crinkles beside his eyes, then noticed that the expression made her look a lot older than fifty-three. "Four years since you showed up on my doorstep, and I still can't always tell when you're joking."

His face relaxed fully into a smile, his arms fell away. "May I shower now?"

"Make it quick, if you're going with me." She shoved the drawer in, gave a last glare at the too-modern haircut, then ducked out before his T-shirt came off and his back came into view. Her fingertips might find that intricate ritual of scars bizarrely compelling, but her eyes saw only the slow pull of a stone blade through flesh.

THIRTY YEARS AGO
GORDON: HIS STORY (1)

All kinds of human flotsam washed up in highland New Guinea in the 1980s, riding the tides of God, or gold, or anthropological glory: missionaries seeking heathen sheep for the fold; multinational corporations eager for riches gouged from the earth; scholars re-writing their disciplines in light of these modern Stone Age people. Then there were the misfits, in search of adventure, or fortune, or simply an escape into the earth's last wild frontier.

Linda McDonald was one of the missionaries.

And when the tiny Air Niugini prop plane turned to taxi away down the Mt. Hagen runway, it was all she could do not to bolt down the rutted tarmac in pursuit.

She told herself that it wasn't fear making her heart pound, it was disorientation. Simple jet lag. The past two forty-eight hours had been Linda's third time to leave

Indianapolis in her whole life, and her first-ever venture out of the United States. She had crossed a continent, an ocean, and half of Australia before she'd hit the stupefying heat and humidity of Port Moresby — only to stand appalled before a wall in the terminal that seemed to be splashed with blood. Yes, the Papua New Guinea highlands had been home to cannibals a generation or two ago, but the missionary school hadn't said anything about violence in the capital city. Maybe it was some weird kind of animal sacrifice? Primitives fearful of the jet age, ensuring a safe arrival through blood-letting? In that case (her fatigued brain went on) shouldn't there be actual dead animals in the corners, or pens of live ones waiting . . . ?

Her hallucinatory speculations were interrupted by a citizen, black of skin and short of stature, who strolled past one particularly gory wall and shot a precisely aimed stream of red spittle from between his teeth.

Ah: betel nut. She'd heard of that.

The plane out of Port Moresby — which was either the morning flight leaving very late or the afternoon one half a day early — worked its way up-country, landing in Mt. Hagen distressingly near dusk: an hour, apparently, when any sensible human, expatriate or local, was sitting down to dinner: the airport was deserted. The air smelled of smoke, and rain, and a whole lot of green.

The plane had laid tire-tracks across one of her Samsonites when it circled to leave.

Linda pulled her inadequate rain jacket together, shivering and bewildered. This was an airport, with buildings all around: why was there no sign of life? She wanted to sit on her luggage and weep. And might have, if it hadn't been so cold — this was the tropics, but Mt. Hagen was a mile high. *Come on, Linda: moving will warm you up. And you're sure to find* someone. *Someone who isn't a cannibal.*

She picked up her two suitcases to stagger in the direction of what looked to be the Mt. Hagen terminal. Within ten steps, she was dripping with a horrid mixture of sweat and rain. The handles of the heavy cases became increasingly slick, and at one stumble over a rough patch of tarmac, the left one slipped from her hand, splashed down in a particularly deep pothole, and vomited its T-shirts and Keds into the mud. She said a word that missionaries do not say, and let the tears spill.

She managed to force most of the sodden contents back inside, and was struggling with the clasp when motion caught the corner of her eye: a scrap of yellow flitting rapidly behind the buildings. She forced the latch shut, clawed her wet hair from her eyes, and waited for the vehicle to zoom on by — but miracle of miracles, it turned in, roaring down the runway as if intending to sprout wings and take to the skies. Instead, it came to a halt next to Linda's bedraggled self.

"You look rather stranded." The man's voice sounded too posh for an Australian.

He was a heavily tanned, clean-shaven, stoop-shouldered expatriate in his forties, high of forehead and bad of teeth; one glance and she was touched by a powerful aura of malaria-racked Victorian expeditions into West Africa, of the besieged administrators of troubled provinces, of wild-eyed Englishmen pressing into the desert on camels or the Antarctic on dog-sleds. Or highland New Guinea in an open-sided yellow jeep. The stranger set the hand-brake and stepped jauntily from the open door, dressed in a button-down, short-sleeved blue shirt, flip-flop sandals, and the sort of khaki shorts that everyone but that kind of man looks ridiculous in.

Later, making subtle inquiries that fooled no one, she would uncover few facts about him, and much rumor: He'd come to teach,

79

and been fired — or quit in disgust. He was on the run from the law of Angola, or was it Albania? He was the father of three, fleeing a dangerous marriage to a drug lord's daughter, or an aristocratic homosexual escaping repressive laws and social condemnation. He was a mercenary wanted for war crimes in some dry African nation.

He was, of course, English, the sort of Englishman who could only have been formed on the playing fields of Eton, his spine stiffened by a regime of genial parental abandonment followed by institutionalized brutality: unsparing of himself, impervious to mere bodily discomfort, and always a step removed from intimacy with his peers. Later, Linda came to realize that both his bone-deep humanity and his utter disdain for authority had been driven into him by the same rods of discipline.

But she knew none of that then; she merely grasped that rescue was at hand. Also, that his eyes were an interesting shade of hazel, or perhaps amber. "Well, yes, it looks like I am kind of stranded. I thought I'd be met, but I'm not quite sure what day it is, and the plane seemed to just sort of collect passengers, and someone told me that we were stopping at a place we weren't scheduled to —" Linda heard her mouth babbling, and shut it.

"Well, we'll soon have you sorted," he said briskly. And indeed, half her possessions were already inside the jeep. She handed him the plastic bag with her hair rollers, which she hadn't been able to jam back into the suitcase, and walked around to what was here the passenger side.

"Just got in from Moresby?" He turned the key, put the vehicle into gear.

"That's right."

"Which mission are you with?"

"The Lutherans."

"Whereabouts?"

"In Wape . . . er."

"Wapeladanga? Father Albion?"

"I think so. Yes, of course. I'm sorry, I'm not too on the ball."

"Understandable. You may not get up there for a day or two, I'm afraid. The S.I.L. lost a plane, and they're flying in another from Oz."

Oz: Australia. *Lost,* as in crash. As in, the plane they'd apparently intended Linda to get into. "There isn't a car?"

The man had a nice laugh, even though it was at her expense. "The only way you'd get a car up there is if you lifted it in by helicopter or had it portaged a piece at a time. No roads." He glanced over to see if she understood, but she must have looked lost, or near to breaking down, because his grin faded and he put out his hand — slowly, as if to a frightened child. "Terribly sorry, don't know what's happened to my manners. The name's Gordon Hugh-Kendrick."

She shook his callused palm. "Linda McDonald. Are you with one of the missions, then?"

"Oh no, no. Just a civil servant. Government employee. Glorified clerk." He pronounced it *clark*. Circling the last of the terminal buildings, they came out on what was identifiably a road. "You'll need a place to stay. You can contact the mission on the radio tonight and ask for instructions."

"If you think that's best." Her voice wavered a bit.

"Happens all the time."

"It must, if the airport is always deserted."

One eyebrow lifted. "In fact, I've never seen it like this, not during the day. Must be something going on in town."

And with that, they cleared a corner and the jeep stood on its nose to avoid plowing into Mardi Gras. The closest ranks of onlookers weren't particularly colorful, being composed of children wearing nothing but a length of cord around their protuber-

82

ant bellies and drably clothed women with heavy string bags hanging off their foreheads — *bilums,* they were called. But toward the center of the crowd came the men, and although some wore grubbier versions of what Gordon Hugh-Kendrick had on — and half a dozen displayed the Air Niugini uniform, which accounted for the deserted terminal — others wore skirts made of brilliant leaves, magnificent headdresses, face paint, and elaborate necklaces. Most of these figures had some object strung through their noses as well: bright feathers, long twigs, curling pig tusks, a yellow pencil. Linda gaped, and wondered aloud if a parade had just broken up.

"Why, the dress? Oh no, they just like to wear their best when they come to town. *Gudai, yupela.*" Mr. Hugh-Kendrick was greeting a tiny man with intensely black skin and a hugely ornate wig. *"Watpo algeta dispela manmeri i stap hia?"*

The man turned to glare, revealing a wide moustache studded with brilliant yellow feathers — and his fierceness split into a huge, betel-stained grin. "Eh, Gordon *pren! Langtaim mipela no see yupela.*" He shifted the stone axe he was carrying into his left hand, thrusting his right through the window. Gordon shook it vigorously, and the two exchanged greetings in a language that Linda did not think was Pidgin, although at that speed, she could not have been sure. Eventually Gordon turned to her.

"Do you speak Pidgin?"

"Liklik tasol." Only a little.

Introductions were made, then to her surprise, Gordon waved the feather-man around to the back. Half a dozen others climbed in as well, squatting down on her suitcases, admiring the pink hair rollers, giving off a powerful miasma of wood smoke, damp, and primal maleness. Each one carried some deadly object, be it stone axe, spear, or bow and arrow — or a combination, such as the two-headed weapon that passed alarmingly close to her nose, with a lovingly polished wedge of black stone on one side and a viciously sharp claw-like object on the other.

Half the men wore shorts, the others nothing but leaves, and it was difficult to know how to greet them without confronting portions of their anatomy an Indiana girl was not accustomed to greet. So she focused on their hair decorations, which ranged from one man's short afro threaded with feathers and bright flowers to his neighbor's three-foot-wide crescent-shaped hat made of matted hair, shells, and black, glossy feathers.

Gordon announced her name to his passengers, politely nudged a quiver of arrows away from her face, and put the jeep back into gear.

The conversation that followed was far too rapid-fire for her kindergarten-level Pidgin, but by the time they had cleared the crowd, Gordon had found out what was going on in the town.

"It would appear that a white man has been found dead."

"Oh, how awful! What happened?"

"They're saying it's murder, although it sounds to me like a climbing accident. They found him at the base of a cliff."

"Murder! Is there a lot . . . I mean, is murder commonplace here?"

That sparked another over-the-shoulder discussion before he replied. "None of these gentlemen can remember when the last *waitpela* was killed."

"And you don't remember it happening?"

He gave her a startled look, then his face cleared. "The last murder, you mean? Oh, I've only been in the highlands for a few weeks — certainly there hasn't been one in that time. But you can ask Mrs. Carver. She'd know if anyone does."

"Who is Mrs. Carver?"

He turned hard down a street and braked

in front of a low, wide building with a rusting tin roof. The door opened and out stepped a rangy six-foot-tall woman with graying brown hair, hands on her hips and a scowl on her face.

"That's Mrs. Carver." The innocent phrase suggested a joke, hidden deep. "Maggie. This is her boarding house."

Linda's heart sank at the lack of welcome in the woman's posture — but to her surprise, Gordon jumped out to trot up the stairs, seize the man-sized hand, and kiss it. The woman melted instantly into a near-simper; Gordon was no stranger here.

An assortment of passengers tumbled out of the back, each holding his weapon in one hand and something of Linda's in the other. They meandered toward the house to heap the bags near the steps before climbing back inside the jeep. Gordon turned Linda over to the woman, politely refused her offer of tea, then walked back to the car amidst a hail of Pidgin.

Linda stood on the graveled walk in front of this nondescript house, the air spiced with the foreign odors of rain and smoke and jungle, and watched the spattered vehicle drive away. Just before it rounded the corner, a tanned arm in a blue sleeve emerged from the yellow jeep, two fingers raised like the touch of a hat-brim. It was a gesture of casual farewell rather than permanent goodbye. Obscurely comforted, she took a deep lungful of this foreign air and turned to meet the next challenge.

Things were indeed sorted out, as her knight-errant had promised. Mrs. Carver proved more maternal than Linda's own mother (though that wasn't saying much). She ordered the rooftop hot water tank stoked so Linda could shower, fed the newcomer a meal of rice and some stewed meat, then sent her to bed, assuring Linda in a broad Australian accent that she'd make radio contact with Linda's mission when they came on that night. Twelve hours later, Linda woke to a cool, misty morning, the smell of cook-fires and diesel fumes in the air, the singing of children outside her window, and a mechanical thumping from somewhere in the building. A delicate green lizard hung from the ceiling beside the light fixture.

Downstairs, she found six guests dawdling over toast and eggs. Introductions were brisk: an American missionary couple on their way to a month in New Zealand, a trio of Catholic priests headed for a conference in Goroka, and a breezy Australian with ingrained grime under his nails and a proprietary attitude toward Mrs. Carver. This last held out his hand for Linda to shake. "G'day, name's Barry. I service the planes here."

It was on the tip of her tongue to ask, *Including the one that went down?* but she was saved from that faux pas by the American woman.

"Did you hear about our murder?"

"I heard a man died, but I thought it was an accident."

The reply came from Barry. "They've got the bloke on ice until the coroner can get here from Moresby, but since no one seems to know what he was doing up there, and since he's got important friends, they're playing it safe."

"I'm so sorry, I didn't realize he was a friend of yours."

"God, no. He worked for the mines."

"Do they know what happened?" But what "they" knew proved little more than what Linda's rescuer had learned from his passengers the previous evening: a man named Dale Lawrence was found by some locals, at the base of a cliff a hundred yards from the road, his head bashed in. Lawrence had been in the highlands about five months, had worked in the upper Sepik

River area before that, and nobody much liked him.

When Mrs. Carver came in with Linda's breakfast, Barry's flow of information cut abruptly off. After the landlady left, he leaned over and lowered his voice. "Maggie doesn't like it when *waitpelas* are rude to her staff. This Lawrence fella was here a coupla days — this was three, four months ago — and after she kicked him out, we heard he'd been in trouble up in the Sepik."

"What kind of trouble?"

Barry looked uncomfortable. "Well, not him, exactly. Seems a friend of his attacked a woman there. A local."

"Attacked?"

"Raped. And killed her."

"*Killed* her?" Linda squeaked. "Did the police catch him?" What was done with foreign criminals here? Were they handed over to the Australians? Or tried by a jury of men wearing tusks through their septums?

"Sure. Though of course nothing happened."

"Why on earth not?"

"He worked security, for the mines." Barry saw that more explanation was needed. "Brutal bastards, all of 'em, pardon my French. 'Course, he *said* he was an engineer, but I've never met an engineer who wore a gun. Name was Abrams. He and Lawrence and another fella — Turner? No, Taylor, I think — they all stood up for each other. And wasn't there something about a pen-knife? Ah, right — fancy little silver thing they found in the corner of the woman's hut, like it'd been kicked there. It belonged to Abrams, but all three of them swore it'd been stolen the week before. The *kiap* couldn't prove otherwise."

Kiap. Linda's stateside training offered a translation: cop — singular or plural. "So he just went free — Abrams did?"

"Not for long. The mine's lawyer bailed him out of the *kalabus,* but a coupla weeks later he went missing. They figured it was the girl's relatives, took 'em in for questioning, big palaver for a while, all kinds of accusations flying. They found him eventually in a place it was unlikely the family'd have got to, and it looked like an accident though the body was . . . well, it was hard to tell. Anyway, nothing much came of it except the other two, Lawrence and Taylor, were sent out of the Sepik area. Girl's name was something flowery. Hibiscus? No: *Jasmin.*"

One fatal injury, and now another a few months later. Linda thought of those stone-headed weapons bobbing around the jeep, and shuddered. What kind of place had she come to?

BRENDAN

Brendan Atcheson narrowed his eyes into slits, then tried raising his chin. No, he still didn't look anything like Jason Bourne. He just looked like a stupid squinting teenager.

Nothing about the figure in the bathroom mirror was heroic or sexy, or even very manly. Except maybe his height. And his chest wasn't too bad, between the pec muscles and the beginning of some hair. Not that you could show off a bare chest at school. With a shirt on, he had to be the least sexy person at Guadalupe Middle School, and that included the teachers. (Even Mr. Kendrick was sexy and he was, like, *ancient*.)

Still, it was weird, because Brendan was pretty sure that when girls giggled, it meant they thought a guy was hot, and girls sometimes giggled around him.

Not Mina Santos, of course. Mina didn't giggle, and she didn't seem to find him hot.

Then again, why should she? So clumsy he'd trip over his own feet (except on the basketball court) and with a mind that went completely blank when he stood in front of someone like Mina. So he scowled. And according to the mirror, it wasn't even a sexy scowl. Plus his ears stood out and his beard was pitiful.

But at least he didn't have to ride on the Big Yellow School Bus anymore. *So* humiliating to be the only eighth-grader on board. (It still pissed him off that he couldn't use Jock's gift toward a better bike, but Sir would've known.) Well, maybe a few others still took the bus. But none of Brendan Atcheson's friends.

The face in the mirror jeered at that. *Yeah, like you have friends.* He didn't. (Other than Jock, of course.) The only place he wasn't the Invisible Boy was on the court. If he got snatched away like the Cuomo girl, nobody'd even notice until the next game. And the other players would be just as happy to have him gone — until they looked at the scoreboard. Just like people were going to notice Brendan Atcheson once he and Jock moved from plans to action. Soon, soon.

He watched as his fingers ran thoughtfully along his jawline. Should he shave? He'd done it just two days ago, but his face was so smooth, it might have been two minutes. With hair as dark as his, you'd think he'd need to shave every day. He probably would eventually. (Maybe twice on nights he had a date.)

Yeah, right. He'd be dead long before he had either a beard or a date.

OLIVIA

Olivia Mendez pushed the cruiser's rear-view mirror back into position, satisfied there weren't any scraps of breakfast between her teeth. She checked the car for loose possessions (protein-bar wrappers scattered across a police cruiser's dash looked *so* professional) and got out, dragging the duty belt after her.

Male uniformed officers tended to drive wearing everything but their nightsticks, but getting into the cruiser ten minutes ago had been a sharp reminder of how all those handles used to leave bruises along the bottom of her rib cage. Was it because she had hips? Or because she was six inches shorter than anyone else in the Department?

Anyway, after this morning's jab she'd hastily unbuckled the belt, grateful that these days she was usually in plainclothes.

But not today. After lengthy discussion and much heart-searching, Linda decided that she wanted Olivia front and center, rather than moving quietly around the edges of the school as she'd done much of the past fifteen weeks, and in her uniform rather than plainclothes. So Olivia drove the cruiser — which she'd run through the car wash yesterday — and parked in a prominent spot in front of Guadalupe Middle School.

Buckles fastened, radio on, nightstick retrieved and dropped through its loop, Olivia wiggled the belt into place as she looked around her. Kids were piling off the early bus, still looking sleepy. Across the road, a field crew was already bending over their labors, planting out . . . broccoli, maybe? No one she recognized from this distance, but she waved anyway, then turned back to the hodgepodge of buildings that made up Guadalupe.

What did it say about her life that she was actually looking forward to the day? *You're a sad case, Sergeant Mendez.*

And yet, as she crossed the driveway in front of the school, she found she was enjoying the return of the cop swagger. And, she realized, the excuse the uniform gave to poke her nose into everyone's business.

But seeing as how she wasn't entirely comfortable with the Big Bad Cop routine, maybe she'd pop into the library and see if the Parents' Club had the coffee machine on.

There was nothing that said Friendly and Casual Neighborhood Authority like a cop with a cup.

MINA

Mina Santos had three mirrors in her bedroom, and they all showed a different person.

The one she was looking at now, hanging on the back of the door, showed a Nice Girl — at least, down to her ankles where the boots started. Long black braid, orange T-shirt, plaid skirt that reached her knees, black tights. Pretty much the same girl it showed last year, and the year before: a girl so short and fresh-faced, you'd think she was a child if you didn't notice her chest. (One reason she wore baggy shirts at school.)

The dressing table mirror, the one with the circle of bright light to help her judge when she had more makeup than Mâmân would permit, showed Mina her too-large nose, coarse pores, and (oh, God!) what threatened to become a moustache.

The third mirror was on the wall next to

the closet. Not much bigger than an iPad and surrounded by a pretty enameled frame, the mirror itself was so old its glass was dim, with freckles along the edges. It had belonged to her grandmother, who'd received it as a present for her thirteenth birthday back in Tehran. It was about the only thing Mâmân had from that whole family, and she gave it to Mina last year, when *she* turned thirteen.

At the time, Mina thought that was sweet. Then she worked out that two months later, her grandmother had not only been married, but pregnant, too. Mina didn't look at this third mirror much now. It had a way of showing her the face of a grown woman, which was more than a little creepy.

Anyway: three mirrors, and none of them gave her the same truth as the mirrors at school.

Mina sometimes thought that she and Sofia should just change bodies (Sofe had been like a sister for years, though now it was complicated). That would make Mina as strong as she felt and force people to look up at her, and let Sofia be small enough to ignore, like she wanted.

As if Sofe had heard her thoughts Mina's phone gave its Sofia-cheep. Mina picked it up and read:

Bus stinx like old sox reeeelly looking forward to high school and boys with cars yasss!!!

Mina texted back:

Yeah boys cars that stink of old sox and dead things.

She waited — Sofia always sent at least three texts on the bus.

I swear im only gonna hang with boys who shower.
Speaken a dead things u see this mornings #speakforbee?

Mina flipped over to the hashtag for a look, and was a little sorry she did.

Really gross did u do it?

Naturally, Sofia hadn't.

As if. Not sure its anyone in school.

It was true, the hashtag that started as a way to torment Bee Cuomo's father had begun to show the kind of pictures not even the more hardcore middle-school students would come up with.

Totally creeps. Gotta go see u soon.

Mina dropped the phone. Funny how little Bee Cuomo — who'd been a sixth-grader (and a strange one at that), which meant she was only at Guadalupe a couple of months before she vanished — had more people talking about her now than when she'd actually been there. Would that be so, if she'd been straight-out killed? Sure, everybody figured Bee was dead (except maybe Nick Clarkson) because really, where would an eleven-year-old go on her own? But without finding her, it was like . . . like walking down a step that wasn't there, or having a cut that wouldn't close. How did families manage to go on, when one of them disappeared? It happened all the time, governments disappearing people. Her mother's own family . . .

She made a face at the mirror. Maybe if she did something with her hair? Hack it off and dye it some outrageous color? Use the scissors — right now!

Yeah, right, might as well pierce her nose and give Mâmân a heart attack. But there had to be *something* she could do about that braid. Shouldn't Career Day include how to

101

look professional?

There must be cops with long hair. Did they pin it up tight? Not that she'd ever be tall enough to be a cop. Or old enough to put her hair up, for that matter — not if her parents had any say in the matter.

Her parents' traditional backgrounds surfaced at the weirdest times. Whenever Papá remembered he was Brazilian, he got all patriarchal. And sometimes Mina thought her mother wouldn't object to putting her into purdah. Like after the Taco Alvarez thing last year — Mina'd be paying for *that* until she was thirty.

The trick was for Mina to *look* like she was being absolutely open about absolutely everything — friends, clothes, school — while doing what she wanted behind the scenes. Like changing clothes every morning. Or like her schedule for Career Day, when she'd allowed Mâmân to override her fourth-period choice of Sergeant Mendez and sign her up for some University Professor — because giving way on that meant that Mina could have Sports Medicine for fifth period. Of course, Mina hadn't mentioned that the reason she wanted that session was because Brendan Atcheson would be there.

Not that Career Day mattered a whole lot.

She was going to be a police officer, period. And it wasn't hero worship, as Mâmân insisted. Yes, Mina would never forget the sight of Olivia Mendez coming through the mouth of that cave, but it wasn't that the sergeant had been terribly heroic, or even very impressive, dressed in old hiking shoes and mud-stained pants.

It was the look on the sergeant's face — relief and fear and outrage and authority, all mixed together and shoved at the world: this is who I am and what I care about, so live with it.

That was strength. *That* was something Mina couldn't imagine seeing in any mirror, ever.

NICK

The last few months, Nick Clarkson had taken to leaving the bathroom mirror standing open while he brushed his teeth. For one thing, that way he didn't have to stare at his own face, which since October felt like it had *COWARD* tattooed across it. But he'd *started* leaving it open (and this was something he was *not* going to tell Dr. Henry!) because for a while after the Weirdman house, he kept seeing . . . *things* in the glass. Shadows, like, out of the corner of his eye. Sort of the reverse of vampires, who don't show up in mirrors.

Or like Death in the Terry Pratchett stories: Death isn't invisible, just that people don't want to see him so they don't. Except maybe cats and little kids. And crazy people. For a while there, Nick almost expected a voice to start TALKING IN CAPS IN THE BACK OF HIS HEAD, ASKING HIM

WHAT HE WAS GOING TO DO ABOUT BEE.

Lately, the shadows had stopped moving and the mirror had gone back to being just a mirror. Still, the face there wasn't someone he was really proud of. Not someone a friend could count on.

So Nick only closed the mirror after he'd put away his toothbrush, then went back to his room.

He liked his new bedroom, a lot. They'd moved here just before Christmas, and Grams and Gramps bought him a new mattress that wasn't lumpy, and even a bookshelf. It wouldn't last. Nothing did: houses, families, friends.

Was it normal to think so much about death? (The non-Pratchett kind.) Maybe everybody did. Even people whose best friend hadn't vanished into thin air.

"Ready, Nicky? Oh, sweetie, your hair! A person would swear you didn't have a mirror. Come here and let me comb it."

"I don't know why I have to go to school this early, Mom."

"Sweetie, I need to be at work at 7:30. Wear your coat, hon — it's chilly this morning."

"Mom, the sweatshirt's fine. School's out of your way, and I don't mind the bus."

"Let's just do this today, and we can talk about it over the weekend, all right?"

"Yeah, okay."

"Nicky, you'd tell me if you had a problem at school, right? Or on the bus? If the kids were, you know, bullying you or anything?"

"Mom, I'm fine. School's fine. They don't bug me on the bus anymore. Stop worrying about it."

"You're the most important thing in my universe, Nicky. There's nothing I wouldn't do to make your life easier."

"Then let me take the bus."

"Well, we'll talk about it. Check the door, that it's locked? So, you're seeing Dr. Henry this morning?"

"Second period."

"You like her?"

"She's fine."

"You'd tell me if —"

"Jeez, Mom, I promise, if anything ever goes the teensiest bit wrong, I'll tell you and Gramps and Dr. Henry and Ms. Mc-Donald and all six of my teachers and Tío the janitor and Mrs. Hopkins the secretary and the lunch ladies and —"

"Okay, I get it. It's hands off Nick Clarkson. Fasten your seat belt, sweetie."

Nick sighed. He bet Death didn't have a mother.

Tío

Tío clicked shut the seat belt in the car of Señora Rodriguez. He did not like to use the good Señora as a taxi service, but he had needed to be certain of a tidy appearance today, and when yesterday's newspaper predicted rain, he accepted her offer of a ride to the school. He knew by midnight that the forecast was wrong, but with no telephone, Tío could not tell her not to come. So he waited at the end of his drive and climbed into her backseat, giving polite greetings to the other two people she was transporting that day: a pregnant woman with a clinic appointment and an old man on his way to visit his wife in the hospital.

At least Guadalupe Middle School was on the way to the hospital.

The drive took less than ten minutes, and they spoke of various matters — the weather, the giant new store near the freeway, the Taco Alvarez trial, the lamentable state of the county bus service. When they reached the entrance to the school, Tío thanked the Señora, wished the young mother-to-be good fortune at her appointment, shook the old man's hand, and waited politely until the car had joined the road again.

The first buses were arriving. Sergeant Mendez was there to greet the students, resplendent in her uniform, stern in her visage, yet also taking sips from a tall paper coffee cup. Tío gave the sergeant a nod of greeting and headed for the entrance arch, bright with the colors of its newly restored mosaic sides.

As he went in, his attention was caught by an object in the corner of the wall and archway. He worked his way through the stream of noisy children to pick it up: a can of orange spray paint. But none on the tiles — or, perhaps a faint orange mist at one side. As if the task of ruination had been interrupted the moment it began.

The cap lay just inside the breezeway. He placed it and the can into his lunch bag and paced the length of A Quad, then back down B Quad, examining the walls, watching for other cans, and wondering if he should perhaps wait until tomorrow before mentioning this to the principal.

LINDA

Good morning, *bienvenidos,* friends, guests, my fellow teachers, and students. Welcome to Career Day at Guadalupe Middle School. It has been a very difficult year, the one that has brought us here. Only a strong community could have come together as we have. As I stand up here, looking at our Guadalupe family gathered together under one roof, I also can't help thinking of a word that's used a lot these days: *diversity.* I can't help wondering if a part of what makes us strong is our mix of diverse gifts and heritages.

And that brings another word to mind: fascination. It fascinates me to think how we all happen to be here, to think of the tales behind each one of us, the ways our stories not only brought us here, but how they will change the way we go forward, together and apart.

Linda paused to re-read her opening words. Was she right, to touch on the trauma without using the name Bee Cuomo? By now, those syllables were hardly necessary, and she did make specific reference later in the speech. She let the paragraphs stand, although she did cross out the word *tales* and write in *stories.* Better to repeat the word than risk setting off an explosion of adolescent sniggers at the phrase *tales behind us.*

She continued, reading aloud under her breath. "What is your principal's story, then? Well, I began in Indiana, and arrived in California by way of New Guinea, Nairobi, Fairbanks, and half a dozen other places and jobs." She scowled, then remembered how old it made her look and tried for an expression of wide-eyed wonder instead.

Pah. She sometimes looked older than Gordon, who was sixty-seven — at least, his passport said he was sixty-seven. He looked fifty. And acted like the forty-year-old she'd thought him when they met, back in the Dark Ages.

Her pen hovered above the heavily marked-up printout. Did it sound like she was bragging about her exotic past? Most of the audience would never so much as own a passport. To focus on The Linda McDonald Story might actually distract from the purpose of her speech. It might also invite awkward questions.

Better to just introduce the guests and talk about dreams.

She'd already decided not to dwell on the fact that Guadalupe had been through a year of hell. Or that the school had all the huge and chronic problems associated with poverty and immigration — language barriers, divided homes, the harsh necessity of keeping away from the law. Few of her kids owned any books. Less than half could point to a high school diploma anywhere in the family — far less a university degree.

However, Linda McDonald had seen enough of the world to know that compared to some dark corners of the globe, even the poorest of Guadalupe's children had their hands cupped around the future.

Her personal tale — Indiana farm girl to California school principal — would be a perfect illustration of what could happen when a person grabbed at chance. (And oh, those 3:00 a.m. thoughts: *What if I'd done the expected, thirty years ago, and stayed where I was planted?* What if she'd never known New Guinea as anything but some colorful pages of *National Geographic*? Never met a peculiar expat named Gordon Hugh-Kendrick . . .)

Of course, similar mixed histories could be found in half the people at school. When she'd opened the personnel files, Linda found all kinds of unexpected, even startling pieces of information. (And that was just the official ones — Linda still couldn't decide how many of the last principal's private notes were delusional. They were filled with pain — directional signs to the poor woman's coming suicide.)

Which brought her back to the question of whether it was wise to put her own background out there, especially with an eager young newspaper reporter taking notes. And Olivia Mendez. Not that she had anything to hide. Not really.

No, she decided, drawing a black line through the words. Better to stay Plain-Jane Ms. McDonald, just as her office at school was blandly anonymous, with none of her African textiles, Inuit carvings, or Sepik wood figures; no photographs of elephants or Northern Lights or a laughing young Linda McDonald surrounded by small, black, bizarrely decorated men — far less the collection of ornate penis sheaths Gordon had blandly suggested she tack up to her office wall.

It was the same reason Linda had never considered asking Gordon to be one of the day's speakers — although God knew this town would never meet a more "Unexpected Thread" than Gordon Hugh-Kendrick. (Four years since he'd dropped back into her life, and pretty much every day she felt as if she'd spotted a Bird of Paradise at the patio bird feeder. Or a hawk.) She'd had the sense to keep his name off the speakers' list, which went to the *Clarion.* Bad enough she'd absent-mindedly given Olivia his name last fall, as one of the school volunteers. It was the closest they'd come to a real fight, and though she knew he'd forgiven her, she also knew he had not forgotten.

"Penny for them," said his English accent.

"Not worth it. Is that a new shirt?" Crisp and white, perfectly fitted to his long arms, it looked custom-made. Probably was, by some shady tailor in Hong Kong who clothed drug lords and Third World politicians, charging more than she made in a week.

And there she went again! What was it about nerves that summoned the most absurd ideas? Gordon was her husband, he was English, he was as old as his passport said. He'd bought his shirt from an online guy on the East Coast. Anything more was a reflection of her own self-doubt, and noth-

113

ing to do with his honesty — or his past. His *suspected* past.

"Oxford cloth." Gordon flipped up the collar to settle his necktie into place — her Christmas present, uncharacteristically bright and whimsical — and then noticed the direction of her eyes. "Hope this one is okay? I thought a bow tie might be a bit much."

"You'd probably start a school-wide fad for them. Sweetheart, you don't really have to go today."

"I got the impression you wanted me there."

"I do. I mean, it's up to you, but . . ."

"But my presence would give you a bit of support. I'm happy to, Linda."

"You'll be bored to tears."

"Never. I can always go talk with Tío."

Tío, she mused. Yet another example of unseen histories. Several parents (as well as the ubiquitous Señora Rodriguez) had recommended him for the job of janitor after the old one had abruptly retired five weeks into the school year (shown the door by the new principal, whose sense of smell was well honed when it came to alcohol). Tío was not particularly qualified — Mrs. Hopkins, the school secretary who had seen so many principals come and go, later told her that Tío had made his living pushing an ice-cream cart through the streets. But his English was good, he looked her in the eye, and he could start immediately. She hired him on a two-month trial, thinking to find a more solid candidate, but the man proved reliable, and the possessor of some unlikely skills, from rewiring a sparking outlet (against union rules) to coaxing conversation from kids who gave no one else the time of day. He'd been there since October, and was now indispensable. More than just a janitor, somehow. It almost felt as if *he* was the one who'd hired *her.*

"Are you sure . . ." *No.* Her chair scraped as Linda rose to carry a half-eaten bowl of cereal to the sink.

"Am I sure what?"

"Gordon, you talk with Tío. You'd have spotted if he was up to something, wouldn't you? You'd have told me?"

"What sort of something?"

"He just . . . he seems to spend a lot of time with the kids, for a janitor."

"Tío Jaime is no pedophile."

"I was thinking more along the lines of . . . supplementing his income."

"Drugs? No. Absolutely not."

"Good. I like him, he's just, well, *odd.*"

"Linda, I know this has been a tough year,

but there is no call to see hobgoblins behind every push-broom."

"You're right. Lord, look at the time!"

As she checked her bag for the day's necessaries, it occurred to her that Gordon hadn't exactly answered her question. But then, silence was woven deep into their relationship, and had been from the beginning. Silence, and trust.

He would tell her, if there was something she needed to know. There might be a lot of gaps in Gordon's history, but she knew him well enough to be sure of that.

GORDON: HIS STORY (2)

Linda was given little time to speculate about what kind of place this was that she'd come to, because Mrs. Carver came in to say that the mission's replacement transport had arrived from Australia, and would leave at noon. In the morning, Linda repacked her clean, dry possessions and was driven to the air strip — where she was faced not with an Air Niugini plane, but a winged contraption so tiny the pilot had to haul off a sack of potatoes to compensate for her weight.

The thirty minutes that followed were terrifying, spine-bruising, ear-splitting, and unforgettable. However, once that had been survived, her life became surprisingly tranquil. Within weeks, it was the letters from friends and family that began to seem exotic. She worked hard, ate simply, learned more than she taught, and made friends not only with her white countrymen, but with the local people. These hillmen lived on the edges of malnutrition, surviving on corn, plantains, and the sweet potato they called *kaukau,* calories supplemented by the occasional scrap of protein brought home by hunters. She was there to teach English and basic medical realities to tiny aboriginal people one narrow step out of the Stone Age, the oldest of whom vividly recalled the first white face to appear in their mountain fastness. She discovered a people who understood both joy and hardship — more alive, more human, than many of the college students she knew.

The mission was, as Gordon had warned her, all but unreachable by land. Their only contact with the outside world was the toy-like plane that dropped out of the heavens twice a week onto a patch of cleared mountaintop with necessities (rice and tinned beef) and luxuries (soap, weeks-old newspapers, toilet paper — of coffee they had plenty, it and peanuts being the two cash crops that would grow here). In addition to Linda, who was a combination full-time schoolteacher and part-time nurse, the station consisted of five people. Albert Haines, known throughout the highlands by the deceptively Roman nickname of "Father Albion," was a lively Chicagoan who admitted to sixty-five but was probably much older; he had been in the country since before Linda was born. His devoted assistants, Alice and Tom Overhampton, had come for a six-month stay three and a half years ago. The other two places were filled by a series of short-term missionaries, male and female: all of them young, all of them terrified, none of whom remained long enough for her to learn more than their names.

Unlike Linda. Within a couple of weeks, her life in Indiana seemed like a distant dream. Her Pidgin grew more fluent. She laughed easily, not only with her co-workers, but with the locals. She had never been happier.

Still, happy or not, a person could only stay so long in the bush before the hills started to press in. Only Father Albion seemed impervious to the claustrophobia of having one's every move an endless source of scrutiny and amusement to the locals, of being followed to the outdoor privy and back, of having any conversation punctuated by the giggles of children beneath the floors. So every few weeks, one or another of the staff would hitch a ride on the supply plane back to Mt. Hagen, the metropolis of fourteen thousand souls that boasted such cultural riches as videotape movies, cold Cokes, and hot showers. The fleshpots were restorative, necessary even to those doing God's work.

Linda had been in the highlands for two months when her turn came. On the second of her seven allotted days in Mrs. Carver's boarding house, spent reading novels, drinking two cold beers each evening, and taking two hot showers a day, another guest brought news of a sing-sing being held thirty miles away.

Sing-sings were Papua New Guinea's ultimate spectacle of male vanity, a Stone Age version of NFL football or Brooklyn bar mitzvah. They were also celebrations: of marriage, or a son's return from the university at Moresby, or an unexpected (i.e., sorcery-assisted) recovery from an illness. The men painted themselves all over, primped like Miss America contestants, stripped the forests of Bird of Paradise plumage, and generally made any woman in sight seem a dull sparrow indeed.

This sing-sing, according to Beth (Vreiland, a schoolteacher from Perth) would include a pig kill. Pigs were the traditional measure of wealth here in the highlands, nurtured and sheltered and made more of than a family's child. Men might own them, but women raised them, sleeping with them, coddling them, even (rumor had it) nursing piglets at their breasts. And although protein was scarce here, a boar was valued as much for its tusks as for the meat itself.

Beth was nervous, but Linda leapt at the chance. She went to consult with Mrs. Carver, font of all Hagen knowledge, and came away with the keys to the local schoolteacher's ancient four-wheel-drive Subaru, a box of provisions, and a hand-drawn map. Early the next morning she and Beth drove off into the bush.

Where they got lost. Easy enough to do, with no signposts and little paving. Still, as she assured Beth, it was only thirty miles, and they both spoke enough Pidgin to get by.

But the third time they got lost, the car sputtered and died, in the least populous bit of track they'd struggled through since leaving Hagen.

The starter whined, and they sat, debating options — rather, Beth debated options with herself while Linda kept her mouth firmly shut lest an un-Christian sentiment escape. She knew more or less where she was: they just had to finish sliding down the hillside into the river and grind their way up the other side, and she told her passenger this. Beth unhelpfully pointed out that, while sliding down to the river was certainly an option, the only thing grinding up the other side would be their teeth.

"Help you ladies?"

They both yelped at the plummy English voice at their backs, and whirled to peer into the gathering gloom, where Linda saw, with a sensation of inevitability, Gordon Hugh-Kendrick, dressed as before except for proper shoes on his feet and a lightly laden *bilum* over his shoulder.

She found her voice first. "We were headed for the sing-sing, but the car seems to have other ideas. I think something's broken."

He nodded at the hood. "Pop the bonnet." Linda searched around for the latch and pulled it, and he disappeared into the engine, which succumbed to his charm within moments — even internal combustion could not resist this man for long. What did take her aback was finding that her ill-tempered companion had submitted as easily as the Subaru. When he let the hood drop on the sweetly humming engine, Beth all but batted her eyelashes at him.

He gave her a distracted smile and turned to Linda. "Do you know where you're going, then?"

"I thought we did, but the instructions for Holyoke must have been wrong."

"You're only one turn off the mark. Shall I show you?"

"Where were you heading?"

"That's as good as any. I'll catch a ride back to Hagen from there."

"But where's your car?"

"Oh, I'm on foot."

Linda glanced at his shoes, which were rimed with a grayish mud and spattered with betel, and wondered how long he'd been on *wokabaut*.

"Would you like to drive?" She threw open her door before he could refuse. Gordon dropped his *bilum* through the rear window — it seemed to hold nothing but an orange, a handful of peanuts, and a change of shirt — and slid behind the wheel, turning the Subaru around in a space Linda would have sworn was too small. Half a mile back up the track he launched the car at a sparsely grown patch between two enormous trees — and there was the road to Holyoke.

Linda let out the breath she'd been holding for the last half hour. Spending a night in a car with the jungle pressing in, even with a resourceful Brit on hand to conjure up fire and food, was not an enticing sleeping arrangement. She was grateful for the

123

simple meal that followed, and for the unoccupied corner of a mission bedroom.

She didn't hear where Gordon planned to sleep — in the car, for all she knew. The missionaries had greeted him as a long-lost rogue of a son, but when they asked if he wanted a bed for the night, he shook his head and said he'd got some friends to stay with, then slipped away before they could press him further.

Beth snored.

Life stirred outside the mission houses long before dawn, a growing ripple of noises and movement. When the sun rose, Linda joined it, following voices to the kitchen. There she found her hosts with an enormous pot of tea on the table and Gordon Hugh-Kendrick in a chair, exchanging local news. He was clean-shaven and his thin hair had been combed, but his eyes were bloodshot and he gave off a powerful aroma of hut-smoke: his friends had been locals.

Breakfast was reconstituted eggs and some of the rock-like but highly nutritious biscuits that the mission wives were experimenting with, an attempt to make something tasty out of the peanut. Gordon shot her a look of commiseration as she accepted one.

Mrs. Wilson pronounced judgment. "They need salt. Don't you agree?"

124

Gordon nodded, his mouth somewhat preoccupied with inadequately ground peanuts.

"Now, as you know, Gordon," the missionary went on, "we're trying to come up with nutrition that doesn't have to be brought in. The women here can grind the nuts with a mortar and pestle, even cook it on a heated rock if they haven't a pan, but I can hardly ask them to use half a teaspoon of Morton's iodized."

Gordon washed the mouthful down with a manly swallow of the excellent local coffee, and managed speech. "Well, it is *edible* without salt."

"So I was wondering if you could get me some from a salt pond?"

His face went wary. "Why? I mean, why me?"

"I keep asking our people about pond salt, but no one has any."

"I imagine they have it, it's just so laborious to produce. It's also pretty nasty stuff. Mostly ashes. It won't improve your biscuits any."

But Mrs. Wilson was determined, so Gordon said he'd try to come up with some. Personally, Linda thought that even with Morton's, the biscuits would be better fed to the pigs and turned into pork roast.

The sing-sing began as soon as Reverend Wilson finished his Sunday morning service — forty minutes, start to finish; in Linda's experience, a record from an evangelical. The congregation spilled out of the open-sided church, the men making for their outdoor dressing rooms, the drums summoning the crowd, the doomed pigs squealing from their stakes along the side of the rough football field.

Down in Moresby, Linda had been told, sing-sings were put on for the tourists, with clans of men in similar costumes — Goroka mudmen in one place, others festooned with shells from near the sea, highland clans sporting variations on the same brilliant feathers and rich furs. Here, it was every man for himself. Strings of shells or huge shell breastplates covered every chest. Pig tusks were given pride of place. Feathers from emu to Bird of Paradise bristled out of every headdress; every man's septum was pierced by tusk, shell, or feather; every solemn face was covered by paint of every pigment under the heavens. There were even design iconoclasts, such as the man with half a dozen Bic pens arrayed in his headdress, or the man with dozens of tiny plastic baby dolls around his neck. Ironically, this evocation of the goddess Kali was one of the few costumes that didn't carry with it a trace of threat: those painted and bewigged figures were gorgeous, sure, but they were also really spooky.

Beth had brought her camera, with enough film to stock a convenience store. Gordon was there for a while, standing among the missionaries and chatting politely, or squatting on his heels with the locals. Linda soon lost sight of him, but he was back again in the evening, when the smoke of the cook-fires gave an air of the netherworld to the slaughtering of pigs. The sounds were appalling, shrill squeals followed by the meaty thuds of killing clubs, but in the end the hunks and quarters were ceremonially distributed, clan by clan. Lengthy speeches were made, and the dancing picked up again. Drums and shouts continued through the night, with the vibration of dancing feet rising through Linda's thin mattress.

The next morning, everything started anew — if anything, the energy was building, and apparently would for days. Linda had regretted promising to get back for the Wednesday plane, but by Tuesday morning, after two days of sensory overload and three ill-slept nights, she did not regret having to leave. Unfortunately, Beth was not interested.

Linda stared at her. "What do you mean, you're not going back?" Would she have to make that drive through the bush all by herself?

"Not for a day or two. I, er, I heard there's a new group coming in tomorrow. I thought I'd photograph them."

Linda narrowed her gritty eyes at Beth, who had spent much of the previous day with a good-looking young pastor. "You mean you don't want to leave Father Harmon yet."

"Yeah, okay, I'm interested in seeing more of him. What of it?"

Only someone like Beth, Linda reflected, would come to highland PNG in search of a mate. She shook her head. "Okay, I'll ask around and see if there's anyone interested in a ride to Hagen."

"Gordon's probably ready to leave." Beth all but waggled her eyebrows at the suggestion.

"I doubt it," Linda said repressively. She was not in the market for a husband.

However, Gordon was indeed ready to go, or would be at noon. By which time Linda was more than happy to hand him the Subaru keys, letting the drums, whistles, bells, songs, and squeals fade behind them.

Linda dozed, head thumping against the door frame as they climbed and descended a series of hills. It wasn't until they forded a stream that she woke.

"This isn't the way we came." *Oh, Linda,* nagged her mother's voice in her head. *What have you done, setting off into the back of beyond with a strange man?*

"No, but it's not much further, and I thought you might like to see a salt pond. Since I promised Mrs. Wilson."

"The substitute for Morton's? What are they, anyway?"

"Patches of salty mud, basically."

"Attractive."

"The body requires sodium. And although one would think that trade with the coast would be a simple matter, it being less than a hundred miles away, as I'm sure you've seen the highlands are like a thousand tiny nations. What is it — a tenth of a percent of the world's land, with more than twelve percent of its total languages? This country's most basic characteristic is xenophobia. Trade with the coast is hard. Thus, one takes salt in whatever form one can find it."

"I saw a lot of sea-shells back there."

"Some of which represent a family's yearly income."

Surely, she thought, *if this Englishman intended to leave my ravaged body under a tree, he wouldn't have begun by driving off in full view of twenty missionaries and some four hundred locals?* "So why do they do it?"

"Wear shells?"

"The sing-sing. It seems an expensive sort of party. Like the families who go into debt for a wedding."

"It's less a party than a military campaign." Gordon had stretched forward to peer over the wheel as their route climbed sharply up from the stream-bed, and now settled back as they successfully emerged from the jungle onto what looked like a mountain-goat track beaten into the side of a cliff.

"Sorry?" Linda was somewhat preoccupied by needing to hold the car to the track by fervent prayer and willpower.

"A sing-sing is sublimated warfare. Highland society is built on war — raids, alliances, stealing women, killing the men — probably eating them, at least in part — and raising the children as their own. Then the *waitpela* came and said, *No, you can't do that any longer.* So now the clans wage economic war instead. Like the potlatch of your Pacific Northwest: throw a huge feast for your neighbors — your primary rivals —

130

and you're not only one up on them, they're forced to stage an even greater feast, which if you're lucky will force them to borrow and go into debt for the next generation or two. Fifty years ago, the big men might have had a collection of human skulls in their homes. Today they all wear the *omak* — you saw those? That bib made from *pitpit* cane? Each length of *pitpit* represents participation in a pig kill. Ten lengths would be the sign of a wealthy man."

The bib worn by the head man of the pig kill — a man with six inches of pig tusk through his nose — had stretched down to his leaf-apron. Linda thought about it, then chuckled aloud.

Gordon glanced at her. "It's true!"

"No doubt. I was just thinking, what if the US and Russia adopted potlatch warfare?"

His face wore a smile as he turned back to the goat-track. "Aerial bombardment of canned hams and television sets."

"And for a really big strike, they'd drop an entire school or hospital: Take that, Commie scum!"

"Might have made quite a difference in Vietnam."

At last — the chance to learn something about Gordon Hugh-Kendrick that was not rumor. "Were you there? In Vietnam?"

"I was, yes." It was either a reluctant admission, or Gordon was uncertain about the Y-junction ahead. He chose the right-hand track. "Three years as a military —"

But she was not to hear what his role in that bloody conflict had been, because with an exclamation she hadn't heard for months, Gordon slammed his foot onto the brake and fought the little car to a standstill between the Charybdis of the river below and Scylla in the form of a four-foot-tall, leaf-clad individual with a spear in his hand, who materialized on their left. They missed hitting him, and missed becoming airborne; after a while, her heart settled back into place.

The local had not moved a hair; the front bumper had stopped two inches from the planted spear.

With admirable English aplomb, Gordon cleared his throat. *"Gudai, yupela."*

The small black figure replied, not with a "Good day" of his own, but with a statement. *"Mipela painim onepela waitpela long raunwara bilong sol. Em i dai."*

"I dai?" Linda repeated in disbelief. The man was informing them — informing Gordon — that a dead white man had been found in a salt pond. However, *i dai,* which

literally meant *he's dead,* could also simply indicate that someone was sick or injured.

But the local continued, *"Em I dai pinis."*

To "die finish" meant at the very least that the white man was mightily ill.

Gordon's face was a study in . . . actually, Linda couldn't tell what he was thinking. It looked almost like chagrin — but perhaps he was just wrestling with how to protect her sensibilities. He stretched an arm over the seat to grab his *bilum.* "You go on without me. If you head straight for a half mile, the track gets —"

"Oh, no. I'll go with you. I'm a trained nurse — I might be able to help."

He protested, but Linda already had the car's first-aid kit in her hand and the door open. She had no intention of driving ten feet down that slick path, much less half a mile — although Gordon, having watched her inch her way around the car to solid ground, appeared to credit her more with fearlessness than its opposite.

Without a word, the local settled his stone axe more firmly into his vine belt and set off down the left-hand side of the Y. Gordon threw up his hands, then took the first-aid kit from Linda and followed on his heels, leaving Linda to keep up with them. Half a mile along, they left the track to climb a trail as slippery as greased glass, then pushed through impenetrable bush to the accompaniment of cries from unseen birds and the buzz of a thousand varieties of insect. Twenty minutes later the bush opened up and the unlikely trio stood looking at an expanse of swampy gray water with a lot of dead tree-trunks in it, some lying flat, others hammered upright to fence off squares of various sizes. Three sulky little fires smoldered on the opposite bank, the smoke drifting around Gordon and half a dozen locals who were looking down at something in the water. Linda joined them, then wished she hadn't.

Little need for her first-aid kit to treat this *waitpela*. He was very much dead-finished.

LINDA

"Would you like me to drive?" Gordon asked.

Linda blinked at the bright flare of California sun off the car window. "Oh, no, I'm . . . Well, yes — that would let me do a last polish on the talk." Their paths crossed around the back of the car. Some husbands automatically assumed control of any car voyage: not Linda's.

"I told you that Sergeant Mendez would be at school all day, didn't I?" The other Career Day speakers would arrive in time for the school-wide assembly at 10:00.

"You did." Gordon pushed the seat back and adjusted both mirrors before pulling out of the driveway. Linda got halfway down the first heavily amended page before letting the file drop to her lap.

"She'll be in uniform. Sergeant Mendez. We thought it might be more interesting for the kids." And a more visible presence of authority. Linda glanced sideways. "I said you'd be available, if she needs a hand with anything."

"That's fine."

"She's nice."

"I'm sure she is."

"I know you don't —"

"Linda, it's fine. I know Olivia. I'm happy to talk to her."

"Sorry. Stupid to be so nervous."

"Understandable. Big day, lots of pressure, you'd be a fool not to be nervous."

Fool. "That reminds me, if you need to make conversation with the good Sergeant" — *if you need to distract the cop* — "ask her about her Fool."

"Her Fool?"

"Yep. It's a part of the Gloria Rivas story you may not have heard. Gordon, was I wrong to tell the Parents' Club that I wouldn't support a fund-raiser for a Threat Assessment and metal detectors?"

"No, it was the right decision. Your childhood imagination wasn't entirely wrong — the threat you see may not be the one you should worry about. Anyway, metal detectors by themselves are useless, since anyone intending to bring a weapon onto school grounds won't care about setting off alarms on the way in. Will the parents pay for an unscalable wall around the entire school? And for staff to man the gates?" Before Linda could voice her own objections to the plan — the emotional impact on the kids — he continued with just that. "And as we both know, that kind of overt paranoia only makes kids feel more unsafe. An hour of listening is worth a foot of wall, any day."

Sometimes, Linda almost managed to forget that Gordon had worked for an organization that got its start enforcing the rules of Third World mining companies and grew into the dark category of private armies. Four years ago, when she'd been considering Gordon's proposal, she began a search of the three TaylorCorp Security names — and then stopped. Trust — with a school or with a husband — worked both ways.

"Just try and explain to some of those fathers that having the kids love their school and feel invested in the community is worth a dozen metal detectors or armed guards."

"After all," he pointed out, "Bee Cuomo didn't disappear from school. Although it's probably better to stick to the price-tag argument. Any particular difficulties you're anticipating today?"

"More than I can count. I decided in the end that I'd let the *Clarion* send its reporter to the assembly, and use her as a speaker for the following period, but she's not allowed to interview anyone until school is over. And she has to stay off school grounds before and after."

No need for Linda to add: *So make sure you keep out of her sight.*

"I'm surprised they agreed to that."

"I got the feeling they're just giving the young woman something to do to keep her away from the Taco Alvarez trial. Which is exactly why I said she has to be off the premises, since I'm pretty sure she's aware we have one of Taco's cousins here — you know Chaco Cabrera? — as well as the victim's younger sister."

"Mina's tall friend."

"Sofia does stand out. At least the kid who actually witnessed the killing isn't around — Danny Escobedo. He's living out of state until he has to testify."

"Which I understand will be today or tomorrow." Gordon signaled to turn left across the morning traffic.

"Did Mina tell you that?"

"She did."

"Is she frightened?"

"For the boy? Because he's testifying? I don't think so."

"I meant personally." Linda had spent

upwards of a hundred hours in meetings over the Taco Alvarez problem since last summer, everything from gang dynamics to witness protection. Gordon's protégée, Mina Santos (Guadalupe's designated Goth), was doubly involved, being both best friends with the dead girl's sister and an unlikely but determined supporter of the young witness. "If I were Mina's mother, I'd have pulled her out long ago."

"I suppose people who have faced true militant thuggery find it hard to take mere gangs seriously."

Linda shook her head. "Ironic, to come to San Felipe thinking it was a safe haven."

"Isn't it, though?" His tone made her glance over, but he was studying the road.

"Well, I guess for them, it was safe. A town this size is not exactly a prime target for international terrorists."

Linda had first met Mina's parents the previous summer, when she'd asked them to come in for a talk about possible threats to their daughter because of the Alvarez case. To her surprise, the tiny, nervous-looking mother had listened with a patient expression — and then gone on to explain her own family situation in such daunting detail, Linda might have suspected clinical paranoia were it not for the newspaper

139

articles she put in Linda's hand. One of them talked about some recent testimony Mrs. Santos had given to a war crimes and reparations tribunal in Brussels. Another had to do with a killing in London.

At the end of it, Mrs. Santos had turned Linda's question around on her: Perhaps Linda would prefer not to have *Mina*'s dangers brought to *Guadalupe*'s door?

It wasn't that Linda didn't believe her. It was just that the problems Mrs. Santos envisioned seemed so very . . . distant. International assassinations, in a quiet farming community? Not what she'd call an immediate concern when compared to the very real Taco Alvarez — but then, the communities of Boston and Oklahoma City and Littleton hadn't expected to see themselves in three-inch headlines, either.

However, whether the danger was faraway or close to home, it was blazingly apparent that the small, nervous Iranian woman had a core of steel, and refused to back down from any threat. Which Linda considered little short of awesome. It was one thing to risk your own skin, but another entirely to do so with your only child.

At any rate, Mina Santos was still in school.

"How are her lessons going?"

140

Gordon smiled. "Her Pidgin English is better than mine. That child is seriously bright."

And gorgeous, under all that makeup and baggy clothing. "Even without the trial, I'm not sure how much longer her parents will keep her in the public system."

"I rather doubt Mina will permit *them* to make that decision. Any other problems I should know about?"

"Something more exciting than gang warfare, you mean? I had a call from Bee Cuomo's father yesterday. Ten in the morning, and he sounded drunk. On the edge of abusive, although he stopped clear of actual threats. He thinks our kids are spreading rumors on social media, suggesting he killed his daughter."

"Which kids?"

"Mostly Nick Clarkson. The boy who had the nervous breakdown last month?"

"I remember."

"It surprised me, since the boy seems to be doing well. He sees our psychologist every week."

"Is it possible Cuomo actually is responsible for the child's disappearance?"

"Olivia says he's not an official suspect, and has no history of violence or abuse, other than being picked up once or twice for being drunk and disorderly. Although that in itself is a little worrying."

"So, add an irate Mr. Cuomo and nervy Nick Clarkson to Iranian terrorists and police sergeants."

"Along with the usual illicit drugs, budget cuts, leaky roofs, kids in divorces, the upcoming school assessment, and general adolescent hormones. Oh, and twenty-three guest speakers. One of whom — the weaver — is nearly blind from glaucoma and absolutely reeks of dope. I know it's legal, but I told her she'd have to lay off it before coming here."

"Isn't a blind weaver rather like a deaf musician?"

"Hey, it worked for Beethoven. And she's famous."

"Still, I wouldn't have thought weaving a career you'd encourage students to pursue."

"I wanted an artist. Besides, with her among the speakers, I get to use that analogy of 'woven threads of community' in my speech." Linda caught his quick grin at the admission, then lifted one of the pages from her lap. "What do you think of 'the warp of hopes woven on the weft of reality'? A bit much?"

"Might be." He smiled as her pencil drew an obedient question mark in the margin.

"So: drugs, death threats, and bureaucratic nonsense. Business as usual, at Guadalupe Middle School."

Linda laughed at Gordon's laconic understatement. She'd probably never know why he came back into her life, four years ago. Or even why she'd decided to let him. But there was no doubt: despite everything he was and had done, this man made her feel as if the world made some kind of sense.

The service crew came on at seven. At twelve minutes after, a woman in company uniform got behind the wheel of the third in the row of white commercial vans. She started it up and drove down the lot to the car wash.

The boss liked his delivery vans clean, even when they didn't have the company logo on the side.

MINA

"Mina, if you are not in the car in thirty seconds you will have to walk to school."

"Fine, I'll walk. We live, like, two minutes away."

"Even if you ran, you would still be late. Especially in those boots."

"Let's try."

"Mina, child, *I* do not wish to be late."

"Yeah, okay. Where's my schedule? Did Papá leave it on the — ah, got it!"

"Thank you. That orange is pretty on you. Although I do not know why you insist on wearing Sofia's old coat. You look like a homeless person."

"It's cold."

"But I bought you — oh, never mind. You have your telephone?"

"One of these days they're going to catch me with it."

"Principal McDonald does not mind unless you use it in your classes. Do you?"

"Of course not. But Sofia was using hers outside during lunch last week and Ms. McDonald confiscated it."

"Our situation is not the same as Sofia's."

"I'm not sure that'll matter."

"Mina, if the principal takes your cellphone, I will speak with her. Or you can take one of the house phones instead."

"Those things barely work!"

"Yasmina Santos, you will *not* leave home without a means of contacting me. And you will send me a text before the first bell. And during the lunch hour."

"Don't I always? Even though you can always see where I am."

"I can see where your phone is. How do I know if you are with it unless you tell me?"

"You do realize normal parents don't track their kid every minute, right?"

"Yet again, our situation is not normal. Is it, Mina?"

"I know, I know. Mâmân?"

"Yes, Mina."

"You said you'd talk to Papá about letting me bike to school."

"I did. And he and I agreed it was not safe."

"But there's a bike lane almost the whole way!"

"Not the last half mile."

"I'd be really careful."

"Perhaps you can ride to school the final week."

"But that's four months away!"

"Yes. Tell me about your speakers today."

"You know the schedule."

"Why did you choose to hear Dr. Henry?"

"I'm interested in psychology."

"It's not because she treated the boys who were involved with Gloria Rivas' murder?"

"Danny and Carlos weren't *involved* in it. Any more than I was. And I don't think the physical therapist in period five is a criminal mastermind, and I'm sure the professor in sixth period isn't an assassin."

"Mina!"

"Sorry, Mâmân."

"Our safety is no laughing matter! You know that. Or perhaps you've forgotten. Perhaps it is time for another review of what has happened to half your family, your grandparents, your uncle —"

"Ma, I'm sorry. I do understand. I was only making a joke — a very *small* joke."

"A joke is funny. Our lives are not."

"No, Mâmân."

"Mina, why is there a police car in front of your school?"

"It's only Sergeant Mendez. She's one of the day's speakers, remember? Can you

147

drop me up front?"

"So you can speak with her? We've been asked to use the drop-off around the side."

"But this early it doesn't matter — and look, there's Tío. I can practice a little Spanish before the bell rings."

"Won't your friend Sofia be expecting you at the drop-off?"

"So?"

"Ah. You are finding her . . . clingy?"

"She's getting better."

"Mina, my flower, you are a good friend."

"Better than I am a daughter?"

"You are the very best daughter a woman could have. Now give me a kiss, child, and go have a good day."

"You too, Mâmân."

"Text me," her mother urged.

But the car door slammed, and Mina was gone.

7:16
Tío

Tío had made a complete circuit of the school without finding another trace of orange paint, ending up at his office.

The janitor's room stood between the cafeteria and the gymnasium. It was not a comfortable space, since it had no outside door and its solitary window was both narrow and high. Indeed, the entire cafeteria seemed designed by an architect whose fear of vandals overcame his desire for fresh air or daylight. And Tío thought he was not the only one to find the place unwelcoming: those brightly painted illustrations on the walls, installed by successive administrations, were too large and vehement to be accidental. Even the students tended not to linger inside.

This early in the day, however, sunlight was still pouring through its long strip of high windows, emphasizing the wear in the linoleum and the age of the faded velvet

149

curtains across the stage. Normally, Tío would have remained for a time, his presence reminding the students to be aware of the need for order and cleanliness. However, Mr. Chaco Cabrera was one of those who received school breakfasts, that they might better concentrate on the day's study. So today, Tío would perform a few of the morning's other tasks, and return to the cafeteria when he estimated young Chaco had eaten.

Tío of all people would not wish to interfere with the boy's education.

By way of reward for his thoughtfulness, Mina Santos arrived as he was hooking the flag to its rope. This early, she was still wearing the face she was born with instead of the mask she would soon paint on. The girl trotted across the busy tarmac to the flagpole, dropping her oversized bag and taking the folded California flag from under his elbow. Mina was a young swan in a clutch of mallard ducklings, down to her name — which sounded as Spanish as her classmates', although it was not, and nor was she. Not that there was a single thing wrong with ducklings. He just wished the child did not feel the need to hide her qualities quite so emphatically.

He thanked her, and asked after her health.

"I'm fine. Though the trial is making my mother crazy. I'm so sick of hearing about it I could scream."

"When does your friend Danny give his testimony?"

"It might be today. He's not sure." With the US flag clipped and run a few feet up, she handed him back the bear flag. "Why is the state flag always under the American one?"

"I imagine it is to do with priorities."

"We're Americans before we're Californians? I guess that makes sense. Are you a citizen?"

"I am."

"That explains why you know more about the country than most of the people born here." He smiled. As he pulled, hand over hand, the limp cloth began to stir, bringing the bear into view.

"The American flag used to be a snake. 'Don't tread on me.' "

"And Mexico chose an eagle eating a snake."

"Ha! The Persian flag had the lion and sun. Even modern Iran couldn't come up with something on their flag that would eat a lion."

"A strong symbol indeed."

"People die for flags, don't they?"

"People die for what they represent."

With the breeze thirty feet up, the flags rippled: stars and stripes; bear with the lone star. The girl's thick braid swung free as she tilted her head back. "When I grow up, I want a flagpole. I like the noise."

After a minute, she drew her eyes from the heavens and bent to catch up the strap of her bag. They moved across the drive toward the parked and rumbling buses. "Thank you for your help, Miss Santos." He paused to let her go ahead of him. "I wish you an interesting day."

"It's not going to be as interesting as I hoped."

"Oh? Why is that?"

She nodded toward the short, tough-looking woman in the immaculate uniform, who watched over the chaos with sharp eyes. "My mother doesn't want me to go to the session Sergeant Mendez is giving. She thinks I've had quite enough of the police in my life for the time being."

"I can understand your mother's concerns."

"I guess. Anyway, I can always talk to Sergeant Mendez on my own." With a grin that made her look her age, just for an instant, Mina turned away to join her duckling friends.

CHACO

Chaco was on the side of the bus near the school when they came down the road, so he saw Tío at the flagpole, talking with Mina Santos, who must've just got here 'cause she still looked like a kid and not a wannabe rock singer. Why'd a girl as hot as her dress like that, anyway? Or hang around with old guys like Tío and the principal's husband? Pretty much every boy made a play for Mina at one time or another. But only once. Girl had a tongue on her. Things she said could leave scorch marks. They'd *excoriate,* which meant taking the skin off something.

Mina wasn't bad for an eighth-grader. Nowhere near as hot as her best friend, Sofia, of course, but she was okay. Before Sofia's sister mouthed off at Cousin Taco last year and dumped them all into la mierda, the girls would sometimes talk to him. That was then. Now, Mina was not only friends with Sofia, she was sticking up for that little punk Danny Escobedo, who was gonna testify for sure against Taco. Which made Mina The Enemy, a person to be dissed every chance Chaco got.

So he did — but she didn't even seem to notice! Which pissed him off, partly because, hey, he should be the one who got to do the ignoring here, but also because she *should* be scared of Taco and didn't seem to be. So how was that smart?

Maybe Mina *wasn't* all that bright. Like, she had a thing for Mr. Basketball Star, Brendan Atcheson, who, yeah, was good-looking, but he was also trouble with a capital T. And like her, Brendan seemed to be both smart and stupid, 'cause he didn't even see Mina flirting with him. Or maybe he was just ignoring her.

Well, there wasn't anything Chaco could do about any of it, and anyway she'd find out how things worked soon enough. Serve her right, the little puta.

But man, life could be so . . . *perplexing.*

The bus doors hissed open. Normally, Chaco was one of the first to shove down the aisle. But Mina and Tío were crossing over in front of the bus, so he sat at the window and watched them.

If Tío'd been any younger, Chaco would've made trouble for him by spreading rumors he was a pervert — like that hashtag thing going around — but honest, who'd believe it? The old guy didn't even eye the girls like Sofia who already had tits. Tío had pets, that was all, boys and girls. Like Esme, after that gum thing back in January.

Everybody knew who was dropping the wads of gum in front of the cashier's window — everyone but the teachers. Esmerelda Gustafson hated the cashier, who'd spotted her chewing one day and given her a hard time about kids leaving it on trays and the mess it made in the dishwashers, and when Esme told the woman it wasn't her, the cashier just got pissed and pretty soon the two of them were shouting and the cashier reported Esme and got her in trouble with her mother. So Esme (who really *wasn't* one of those leaving gum on the trays) starting saving her gum up just so she could let it fall in front of the cashier's window.

Until Tío caught her.

Chaco happened to see the whole thing, though nobody else did. He came through the cafeteria door and there was Tío standing straight as a soldier next to his mopcart, staring across the tables at Esme, who was looking like that nature program in science class about the mouse frozen in front of a snake. *Hypnotized* was the word. And Chaco didn't see Tío make any move, but after a minute Esme left the line and walked over to stand in front of him. Tío said something, she answered back — polite, not smart-ass — and the old guy said something else. Esmerelda nodded, and got back in line. Tío pulled out his scraper and went to work on the gum. But after the final bell, instead of getting on the bus, Esme headed toward the school yard, where Chaco saw her sitting at a picnic table, across from Tío. Talking. She never said what had happened, but she didn't spit gum on the floor anymore.

Chaco'd even seen her doing homework one afternoon in the cafeteria while Tío mopped away at the other end. He didn't know why, but it made him think of his mother and Auntie Isabella, working in the rows of tomatoes and chilies in Isa's garden, separate but somehow together.

Which was weird.

Hell, Tío was weird. He'd only been here a few months, and couldn't earn as much as even a teacher, but it almost felt like he ran the school instead of Principal McDonald. Maybe it was that quiet thing of his, *ominous,* like, but Tío reminded him a little of cousin Taco, the way Taco would walk into a room and everybody'd kind of watch him. Which was stupid, 'cause Taco was a big man in San Felipe, with money and guns and scary Angel to back him. Tío was just this indio in a turd-brown uniform, scrubbing out toilets.

Anyway, what with Mina and Esme, there was a lot about the janitor that confused Chaco. The old man was a . . . an *anomaly,* meaning something that didn't fit. Tío didn't fit.

But he was there, all the time, sneaking around behind his quiet cart. And those black eyes of his, they saw everything — a lot more than Principal McDonald's blue ones.

When Tío and the second-hottest girl in school had passed by the front of the bus, Chaco stood up at last to join the kids shuffling down the middle. Although he checked to make sure the janitor had gone on into the building before he pushed forward to the steps.

Not that Tío would guess where that can of spray paint came from. Not unless the old guy knew how to do fingerprints.

158

GORDON: HIS STORY (3)

The news of a strange man who was dead-finished in the salt pond brought a crowd as the bush-telegraph spread the word of this gratifying event. Men with hastily-arranged decoration, women with *bilums* loaded with *kaukau* and *pikininis,* older naked children at their feet — and all of them including Gordon seemed to feel that the dead man was the responsibility of the two *waitpela*s. All ignored Linda's protestations that the police should be called.

With a sigh, Gordon began to undo the buttons on his shirt. "There'll be nothing left of him by the time they get here. And he's already spoiling the salt."

"But surely these people —"

"They've gone for something to wrap him in. They'll take him down to the main road for us, but I'll have to get him out for them."

He handed his shirt to the man with the spear, slipped out of his shoes, and waded cautiously into the murky water. But Linda scarcely noticed his manipulations of the gruesome object, because as Gordon turned away, her eyes were riveted by the skin on his back. He had been scarred, deeply and thoroughly, in a pattern of great raised welts from shoulder to waist. She had read about this, the crocodile-marks of tribal initiation. Where the hell had he submitted to those? And why?

Gordon wrestled the corpse to the bank, where a threadbare blanket had been stretched out to receive it. When he had it at the water's edge, hands joined in to help roll the body into the blanket, wrapping the resulting bundle with bits of vine-rope and commercial twine, using a pair of machete-trimmed saplings to turn the muddy corpse into a package with handles. A package with two naked feet emerging from one end, the dead man's shoes having been claimed by one of the rescuers.

With great good cheer, now that the problematic corpse had been transformed into a ceremonial object, four men seized the ends of the branches and heaved the burden up from the ground. They and a dozen others made off with it, chattering and shouting. Gordon sluiced himself with water from the cleaner end of the pond, then resumed his shirt, squatting down on the grass-covered bank to dry his feet and speak with the spear-carrier about the discovery of the body. Linda walked along the bank to look at the fires, and realized this was what Gordon had been telling Mrs. Wilson about, back in Holyoke: pond salt was a far cry from the supermarket variety. Logs were weighted down in the mineral-rich *raunwara* to soak up all they could, then propped up to dry, and set alight. The little heaps of ash were no doubt salty, but Linda couldn't imagine the tidy Mrs. Wilson spooning that into her peanut biscuit recipe, no matter how authentic. She also wondered, somewhat queasily, how long it would be before minute traces of *waitpela* ended up in someone's dinner — although, come to think of it, the body was near the pond's trickling outlet.

What was the man doing here, she wondered. Had he drowned — in knee-deep water ten feet from the bank? Perhaps he'd had a heart attack.

While she wandered up and down, trying to push these morbid thoughts away with a close examination of the salt enterprise, she was interrupted by a smothered burst of laughter. She looked up, startled, to see Gordon sitting on the grass beside a boy of about twelve, their heads together as they watched her, their faces holding identical expressions of impish humor.

Her own disapproving-missionary face shamed them instantly into solemnity. Gordon got to his feet, clapping the boy on the back, shaking hands with the remaining menfolk, rubbing the heads of the small children, and taking verbal leave of the women in the background. He tucked his shoes under his arm for the slippery journey back to the jeep. Once there, Linda scraped the muck from her own footwear while Gordon washed his feet off with water from the five-gallon can lashed to the back.

When they were moving again, she hardly noticed the precipitous cliff at her elbow, all but forgot her disapproval at the insensitive laughter. The scarring on her companion's back seemed to press through the very fabric of his shirt at her, until finally she couldn't bear not knowing.

"Those cuts, on your back . . ."

He shot her a rueful grin. "You know how sailors get to port and wake up with a tattoo? Well, I didn't realize how strong the local hooch was."

You'd have to be catatonic for a week, for that much cutting. "An initiation?"

"More or less. None of us took it very seri-

162

ously — once it healed, that is." She thought he was lying, but to what extent, or why, she did not know. Before she could go any further, he asked, "So, why are you in New Guinea? You don't seem much of an evangelical."

"I caught my fiancé in bed with my best friend, and missionary work was the first escape I came across."

He gave a cough of laughter. "Bit of a shock, that."

"Galvanizing." At her dry agreement, he glanced over. She smiled. "What about you? Are you married?"

But that was a step too far. His face shut down, his focus on the road ahead resumed. When they had negotiated their way around an unremarkable gap in the road, he gave her the briefest possible answer.

"I was. She died."

"Oh, Gordon. I'm so sorry. What was her name?"

This silence was even longer. "Mary. Her name was Mary."

Linda heard the name as *Meri — how odd, to name a girl Woman* — before her native tongue reasserted itself to identify it as a proper name. "Was she English?"

"No." The finality of the word made it clear that the topic was at an end.

When they reached town, Gordon insisted on dropping Linda at Mrs. Carver's before he went on to the police station. Linda shivered as she watched him drive away, and continued to feel so shivery that Mrs. Carver called the doctor, to check her for malaria.

She was better the next morning, when a *kiap* came for her statement. She had little to tell him apart from having been with Gordon Hugh-Kendrick when the dead man was taken from the pond, but he wrote it down and had her sign it, then told her that there was no reason she couldn't get on the plane that afternoon.

"Do you know who he was?" Linda thought the chance of any white man going unidentified for long here was tiny.

"ID in his pocket said John Taylor. But it'll be a while before we're sure. Have to send for his dental records in Brisbane. Nothing to worry about, miss. Accidents happen."

He left.

But as Linda retrieved her things from the laundry, as she packed her bags and went over Father Albion's shopping list, she could not stop thinking about all she had seen and heard. John Taylor. Dale Lawrence. Their friend Abrams. Gordon Hugh-Kendrick's initiation scars and his marriage to a woman called Woman. His wife's death, and his subsequent arrival in the highlands. The gray mud and splash of betel on his shoes the afternoon he appeared out of the bush. His easy camaraderie with men dressed in leaves, whose heads did not reach his chin.

When her suitcase was packed, Linda went to the kitchen and asked Mrs. Carver if there was any way to get a message to Gordon. The landlady said that one of her employees was sure to find him, if he was in town, so Linda wrote a brief note. *I need to speak with you before my plane goes at 3:00.*

And sure enough, at 2:30 there he was, leaning on the side of the yellow jeep and chatting amiably with one of Mrs. Carver's houseboys. When Linda came out onto the veranda, his eyes lit on her, and he managed to dismiss the young man without seeming to do so.

"Take you to the airport?" He was already reaching for her bag. He held the car door for her, and she did not hesitate to get in. As he drove back through the town, she studied his face. Another man would have looked apprehensive, or even curious about why she had asked him to come. Gordon merely looked bone tired. As if he had just finished a long and arduous task, and wanted nothing but to rest.

"I have a question."

The side of his mouth quirked. "Only one?"

"I think so."

"Ask."

"Your wife's name wasn't Mary. Was it?"

"No." He drew a breath, as if his last as a free man. "Her name was Jasmin. We were expecting our first child when they came through — Lawrence, Abrams, and Taylor. They worked for TaylorCorp. Private security contractors that the mines use to keep their workers in line. Mercenaries, really. The founder was convicted in absentia of war crimes in Africa. John was one of his sons. I did some work for them a couple years back, and stepped on a few toes when I quit. When John heard I was in the area, he and his friends came looking for me. They found Jasmin instead. I got home six hours later, just in time to watch her die."

Linda had always found forgiveness the most difficult precept of the Christian faith. Who holds the power to forgive? When is the refusal to punish a sign of forgiveness, and when is it cowardice? And if she said nothing, did that make her an accomplice?

What did God want Linda McDonald to

do with this stranger's confession? Could she possibly condone the cold-blooded murder of three men?

But charming accent and appealing smile aside, she felt to her bones that Gordon Hugh-Kendrick was a good man. She had no doubt that if she told him they needed to speak to the police, he'd merely nod tiredly and head back into town. On the other hand, from what she had heard about those three men — what she had seen of the mines during her months in this country — it was clear that they had turned their backs on God's repentance.

The jeep came to a halt on the runway tarmac. Gordon sat back with his fingers on the lower edge of the steering wheel, watching the slowly rotating propellers of the tiny plane for a bit before turning his eyes to her. They were golden, she realized, not green. "Is that the end of it, then?" she asked him.

"There is nothing else that needs doing."

After a moment, Linda held out her right hand. "If anyone puts it together, it won't be because of me."

Equally deliberately, his hand clasped hers. He looked puzzled, rather than relieved, then suddenly his fatigue seemed to drop away, the lines beside his eyes crinkling

167

into a smile. When he leaned forward to kiss her cheek, his skin smelled of coffee and hut-smoke.

Gordon helped Linda into the plane, handing up her suitcase and the string bags filled with the mission's marketing. He stood on the tarmac until she was in her seat by the window, then climbed into the yellow jeep and drove away. As he went, his arm came up in a two-fingered salute.

The next time Linda came down from her mountain perch, he had left Mt. Hagen. The *kiap* were looking to talk with him further, Barry told her, but Gordon had gone home, to New Zealand, or England. Or was it Scotland? Privately, Linda thought that Gordon Hugh-Kendrick had indeed gone home, but not to a land where English was primary.

And that was that.

She thought of him often, over the years. Any number of times she took out her memories and turned them over and over in her mind, wondering if she should have spoken aloud her suspicions, wondering if it was too late . . .

But in the end, she had not. He was gone, back into the wilds, and — the implied promise of that wave notwithstanding — she did not expect to see him again, ever.

Twenty-six years later, and half a world away from Papua New Guinea, she did.

BRENDAN

The text came while Brendan was eating his cereal at the kitchen table. The name on the header was Jim Cooper, but it was Jock, one of the burner phones he'd got so Sir wouldn't catch the forbidden communication.

Hope you pick up some good tips today, wish I was in your sessions.

Brendan replied:

Like anyone would trust you w a job.

Jock texted back:

Yeah and you'll look adorbs in a nurses uniform.

Brendan snorted, just as Sir came into the kitchen. Naturally, he wanted to know who it was.

170

Brendan closed the message function but took care to leave the phone, oh so casually, lying next to his glass. "Nobody. Just a friend."

"I was beginning to think you didn't have any. Brendan, I had a reminder of your dentist appointment next week. Have you been flossing your teeth?"

"Yes, Sir." *No, Sir. Put your Glock to your head, Sir.*

"Maybe if you got on with your breakfast you'd have time to floss, instead of fooling around with your friends."

"Just finishing, Sir." Brendan shoveled in the last mouthful and stood, slipping the phone (oh so casually) into his pocket before Sir could investigate.

Coach Gilbert

Joe Gilbert sat in the breakfast nook stirring his coffee, oblivious to the sound, the sunlight, and the presence of his wife at the stove. Carol had to speak his name three times for him to look up.

"Sorry?"

"I said, why are you stirring your coffee? You don't use sugar anymore."

He looked at the spoon and laid it back down next to the knife. When he picked up the cup, it had gone oddly cool.

She frowned at him, dish-towel in hand.

"Joe, is something wrong with Nick? Trouble at school?"

"Nick? No, Nick's doing great. In fact, if anything I'd say he's becoming something of a hero."

"Really?"

Coach could understand his wife's reaction. Sure, *they* loved the boy, and had since they'd first laid eyes on the tiny,

172

wizened creature in the neonatal intensive care unit, but Nick wasn't exactly the first kid who came to mind when you said the word *hero*. And there had definitely been problems at school, early on. There were always problems. He still didn't know why the whole school hadn't risen up and started laughing at his grandson as soon as his crazy story got out. No, Coach would never understand middle school students. Or maybe there was something in how the principal was running the place. "Bee Cuomo seems to've been a popular girl. Anyway, Nick's something of a celebrity now. Like if he'd had a UFO land on his lawn."

"So if it's not Nick that's bugging you, Joe, what is it?"

He took a deep breath. "I think maybe I've got a pervert coming to watch the team practice."

She laid the dish-towel on the sink and came to sit across the table from him. "Are you sure?"

"No. But the guy isn't there to pick someone up. He comes in and sits in the stands, then he drives off without a kid in the car. And he doesn't work at the school — I'm pretty sure I know all the faces by now."

"Does he . . ." Reluctantly, he lifted his gaze to her, and the two of them consulted silently across the table on the possible endings for that sentence: Drool? Breathe heavily? Play with himself? ". . . *do* anything?"

"He watches. And he wears a raincoat." Immediately, Coach felt ridiculous.

"It has been raining."

"I know, I'm overreacting. He's just . . . strange. Intense, I guess."

"Is there any kid in particular? Or the team in general? I mean, could it be a scout? Another coach, looking for tips?"

He stared at his coffee, wondering, as he had for a couple of days now, if it wasn't just his own sensitivity to the boy in question. He answered her reluctantly. "I think it is one kid in particular. I think he's got his eyes on Brendan Atcheson."

Coach Gilbert had only noticed the man in the stands a week ago. He might have been there all along, but Coach had been rather preoccupied. New school, catch-up work in the classroom, a team in shambles: it was understandable he didn't see the man earlier. But once he'd seen him, once Joe Gilbert really saw the man's posture and the . . . hungry expression on his face, it was hard to see anything else.

Coach Gilbert was a hasty hire ten days into the new year, after the math-teacher-slash-basketball-coach skied himself into a tree over Christmas vacation.

Joe Gilbert, retired teacher, volunteer tutor, grandparent of troubled sixth-grader Nicholas Clarkson, was there for the asking — and Linda McDonald had asked. She'd begged. And even though Coach was doing just fine in retirement and had no intention of taking another job, he ended up telling the principal that he'd fill the position until the skier was back. If nothing else, it meant he could be near Nick without either of them feeling like Gramps was being a nurse-maid.

In any event, Coach found a lot to like about Guadalupe Middle School. Oh, the school had more than its share of problems, but its teachers were mostly young enough to still care, the principal was nowhere near as corn-fed Ohio as she looked, and the kids (most of them) had a certain amount of respect for their elders. He'd spent much of his life teaching in the inner city, until he and Carol made a hasty move back to San Felipe in November to help their daughter with Nick. And unlike in LA, he didn't feel like he should wear a Kevlar vest to work.

Still, Coach had been a Marine and a

teacher of adolescents long enough to know that he had to walk in the door with a bang. So he'd come in to first-period math, found a riot in progress, and responded like a drill sergeant: no fear, no doubt, no hesitation at getting right up in their faces. Riot quelled, kids wary, books on desks, Coach was boss.

The same on the court that afternoon, once he'd dismissed the three bickering volunteer-coach dads with brusque thanks. He'd stood with his arms crossed and glared down at his motley collection of twelve- to fourteen-year-olds, tall and short, flabby and muscled, brown and white and one lone black kid, letting them know that Coach Gilbert was a tyrant, by God, and unless you wanted off the team or to have a part of your anatomy verbally shredded or ripped away, you did what Coach wanted. *Now.*

But there was always one kid . . .

Well, that wasn't true. Some blessed years his only rebels had been the usual testosterone-fueled boys who couldn't help pushing the boundaries. He'd learned to deal with those by a show of Alpha-male domination followed by a dose of humor, to establish a sense of shared masculinity. He'd found that the troublemakers often turned out to be the most helpful assistants and players imaginable. But then there were the

176

others, those kids with some bleak space in their psyches, who made life a constant painful battle — not for domination, but for salvation.

Coach wouldn't use a word like *salvation* out loud, of course, except maybe after a couple of beers, and then only to his wife. But that's how he thought of it. And he knew, deep in his soul, that the basketball court — or the baseball diamond or the playing field — was where, for a boy that age, salvation lay.

What hurt was knowing how rare it was to actually save one of them. He'd had maybe a dozen such kids over the years, kids with dead patches in the depths of their eyes and nothing but hate for the world. He'd saved two of them — he personally, using the court, the kids' skill, and his own teacher's soul, had saved two young men from defeat, turning them into productive human beings who'd gone on to lend a hand to other lost boys. Another four of the dozen had some-how fumbled their way out of the morass to become what looked like normal men, with drinking problems maybe, but carrying on. Some of the others had slipped out of his view, which he tried to take as a good sign — at least their names hadn't appeared in the headlines. But for three of these kids, it had been a matter of too little, too late. One to drugs. One to a bullet out the window of a passing car. One to a homemade knife in prison. Three of his boys, he had failed.

And now he was faced with another arrogant fourteen-year-old with deadness creeping over his eyes like spiritual cataracts. Brendan Atcheson's entire being seemed to beg the world to kick him and justify his own self-loathing. All Coach could do was keep an eye out for reportable bruises, and remind himself that the boy was *here,* willing to play ball, willing to risk a commitment to the game: the kid was not lost yet.

So all in all, what with wrenching unruly classes into line and hammering those adolescent minds onto equations, while figuring out the workings of this particular school and a new set of colleagues, then scrambling to knock the basketball team into some kind of order (undoing the lessons of that trio of well-meaning idiot dads) on top of all the hours of paperwork, meetings, and phone calls that teaching and coaching entailed — to say nothing of many, many hours spent with his grandson Nick — it was little wonder that three weeks went by before he raised his eyes far enough to notice the man in the stands.

Yes, Brendan Atcheson was this year's official Problem, no doubt about it — all three of the dads had taken pains to warn him. He'd had two complaints about Brendan in the first week, from parents who disliked the kid's attitude toward them — and toward his teammates. At the games, Brendan always managed to get himself fouled by players who were fed up with his sneers.

The trouble was, Brendan *was* damned good, on the court, anyway — tall, fast, and ruthless, with a decent arm and an unerring eye for the smallest gap in an opponent's attention. Wickedly bright. It didn't help that he was blessed with dark and brooding good looks *and* a rich hot-shit of a father. All of which meant that Brendan Atcheson was not interested in being a team player.

Coach had had gifted kids before, and found them a mixed blessing. These boys were always disdainful of their teammates until they'd had it beaten into their thick noggins that one player could win a point, even a game, but he couldn't win a season. The trick was convincing the kid before the season had gone too far to be retrieved.

The first step was to make it clear that for Coach, the team was more important than one fancy player. To establish that maybe past coaches hadn't been willing to kick the top scorer off the team, but things had changed.

Once that weapon was out of the boy's hands — once Brendan accepted that Coach meant it when he said, *I'd like you on the team, kid, but not if you can't play nice* — he'd have a chance to reshape the boy. The trick was not pushing matters so far that his star player quit the team.

So the games and practice sessions went by, Coach benching the kid whenever he got out of line, and Brendan acting like it was all the same to him if he was kicked off entirely (which Coach didn't believe for a minute) while waiting for Coach to lose his temper and lash out at his lack of discipline, his waste of talent, his unwillingness to use his gifts . . .

So Coach refused to moan and plead. Refused to show how much he was counting on Brendan's presence. Instead, he acted even more casual than Brendan about whether or not he stayed on the team. That attitude puzzled the boy, a lot. Which was just fine with Coach.

In the meantime, practice was a battle-ground. Games were worse, with the kid pressing the bounds every moment, and Coach always there to check his challenges. Sometimes Coach sent him to the bench just so he could give the other players his attention. He was grateful that Brendan was not one of his math students, as well, and wondered if he had the strength, what with everything else, for the war of attrition Brendan seemed to have declared.

Then at last week's practice, Brendan fouled another player so subtly that the kid picked himself up from the floor thinking he'd tripped over his own feet. Even the sharp-eyed mothers hadn't caught it. But Coach blew his whistle and called Brendan over, pitching his voice too low for anyone else to hear. "That was clever, Atcheson, but if I were you, I'd save it for an actual game. Too much practice'll give it away."

The open-eyed expression of innocence that the boy had put on at the whistle's blow gave way to honest surprise, with a thread of something more, some emotion darker than the usual mix of challenge and scorn: Coach almost thought the boy was about to take a swing at him. He managed to keep still and reveal nothing of his impulse to self-defense; then the expression vanished, and the cocky confrontational kid was back.

Coach held Brendan's eyes for another couple seconds, then sent the boy back into play and let the game go on, wondering what exactly he had seen.

It was twenty minutes later when Coach

noticed the man in the stands. Practice was nearly over, with parents and younger siblings drifting in to watch the end of the mock game and catch up on gossip. Coach was happy enough for their presence — players had to get used to an audience — but no question, it made for more distractions, for the players and for him. Which meant that he didn't see the water bottle coming or where it came from, merely a shiny object cartwheeling through the air above the rapidly-moving pack to explode on the wooden floor at the very feet of the front-man, Brendan Atcheson.

The boy whirled and nearly went down. The ball careened off into the hands of an opposing player while Brendan stared, white-faced, into the stands. Only for an instant: the shamed outrage of a mother and an appalled chorus from the malefactor's friends made it clear what had happened, and Brendan pivoted to sprint after the ball. But that brief, unguarded look up into the stands left Coach searching the bleachers until his eyes settled on the solitary man.

Tall guy, mid-forties, dark hair going gray, thin under the trench-coat he wore. A guy who just sort of faded into the background of dads looking on and moms waiting to give rides. This time, however, Coach kept an eye on him. He saw the man stand up at the end of practice, pull his coat together, and walk easily down the bouncing metal stands to the door and out into the parking lot. He didn't wait for a player. He drove off alone.

The twist in Coach's gut almost took his mind off that expression of horror on Brendan's face.

In the two practices and one game since then, he'd watched. The guy showed up every time. He always sat in the same place, never too close to the cluster of moms near the floor, never too far from the dads who sat with their elbows propped on the seats behind them. He came in before practice began, left when it ended, never acknowledged the presence of another adult, never showed any expression — no pleasure in a clever score, no sympathy when the Peralta boy injured his knee, nothing.

The guy just watched.

"I think he's got his eyes on Brendan Atcheson." Coach looked across the table at his wife.

"Your bad boy."

"I don't know that he's a bad boy." He probably shouldn't have told her about Brendan in their various so-how-was-your-day dinner conversations since he'd started at Guadalupe. "Just a smart-ass."

"Sounds like more to me."

"If you condemned every kid who sneered at his coach, hell would be full. Anyway, I still have a responsibility, Carol. He's only fourteen, even if he acts like twenty."

"This is Thomas Atcheson's son, right? The man's not quite in the Bill Gates category, but maybe he thinks the boy needs a bodyguard? Or could it be a relative? A dad who's lost custody, or something?"

"If they know each other, why don't they talk? You'd think Brendan was completely unaware of him — except last week, when some kid threw a water bottle out onto the court? Brendan stopped cold and looked straight up at where this guy sits."

"Wait. You mean the boy assumed this adult in the stands threw something at him?"

"Sounds crazy. But it's more than that. He seems . . ." Coach stopped, embarrassed. "I get the feeling Brendan's aware of him all the time, even though he never looks up there. Like . . . like the way a kid'll play to a girl he wants to impress, without showing it openly."

"So Brendan knows the man, but doesn't want to let on?"

"Pretty sure."

"You think he's flirting?"

Coach pushed down the surge of revulsion, and got up to put his coffee cup and spoon in the dishwasher. He closed the door and propped his backside against it. "If the kid is . . . 'flirting,' it's more like his attitude toward me than anything more . . . overt. When Brendan pulls one of his tricks on the court, he's watching out of the corner of his eye to see if I notice. Testing, like. I mean, I don't begin to understand how gay men think, much less pedophiles, but it's more like Brendan's saying, *Look at what you can't have.*"

"So maybe the guy made a pass at him, and Brendan turned him down and is rubbing it in?"

"I don't know. I suppose it's possible. Ah hell, Carol, what am I going to do?"

"If it were me, I'd call the police. Knowing you, you'll probably want to have a private conversation with the man first."

"Yeah. It's just, if I'm wrong, if he's just some innocent fan or something . . ."

"Then you're both going to be horribly embarrassed and you'll avoid each other for the rest of your lives. At least bring in the principal."

"I'd like to be a little surer, first. Today's

185

Career Day, and next week there's a state evaluation — they're making Linda crazy."

"This wouldn't be one of the evaluators, would it? Checking on school security?"

"I've never heard of them doing that."

"No, but after last year's problems . . . You know, you could just ask Brendan himself."

He shook his head slowly. "I'm not sure I'm in any position to do that."

After a minute, Carol broke the silence. "It might be good to find out. In case this is someone testing how well the school protects its kids."

"Oh, yeah, I really need that hanging over me!"

She walked over and gave him a quick kiss. "Joe, you know it'll turn out to be something simple. You'll solve it. Stop worrying about it. You better go if you want to be there by first bell. And you'll give me a ring if you think the day's getting too much for Nicky?"

"Absolutely." He only wished his grandson was the least bit interested in sports. Of all the activities he'd tried, from fishing to football, the only thing Nick had responded to was range shooting. Which his mother had immediately banned.

Without some kind of a sport in common,

Coach really wasn't sure what to do with the boy.

NICK: HIS STORY (1)

CLINICAL CASE NOTES AND TRANSCRIPT: NICHOLAS CLARKSON

The following is provided as evidence, as requested by the Superior Court of California, concerning events leading up to the Guadalupe Middle School incident. As per my conversation with Judge Stanley, only specifically relevant portions of the transcripts are provided here.

— Dr. Cassandra Henry

Client information:
Nicholas (Nick) Clarkson, eleven-year-old Caucasian male, parents divorced. Nick's grandparents are close to him — they returned to San Felipe in November following the events described below.

Client history:
Mrs. Clarkson came on the recommendation of Nick's principal, Linda McDonald. Mrs.

Clarkson, who might be called a "free spirit," was agitated by her son's condition, describing him as delusional, withdrawn, and possibly suicidal over the disappearance of his friend, Bee Cuomo. When asked for details, Mrs. Clarkson said it was "just a feeling," and later admitted she was exaggerating matters as a means of persuading me to fit Nick into my schedule.

Nick's first session, January 25, was cut short by the boy's distress.

1 February: first full session.
Nick's grandfather, Joseph ("Coach") Gilbert, brought him in, Mrs. Clarkson being at work. Nick presents as a quiet boy, small for his age, intelligent but shy, possibly due to a lack of stability in his home life. I started by asking comfortable questions about books, sports, school, etc., before asking about his friends.

DRH: Tell me about starting school last summer. It's never easy, being the new kid, is it?

NICK: No. Well, we moved here in June, me and Mom. And the only place she could afford was miles from anywhere.

DRH: So you didn't have any neighbors?

NICK: I didn't meet anybody until the first day of school.

DRH: Your grandparents weren't here yet, were they?

NICK: No. They said something about coming in a few years, when Grams retired, if we were still here. But then she got a job at the hospital, so they came in November. Anyway, that's what they said.

DRH: You don't think that's why they moved?

NICK: They came back because of me and the . . . thing.

DRH: Don't you feel they're happy here?

NICK: I guess. I just, they look at me sometimes like they wonder if I'm about to cut my wrists or something.

DRH: Are you?

NICK: 'Course not. How could anyone do that?

DRH: Because if you think —

NICK: I don't! Jeez, how many times do I need to say it!

DRH: Okay, Nick, let's move on. How did you feel going to a school where you didn't know anyone?

NICK: It sucked. It always sucks. But this time, at lunch the first day, this weird girl just marched up to talk about a book she'd seen in my backpack.

DRH: Bee Cuomo. "Weird" in what way?

NICK: You never met her?

DrH: Not that I remember.

Nick: Oh, you'd remember Bee. Not by how she looked — she looked just . . . like a kid, I guess. Glasses, braces, and what d'you call them — pigtails. But she'd say things, do things nobody'd expect. Even the teachers sometimes looked at her like she was from another planet.

DrH: Well, it was thoughtful of her to break the ice that way.

Nick: That's Bee. That *was* Bee.

DrH: She's only missing, Nicholas.

Nick: I don't think so.

DrH: Tell me about the day when you and Bee and your other friend went into the Weildman house. What were you doing before you went in?

Nick: Talking about names. Like if your parents name you Bruce, you're stuck with being a Bruce.

DrH: What did that have to do with the house?

Nick: Because people call it the "Weirdman" place.

DrH: And the house is weird?

Nick: Yeah. Well, and it's awesome. You've seen it, right? Really big, these turrets and things on the corners and that wooden lacy stuff Grams calls gingerbread. And old, maybe the oldest house in the whole county. But the real name is *Weildman*. There was something in the papers just after we moved here, people raising money to fix it up, and then I saw the name on some pictures in the historical museum where Bee dragged AJ and me when we went to the fair, back . . . back in September. I . . .

[Silence.]

DrH: We don't need to talk about the museum yet, Nick. Do you want a tissue? You were saying, about the names.

Nick: Yeah. Okay. I said maybe it had started as a typo or something, and then people started thinking it was weird and haunted, but Bee said she thought the house would be weird even if the family that owned it was called Smith. "Weirdman comes from the vibes, the vibes don't come from the name."

Bee used to talk like that — *vibes* and *far out* and stuff. I think it was 'cause she loved the past, the clothes and the people and words. She *had* modern stuff, more than I do — smartphone and laptop and all — but she'd ride around on this old clunker of a bike instead of the fancy one her dad bought her, and she used a fountain pen even when it leaked, and a real camera —

well, a digital one — instead of her phone. She'd even edit the pictures on her computer to make old-looking black-and-white prints. Anyway, Bee called us the geek patrol, her and me and AJ, and the Tim twins if they didn't have piano lessons or something. Sometimes others, but mostly us.

And that's how we were standing there inside this giant hedge that grows around the Weirdman house. The garden's mostly weeds, with a couple giant rose bushes climbing up the house. Bee said it was like one of her favorite books.

DrH: *The Secret Garden?*

Nick: That's it. She gave it to me, but I didn't get far. The kid in it's really annoying.

DrH: You like to read, don't you, Nick?

Nick: Sure. But Bee was *always* going on about some book nobody'd ever heard of. Anyway, that's why we were there. She'd said something about the Weirdman — sorry, *Weildman* — family, and asked if we knew the story, and then just started in on it. How the last Weildman up and disappeared, way back in the Fifties. The mail piled up, the dog was howling, finally somebody called the cops and asked them to check on the old lady. And they never

193

found her.

So I told her what *I'd* heard, that the old lady had the Alzheimer's and wandered off, and they found her down in Monterey and put her in a home. And Bee said where'd I hear that, and I said Mom told me, and she got all superior and said something like maybe Mom said that so I wouldn't have bad dreams.

It made me mad, but she was right. My mom's always trying to keep what she calls my imagination under control. Even before . . . this.

DrH: Do you think your mother is justified, in saying you're a little too imaginative?

Nick: No! I'm not nuts! I know —

DrH: Nick, I didn't —

Nick: — the difference between fiction and real. And I don't lie to my mom, not about important things.

DrH: So your mother knew that you and your friends were trespassing on the Weildman property?

Nick: Well, no, but . . . I didn't want her to worry. I mean, all moms worry, but single moms do more, especially when she has two jobs. It's easier if she thinks her kid isn't getting into trouble. Yeah, well. So much for that.

DrH: You were saying that you and your

friends went to the house.

NICK: Yeah. I forget who said it, but we were thinking we could make it our group project for Social Studies. So we were in the garden, and AJ said, "Do we have to go in?", and I didn't want to so I said there wasn't a lot there, and he asked how I knew, so I had to say I'd been in there loads of times, right? And then Bee said, "Twice." And I wanted to hit her. Which would've been really great, to hit someone whose father beat up on her, but good thing —

DRH: Did Bee tell you that her father abused her?

NICK: No, but I could tell. Things she said. How she said them.

DRH: I'm sorry I interrupted, Nick. So, you felt angry when Bee corrected you. Had you actually been inside the house?

NICK: Yeah. Twice, like I told her.

DRH: Want to tell me about those visits?

NICK: Not really. But . . . Look, I know this sounds stupid after . . . everything, but I'm not a space-cadet. Nothing like AJ, who goes around in a dream all the time.

DRH: Okay. Tell me about those earlier visits.

NICK: You really are going to think I'm nuts.

DRH: Nick, I promise to reserve judgment.

NICK: Right. Well, the first time was in June,

a couple weeks after we moved here. Mom was at work. I was bored, so I went down the road and managed to push through the front gate. It made me nervous, not only 'cause the metal was rusty and had jagged bits, but 'cause I kind of expected somebody to jump out at me — a homeless guy or meth head or something. But there wasn't any sign of people. Some junk in the garden, cans and stuff, but the house looked almost like someone was living there. Like, all these windows that would've been so easy to smash and climb in through, none of them were even broken.

And the garden was kinda cool. All Mom and I had was this little patch of dead lawn, but this one was huge and smelled good, and there was this tree with a low branch that looked perfect for reading. So the next day I took a book down, and the next. Then one time I finished my book and looked up and saw a way in.

This is where things start to get crazy. You see, all those hours hanging around the place, I never noticed that the outside wall had this square in it, a couple feet high. Like a dog-door, only way up off the ground. I'd just never seen it until then. You keep asking me how I feel, and what it *felt* like was

the house decided to show me a way in.
Now you *really* think I'm nuts.

DRH: Nick, I've never used that diagnosis in my entire career. There are all kinds of reasons for feeling something, but until you tell me what you remember, we can't know what caused it. So, you felt the house was . . . aware?

NICK: Like something out of Stephen King, I know. And it should have been major creepy. I mean, I'm not a coward, exactly, but you know. In a book, when there's a house that invites someone in, bad things always happen. But it just didn't feel like that. What it felt like was . . .
[Pause.]

NICK: You know how in the first Harry Potter book he's living under the stairs and he gets an invitation to go to school? And yeah, that's a story and no I'm not telling you I'm a wizard or anything, but that's how it *felt*. Like this big old house was offering me a . . . an adventure. All right?

DRH: So you went in through the little door?

NICK: Not then. It took me a couple days to work myself up to it. Because, duh: big old lonely house. And I took the pocket-knife Gramps gave me for Christmas.

Which was a good thing, because the door was stuck and I had to pry at it with the littlest blade. But then it kind of . . . sighed, and gave way.

Right inside was a big metal-lined box that I guess was for firewood, 'cause it was next to this ginormous fireplace. Spiderwebs all over, and so much dust I left tracks, but the wallpaper was still mostly up, and this fancy chandelier overhead.

The next room was a kind of library, all these empty shelves. There was another room that still had curtains on the windows, but they looked so dried-up that if you touched them, they'd fall apart.

There was a kitchen that looked like an old movie, and I was about to go into the next room when I heard something outside. I went over to the window to listen and it was Mom, sounding a long way off, calling me.

I ran back to the wood box, but when I pushed at the door (which I really don't think I'd shut behind me) it was stuck. I knew Mom would have a cow if she found me here, and plus that there had to be some reason for her to be home early since she wasn't due back for a couple hours. I was probably doing something stupid like pushing the frame instead of the door itself, but it didn't move, not a hair, and for a minute I thought that . . . that the house wasn't going to let me go. I know, right? But then I shoved really hard and it slammed open, and I sort of fell out and ran across the weeds to the gate. When I turned to squeeze through, I saw the door was invisible again.

I ran hard, circling around this storage shed near the main road, so when Mom saw me, she'd think I was coming from there. She gave me hell for poking around the shed, made me promise never to go there again, and took a while to settle down.

Because the really weird thing?

She'd been home for more than an hour, looking for me the whole time. She was about to call the cops. And all I'd done was find a door and walk through three rooms.

DrH: That must have been a good book.

NICK: I wasn't reading! I wasn't, I swear, just a couple chapters and then I saw the door, and — oh *why* doesn't anybody believe me! I'm —

DrH: Nick, Nicholas, hon, settle down. I'm not saying I don't believe you. I don't know what to believe yet. That's why you're here, isn't it? Okay? Do you want to continue, or have you had enough? Nicholas?

[Session ended.]

The white van, water beaded down its sides, traveled back up the commercial lot to take its slot behind the building. The company woman got out, paused for a minute to chat with a coworker, then continued inside. She hung the van's keys on the board, and pulled down the keys to the next one.

The van stood clean and cleared, ready for its day.

7:20
OLIVIA

Olivia stood on the school lawn sipping her weak coffee, watching the kids tumble from the buses, her casual stance and friendly manner somewhat undermined by the sharpness of her gaze.

The school's pulse was elevated. Which was only to be expected — but was it excitement? Or tension? She knew all the usual troublemakers: did any of them look more shifty than usual, less willing to meet her eyes or walk in front of her? Or the reverse, equally telling — did any of them greet her with defiance and a secret contempt for what she did not know?

A short cop drinking her morning coffee with a smile on her face, while behind her eyes was a brain thinking, *Is it you? What are you planning? What do you hope I'm missing?*

CHACO

When Chaco stepped down from the bus, Sergeant Olivia Mendez in full uniform was looking straight at him.

His legs went frozen — until Javi gave him a shove and Mendez looked away, and Chaco started to breathe again.

He turned and punched Javi, not hard, and the boys jostled their way into the stream of students. Right past Mendez. She didn't even glance at him.

(Which was what he wanted, of course it was. If Chaco couldn't tell his own mother, it wasn't like he was gonna rat Angel out to the sergeant. Not unless she did one of those TV *interrogations* the cops did to trick it out of him. Anyway, if Mendez hadn't figured Angel out by now, she wasn't as clever as a TV cop.)

And she wasn't going to figure out about Chaco's tagging, either. Nobody was. Like he thought, there wasn't no camera — or if there was, nobody'd bothered to check it. And they wouldn't, since *nothing happened.* And anyway, those things only saved for a few days, so it would be gone soon.

Of course, Javi and the others knew Chaco'd been going to the school last night, and they'd already started giving him a hard time on the bus, but it wasn't like *they* were tagging any school walls. Anyway, it was only a first try, he told them. Next time, he'd aim for something bigger. More *consequential.* This was like a *reconnaissance* (not that he used the word) and they all agreed that old McDonald must be pissed (*irate*) this morning, after her carefully laid trap gave up nothing. Although it was too bad she (and old man Tío!) hadn't had to deal with a bright orange tag, today being her Great Day and all.

When he and Javi walked into the cafeteria, Chaco had the kind of cool sway in his hips like cousin Taco. When you saw a man walk like that, you knew what it meant even if you didn't know him. People moved that way when they wore a gun.

Chaco felt tall this morning. Sure, he hadn't slept much, and yeah, he'd left the spray can behind (*With your fingerprints, really smart there, Chaco!*) — but again, what did it matter? They weren't about to fingerprint the whole school. And how else would they pick him out? Of course, if they did decide to start fingerprinting everyone, he'd be in la mierda, but they wouldn't go to all that effort for a tag he hadn't even got around to doing.

No, he was safe enough, and walking tall.

This is why gangs had initiations. You had to *validate* yourself. Prove that you could be trusted, to do what you say. Yeah, he hadn't carried it through yet, but he would. He *was* loyal to Taco, no matter what Angel thought.

He'd lay low for a night or two, then come back. And maybe he'd do something that people would *really* notice, like . . . a threat. From Taco? Against . . . did it have to be Sofia? It really should be, since it was all her sister's fault, disrespecting Taco like that . . .

Chaco's mind was flipping through his *options* as he let the server give him the food — another thing he was too old for, really, but if he'd cooked himself eggs that morning, there'd be none left for the little ones by Friday, and when he skipped breakfast he got dizzy halfway through the morning. He and Javi ignored the empty seats next to sixth-grader Nick Clarkson (a weirdo even before his good buddy Bee Cuomo went missing) and moved to the table where the other seventh-graders hung out.

Halfway through the fruit cup, Chaco felt something like a tickle on the side of his mind. He knew what it was, but he ignored it and made a loud joke at a sixth-grader going by and said some things about a movie he hadn't seen, until finally Javi leaned forward. "Hey, man, Tío's watching you. Think he knows?"

Chaco whipped his head around and made his eyes go all mad dog like Angel's. "Javi, you shut your face. Anybody finds out, I'll bust your head."

Javi shut up and picked up his things, not looking at the janitor as he dropped his garbage and tray and hurried off. Reluctantly, Chaco climbed out of the bench.

The janitor watched him approach. When Chaco dumped his tray onto the surface, Tío said his name. "Mr. Cabrera." Just like that — no first name, no Spanish.

"Yes?" Chaco tried to say *Yeah,* but had to fight to keep it from coming out *Yes, sir.*

The dark eyes were like tiny caves. "Mr. Cabrera, you and I need to have a conversation."

LINDA

Linda McDonald made a last correction to the speech and stuffed the crumpled pages back into her carry-all messenger bag. As she straightened, a cliché came into her mind: *Gordon, we need to talk.*

As a teacher, and as a person, she had always tried to avoid clichés. Maybe because her entire life looked like one? Midwestern farm girl, escaped to the big world, discovered the rewards of teaching, never had kids of her own . . .

So no, she would avoid the phrase itself when she confronted Gordon. However, his restlessness was becoming too obvious to overlook. She'd begun to find herself wondering, as she drove off each morning, if he'd be there when she got home. If he carried his passport in his pocket whenever he left the house. If her blunder over the volunteers list had poisoned everything.

Even wondering if she'd made that slip in

the first place because she suspected that *not* investigating him was irresponsible, when it came to her kids . . .

We need to talk. She had every right to ask Gordon if he was planning to move on. She dreaded argument, and confrontations made her ill, but she'd spent her life fighting timidity. If Linda accepted some matter — something like Gordon's history — she did so deliberately, rather than through fear of knowing.

When today was over, she and Gordon needed to talk. Preferably without clichés.

CHACO

The idea of a conversation with Tío made Chaco want to crawl under the nearest table. The janitor didn't look like an old guy in a turd-colored uniform now. More like cousin Taco when he was starting to get mad — or Angel, when he went quiet.

Chaco fought to hang on to the scorn — *contempt,* he thought desperately; *derision* — but he felt himself shrink. Felt the manly swagger of two pounds of steel tucked into his belt shrivel away to nothing.

The cafeteria was emptying now, but before Tío could start in on him, they were interrupted by Esme Gustafson, carrying a greasy paper bag. "Mamá made these for you."

Tío sat down on the bench of the nearest table. He opened the bag like a birthday present, and looked in. "Tamales!"

"Mamá's molé chicken. I hope you like them?"

"Tell your mother I have dreams about her molé chicken tamales. Thank you, Miss Gustafson."

Esme ran off, smiling. Tío rolled down the top of the bag, put it on the bench next to his leg, and turned to Chaco. Those dark eyes of his seemed to jab at Chaco's knees, so he sat down on the bench, well clear of Tío's reach, intently studying the frayed rubber on his high-tops.

"Did you have a good breakfast, Mr. Cabrera?"

Chaco shrugged.

"Do you know what your mother earns, Mr. Cabrera?"

"What?"

"Your mother. What she earns, at the cannery."

Chaco shrugged.

"Eleven dollars and twelve cents an hour. Just above minimum wage. Do you know what I earn, Mr. Cabrera?"

Chaco tried to make his mouth say, *You earn shit,* but couldn't get it out with those eyes drilling into him. He shrugged again.

"It is polite to look at someone who is speaking to you, Mr. Cabrera. Thank you. Mr. Cabrera, let us say that I earn one and one-half times what your mother does. How much do I earn per hour?"

It popped out before Chaco could help himself. "Sixteen sixty-eight."

The janitor's eyes went somehow dark, like they had when they saw Esme's tamales. "I work thirty-eight hours a week, forty-eight weeks a year. How much do I earn in a year?"

"How would I know?"

"How much, Mr. Cabrera?"

Chaco lifted his chin. "Thirty thousand, four hundred and, uh, twenty-four dollars. And thirty-two cents, okay?"

But Chaco's attempt at shutting down the janitor didn't have quite the effect he'd intended.

"Mr. Cabrera." The old man's voice was like a purr. "I think I may be able to make better use of you than your cousin Taco would."

And then Tío smiled. A smile that gave Chaco Cabrera a clear illustration for the word *apprehensive*.

LINDA

Waiting for Gordon to turn in at the school's access road, Linda looked past him and saw how much of the staff parking lot was already full. *Oh Lord, I should have been here first thing, what was I thinking —*

No. *You made the decision deliberately, after considerable thought.* Showing the staff that their principal was *not* here at the crack of dawn today, fretting over every little thing, served to underscore the message she'd been sending since day one: *I trust you. We are a community. I am always available, but I will not micromanage your every move.* Trust was vital in rebuilding the school's sense of worth. Even — no: *especially* — on this most complicated of days.

Still, Linda couldn't help feeling as if she were scrambling to join the orchestra just as the curtain was rising. The flags waved from the top of the pole, the last buses were pulling in, and a solid stream of parents' cars were coming out of the side road. Olivia Mendez stood prominently in front of the school entrance, every button of her uniform gleaming. By her side, Mina Santos chatted with enthusiasm.

An aging pickup truck slowed to let the waiting cars turn into the school — Coach Gilbert. Linda gave Coach a wave of thanks as Gordon crossed in front of him.

The slot marked "Principal" faced the open end of the main breezeway — the long part of the capital E of Guadalupe's layout, which comprised a long rectangle of front-facing offices and three cross-wise wings with quads between them. As Gordon pulled into the slot, she glimpsed Chaco Cabrera, slouching along with his usual Bad-Guy Attitude, for once without a group of buddies in his wake. Bright kid, but when it came to resisting the violent romance of gang life, a good brain was rarely enough. Linda reached for the seat belt clasp, then paused as another figure stepped into the walkway, watching the same boy. Hmm. The school janitor appeared to have an interest in young Chaco as well.

Chaco vanished into A Quad. Tío turned, spotted Linda's bright yellow Mazda, and gave one of his oddly formal nods before he, too, moved out of sight. An instant later, as if precisely choreographed, Olivia Mendez stepped through the school entrance at the far end of the central breezeway. Kids gave wide berth to her uniformed figure as she walked toward the staff lot.

"I think Sergeant Mendez is coming to talk to me." Linda pushed the clasp on the seat belt, it clicked simultaneously with the thud of the trunk latch Gordon pulled.

"She does look like a woman with news to impart."

They were unloading boxes when the sergeant came up. "Morning, Linda. Mr. Kendrick."

Linda frowned over the carton in her arms. "Any problems?"

"Things seem to be fine so far. Can I take something?"

Linda put her load into the policewoman's hands, then moved toward the back door.

"I saw you out for your run this morning, Mr. Kendrick." Olivia watched his tall form uncurl from the depths of the trunk. "That's quite a circuit you make."

"I'm fortunate that San Felipe is so flat. Here, Linda, let me have that one."

"Those are more paper cups, for the library. Oh, and this bag of spoons and such. Let's hope they don't discover anything else vital at the last minute."

"If so, I shall volunteer to fetch." He gave Olivia a polite nod, and moved off in the direction of the library's coffee machine.

"You're a lifesaver, Gordon," Linda called at his back.

His left hand swung up, two fingers raised in a kind of salute. The women watched him weave a path through the same students who had parted like the Red Sea at the sight of Olivia's uniform.

"Could you . . ." Linda held out a box hand-labeled Teacher Memos. Olivia turned to take on another layer, and spotted a gray-haired man climbing from an old pickup truck, half a dozen spaces away. "Morning, Coach! We going to win next week?"

"Hello, Sergeant. I hope so. The boys are looking good."

The policewoman seemed about to ask another question, then hesitated, and lowered her voice to ask the principal instead. "How is Coach's grandson doing?"

"Nick? A lot better than I expected. I still haven't figured out if the kid has real problems or just a particularly vivid imagination."

"He's seeing Dr. Henry, right? What does she think?"

"She doesn't seem in any hurry to diagnose, but she did say the boy shows no further signs of delusions beyond Bee's disappearance, and no overt signs of acting out — against himself or others. Except maybe when it comes to Bee's father. Nick is still convinced that Mr. Cuomo was abusing his daughter."

Olivia shook her head. "We pushed the man pretty hard during the investigation, because of what Nick said. We got nothing. The only suggestions of abuse were those stories on Bee's computer. And since those were clearly made-up and not an electronic diary, they couldn't be considered evidence."

"I know. But I had a call from Mr. Cuomo complaining about a social media campaign against him. You know anything about it?"

"No. What kind of campaign?"

"Seems to be the online equivalent of graffiti. Rude words, childish drawings. He says there's a hashtag about them."

"Does he know who's doing it?"

"He blames Nick Clarkson, but I haven't had a chance to ask the boy about it yet."

"Okay, well, send me the link, I'll have a look."

Linda clicked the key fob at the car and the two women started out of the parking lot.

"Something else I should mention." Olivia's low voice warned Linda to brace herself. "It could be nothing, but I heard last night that the district attorney is starting an investigation of Tom Atcheson's company."

Linda stopped dead in the middle of the drive. "No. Not *today*?"

" 'Fraid so. I know he's one of your speakers."

"What's being investigated?"

"I don't have any details, just that it's both Atcheson and his company. I'm afraid it'll be public knowledge very soon. I did ask the DA if he could delay letting it 'leak' until tomorrow, but he didn't promise."

"Crap."

"I'm sorry."

Linda realized that they were stopping traffic. She gave the waiting car a quick smile — one of the lunch ladies, Susanna — and hurried toward the breezeway.

"Could you possibly find out when? If it's today, I should offer to let Mr. Atcheson cancel rather than force him to run a gauntlet of reporters. But if it isn't . . ."

". . . then telling him is going to make for a really awkward conversation. I'll make a call."

"Thanks, Olivia. And as soon as possible?"

"Offices don't open until eight, but I'll see if anyone's in yet."

"Bless you. Oh, that poor boy."

"What, your basketball player?"

"Brendan, yes. A real porcupine of a kid." Troubled, and troubling.

"It's a hard age."

"Harder for some. Anyway, thanks. I guess."

Olivia gave her a sympathetic smile, and stretched a hand out for the office door.

COACH GILBERT

Coach transferred his much-mended, forty-year-old briefcase into his left hand and thumbed the pickup's key button, watching to make sure the locks went down. When he was satisfied the infernal things weren't about to sneak back up again, he pocketed the keys and made his way from the staff parking lot.

Ahead of him, the principal and Sergeant Mendez were walking down the breezeway. He'd met Linda McDonald six or seven years ago, although he didn't think she remembered — a back-to-school night he and Carol happened to attend for a nephew's two little girls. Linda was the school's vice principal, and he'd vaguely figured her for a lesbian. Which was fine — his own kid sister was happily married to a great woman who went to Giants games with him sometimes — but when Linda hired him as a temp here back in January, he'd found out she was married. To the man who'd been driving just now. Retired guy, a little older than Coach, and solid despite the hoity-toity accent. In good shape, too. Didn't know much about basketball, but he managed to keep up with the kids during lunch hour games. (Better than Coach did, truth to tell.)

And not just physically. The kids seemed to respect him — like him, even. Maybe he could talk to Gordon about the man in the stands?

Soon as this Career Day circus was over.

LINDA

The main office was packed. Linda peered across the seething mass of heads at the school secretary, wondering if she needed to plunge in to the rescue. Mrs. Hopkins had her students well trained, but today there were strangers in the office, adults who had clearly yet to meet the withering gaze of authority from across the high counter. However, Mrs. Hopkins seemed to be handling the chaos with her usual firm competence, allowing the principal to make a cowardly retreat.

"Let's use my door," Linda told Olivia. They circled a pack of students gathered around the school notice board with its Career Day session assignments, and Linda managed to work the key and reach her desk without losing too much of her armload.

Olivia put her boxes on the low table, added the papers that she'd retrieved from the floor, and nodded her head at the clamor from next door. "You think she'd like me to go out there with my gun drawn?"

"That might be a little excessive. Although maybe you could just clear your throat a bit?"

Sergeant Mendez took hold of the knob. As the principal's door opened, the voices surged — then fell away sharply as the uniform came into view.

"I know we all want to make an example of our good manners in front of the students." Silence. Olivia, eyes shining with mischief, stepped back into the office and shut the door. "I'll go make that phone call now. See if there's anyone in the DA's office who can tell me about the Atcheson leak."

"Flip the latch so you can let yourself back in." Linda picked up the receiver to begin dialing from the pink message slips (divided into Urgent, Today, and If-you-don't-reply-they'll-forget-about-it). When the door opened again ten minutes later, she quickly finished the conversation — and saw the bad news on Olivia's face.

"I'm afraid the Atcheson mess will be in the afternoon news. And the *Clarion*'s reporter is already parked out front."

Linda groaned. "Oh, Lord. And she's one of the speakers, so it's too much to hope that she doesn't hear about it. This is going to be a long day."

"I thought I'd ask for your husband's help in keeping an eye on the back of the school, in case our Lois Lane out there decides to get creative."

Linda wasn't overjoyed at the idea of Olivia asking Gordon anything, but it made sense. "Make sure you tell Tío as well — he's got eyes all over. I'm already sorry I didn't let you talk me out of Career Day."

But the cop surprised her. "I wasn't trying to talk you out of it. I think it's great that you're going ahead. I was only making sure you were clear on what you could be getting into."

"I thought I was." Grim humor seemed to be her fallback position for the day — for the year, really, through a paint-to-policy school reorganization, three arrests for drugs and two for weapons-on-campus, one vanished student, a rat infestation, and a murder trial.

But just as the absence of metal detectors was an assertion of openness, so was Career Day a determined effort to force the students to look past their school's problems. Even if it meant a reporter camped on the road and Olivia Mendez wearing a gun.

Olivia was watching her with sympathy. "I've got every officer on the job today. And cruisers will drive by regularly."

"Thank you."

"I wanted to ask, how are my two musketeers doing?"

"Your two — you mean Danny Escobedo's friends? Carlos seems to be fine. And Mina — that child is amazing. I don't care if she does look like some punk rocker, she's got a lot of . . . presence, I guess."

"The look is new since last year — she'll grow out of it. I just hope I live long enough to vote for her when she runs for president."

"She may have too much sense for that."

Olivia laughed and stood up. "I'll go check on the reporter, make sure she's staying put. I told her that the road may be public domain, but I don't want to see any student names or faces in their reports."

"Just try not to draw your gun when you talk to her." As a joke, it came out a little flat.

"I find that resting my hand on it tends to be enough for most purposes." Olivia smiled, a five-foot-seven bulldog with a dangerous little glint in her dark eyes. Nothing like Gordon — yet oddly similar.

"Thanks, Olivia. And make sure you drop by the library before the first bell. I was promised donations from that new French bakery down on Main Street."

And, Linda prayed as the sergeant left, *please be just a little bit blind and deaf today. Please don't get too curious about my husband — or my janitor. Or any extracurricular activities of your fellow speakers. Not today.*

What time do important men like Tom Atcheson get to their office? she asked herself, and reached for the next call slip.

BRENDAN

Brendan squeezed the toothpaste out onto his brush. *Can a dentist tell when you haven't been flossing? And wasn't there some kind of patient confidentiality that they had — oh, crap!* He leaned in for a closer look at his chin. *Is that a zit?* Only losers got zits. Mina Santos never had a pimple in her life. Her buddy Sofia, equally perfect. Even that weird Cuomo girl hadn't had explosions on her face. But then, the kid had been impervious to everything. (Until she wasn't.)

Brendan put down the toothbrush. Rubbing in zit cream, he thought about Mina, and about Bee Cuomo. Not that he'd been interested in *her* — she was only a sixth-grader, and looked even younger — but he was, you know, *interested.* It was like one of those urban myths: The Disappearance of Bee Cuomo. Everyone crying, waiting to hear some hiker had found her body — and then that story starting up, which should've

225

sounded crazier than it did. Then the hashtag.

What *did* happen to the kid, anyway? She'd been seen in broad daylight, then she was gone. People might have started to forget about her after Christmas vacation (she'd only been at Guadalupe for a few weeks, after all) except that Nick kid flipped out on the field trip. Talking about where she'd gone.

Watching too many movies about people stepping into alternate universes, it'll do that to you.

Brendan put away the zit cream and shoved his toothbrush back in his mouth. Man, if there *was* a way to step out of the world, he'd do it in a flash. Walk right across that border, let the world zip up the place where he'd been. Leave people wondering. Become an urban myth himself. He'd do it today, if not for —

The toothbrush stopped moving at the sound of shoes coming down the hallway.

"I'm going now, Brendan." Sir's voice, just outside the bathroom door. "You need to leave within four minutes or you'll be late."

He hastily spat his mouthful of foam into the sink. "Yes, Sir, I'm just finishing." *You bastard. I haven't been late once since I got the bike.* He mouthed the words at the

226

bathroom mirror — letting not so much as a whisper of sound emerge. That "god-damn" last night had been . . . not scary, but . . . (Yeah: scary.) Sir must have a real hair up his ass, to let fly with an actual curse word. The thought of Sir losing it made Brendan want to pump his fist in the air. (And then lock himself in the closet.)

"As I told you, I will not be at your school until 12:40, after lunch."

"Yes, Sir."

"And you're certain you want to listen to this physiotherapist instead of coming to hear me?"

Brendan froze. He half expected the door to open so Sir could fix him with that icy, disappointed gaze. "If . . . you don't mind," he managed. "I'm really interested in —"

"Yes, I suppose, that kind of technical training might be for the best." *For you, my chief failure, who can't be expected to suc-ceed at anything more demanding.* "In any event, I may be late coming home. If you don't hear from me, take a dinner from the freezer."

"Yes, Sir."

"No television or video games until you have studied for your math exam. You need a good grade. Even, I imagine, for 'sports medicine.'"

"Yes, Sir."

"Brendan, I have a lot going on at the moment. I need you to carry your weight around here. Do *try* not to disappoint me. And for heaven's sake, make your bed."

And his footsteps retreated along the hallway and down the stairs beyond.

Disappoint! Try — not to *disappoint?* Rage welled up out of some deep reserve, a red-hot tide that made Brendan's fingertips go white gripping the edge of the sink. Usually he had to break something — or hurt himself — to get it to subside. This time he stood staring into his own eyes, letting the rage come, and come. He could smash his fist into the mirror, slicing his hand to bits again, arrive at school (*on time!*) covered in blood. Or . . .

As he watched his dark eyes (Mom's eyes) glare back in fury, he felt the tide begin to retreat, all on its own. Down it pulled, away from view, into the depths. Only this time, instead of feeling beaten and small, he felt cold. Hard. Like a forged blade. Like the polymer and steel Bodyguard, locked in the gun safe downstairs.

Disappoint? Yes, you *fucking tyrannical bastard,* I'll *disappoint* you, all right.

And with no more warning than that, Brendan Atcheson stepped out of the world and into a decision.

All those months of fantasy and frustration, nobody but Jock to share his plans. The hidden lists and sketches, all those long hours staring up at the pattern of light on his ceiling and wondering if he'd done a good enough job covering his tracks — but all it took (*Now!*) was a single word (*disappoint . . .*) and the planning was over.

The load that lifted from Brendan's shoulders was so huge that he had to lean on the sink to keep from staggering. *Today? My God, it was actually going to happen — today!*

The car started up in the drive. (Had it been only seconds?) Sir backed, shifted, accelerated away down the street. (For the last time?)

Brendan looked down, on this, the last (normal) morning of his (old) life, and saw that he was still gripping the toothbrush. He dropped it into the glass unrinsed; foam dribbled down to the porcelain below. He turned on the tap to rinse his mouth, then changed his mind and wiped his face on the towel instead, stretching it out so the smear was displayed. He walked out of the bathroom, leaving the tap running, the light on, the toilet unflushed, lid up. A string of punishable offenses.

One of his four minutes was gone. Brendan grabbed his backpack by the bottom and jerked, watching with joy as the books and papers exploded across the bed and chair and carpet. He then yanked open drawers to replace the books with what he'd actually need today. He opened his laptop, followed the route to his most hidden files, and hit PRINT. While the old machine was creaking into life, he ran downstairs to Sir's forbidden study, and came back up: two minutes left.

At the desk, he signed his name (his real name) on the long-planned document and folded it into an envelope. When he'd addressed it (Who'd find it first?) he reached up to the row of plastic cases with video games and DVDs: fourth one from the right. Anyone who didn't know — Sir, if he'd looked — would think this was just a pirated game. (Probably not a very good one.)

Brendan popped open the case to be sure the disc bore the same words as the one he'd put in his pack: nothing more than his name — his real name, not "Atcheson."

Brendan James Connelly.

He closed the cover, scribbled a sticky note on it, and propped it with the envelope against a glass he should have taken down to the dishwasher (another offense). He swung the heavy pack onto his shoulder, and took a moment for one last look at his childhood: unmade bed, old tired carpet, books and papers vomited across both. At his feet lay a page with his Career Day schedule, the speakers he'd been going to hear.

Nothing in this room he would need, ever again.

Brendan left his bedroom light on. Walked out the kitchen door without locking it. Strapped the backpack onto his bike and wheeled it into the drive, not even closing the gate behind him.

Helmet on, Brendan pulled out his phone . . . and paused.

Could he believe Jock? What if all his talk had been just bullshit? What if, when it came right down to it, Jock had somewhere else to be? Could Brendan do this by himself?

Time to find out if the dude was solid or not.

Brendan had chosen his future. The past was back there in his room for Sir to find — Sir, and the San Felipe Police Department: a letter and a disc, concealed by Brendan's homemade illustration of a mock game called First Person Shooter.

He opened his cell and typed out a text.

It's today. Be ready.

Brendan's thumb hovered over the surface
of the phone. Maybe he should . . .
No. Be a man. Today, or never.
His thumb came down on SEND.

OLIVIA: HER STORY

"Sergeant Mendez, there's some nut case on the phone. Can you figure out what he wants?"

Olivia Mendez did not reply, so deep in the maddening details of the Rivas murder file that she didn't notice the uniformed officer in her doorway.

"Ma'am?"

It was shaping up to be one of *those* cases, the kind that brought you in on your days off and laid in wait until 3:00 a.m. rolled around on the bedside clock. *What have I missed?*

Gloria Rivas: Sixteen-year-old babysitter, dead from a bullet in her chest, shot eight days ago on the front walkway of the Escobedo house.

Danny Escobedo: Gloria's charge, eleven years old, missing since the night of the murder.

Thomas "Taco" Alvarez: twenty-three

233

years old, local punk and gang member, threatened Gloria Rivas the night before she died, after she publicly disrespected him by refusing to go out with him, then further compounded the insult by bad-mouthing Taco's whole gang. Taco hadn't been seen since that night, when he'd filled his car at the Shell station near the freeway and withdrawn $300 from the station ATM.

"Um, Sergeant Mendez? The telephone?"

The first time Olivia had arrested Taco Alvarez was for tagging, back when he was a smart-mouthed fourteen-year-old headed toward a gang initiation. Nine years later, she wouldn't be surprised if he'd shot others before Gloria. Nor was she surprised that he'd successfully fallen off the map: Taco was not without smarts.

What didn't fit was Taco saddling himself with eleven-year-old Danny as a hostage. Taco's brother, Angel, sure. Angel was the true psychopath in that family, and might do anything that caught his fancy, but Taco?

Still, if Taco didn't have Danny, who the hell did? She'd even wondered if the boy's mother had whisked him out of sight from Taco's homies, but if that was so, the woman was a hell of an actress.

"Sergeant?"

"What!"

234

"You got some whack job on line two. I hung up on him once but he called back. I thought maybe you could figure out what he wants."

Olivia stared at Marcoletti for a moment, then flicked her eyes to the phone that lay buried under Post-its, notebook pages, unfurled California maps, and scraps of paper. The phone's light was blinking, which meant that at least the caller was safely on hold and couldn't have overheard the insult. "Why give it to me?" she asked. Stupid question. She was the only detective obsessed enough to hang around the station on a Saturday morning.

"Because you're here?" Marcoletti sounded like a teenager — with just enough sense not to add "duh" and a roll of the eyes. Were uniforms this casual in a big-city police department?

"I'm busy. Paul's the one on call today." She looked down at the scrap of paper in her hand, where she'd written:

March 4: Mrs. Escobedo hysterical.
March 5: Mrs. Escobedo phoned seven times.
March 7: Mrs. Escobedo did not phone, is not answering calls.

She didn't want to make another run at the Alvarez family yet. She was pretty sure Taco was still in the area, but if she gave that vicious little brother of his — Angel, what a joke of a name — another day to think he'd got one over on the cops, it might make him cocky enough to slip up. And she wanted another talk with the victim's sister, Sofia, but the family needed a weekend to themselves. Sofia's best friend, Yasmina Santos, seemed to know more than she was telling — or it could just be that Mina Santos seemed to know more about everything. Mina was tiny, yes, but it was hard to believe she was only twelve — or, no: thirteen, as of Tuesday.

Marcoletti was still planted in the doorway. "Paul's at his daughter's tournament today, and I sort of thought . . ."

She snatched the receiver and jabbed the 2, knowing she'd regret this. Why on earth had the Department hired this kid who couldn't speak Spanish and therefore interpreted the language as a lunatic's ravings?

"Mendez!" Maybe she could intimidate the caller into hanging up.

Instead, the voice came on, deep and melodic and English: England-English. "What am I? An infant crying in the night."

The voice stopped. Olivia's eyes narrowed:

Marcoletti's diagnosis might not be far off. "Sir, you've reached the San Felipe Police Department. Do you have a crime to report?"

"Man's hand is not able to taste, his tongue to conceive, nor his heart to report, what my dream was."

Her English teacher in high school would have called it a non sequitur — although "whack job" would do. Still, something in the voice, some pressing intelligence, kept her from dropping the phone onto its base and going back to her fruitless search for ideas over who killed Gloria Rivas and who had Danny Escobedo. "Sir, I don't understand."

"Words are like leaves, and where they most abound, much fruit of sense beneath is rarely found."

She pinched her fingertips into the inner corners of her tired eyes. When did she last have a solid eight hours? Gloria Rivas died on March fourth. It was now the twelfth. Eight days of evidence and interviews, one blank wall after another. Long unproductive conversations with the police of Chiapas, where the Alvarez family came from and where Taco might be headed, and of Oajaca, where the Escobedos had lived before migrating north a few months before Danny was born. Dead ends for the murder, a complete puzzle about the boy. *Hang up on this guy, Mendez. You'd do everyone a lot more good if you went home and got some sleep.*

But the caller's voice had none of the slurred consonants of drink or the edginess of drugs. His brief statements, though nonsensical (and now rhyming) did not sound like the ravings of a garden-variety lunatic. He was polite, calm, and somehow determined. Maybe it was the accent — she was a softie for an English accent — but the guy sounded like a professor trying to get across a difficult lesson. Okay, see how he dealt with a bright student.

"Well, sir, you called me. If you want me to pick up the fruit of sense, you'll have to drop it where I can find it."

"Truth can never be told so as to be understood."

"Yeah, ain't that the pits? If you can't tell me the truth, sir, why are you calling?"

"For now we see through a glass, darkly, but then face to face."

This, anyway, was something she recognized. Although what First Corinthians had to do with leaves and fruit, she hadn't a clue. "Sir, if you want to discuss the Bible, why not go down to St. Patrick's and have a nice chat with Father —"

"An infant. Crying in the night."

She paused. "Are you telling me there's a child in danger?"

"It needs a very clever woman to manage a fool!" the voice boomed in approval.

Fool. Something about that word made the back of her mind twitch, a brief pulse of recognition, or apprehension . . . then it was gone, leaving her to loop back to where they'd started. "Sir, perhaps you'd like to come in to the Department and tell me all about it."

"So near, and yet so far." He sounded wistful.

She looked at the number on the phone's display: local in both area code and prefix, so he couldn't be too far away. No car? Disabled? Other than mentally, that is. "You want me to come to you?"

"Come before his presence with song."

She hoped this wasn't a sign that her caller thought of himself as God; she really didn't have time to get involved with the paperwork of a psychiatric hold. Damn it, she wasn't even on call today. "Where are you located?"

"Absent thee from felicity for a while, and in this harsh world draw thy breath in pain, to tell my story."

Her cop's mind snagged for a moment on

239

the word *pain*. Then it moved on to the possibility that *tell my story* might be where the man's emphasis lay. "I'm sorry, sir, I don't think . . ." She stopped. The sounds from the earpiece included the crackle of a bad connection — or of a public phone box — and the build and fade of a diesel engine in the background. Also, the voice of a child in long and unintelligible monologue.

When Olivia Mendez was a girl, not much older than the owner of that piping voice in the background, two cousins had been killed by a drunk driver. Her aunt had responded to the agony by joining a church, one of those that lived and breathed the Bible, that regarded Proverbs and Job and the Book of Romans as immediate as the daily news, who referenced any decision, from ethical action to choice of breakfast cereals, by summoning a verse. They could be strikingly apt — the Bible is, after all, a large and diverse book — but often any meaning was stretched past the snapping point, leaving the aunt and her audience staring at each other, dumbfounded. Rather as she felt with this man on the telephone, in fact. "Are you by any chance talking about Felicia? South of San Felipe?"

"My *library* was dukedom large enough."

"You're at the Felicia library?"

240

"I give you a wise and understanding heart." The voice's instant approval made her feel oddly warm. Anyway, it wasn't like she was getting anything done here.

"Okay, it'll take me fifteen, twenty minutes to get there. Will you wait for me?"

The phone went dead, which she supposed meant *yes.*

She sat for a minute, tapping her middle fingernail on the desk, wondering what the hell she'd just been listening to. There remained the tiny, faraway sense of familiarity in the back of her mind, but for the life of her, she couldn't tease it forward. Something years back and not here, but an echo . . . The Bible, snippets of poetry, Shakespeare — she'd caught both *Hamlet* and *The Tempest* in his words: an odd conversational form, to be sure. But conversation it appeared to be, albeit of a convoluted and inadequate style. She felt a stir of interest, at this welcome distraction from frustration — and then caught herself.

She had to be careful. This thespian-voiced Englishman could be some honest-to-God nut case setting a trap for a cop. A backwater town like San Felipe might not shelter as many toxic individuals as a big city, but that didn't rule anything out.

When in doubt, take backup.

And always be in doubt.

Olivia closed the Escobedo file. She opened her computer, hunting for the location of the Englishman's number. Yes: the little Felicia library's public telephone, as he'd said. Sort of said.

She shut down the computer. "Marcoletti!"

"Yeah?"

"Yes, Sergeant Mendez, ma'am." She was muttering as she pulled her shoulder holster from the desk drawer. Muttering wasn't a good sign.

"What?"

"Nothing. Who's on patrol down in Felicia?"

"What, you mean *now*?"

She glared from the doorway. "Yes, I mean now."

"Um, let me see." He pawed through the mess before him, came up with the right piece of paper, and read from it. "Torres and Wong."

"Patch me through to them, will you?"

It only took him two tries. When she had Alex Torres on the line, she asked if the two patrolmen could swing by the front of the Felicia library in fifteen minutes, to provide a little probably unnecessary backup.

"Funny, that's where we are now."

"What, at the library? Why?"

"Someone called in a report of a suspected terrorist in Arab robes hanging around out front."

"A Muslim terrorist? In *Felicia*?" Every cop's nightmare: an incomprehensible threat dropping out of the blue to splash some backwater town across the nation's headlines, just because some maniac — wait. "I don't suppose the guy has an English accent?"

"Don't know about the accent, we just pulled up, but there's a white-haired male sitting on the bench near the phones. He's got a knapsack on the ground next to him, but I got to say he looks more like a monk than an Arab. Doesn't have a turban or anything."

"Look, would you mind not approaching him until I get there? Unless he's actively causing problems, that is. I'm leaving the station now."

"Sure, he's just sitting there. Looks pretty harmless. You want us to watch him from the car, or from the café across the street? It has a clear line of surveillance."

"Why don't you go ahead and take your break? But sit where you can keep an eye on him. I'll be there in twelve minutes if I make both signals."

"Take your time, Sergeant. Wong's got the prostrate trouble, he's happy to piss for a while."

The line cut off, but not before she heard the beginnings of an outraged partner's voice. She smiled, figuring that Wong, not yet thirty, had no "prostrate" trouble at all. Torres had no doubt heard that Olivia Mendez was unattached again, and was pulling his unmarried partner's leg.

The Felicia library was a tiny building with a few hundred books, two computer terminals, one part-time librarian, and a regiment of volunteers, mostly Latinas with young kids. The Felicia district of San Felipe, surrounded by fields of strawberries and lettuce, was the kind of neighborhood where few homes had computers (or books, for that matter), and the only other forms of entertainment in walking distance were the roadside bar a mile south and the dusty general-store-and-café across from the library. That made the Felicia Public Library the de facto community center, the place to go for homework, after-school gatherings, job searches, ESL classes, casting a ballot, and visiting-nurse clinics. It also made for some great numbers to show the state auditors, and its high percentage of non-English-speaking, low-income patrons generated a regular trickle of state and federal grants. Without a doubt, the people here adored the place, and kept it both busy and spotless.

Which might explain why some concerned patron had called in a stranger hanging around the public phone out front. As Olivia pulled into the pitted but freshly swept surface of the small parking area, a mother and her two young kids were coming out of the library door. All three patrons gave the odd figure a wary look. The white-haired man lifted his hand, two fingers raised like a benediction, and the uncertain looks turned to smiles.

When Olivia got closer, she could understand why. The man in the brown robe — which was no more Arabic than the checked shirt and khaki trousers she was wearing — resembled a tall, thin, brown-clad Father Christmas, down to the twinkle in his eye. There was, as Torres had told her, a blue nylon backpack tucked under the front edge of the bench, and a tall walking stick leaning against its back. A pair of nearly white running shoes peeked out from the hem of his robe.

The old man watched her climb out of the Department's car (unmarked, but so anonymous it could only belong to the police), showing no sign of the defiant manner that raised a cop's hackles.

Seconds later, Torres and Wong emerged from the Felicia Mercado, a onetime garage now plastered with neatly painted signs advertising "Strong Hot Coffee," "Breakfast Burritoes All Day," and "Menudo Ever Tursday." The two uniforms hitched up their duty belts as they crossed the deserted side-street. They joined her at the car, only taking their eyes off the man for the brief moment necessary to greet her.

Torres she had known forever. Wong had been with the Department just under a year. Torres spoke first.

"He's just been sitting there. Says hi to the people going in and out, but otherwise just cooling it."

"Okay, I don't think there'll be a problem here, you might as well go back to work."

"In a minute." The men followed her up the library's walk.

The bearded monk stood as she approached, a motion less like a flight response and more like the compulsive manners of her mother's father, who'd been unable to sit when a lady came in the room. Any resemblance ended there: her grandfather, shaped by childhood malnutrition and a lifetime of work in the fields, hadn't been much over five and a half feet. This man towered well over six, though so gaunt, there were hollows in the cheeks above his beard. He was probably homeless, what with being a stranger in the area and carrying that worn knapsack, but if so, it was a very clean and tidy homelessness. He reminded her of a saintly portrait in church school.

"Sir, I believe you called the police department?"

"When there are constabulary duties to be done." One eyelid drooped infinitesimally, a near-wink.

"Could we have your name, sir?"

Instead of answering, his right hand went toward the side of the brown robe, where a pocket might be; instantly, both young officers leapt forward to seize his arms hard, making the old man gasp.

"Stop!" She stepped between the monk and Torres. "He's probably got arthritis. Sir, do you have any weapons in your pocket? Anything sharp?"

He shook his head.

"Do we have your permission to check for ourselves?"

He nodded.

"Would you please lean with both arms against the back of that bench?" The two uniforms let him go, and the old man

247

turned to place both hands on the bench, automatically spreading his feet apart as he did so: he'd been patted down before. Then again, anyone who looked like this would have been picked up regularly, no matter his appearance of a thin Kris Kringle.

His pockets, accessible through slits in the seams of the brown robe, held no weapon, only coins, a pencil stub, some folded sheets of paper, and a nearly flat wallet. She signaled for the officers to let him go, and held out his wallet to him. "Is this what you were after?"

In answer, he took it from her and opened the billfold portion. No money that she could see, but he selected a piece of folded newspaper and held it out.

Torres, meanwhile, had his hand on the backpack. "You want us to look through this?"

She met the brown eyes above her. "Sir, do you mind if we take a look at your belongings?"

"What's mine is yours, and what is yours is mine." The monk watched as Torres unbuckled the top. Gingerly, Olivia began to peel apart the ancient piece of newspaper.

It was the upper half of a front page from the *San Francisco Chronicle*. In the center was a photograph showing four people, standing in conversation.

Although the page was all but worn through on its fold lines, Olivia recognized the figure with the white hair. He was wearing the same robe, or an earlier version of this one, and had a tall walking stick with a knob on top — currently leaning against the end of the bench. In the grainy newsprint, the stick was tucked into his shoulder as he stood listening to a dark-haired woman who barely came to his chin. To her left stood a distinctive black man in a dashing hat who could only be the former mayor of San Francisco. The picture's fourth figure was a middle-aged man whose face was vaguely familiar.

When she read the caption, she realized why:

Mayor Willie Brown, Inspectors Martinelli and Hawkin of the SFPD talk with the self-styled "Brother Erasmus" at the funeral of homeless woman Beatrice Jankowski, Saturday, St. Mary's Church.

Hawkin: she knew that name. And Martinelli — they'd been involved with a couple of cases that got a lot of press.

The faint bell of memory rang slightly

louder. Hadn't one of those cases been something extremely quirky to do with the homeless population of San Francisco? Ages ago — a murder case in which a sort of patron saint of the homeless population had played a part? One Brother Erasmus?

She opened her mouth to ask him about it, but suddenly Torres cursed and thrust an object under her nose — a small, thick, leather-bound book with onionskin pages, closely printed in some heavy writing.

"Arabic! And it's got notes to himself in the same language!"

For a moment, just an instant, it crossed Olivia's mind that there might actually be a point to all those idiotic federal terrorist warnings the Department kept getting — but one glance at the old man's face, one white eyebrow raised in a look that was more quizzical than guilty, and the panic faded.

"Let me see." She held out her hand for the book. Torres gave it to her, his own hand on the butt of his gun, the snap flipped away: he'd be ready if the old man reached for the trigger of a vest-bomb. She opened the book, and immediately shook her head — not that she had any idea what it said, but she'd watched enough television news to know what she was looking at.

"This isn't Arabic, Torres, it's Hebrew. And for heaven's sake take your hand off your weapon."

"Hebrew?"

"Sure, it's all square and boxy — Arabic is all curves and curlicues. Haven't you ever noticed the banners and signs on the news?"

"So, what? A Jewish terrorist?"

"This is a Bible. Look, don't bother going through the rest of his pack. I know who this is. They call him Brother Erasmus."

"A muddled fool, full of lucid intervals." His smile was like a beatitude as he held out his hand to her.

"Er, right." She allowed his fingers to wrap around hers, a smooth, strong, warm grip that again evoked her grandfather, who had grasped the wooden handle of a hoe until the last day of a long life. Not that they shared much in the way of appearance — this man's were long and thin and considerably less bashed about. They reminded her of that Dürer engraving of praying hands that used to be so popular when she was growing up. "Sergeant Olivia Mendez."

Erasmus held on for a moment, then let her go.

"Thanks, Torres, you and Wong can get back on patrol. We'll be fine here."

Reluctantly, the two patrol officers retreated to their car. Olivia turned to the man at her side. "Sir, I'm going to need to make some phone calls. Do you mind coming with me to the station house? You could have a cup of coffee or something." She didn't want him to think of it as an arrest.

He stretched out a long arm for the rucksack Torres had left on the bench, retrieved the carved staff, and walked beside her to the unmarked she'd driven here.

She put him in the front, with the staff threaded over the seat back. Neither of them spoke on the drive into town, although it was not an uncomfortable silence. At the station, she helped him get his stick out and led him inside.

"Sir, I'm going to put you in an interview room for a few minutes, and I'll be with you as soon as I've made my calls. Is there anything you need? Coffee? Soft drink? Something to eat?"

"I am glad I was not born before tea." The fellow had a knack for making a statement sound like a suggestion.

"Tea? I'll see what we can do. Officer Marcoletti, would you please make a cup of tea for the gentleman in interview room one?"

"Tea?"

"Yes, there are some bags in the cabinet. And take him the milk and sugar, in case he wants them."

"Milk and sugar?"

"And the package of cookies." She shut the door before he could repeat that, too.

It took four calls to track down Inspector Kate Martinelli of the San Francisco Police Department, finally reaching her at home. A woman answered; a child was talking in the background; Martinelli came on the line, and the noises cut off.

Olivia began to explain: her odd phone call; tracked to a local library; seemed to match the identity of the man known as Brother Erasmus, and she wondered —

"Our Holy Fool is there? In San Felipe?"

"Apparently."

"Good Lord, I've often wondered what happened to him. How is the old fellow?"

"He looks fine. Thin, but healthy."

"I am so tempted to drive down and see him. Tell him hi from me, would you?"

The affection in Martinelli's voice was not the usual reaction of a homicide detective to a witness and onetime suspect, Olivia reflected.

"I wanted to ask you about him, whether you'd say he was reliable, but it sounds like you've already answered my question."

"I don't know about reliable, since he's a man with his own agendas, but I'd say

Brother Erasmus is the most honest man you'll ever meet."

"If you can figure out what he's saying."

"Does he still talk that way? Everything in quotes?"

"Are those all quotes?"

"That's how he talked then. It took us forever to catch on."

"Why does he do that?"

The phone went silent for a minute, before Martinelli answered. "He would probably call it penance for his sins. He lost his family, years ago back in England, in a way he felt responsible for. Personally, I thought he was trying to keep his mind so busy, he didn't have energy left over for his own thoughts. He is actually able to speak directly, in his own words — he finally did when he was helping us with our case — but it seemed to be very hard on him. I think you'll find that, if you listen carefully, his meaning becomes clear. Have you figured out what he's after?"

"What do you mean?"

"You said he called you and said something about 'a child crying in the night.' Has he suggested yet how he can help you?"

"You think he knows something about one of my cases?"

"People open up to him — even the most

unlikely people." The detective made it sound like an admission. "And if he didn't know anything, why would he have called? Do you have a case involving a child?"

Gloria Rivas was nearly seventeen, the edge of womanhood, but Olivia pictured the bedroom of eleven-year-old Danny Escobedo, his LEGO spaceship and Spider-Man sheets. "Yes."

"Well, he had some reason to come to you. You might start there."

Olivia thanked her, repeated the promise to pass her greeting on to the old man, and hung up. She then phoned her priest, at the Catholic church downtown. He knew immediately who she was talking about.

"The children call him Saint Francis, because he has a way of coaxing birds into eating from his hand — literally, although I suppose figurative birds as well. He's been at mass several times over the past few weeks. I'm not sure where he lives, or how he supports himself, although I've seen people slip him money and they often bring him something to eat. He's oddly . . . authoritative. There was a scuffle in the food line one day and he stepped forward to put his hands on the two men's shoulders. They calmed right down. What's more, he had them eating together afterward, talking up a storm while he sat and nodded."

"Have you talked with him?"

"Don't know if I'd call it talking *with* him, but I've talked *to* him three or four times myself. Very restful kind of guy. Knows his Bible better than I do."

"But you'd say he's a trustworthy sort?"

The priest did not hesitate. "I'd say he's a saint of God."

When she hung up, she tapped her fingernail on the desk a few times, then returned to the interrogation room. Glancing through the door's small window, she could see the old man, long fingers threaded together, gazing in silent contemplation at the staff propped in the corner. She opened the door and stuck her head inside.

"I need some lunch. Want to join me?"

He rose and picked up his knapsack and staff, following her out of the station.

The take-out burrito stand down the street was doing brisk business with an assortment of children in soccer uniforms. They waited their turn, the old man beaming down at all around him. She was curious to see how he would order, but rather than speak, he laid a finger on the Spanish-language menu taped to the pass-through window, choosing the vegetarian option, and water. Two minutes later they had their fragrant meals before them on one of the stand's scarred wooden picnic tables. She peeled back the paper from one end and bit in; Erasmus was of the fork-and-knife school, taking a fastidious surgical approach to the object with his plastic utensils. His staff lay stretched out on the top of a low concrete-block wall, and she noticed that the fist-sized swelling at the top was not an amorphous knot of the wood as she'd thought, but a heavily worn carving. Studying it, she realized that when it was new, it must have resembled its owner — beard, flowing hair, hawk-like nose. She smiled.

"I spoke with Inspector Martinelli in San Francisco."

His response came as an affectionate murmur. "Subtle and profound female."

"Yeah, she seemed to admire you, too. Asked me to say hi. She also said you might have some information regarding an active case. That it could be the reason you called."

He put his fork down and reached through the pocket-slit of his robe, pulling out a folded scrap of newsprint considerably fresher than the earlier one. He laid it in front of her, reclaiming his fork as she picked up the clipping.

The Escobedo boy's school picture looked out at her.

She knew what the article said without having to look — the words might have been carved on her heart. It had been published on Thursday, six days after Gloria Rivas was gunned down and Danny vanished.

"You have information about this?"

He gazed thoughtfully at the rice and beans. "Nothing is so firmly believed as that which is least known."

"Look, sir, can't we just drop this whole quotation business? This isn't a game."

"The rules of the game are what we call the laws of nature. The player on the other side is hidden from us." He chewed, watching as she thought it over.

"You're telling me you don't actually have direct information that could lead me to Danny Escobedo." She rubbed her face: even the skin felt tired. "You only have guesses. And I have to jump through hoops to try and figure out what you mean, when I'm so beat that even if you were talking sense, I'd have problems sorting it out. I have to say, if you're trying to help, I wish you wouldn't. You're wasting time that I don't have."

She felt his touch then, firm, dry fingers that came down on the back of her wrist. She looked into his eyes, dark into dark, and saw a reflection of torment.

"To everything there is a season." The words sounded as if no one had ever thought of them before. "A time to weep, and a time to laugh. A time to keep silence, and a time to speak. There is a time for many words, and there is a time as well for sleep. A little sleep, a little slumber, a little folding of the hands to sleep." The repetition of the word alone was soporific; Olivia wanted to lay her head onto her arms right there on the picnic table. "Take up thy bed. And if we do meet again, why, we shall smile."

"You're telling me to go home and have a nap." His eyes crinkled: *yes.* "You're probably right. But you haven't told me what you wanted me to know, about Danny Escobedo."

"Those that have eyes to see, let them see."

"Jesus. Do you have any idea how irritating this is?"

"The discourse of fools is irksome." He gave her a smile filled with apology and empathy.

"So why do you do it?"

"He wrapped himself in quotations, as a beggar would enfold himself in the purple of emperors."

"There's nothing wrong with a beggar's rags."

But Brother Erasmus merely nodded.

259

"Like him that travels, I return again." He set the tip of his first finger against the table to indicate: *here.* Then he spread both hands out against the dented wood. When all his fingers were outstretched, he deliberately folded back the thumb of his left hand, then the first finger.

"You want me to meet you here, at eight o'clock? Tonight?"

Satisfied, he folded the paper around his half-eaten burrito, tucked it and the plastic fork and knife into his knapsack, stood up, and walked away, his staff beating a syncopation to his steps. The carved head, pointing backward, seemed to watch Olivia as it rose and fell.

Ridiculous notion. But in one thing the man was surely right: she did need some rest if she wasn't to be utterly useless. She phoned the station and told Marcoletti that she was going home, and wasn't to be disturbed for anything short of catastrophic. Inevitably, he wanted to know what she meant by catastrophic, but she just ended the call.

She drove home, fed the cat, kicked off her shoes, and crawled into bed, pulling the covers up over her head. And although she expected perhaps twenty minutes of fitful rest, she set her alarm for seven o'clock.

Olivia Mendez slept like a babe in its mother's arms, her dreams filled with the warm brown eyes of wise old men.

When she woke, it was dark, and the bedside clock told her it was nearly seven. She fried up some eggs, onions, and jalapeños, wrapping them in some of the tortillas her mother had made, topped with her sister's fiery salsa. Rested, fed, and warm inside, she then took a long, hot shower, washed her hair, dressed in warm clothes with a jacket to cover her gun, and went by the station in the vain hope that something — anything — had come to light in the case. There was nothing. Not even a phone call from Mrs. Escobedo.

Olivia had no intention of meeting the old man. It was ridiculous, a waste of time when she could be out re-interviewing Danny's friends, or — Oh, that reminded her. She called the Santos number, got Yasmina's mother again, and was told that no, Mina had been in earlier, but she was staying with friends tonight. Did Sergeant Mendez have Mina's cell number? Yes, Sergeant Mendez had it, and now tried it, but the phone was either turned off or in one of the county's many dead zones.

Olivia looked at the clock again: 7:52. Oh hell, why not? If she didn't go see, her curiosity would drive her nuts.

When she turned down the alleyway near the burrito stand, it appeared empty, until the old man stepped out of the shadows, a swirl of dark robes and a gleaming staff. He pulled open the door, slid the stick inside, and tucked himself into the passenger seat.

"Where are we going?" She reached up to flick on the overhead light.

He held out a scrap of paper, a torn-off section of an old map, showing San Felipe and the outlying countryside. Near the upper right corner, eight miles or so from the center of town, was a penciled circle. She pointed at it.

"You want me to go there?"

He pulled his seat belt around him; she put the car into gear and drove off.

She didn't have to check his map again — one thing Olivia Mendez knew, it was this valley. Twenty years ago, she'd learned to drive a stick shift on a farm lane just outside the map's penciled circle. Four years ago, she'd helped dismantle a meth lab half a mile to the north. She'd provided reluctant backup when *la Migra* raided a camp carved into the sandstone hills by men desperate to send every possible dollar back home.

Ten minutes later, she let the car slow. They were a mile from the nearest house, three from a paved road, and the last headlights behind them had vanished.

"Okay." She said it like a question.

The old man's hand appeared in the glow from the dashboard, one long finger pointing straight ahead. She gave the car some gas; in a hundred yards, when his finger shifted to the right, she steered down a graveled track between fields.

They went on that way for about a mile in all, gravel giving way to dirt, then ruts. Eventually, his hand came up — though she'd have stopped even without the signal, because they'd run out of road. Fences lay on either side. Before them lay a dirt turnaround and a wall of greenery, although she knew that behind it was a small creek and a cliff thrust upward by the plates of the earth. The camp of illegals had been very near here, as she remembered — the men had used the creek for water, the hills for shelter, and the trees for concealment. In the end, the smell of the cook-fire had given them away.

As the smell of smoke when she got out of the car gave this encampment away.

She had her hand on the weapon at her side, easing the car door shut with the hand that held the big Maglite. The old man, however, had no such urge to silence. He

263

slammed his door with a bang that could be heard for a mile.

The very air seemed to wince. Her companion merely walked toward the turnaround, speaking over his shoulder. *"Venga."*

She was already moving before the implications of his command struck her. Unless he'd come up with a very short quotation from some Spanish book, he had just addressed her directly. She trotted after him, switching on her flashlight as they plunged into a shadow of a space between some bushes.

Stones had been laid across the creek to ensure dry feet. And yes, the smell of wood smoke grew, along with signs of human occupation — two plastic chairs that looked as if they'd literally fallen off the back of a truck; two black trash bags with their necks tied shut; a neat row of empty plastic milk jugs. At least the place didn't reek like a toilet or meth lab, she thought, grateful not to be getting toxic waste on her shoes.

The ground began to rise. The trees grew thin, the path more defined, and suddenly Erasmus came to a halt before her, raising his voice to call at a patch of vegetation. *"Hola, niños. 'Stoy aqui con mi amiga. Permiso?"*

There followed a long and tense silence,

during which her fingers played with the strap on her gun, and then an answer: *"Vengan."*

She nearly dropped the flashlight at hearing a child's voice — she'd thought Erasmus was using the word *children* as a priest would. She pressed close against the shifting outline of his robes.

An L-shaped barrier of wired-together shipping pallets and plywood scraps jutted out of the sandstone cliff. Inside this patchwork wall stood two fairly expensive bicycles, helmets looped over the handlebars, and the circle of a burned-down campfire; in the cliff behind was the low entrance to a cave, one that had either gone unnoticed when the previous encampment had been destroyed, or been carved anew. Light spilled from the mouth. Erasmus started forward, but she caught his arm to hold him back, stooping to peer inside.

Three children stood in an apprehensive half circle behind an upended plastic milk crate draped with an incongruous square of brightly flowered oilcloth, on which stood a rechargeable camp light. On the right was that tiny firebrand Mina Santos. On the left, Carlos Garcia, one of the dozens of kids she'd interviewed several times in the days since Gloria's murder.

And between them, grubby but standing tall, was eleven-year-old Danny Escobedo.

The woman in Sergeant Mendez wanted to vault the plastic crate and throw her arms around the boy — then grab his shoulders and deliver a tongue-lashing these three would not recover from soon. She wanted to dance and sing and kiss the old monk's bearded cheek and yank out her cellphone to tell all the world the missing boy was safe — *safe!* — but the cop in her nailed her boots to the ground and sent her eyes traveling across the contents of the cave. It was, she had to admit, dry, neat, and surprisingly well equipped. Half a dozen gallon water jugs were lined up against the wall beside a cheap Styrofoam cooler, a second smaller lantern, a large box of candles, and a one-burner propane cooker with two extra canisters. A stack of neatly folded bedding — wool blanket, mover's pad, and a sleeping bag losing its stuffing — sat atop the cooler. Thought had gone into the hideout, and care — most kids would have dumped a pile of charcoal in the middle of the cave and suffocated to death by morning.

Olivia studied the cheerful flowered tablecloth, and wondered if it had been put there to impress her.

Not going to work.

"You guys having fun here?" She made her voice harsh. "The city's spent a fortune looking for you, Danny. Half of us haven't slept in a week because we've been searching for your body. Your family is going nuts." At the last accusation, the boy's gaze flicked over to Mina. There was a blatant lack of guilt on his face.

"God damn it. Your mother *knows,* doesn't she? That you weren't kidnapped? *That's* why she stopped phoning me 'round the clock."

"Mina told Mom I was at her house. I . . . I didn't want her to worry."

At that, Olivia lost it. "What are you *doing* here? Why the hell didn't you come to the police?" The kids' eyes grew wider with every word. "Why are you hiding out —"

Click: she stopped. Realization dawned. "You saw it, Danny, didn't you? *You saw Gloria die.* And you're afraid he's coming after you." In a community dominated by gangs, a minor crime — a passing remark — could escalate into a circle of violence and retribution.

Olivia sighed, rubbed at her face, and started over. "Okay, let's sit down and talk about this."

The boy's last trace of defiance melted, leaving him small and scared. With Danny's friends on either side of him, the kids settled onto the dusty pads. Olivia moved the camping light to the ground and sat cautiously down on the "table." She glanced behind her to see if there was some perch for the old man, but he was not there. Faded into the night like a brown-robed Zorro.

"Dígame." And the boy told her, so eager, his words tumbled in a rush of Spanish and English, with his friends contributing the occasional comment or clarification.

The first thing Danny wanted her to know was that Gloria wasn't really his babysitter, just that his mother paid to have her stay with him whenever she had to work nights. He didn't need a babysitter. But Gloria's family was large and she was serious about getting into college, and she could work more easily in the silence of the Escobedo house, so they all pretended she was a babysitter.

Olivia blinked at the boy's sense of priorities, but did not interrupt.

"So anyway, on Friday night — a week ago — Gloria got this call on her cell. She looked all funny when she saw the ID, and took it outside so I wouldn't hear. I didn't know who it was, but later, after I'd gone up to bed, there was this knock on the front

268

door. I looked around my curtains and there was this guy. I figured he was the one that called."

"What made you think that?"

" 'Cause Gloria was mad when she was on the phone, and mad when she saw him. She wouldn't let him in so they stood in the yard. She made him keep his voice down, so I couldn't hear what they were saying, but I could tell she was real mad."

"Did you know him?"

"I know who he is. Somebody told me he's big in one of the gangs. They call him Taco."

"Go ahead."

"Like I said, I couldn't hear them, but it looked like he was trying to talk her into something, all friendly and joking, like, you know? But she just kept shaking her head, and after a while he hauled off and *hit* her — hard enough to knock her over. I was going to run down and make him stop, but this Taco guy started to go back to his car. And Gloria went after him! She grabbed his arm just before he got to the car, and he turned around really fast and I heard this *bang!* and Gloria fell. I just . . . I kept waiting for her to get up, you know?"

The boy's stricken expression, the tears in his eyes: the first time Olivia had seen a

269

dead person, she'd felt the same way. She nodded.

"Then he looked up and saw me. He started running toward the front door, and he had this gun, and I heard the front door crash, so I got out of there, fast."

"How?"

"Out the window. You can climb out onto the porch roof and down the what-ya-call-it, the trellis, but I sort of just shot off the roof and hit the ground and ran. I hid in a neighbor's garden until he came out. He looked around for a minute, but then I heard sirens coming, and I could tell he did, too. He got in his car and drove off, but I was scared to go home again. I mean, I *saw* him, saw his *face*. He's in a gang!"

"So what did you do?"

"I could tell Gloria was . . . Anyway, the cops were on their way. But I knew they'd ask what I saw, and I just *couldn't*. Mina lives on the next street over, and I knew her a little, mostly 'cause she's best friends with Gloria's sister. And nobody would think of looking for me there. And anyway, I couldn't think where else to go in the middle of the night. So I snuck through the yards and knocked on her window. When I told her about Gloria, she said I was right, and let me hide out in her tool-shed until morning, when I had her call Carlos — I'd left my phone at home — to see if he'd heard anything. He didn't know anything new, but he said he had an uncle who lived down in these caves for a while, before *la Migra* deported him. So we figured I could hide out here a couple days until you guys arrested Taco. Mina had a bunch of stuff she could bring."

"And that was your plan?"

"If I told, about Taco, he'd come after me. And my family. I figured if everyone knew you couldn't find me, they wouldn't blame *me* when Taco got arrested."

In the backward logic of the gang world, it made sense. "So why did you have Brother Erasmus bring me here?"

Danny's look of defiance wavered. "Erasmo saw Mina riding her bike on the levee a couple days in a row, bringing me water and stuff. He followed her, and found me. I was getting — well, these caves are really creepy at night. And he's easy to talk to, you know? I told him about Gloria, and somehow, I don't know, I got to thinking about her. Not just how horrible it was that she died, but how really great she was and how smart, and how much she was looking forward to college. And how my hiding out . . . well, she deserved better."

The trio across from Sergeant Mendez seemed to sit a little straighter, either shouldering their portion of responsibility, or squaring off for the firing squad. Two eleven-year-old boys and their guardian of thirteen, prepared for whatever fate she would march them to.

Must've been some conversation with that old man, she thought, and cleared her throat.

"You know, it would've saved us all a lot of grief if you'd stepped forward the night it happened. But you've done so now, and that lets me get on with *my* responsibility. Which includes protecting you." For an instant, just a flash, she felt an urge to stand up and walk away, to leave these kids to their Neverland, far from vengeful gangbangers and the relentless machinery of the legal system. Ridiculous, of course. They were lucky they hadn't run into some human predator already. Or had the cave fall in on them. Time to take them home.

She told them to gather their things, a process that consisted of picking up two already-full backpacks. She stuck the flashlight in her belt and exchanged it for the lantern, running her eyes across the sanctuary. The two boys hadn't organized this. Young Mina Santos showed signs of becoming a formidable woman. Olivia was almost smiling as she bent to pass through the entrance of the cave, but the moment she straightened, a sound echoing off the sandstone cliff froze all the blood in her veins. Her hands shot out to block the children behind her, and she snapped out a command.

"Back! Get back!"

It was the sound of a shotgun racking a shell into place.

The lamp in her left hand blinded her, but she knew that sound, oh yes, and although it set her guts to crawling and every cell in her body wanted to fling itself to the ground, she was not about to let these three children walk into it.

The kids scrambled backward into the dark and inadequate depths of the cave. Olivia kept her arms outstretched. The gun couldn't be more than twenty feet away: impossible to miss at that range. But maybe if she turned her left side toward it, she could survive long enough to pull her weapon and take him down . . . She raised the lantern a bit, shifting her body to the right as she moved.

A Latino voice came from the darkness. Taco? "I want the kid."

"You don't want these kids. They're just

vagrants camping out here. I'd suggest you leave before my partner arrives."

"You don't got a partner, you came on your own."

So he'd seen her leave the station, though not her stop to pick up Brother Erasmus. "You've been following me?"

"Last couple nights. One of my boys heard you were onto the kid."

"Those were your headlights I saw behind me, on the road."

"Didn't need to follow you closer, I could see where you were coming. Now, get out of the way."

"I can't do that. And whoever you are and whatever you've done, the one thing you really don't want to take on is shooting a police officer." It could only be Taco Alvarez, but if Taco thought she did not know, maybe, just maybe, he might back off, leaving Danny for another day.

She heard a step, then another, and braced herself for action: throw the lamp, hit the ground, pull her gun —

Then came a sound that didn't fit: a patter of rainfall on a dry night, off to the side. Erasmus? She drew breath for a warning. But before the words could leave her mouth there was a quick scuffle, then the explosion she had been dreading, deafening her and burning a black-and-white print of tree branches onto her retinas.

After what seemed a very long time, Olivia lifted her cheek off the dirt. The night had gone black. Over the ringing in her ears she could make out some high-pitched noise, a chorus of — *screams* — the kids, in the cave! She staggered upright, pulling her sidearm, wondering vaguely why she hadn't been cut in half by the shotgun blast, then crashed into something that wobbled and bit at her shoulder: the pallet wall. She put out her left hand, and finally remembered: *Mendez, you got a flashlight!* She grabbed it from her belt and thumbed it on, holding it well away from her body; over the ringing in her ears, the screams seemed to diminish slightly.

Two steps to the cave entrance, and at the beam's end . . .

The kids, pressed against the cave's back wall, wrapped in each other's arms. Terrified, but whole. Carlos was the only one still screaming, his eyes tight shut. The other two blinked into the light, and Mina's lips moved, saying something.

Olivia ducked back outside. The beam skittered in a circle, catching the half-collapsed pallet wall, the smashed lantern, a dark circle of ashes, the path along the cliff

— and legs.

Taco Alvarez lay stretched out with his feet toward the cave, blood in his hair, mouth agape, the fingers of one hand twitching. Her flashlight found another pair of feet: white sneakers beneath a dark brown robe.

Brother Erasmus: wooden staff in one hand, shotgun in the other. He blinked when the beam hit his eyes, but the smile on his face was beatific.

"Was he alone?" She'd snapped out the demand automatically, envisioning the psycho brother Angel taking aim at them all — but the smile did not shift.

"Alone, alone, all, all alone."

She took the shotgun, peeled out the shells, and flung the empty weapon to the side. As she knelt to slap the handcuffs onto the groaning Taco Alvarez, the old man pulled out a minuscule flashlight and walked past her to the entrance of the cave. When she stood up again, the children were clinging to him like limpets on a rock, weeping. He somehow had enough hands to embrace all three of them at once.

Her cellphone, of course, couldn't get a signal. *Next time you drive off with a mad monk,* she raged at herself, *take a Department cruiser.*

She couldn't leave the kids here while she went for help. And she'd be damned if they had to sit in a car with their would-be murderer. In the end, she left Taco — cursing in two languages, hands in cuffs, feet wrapped in duct tape, and a knot the size of an egg on his head — in the gentle care of Brother Erasmus.

"I'll send someone the instant I get in range of a cell tower. You sure you'll be okay with him? I could just tie him to a tree."

"Bright star, would I were steadfast as thou art, watching, with eternal lids apart."

"I don't think it'll be anywhere near an eternity. Maybe twenty minutes, half an hour at the most."

By way of answer, he placed his hand on her shoulder, and smiled down on her.

She looked over at the children, who had passed through the terror phase and were now beginning to talk in a mad tumble of words. She lowered her voice. "Thank you. He'd have pulled the trigger for sure. I should have been more careful."

"There is no fool like an old fool."

She laughed. "You're right about that. The last thing he could've expected was an old man with a cudgel."

"Every inch that is not fool is rogue." In the lamp-light, the old eyes sparkled.

277

"Well, I thank God for that. Okay, I'd better get these three home. I'll see you at the station."

He merely smiled, and leaned on his staff. She gathered up Danny and his two protectors, got them across the creek dry-footed, and into the car.

When she turned back, she saw Erasmus through a gap in the trees, a dark shape in the light of the back-up lantern. A line from some summer Shakespeare play percolated up in her mind, and she murmured it into the night. "I met a fool in the forest, a motley fool."

A mile from the cave, her phone came to life. As she made her calls, she was dimly aware that the kids had moved on from reliving their terror to speculation about Erasmus. Danny thought he was a hero in disguise. Carlos wondered if he'd just dyed his hair and painted lines to look old. But Mina, with the superiority of age and the wisdom of her sex, insisted he was an angel of God.

Olivia Mendez thought all three kids might be right.

Mina

Mina gave a last glance at the girls' room mirror, rolled her skirt a little shorter, then shoved her makeup pouch back into her bag. A little more around the eyes than usual, but Ms. McDonald would be too busy today to notice.

Sofia squinted at her appraisingly. "I like the earrings."

Mina did, too, although they were heavy, and so cheap they'd probably give her an infection. "You ever think of getting other piercings?"

"Like, nose or something?"

"Tongue, lip, belly button. Tit."

Sofia giggled. "Yeah, right. My mom would lock me in my room until I was forty."

"That reminds me." Mina snaked her hand down to the bottom of her bag to feel around for her phone.

"Checking in with Mommy?"

"Sucks, I know." Sofia had a big family.

279

Even after Gloria, she tended to take them for granted. Mina had her parents, period.

Mina's fast-moving thumbs picked out a text to her mother.

Heading to class now no sign of terrorists or gangsters yet, luv m.

OLIVIA

There were times Olivia regretted being a cop. Oh, not the job itself — other than when she had to clean up some horrible thing one human being had done to another, or keep awake on her third shift in a row, or sit surveillance with an exploding bladder. And she always found she drank more on nights when she'd had to ravage some harmless citizen to tears in an interrogation.

No, it was the easy relationships she missed. Bad enough to go to a party and be introduced to a woman you'd busted for prostitution, or wheel your grocery cart past a guy behind on his child support, but she'd bet that secretaries and bus drivers didn't get that moment of hesitation when a new acquaintance heard what you did, or when a long-time friend started to dish the gossip and then realized that she shouldn't tell *you*.

Take Linda. She liked Linda McDonald,

but there was something about her husband the woman didn't want Olivia to look at too closely. Not long ago, that would have been a red flag to Olivia's bullish nature. Even now, her first impulse was to dive in and dig it out, friendship be damned. However, Olivia Mendez had been a cop for long enough to learn that to survive the job, a person had to find a balance. Loneliness was corrosive. Sometimes, what people were hiding could remain hidden, without the world coming to an end.

Her fallback position now was: trust, but keep your eyes open.

The students were beginning to move toward their homerooms, the breezeways emptying with the approach of first bell. Her uniform made it unnecessary to chide anyone against running, as each and every student instantly dropped into a sort of race-walk when they caught sight of her, mumbling a greeting as they scurried by. To give them a break, she went into the library to see how preparations were going — and there, speak of the devil, was Gordon Hugh-Kendrick, arranging plastic spoons on a cheap paper tablecloth.

Did she imagine the brief flicker of alarm, as if checking the surroundings for escape routes?

And if she had seen it, so what? Lots of good people still had reason to be wary of cops. *Trust, but keep your eyes open.*

"Hello, Mr. Kendrick."

"Please, call me Gordon."

"And I'm Olivia."

"How are things going, Olivia?"

"So far, so good. You?"

"I have narrowly averted calamity by locating a packet of artificial sweetener in the far reaches of the staff cupboards. Thus ensuring that our guests may die of some terrible cancer, but years from now and not on school grounds."

"That's all we can hope for."

He held up a cup. "Coffee?"

"Maybe later."

"The speakers were asked to come at 9:30. I give the croissants until 9:32, if you've got your eyes on one of those."

The man was as open and friendly as a stay-at-home dad, she thought. Or somebody's granddad, finding a purpose to his retirement. "Thanks for the warning. Okay, well, see you later."

She moved away before she could see a look of relief on his face, and went back out into the breezeway, where all the kids and most of the adults bounced away like reversed magnets. Nothing like an armed cop to make even the innocent look around for the trouble.

Maybe she should take her uniform away to the furthest reaches of the school and let the kids have their last few minutes of blowing off the morning's steam. Once she was formally introduced, with the other guest speakers during the assembly, her badge and duty belt would become a sort of costume. The kids would relax.

So she sent Linda a text to let her know where she was going, and walked away, down the circuit of chain-link fence that separated the playing fields from a road on the west side, an apple orchard on the east, and the seasonal creek at the back. Not that the fence meant much. It wasn't even continuous, since the school grounds were public property on weekends. The only section that would slow down a determined five-year-old was the hundred or so feet between the baseball diamond and the apple orchard's storage yard. The mowing crew regularly came across used needles.

But then, she supposed that the uniform she had on was largely symbolic, too, when it came to enforcing the law.

LINDA

Linda hung up the telephone and checked her cell for the text she'd heard come in: from Olivia, saying that she was walking the perimeter. She stretched out an arm for the next call slip — and nearly knocked over the box of flyers she'd spent the night fretting about. She shook her head, stood up rapidly enough to bash her thigh on the corner of the desk, muttered dire threats at her stockings not to run, and limped into the office with the flyers.

Mrs. Hopkins, having stemmed the worst of the tide, glanced up as Linda popped into her realm.

"I forgot to give you these — the extra Teacher Memos you wanted? To give the volunteers?"

The other woman at the high counter turned, and Linda's heart sank. "Good morning, Señora McDonald, I wonder if —"

"Ah, Señora Rodriguez, *so* good to see you. Going to be a gorgeous day, isn't it?" Linda took care not to pause for breath — if the Señora got a wedge into the space between words, she would use it to drive home her inevitable list of reasonable and vastly time-consuming suggestions. "Sorry I can't talk, I have a million things to do, I'm sure you understand — maybe you'd take charge of this for me?"

Her distraction succeeded. As Linda retreated inside her office door, she saw the woman reach for a sheet from the box.

Her door closed; the 8:00 bell rang.

Career Day, at Guadalupe Middle School.

■ ■ ■ ■

CAREER DAY

Dream Time

■ ■ ■ ■

TEACHER MEMO —

GUADALUPE MIDDLE SCHOOL CAREER DAY

Remember, **all Period 1 classes** focus on **"The Dream."** Encourage students to consider a career's satisfactions, how they think the job would make them *feel.*

Period 2 focuses on **"The Practical"**: Could I make a living? Would I have a good home life and live where I wanted? How much would the training cost? Etc.

Both Period 1 and Period 2 written assignments are due **Friday.**

Period 3 is the assembly. I will try to dismiss early. All students have classroom assignments for **Periods 4, 5, and 6** — the complete list is posted outside the office. *Please discourage students* from trying to make changes in their classroom assignments. If they have problems, send them to the office.

PERIOD (TIME)	ACTIVITY
1 (8:00–8:50)	Writing assignment: the Dream
2 (9:00–9:50)	Writing assignment: the Practical
3 (10:00–10:50)	Assembly (multipurpose room)
4 (11:00–11:50)	Speakers I
Lunch (11:50–12:40)	Lunch
5 (12:40–1:30)	Speakers II
6 (1:40–2:30)	Speakers III

Thanks to everyone who has worked so hard to make this year's Career Day a success!

Linda McDonald, Principal

The morning bell echoed down the breeze-ways, hurrying the last students toward their first-period rooms. In the office, Mrs. Hopkins took out her pad of admit slips for the inevitable trickle of students with business too urgent to finish before the bell. Back at her desk, Linda picked up another telephone slip. In the school entranceway, Tío pulled a broom out of his cart.

The hallways quieted; an abandoned basketball rolled out from under a picnic table at the end of B Quad. Inside thirty-one classrooms, teachers expert at the herding of cats turned their restless adolescents toward an honest contemplation of dreams.

GORDON

Gordon stood outside the library, head lifted, as the buildings around him fell slowly quiet. It was a moment he cherished whenever it was offered, this sensation of a school full of children settling to their futures. Some days it didn't come. He hadn't expected it today, when the hallways were bustling with adults and excited kids. But here it was, a rare and undeserved gift. Gordon Hugh-Kendrick, surrounded by the sweet and ephemeral beauty of a generation, feeling old and tired.

Feeling, too, that his presence here was a blight on the landscape. What kind of school deserved a man who'd worked for a gang of mercenaries?

He might have grandchildren this age, had Jasmin lived. Three decades ago, he had barely noticed the child's sex on the coroner's report — but the older Gordon got, the more present that missing piece had become in his life. He never spoke of it, even with Linda, but his unborn daughter was often there in the corner of his eye, at the edge of his mind, in the figures of his dreams.

It also amused his English spirit to reflect that those theoretical grandchildren of his could have had skin even darker than those settling to their desks around him.

MINA

Mina fiddled with the end of her black braid while her homeroom teacher droned his instructions about the assignment. Really, why didn't he just say, "Write a one-page essay about your dream job"? But she waited until he'd finished, then flipped her braid back over her shoulder and clicked open her pen.

Dreams are easy. Reality is hard. Still . . . maybe this essay could help with the hard reality, since it would be a thing she could hand her parents, the next time that discussion came around.

AN AMERICAN GIRL'S DREAM

Forty-three years ago, a little girl escaped Iran with her mother and her baby brother. She was too young to understand why her world had ended, too young to know why her father wasn't with them, why her

mother kept crying, why she wasn't allowed to talk to *anyone* on the cars and trains and planes they went on. All she knew was, her room, her toys, her parakeet — that life was gone.

Everything but her mother and little brother.

They went to a place where people made noises that sounded like talk but had no words. And just when some of the noises started to become words, they went to another place where the people made noises. This happened a third time before they stayed long enough for the words to develop in her mind and she could reach out to strangers at last.

My mother was this poor refugee from a rich background. She grew up in London and met my Brazilian father during a riot, when they both took shelter near a police constable armed with nothing but a stick. They married and came to America, a country where bad things may happen, but where good people can still speak up.

Hearing these stories in my childhood taught me that there are two strong things: language, and the law. With one, you can reach out to strangers. With the other, you can try to protect them.

My dream in life is to bring the two together.

Brendan

Brendan's phone had pinged as he was biking down the main road, so he'd stopped, legs straddled as the cars flew past, to read Jock's text:

You sure? When?

At least Jock wasn't blowing him off (not right away). Brendan sent back:

Let you know

When he'd reached school (almost on time) he checked it again and found:

Standing by.

So there was that much, anyway.
But instead of going straight to the school office as he'd meant to, Brendan found himself heading for homeroom, like any other day. He even got to his seat before the

bell finished ringing — only to realize that (*duh*) if he was there, he'd have to at least pretend to be doing this dumb "dreams" assignment. Which meant he'd need to borrow a piece of paper, since everything related to school was on his bedroom floor.

Writing his dreams? What was the fucking point? He sure wasn't going to be finishing the thing.

But if he wasn't going to the main office yet, he might as well scribble words on the page while he worked himself up to do what he (and Jock!) were now committed to.

Sure, like I'm going to write down dreams on this piece of paper for everyone to see. Dreams are just a mix of crap from the back of the brain. People who think dreams mean something are like those religious nuts who see Jesus on a tortilla.

Smith & Wesson Bodyguard 380, now there's a dream for you.

I read somewhere that dreams are how the subconsious tries to make things right, by redoing them, over and over. If that's true, all I can say is, I have a really sick subconsious. Why can't I dream about ~~Mina S~~ some hot actress or something?

And anyway by the time this essay is due I don't think it'll be the first thing on people's minds for me.

I'm only sitting here because I'm working up the nerve to hunt down Ms. McDonald. Get things moving, like I told Jock. Career Day? Who gives a crap?

Your wasting time, Brendan. Stand up and just walk out. Take your backpack to the office. Give it to the principal like you planned.

Your such a coward.

Okay, soon as the bell rings.

LINDA

Linda leaned back in her chair, blowing a puff of air up toward her unruly bangs. A little more than an hour before the guest speakers started to arrive, with a speech to finalize, a stack of pink call slips, and a queue of emails demanding attention. Most of all, the call to Tom Atcheson — she'd Googled his name twice, to see if the DA had announced his investigation, but so far there was nothing.

By tonight, she was going to feel like an old dishrag.

She and Gordon should take off for a few days over Easter vacation. Or what about a nice long trip, over the summer? They'd never had an actual holiday together. And she'd been working 70-hour weeks since May. Could she talk him into going some-where? Fiji, Tahiti . . .

Maybe someplace without international borders. Maui? Two weeks there, doing nothing but sweating, swimming, and reading a suitcase full of trashy novels.

For the next forty seconds, Linda McDonald was on a beach, listening to waves and the clatter of wind through palm trees — until a raised voice from the adjoining office reminded her of life, and her eyes came to focus on the little red circle informing her of 42 unopened emails.

Day-dreams over. She picked up the phone and called Atcheson Enterprises, to ask that the man get in touch with her as soon as he came in.

Tío

A janitor's dreams were not those of a schoolmaster, Tío had found. To say nothing of the extent the world had changed since he last stood in front of a class.

Sometimes he would pause, outside a classroom or near a group of students, to perform some task that allowed him to listen unnoticed.

Guadalupe was an alien world from the one where he grew up. It was not merely the modern inventions — this change from chalkboards to video screens, from shared textbooks to electronic tablets was a matter of surface technology. It was the shift in attitudes that made him ponder.

A school had always been a place to incubate hopes and dreams, in a village like Tío's or in the biggest of cities. But for many of the children here, parental hopes had turned to adult expectations, and the warmth of the incubator felt more like the focused burn of a magnifying glass in the sun. He had first noticed it in the ball games — baseball and what they called *soccer* here. Mothers and fathers screamed at their players, not in appreciation but in command, even condemnation. Did no one still believe that childhood was a time for joy? That *soccer* was a game, not a test of the child's moral strength?

He finished his tidying of the school entrance and slipped the handle of the broom into its slot, turning back toward the cafeteria. Entering the breezeway, he saw a man standing outside of the library, head tipped in attention.

This man interested Tío. The husband of Principal McDonald was one of the rare individuals who looked at a uniform and saw the person underneath. In another (Sergeant Olivia Mendez, for one) this might have made Tío uncomfortable, but from their first encounter, he had felt that he and Gordon Kendrick spoke the same language. That this man, too, had a face he did not show the world.

Once or twice a month, they would have a conversation. About nothing much, and yet, about everything.

Tío gave his cart a little jiggle, causing a rattle that made the tall man turn, startled.

Immediately, his face relaxed into the open expression that (Tío thought) went far to explain how the unsentimental Principal McDonald had allowed this man under her guard.

They exchanged greetings in each other's languages, and Tío asked what it was the Englishman had heard.

"I was listening to the silence."

"Ah." Tío nodded. "The sound of the children at work."

"According to the schedule, they're spending this hour writing their dreams."

"An hour seems very little time for dreaming."

"Hard reality and job planning come at nine o'clock."

"A pity."

The two men smiled, both of them aware of, but neither looking at, the uniformed woman approaching from the far end of the quad. "In Australia, the aboriginals talk about Dreamtime, a place of eternal potential — *entiende* 'potential'?"

"*Potentia* is Latin, Señor."

"Of course, sorry. Dreamtime is where the lives and the knowledge of all our ancestors exist, and where all the acts of our descendants wait, at once."

"A potent assignment, indeed, for one

fifty-minute class."

Gordon laughed. "I don't think I ever asked — do you have children?"

"I did." Tío's voice was calm. "A son. He was killed."

"Oh, Jaime. I'm sorry."

"Many years ago. Some joys are . . . temporary."

"And yet pain seems to last forever."

"And speaking of pain." The two men moved apart to watch Olivia Mendez, coming at them down the length of B Quad.

OLIVIA

When the eight o'clock bell rang, Olivia had been turning the last corner of the fence-line, in a world so quiet, she could hear a trickle of water in the stream behind her. It might have been a Sunday morning — until a girl popped out of a B Wing classroom, crossing the quad to the bathrooms at the end of the gym. And a teacher, head bent over a cellphone, strolled down A Quad toward the office. Someone had come out of the library to stand, in an attitude of listening — and although Olivia's even pace did not change, her interest sharpened.

Gordon Kendrick.

Mendez, she scolded herself, *you're like that kid who just* has *to pull apart a clock to see how it works.* Some people wanted privacy for no other reason than they were private people. She should be glad for the chance to meet someone like Linda's quirky husband.

But she couldn't shake the feeling there was something about him she ought to know.

As she watched-without-watching, he turned sharply at a sound behind him, then relaxed, his posture declaring how pleased he was to see whoever was coming down the breezeway. And that was exactly it: wasn't the reaction just a bit more . . . *edgy* than you'd expect from an amiable British guy? Was it mere chance that he now had his back to the wall? Or was Olivia Mendez about to reduce another lovely piece of machinery to a silent heap of gears?

The janitor's cart came into view, along with the janitor. The two men shook hands like old friends, then stood talking. She was tempted — briefly — to veer aside and sprint down A Quad, so she could listen in on what the unlikely pair was saying, but she squelched the impulse. Instead, she continued her steady approach, across the outdoor basketball courts and through the picnic tables of B Quad.

Gordon appeared to notice her, although she suspected that he'd been watching her all along. Tío, too, looked around, then finished whatever he had been saying to his boss's tall husband. The men stood apart as she came into earshot.

307

"Morning." Her voice was all cop: friendly authority.

When they had returned her greeting, Tío nodded toward the far end of the quad she had just come down. "Does all look well in the school grounds?"

"I didn't see any problems."

"Good. It is troubling, what people will throw over the fences to save paying fees at the dump. Today I found this." He pulled a white plastic shopping bag from the cart. Olivia accepted it gingerly, but when it neither dripped nor squelched, she pulled open the top: a can of spray paint and an orange cap. "It was lying at the entrance to the school. The cap was off, but it looks unused. I have found no paint on the walls."

"Like someone was about to use it, and got interrupted?"

"There is a light in the entrance that goes on with motion, but it has developed a few seconds of delay. I reported it to the District. They have not yet fixed it."

"Okay. Um, has anyone touched this but you?"

"Not that I know of."

"Well, thanks. I'll hang on to it, in case we . . . well, just in case."

He nodded, and pushed his cart down the quad to the cafeteria.

Gordon turned his gaze on the plastic bag. "You could leave that in Linda's office, if you don't want to carry it around."

"Oh, I'll just stick it in my cruiser. How are things going up here?"

Somehow, she found that they were moving in the direction of the parking lot, Gordon slowing his pace to her shorter legs as he considered his reply. "The children seem . . . excited."

"That's understandable. Unless it's something more?" When he did not answer, she glanced up sharply. "Trouble?" *God,* she thought, *I take a ten-minute walk around the fields and something happens?*

But he was shaking his head. "Not necessarily. More as if . . . have you ever stepped into a surprise party? Where guests are hiding behind the sofas?"

She stopped walking, openly astonished at the picture: this man, with friends in silly hats waiting to pounce? "You think the kids have something planned?"

"Not all of them. And not even a plan." He gave her a rueful smile. "I honestly don't know what I mean. It's probably just their reaction to the day's excitements. And speaking of excitements," he went on before she could decide whether or not she agreed, "Linda tells me I'm to ask about your Fool."

GORDON

Innocence was not a word most people associated with the students of a California middle school, Gordon reflected as he walked beside a woman with handcuffs on her belt. These were children who had long outgrown childish naiveté: raised with televised violence, playing games of graphic death, taught by their parents to mistrust any political, economic, or even religious authority. Eleven-year-old girls with braces on their teeth and sparkly unicorns on their notebooks breathed out the cynicism of a nihilist.

And yet, even the oldest, most sneering of these adolescents harbored secret pockets of hope, a hidden belief that the world might still hold out an outstretched hand in place of a fist.

This story of the Fool and the killer, for example. The goodness of three children in the face of murder, their willingness to share danger, made him want to weep — although he took care not to show that to Sergeant Olivia Mendez.

Gordon Hugh-Kendrick had no business walking among these children. His very presence was a threat — to their persons, and to that tiny flicker of hope in each and every breast. He should go before the demons of his past turned an Arctic breeze on the school's small candle — to say nothing of Linda's.

God only knew what kind of creative vengeance a company of international mercenaries might come up with.

And yet, he couldn't quite stay away. Just as he couldn't resist this game of conversation with Sergeant Olivia Mendez. While he listened to her story about San Felipe's visitation from the Fool, his tongue was playing with words as it might with a chipped tooth. It would not take much of a slip: Sergeant Mendez might look like a small-town cop, but her mind was sharp, and curious, and very probably inexorable.

Instead, he listened, and made the expected responses in an open and appreciative manner, with no jarring note, no oddness that could not be explained by his accent. The very model of a principal's English husband.

311

CHACO

What's the point in writing about some pinche *dream job*? The men he knew took whatever work there was. Holding out for something you really wanted to do was just a ticket to Disappointment. Like, someone was going to hire Chaco Cabrera for a job in a fine suit? Oh, sure. Might as well dream about being Spider-Man or the Arrow.

No: what a man hoped for was a life that was *sufficient*. (And maybe one that was long enough to worry about jobs . . .) Like university professor would be nuts but schoolteacher might not be *way* out of reach. Video game designer? (Yeah, sure: more like selling videos at Best Buy.)

Still, the teacher might be right about one thing: "Think about what's easy for you, or what you really love to do." Not that Chaco was gonna blab aloud about that second part, but "easy"?

Math had always been weirdly simple.

Other subjects were slippery, but math was so *effortless* he had to work sometimes to hide it, giving wrong answers so the teacher didn't make comments in front of the class. But what kinds of things used math? (Other than whatever it was Tío had in mind. What was *that* about, anyway?) Maybe math teacher, if he wanted it bad enough, and if he got lucky along the way. Or work in a bank? He'd heard his aunt complaining about the tellers (funny word — what did they *tell*?) who didn't speak enough Spanish to get through a simple thing like depositing a check.

There, Chaco had two skills: math, and Spanish.

'Course, he also had Mamá and the littles and Angel in his life. So he wasn't about to write anything too honest about dreams. Lying was a skill, too.

Dreams are what keep you from sleeping at night. Dreams get in the way of standing on your feet. Dreams are for mothers, who don't really know what's going on in their son's life.

I used to dream. One of my dreams was walking into the house and finding my Dad, only he wasn't my Dad he was someone all healthy and cheerful who

313

looked like him. Or I sometimes had dreams that my Mom was laughing. My father was never happy or healthy, not when I knew him, but Mom used to laugh a lot when I was young.

If I was going to dream some kind of Career, it would be something that would make my Mom laugh like that again. Something that would mean she doesn't have to work so much, and stops worrying about paying the rent, and can take my sister to the doctor when she needs to. Buy herself clothes she likes, not just what she needs.

But it would also have to be something that would keep ~~my cous~~ other people happy, too. Cause there are people with expectations who if I let down, would make things even harder on my Mom.

So will this Career Day give me some kind of job that lets my Mom laugh again, but also keeps my family happy? Cause right now I don't see that happening.

But anyway, that's my dream.

8:23
NICK

"Write your dreams," the teacher said. "Due Friday."

As far as Nick was concerned, this whole year had been a dream. And at other times, it was the most real thing that had ever happened to him.

Bee was gone: *that* was real.

A month ago, he'd been so sure he knew what happened to her, even though he'd seen how careful all the adults were around the subject, like they were afraid to point out how really unlikely it was, in case he broke into a thousand pieces.

He knew it was unlikely. Did they think he believed in Harry Potter or something?

Then the really strange thing happened.

He'd started #speakforbee because he was mad. And sad, sure, but mostly really pissed off, that he couldn't seem to do *anything* for Bee. He could even remember when it started: with that ad in the paper showing Mr. Cuomo grinning like the salesman he was.

What right did he have to look like that when his daughter was *gone*?

Nick had grabbed a felt pen to add horns and fangs to the ad. Then he put little red lines in the guy's eyes and blood dripping down his chin.

But instead of bursting into tears (like he was doing at pretty much everything else right then) Nick cut the ad out and kept it.

The next day he hunted down the ad online and printed off a bunch of copies. It made him feel good to turn the smile into something evil. Nearly as good as hurting Mr. Cuomo himself. It was childish, but so what?

Nick couldn't afford Photoshop, but in one of his schools he'd learned how to edit a photo, so he downloaded a free program and added Dracula fangs onto Cuomo's grin. It looked almost real.

He sent it to AJ as a laugh — well, not a laugh, really. It was too angry for that. But AJ had been Bee's friend, too.

AJ sent it to the Tim twins, and they sent it to some other friends of Bee's, and then somebody — Nick never did find out who — posted it online. Along with the hashtag #speakforbee.

In a couple of days there were four images, only two of them Nick's. In no time at all it went viral. It became a game to see who could make the best image of Evil Cuomo — the one of Cuomo's face mixed with Hannibal Lechter was totally creepy, since the two faces looked a little bit alike.

Anyway, the point was that once the hashtag got going, people at school started to treat him differently. Even the older kids acted like they thought he was almost cool — him, Nick Clarkson! Like he'd brought in a movie and set it down over their heads so they could walk around in it (and not a horror movie with creepy dolls in haunted attics, or the kind of movie where you just knew someone was going to set off a bomb).

The Bee Cuomo Story!

Maybe that was why #speakforbee had sort of caught on. Not because people really cared about Bee, but because they liked being part of a movie?

Not that it mattered why — he was glad it was popular, 'cause it must be making Mr. Cuomo crazy. But he had to admit, the whole thing was getting a little out of hand. Like it wasn't really to do with Bee now. Some of the things you got when you hit the hashtag were, well . . . At the same time, Nick's own images seemed to be going back to the felt pen fangs stage.

Why? Maybe it was how gross the other images were getting. Or maybe it was the way that grown-ups were still tip-toeing around him while the kids had started to treat him as almost cool? Anyway, he'd found himself asking, what really *did* happen to Bee?

Was he still all that sure about what happened? Even last week he'd been convinced of what he saw, but now, after going back to the museum Saturday, he had to wonder.

Was it possible that his mind was so freaked-out at the idea of Bee gone, it added a kind of chapter to the story on its own? A chapter where Bee didn't get hurt or anything, but instead just sort of . . . moved sideways?

NICK: HIS STORY (2)

CLINICAL CASE NOTES AND TRANSCRIPT EXCERPTS, FEBRUARY 8 SESSION, NICHOLAS CLARKSON.

Notes:
From the beginning of this session, Nick exhibited more assurance than during our initial session. He also became more involved with the story, mimicking the voices of his friends as if he were re-experiencing it. He has also relaxed enough into the process that he could respond to, and even make, small forays of humor.

DRH: Okay, you told me about the first time you went into the Weildman House. What was the second?

NICK: That was in August, about six weeks after the first time. We had a TV by then, plus we were going to the library a couple times a week, and Mom got a reading list from the school so I wouldn't be behind, but the whole time the house was just sort of . . . waiting. So the Friday before school started, I went back.

The little door was still hard to open, but this time I propped a stick in it so it wouldn't shut on me. I could tell no one else'd been in — you could see my footprints. I stood in the living room a while, looking at that humongous fireplace. It was so big, you could burn like a whole tree in it. I was trying to imagine the family, these ladies knitting or something, a guy with a beard, that chandelier burning. A piano, maybe? What would you do, without TV or games? Books, yeah, but how many hours a day could you read? It was hard to picture. Then when I turned to walk out, I kind of . . . out of the corner of my eye, like, there was a sort of a flame, flashing up in the empty fireplace. Not only that, I heard a sort of a creaking noise, like a rocking chair.

I turned around fast, but there wasn't anything there.

And a little while later, the same thing happened in the kitchen. I was checking out the empty cabinets when I felt heat on my back, and the air smelled like coffee and there was a man's voice — less than a second, there and gone.

And when I looked the stove was just this rusty black thing, and the air only smelled . . . stale.

That's when I left, and I didn't go back.

DrH: Until you brought Bee and AJ.

NICK: Until Bee brought us, you mean. I thought maybe the house wouldn't . . . you know. Show us the door. But it did. For some reason, Bee spotted it the second we came through the gate. I told her and AJ we didn't have to go in, 'cause it was dirty in there, but she wanted to see it. And anyway, there was the Social Studies project we had to decide on. And then she said, "Besides, if we don't go in, it's going to bug you forever."

I told her I thought it might bug me forever if we *did* go in.

DrH: What did you mean by that?

NICK: Just a joke. Well, meant to be. But she gave me a look and stuck her fingernails under the edge of the little door. I was about to get out my pocket-knife but it just popped open. I had to help AJ climb up — he's kind of fat — but we followed her in.

We went all through the house that day, even upstairs. Most of the rooms were empty, except for some bed frames in some of the upstairs rooms, and one mattress that was like a mouse condo. When nothing happened, I decided that whatever I'd seen — whatever I *thought* I'd seen — it was only my imagination.

Oh, but did I say it was morning when we got there? It was. Bee's housekeeper dropped her and AJ off at nine, and we walked to the house, looked around the garden for maybe two minutes, then went in. So, I was standing in the middle of the living room again, glad there weren't any weird voices this time, when AJ said, "It's late, and I'm hungry."

I told him he was always hungry, but then I looked at the window and he was right: the whole day was gone! It felt like a couple of hours, but when we got back to the garden, the sun was way low.

When we were helping AJ get through the gate, Bee asked me if I'd seen anything this time.

DrH: You'd told Bee, about hearing the sounds?

Nick: Yeah.

DrH: What had her reaction been?

Nick: She didn't look at me like I was looney tunes, I'll tell you that.

DrH: Nick, I don't —

Nick: It's okay, really. But Bee just said, "Yeah, it's a puzzle," and let it go at that.

So this time, when I said no, I didn't see anything, she said maybe there was too much going on, with all three of us. I said maybe there was nothing there the first time. 'Cause even then I knew how nuts it sounds.

DrH: How did she respond?

NICK: She said, "I don't see any reason to doubt your senses. And the house *does* feel strange."

DrH: It must have been reassuring to have someone agree with you, even if you weren't entirely sure?

NICK: That's why Bee was so great: she made you feel like there were two of you in the world. I asked her if she'd felt the weirdness, too, and she said sure, and something like, "Think about it: When people die, where does their energy go? When a family lives in a house for years and years and they go away, what does the house think?"

And then AJ said, "Like when you trash something on your computer, it stays there on your hard drive until it's written over. Maybe it's the same with people and houses."

AJ sometimes comes up with the most amazing ideas.

Anyway, when we were walking back to

my house, we decided to do our group project on the Weirdman House.

DRH: How did you feel about that decision?

NICK: I guess fine. I mean, it was better than some. What kind of teacher thinks it's a good idea for middle school kids to learn all about toxic plants?

DRH: *[Laughter]*

NICK: Yeah. Anyway, the next Saturday we found ourselves back in the jungly garden. And that time, we saw the Weird Man.

We met at my house early, at eight. Bee and AJ and me — the Tim twins were supposed to come, but their parents had some kind of party they were going to in San Jose. Mom had work that day and left even before that, so when the others came, we got together a bunch of food and drinks and put it in a backpack. And the big flashlight Mom keeps on top of the fridge, in case we wanted to look into a closet or the basement or something.

The sun was out, I remember that. We'd had some rain, so the weeds in the garden were turning green and that rose bush that covered half the front of the house had a few flowers that smelled really sweet. Bee took some pictures with her camera and put some petals in her pocket.

We'd brought one of those plastic milk crates to make it easier to climb in. Bee went first again, but I wasn't as nervous this time, with her there. You could see our footprints from the first time, going all over. She took pictures of them. Took pictures of everything, really: the wallpaper, the chandelier that was like a giant ball of cobwebs, the kitchen, the library shelves.

On one side of the kitchen there were two sets of stairs. One of them went down into the basement, this black pit that smelled like mildew, and the other went up. I asked Bee which she wanted to go on, hoping she wouldn't choose the basement, and she was just starting to answer when something behind me surprised her and her voice went all tight. AJ and me whipped around to see what she was looking at, but there wasn't anything, just a corner of the dining room with its curtains that looked like they were made out of dust.

I asked her what she saw, and she said it was probably just some reflection.

And AJ said, "If you guys are starting in on the ghost stories, I'm going home." He didn't sound very happy.

So I said it was probably a bird, and

maybe we should go upstairs.

The stairs near the living room were wide, but these ones were really narrow, and steep — Bee said they were for the servants. She took a bunch of pictures. At the top was this little landing with a door. The hinges creaked like some horror movie.

The second story was mostly bedrooms, we decided, and two bathrooms with these old-fashioned tubs with feet, and the kind of toilets that have pull handles on a chain. There were mouse droppings all over.

We went up to the top floor, too. There were all these little rooms with slanty ceilings and rusty metal bed frames that Bee said was probably where the servants lived. You could tell that made her sad. It was getting hot, so Bee went over to this teensy window, and even though the windows downstairs were all painted shut, maybe they didn't bother doing the servants' floor because the window slid right up.

The temperature dropped right away, but Bee stayed by the window, and after a minute she said, "Who's that?"

I went over, and there was this man down in the garden, looking straight up at us. He was wearing a faded plaid shirt and baggy pants held up by suspenders, with dirty boots and a battered hat. Bee took a picture, but I said, "Crap, we're busted!" I figured he was one of the people working on the renovation project.

But Bee said, "I don't think so. Look at him."

For some reason, I couldn't see him very well. He was . . . fuzzy, kind of. I rubbed my eyes, thinking the dust had got in them. When I looked back, the guy was taking off his hat, like he was trying to see us better, too. I tried to pull Bee away, but she just kept staring down.

So I took another look. He still wasn't very clear, but without his hat, he was younger than I'd thought. Maybe high school age? But his clothes were really old-fashioned, and he had long blond hair, and he just stood there staring up while Bee and I stared down.

And then AJ came to see what was going on. He took one look and jumped backward, straight into one of the beds. He sat down hard, and there was this incredible noise — and when Bee and I had got him up and went back to the window, the guy was gone. We kind of tiptoed downstairs — my heart was beating so hard I thought I'd throw up, but there wasn't any sign of him. Not even any boot marks in the dust.

Bee looked all over the garden, but you couldn't tell he'd been there, not even right where he was standing. And the ground there was soft.

I said something like, where the *hell* did he go, and Bee said maybe he wasn't really there. And AJ looked kinda creeped out and said, What, that was a ghost? And Bee said no, but I just said I hope she'd got enough for the report, 'cause *I* wasn't going back inside.

"Is Nicky scared?" It sounds like a really mean thing to say, but from her, it wasn't somehow.

So I asked her, what if that guy'd been some psycho serial killer? What if he'd had a gun? I mean, I know I'm a . . . a coward, but aren't girls supposed to be even more careful than boys? Plus, Bee was older than AJ and me — she should've known better.

"I just wish I knew who that was. Did you see the way he was dressed? He must have been some kind of re-enactor, in period costume."

And then she gave me this . . . look. Like she was daring me. Not just to go with her. It was more like she was saying, *Are you with me?*

All I could think of was how I should never have shown her the house. I told her the guy was probably just a hippie. Running one of those organic farms, plowing with horses. Mom and I lived in a place like that once.

DRH: *[Prompt after a long silence.]* How did she react?

NICK: She was . . . disappointed, I guess. She just said something like, "Even that would be interesting." Anyway, when they left, I told Bee to email me the pictures. And she said, "Sure. See you Monday."

But she didn't send them. And on Monday morning, she wasn't at school.

NICK

Nick stared at his blank page. "A Dream," he'd written, then sat there spacing out about #speakforbee.

Either something awful happened to Bee, or she walked away.

The first was a nightmare. But the other, that was its own kind of awful.

People did disappear, and their bodies turned up years and years later: Nick knew that. And he knew — a part of him knew — this could be what happened to Bee. That when he was twenty (or forty, or ninety) they'd find a skeleton and he'd finally know.

But if she'd walked away, well, that was a kind of nightmare, too — because Nick had thought Bee was his best friend, somebody who'd never leave without telling him, but why? He'd only known her about nine weeks. Sixty-two days.

One thing he was sure about: Bee cared about people. She cared about Nick. If she'd left without telling anyone, there was some good reason.

Not knowing was awful. It hurt like hell. But maybe if he could just remember how she'd been, how cool and weird and strong she was instead of how she walked into a hole, he could hang on to her as a friend even if she wasn't around any longer. Think about Bee, not about #speakforbee.

He realized that the teacher was making the rounds through the silent classroom, checking to make sure everyone was writing. Nick glanced at the clock, then set his pencil onto his piece of paper.

A DREAM
By Nick Clarkson

I think when I grow up, I'd like to be a teacher, probably of history.

I once knew a girl who loved history. She was also a really clever photographer. Sometimes she would make her photographs look old, like they had been taken with one of those machines that have the black curtain over the photographer's head.

LINDA

Linda had just hit PRINT for the final (!) draft of her assembly speech — the one that left out "warp of hopes" and a principal's exotic travels — when Mrs. Hopkins knocked at the door and stuck her head in. "Dr. Henry is here to see you."

"Good, send her in. Hi, Cass." Linda came around the desk to shake the hand of the school district's psychologist. "Thanks for dropping by, have a seat. I wanted a quick word about Nick Clarkson."

"I'm seeing him in a few minutes."

"I know. This is your, what? Fourth session?"

"Yes, although only the third of any substance."

"Would you say he's doing okay?"

"Remarkably so."

Linda gave her a sharp look. "You don't sound like that's a good thing."

"Nick Clarkson lost his best friend. Too

much calm can be worrying. Would you like to read the session transcripts? His mother said I could show them to you, and it might help explain where the boy is coming from."

"Then, sure."

"I'll email them to you, when they're typed up. Was that all you wanted?"

"No — it's about Bee's father. Next week you and I should sit down and figure out what to do about him."

"Do you mean Bee's memorial?"

"I suppose, but —"

"Linda, I know the man has refused to be involved, but there has to be some kind of school acknowledgment, for the sake of the kids. You've started to wince away from her name as if it's a sore tooth, and that's not fair to the kids."

"They need closure."

"I know — I don't care for the word either, but the school needs to recognize the loss of one of its own. In some fashion."

"The one time I could really use a clear-cut district policy on something . . . But look, I had a call from Mr. Cuomo yesterday accusing Nick of spreading online rumors about him."

"Ah."

"Is it true?"

"Online stuff? I don't know. I do know

that Nick believes Bee's father hit her. Nothing sexual, so far as he's said."

"Do you think he's right? Or could it be a part of his . . . fantasy?"

"I can't tell you that yet. I wish I'd met the child herself, so I knew if she'd exhibited any signs of problems at home. Did you know her?"

"I'm ashamed to say that the first weeks of school are such a blur, my only memory of that little girl is that she liked to watch the guy restoring the school mural. She'd have made more of an impression if she'd been a troublemaker. You should talk to Gordon — he remembers her."

"I will. And maybe her teachers as well? I know there's privacy issues, and if Nick were an adult I'd hesitate to step outside our actual sessions, but this is one of those cases where it might be good to know if the school missed any obvious clues."

Both for Nick and for the school, thought Linda: liability issues could be a major pain. *As if I needed something else to worry about!*

"Mrs. Hopkins can give you the names of Bee's teachers."

"Thanks." Dr. Henry stood. "See you in the gym — and good luck!"

■ ■ ■ ■

CAREER DAY

Cold Reality

■ ■ ■ ■

LINDA

Linda found Sergeant Mendez at the far end of B Quad, standing under the window of the girls' restroom. "There you are!"

Olivia looked alarmed and fumbled at her shirt pocket for the cellphone. "Sorry, did I miss a text?"

"No, it's fine, I needed a breath of air anyway. I sent you a text with the Bee Cuomo thing. The hashtag."

Olivia thumbed open the text function.

Hi Olivia, that hashtag is #speakforbee

"Okay, thanks, I'll look into it." She searched for the VOLUME button on the side of the phone.

"I also wanted to ask: you said Bee Cuomo's father has a history of drunk-and-disorderly. If he thinks Nick Clarkson is behind this . . . whatever it is, do you think I ought to warn Nick's mother?"

"We should warn her that the kid's going

to get into trouble if he doesn't lay off."

"I mean from —"

"I know what you mean. But like I said, we've been digging hard for four months, since she went missing. Cuomo's lawyer is talking harassment, and we've found nothing. No history of family violence on his sheet, just social stupidity."

"Okay, thanks. Everything fine out here?"

"Sure." But the police sergeant then continued in a voice loud enough to be heard in the next quad, much less inside the girls' room. "Everything's fine so long as I don't catch any girls using their phones in the toilets."

After a moment of dead silence, hushed giggles rose up again and a handful of girls came scurrying out, looking any place but at Sergeant Mendez.

Linda laughed, and told Olivia to have fun.

MINA

Mina and Sofia stood at the middle of A Quad, comparing their schedules. Mina held hers out so her friend could see.

"I have University Professor, Sports Medicine, and Psychology. I wanted Sergeant Mendez in fourth period but my mom said no."

"You have Sports Medicine for fifth? I thought you picked Software Development?"

"Yeah, I don't know how that got changed." Mina had changed it herself. And she hadn't told Sofia because . . . well, Sofia didn't have to know *everything*. "That's okay, we both have the history professor in fourth period. What's your sixth period?"

Sofia frowned at her page. "Organic Farming."

"Organic *farming*? How random! Can you imagine what your mother would say if you wanted to be a *farmer*?"

" '*Mija,* you're goin' to college so you don' have dirt in your nails!' " Sofia's mom didn't have an accent that strong, but Mina laughed anyway. Sofia was finally starting to lose that haunted look she'd got after Gloria's murder, but her sense of humor had been slow to return.

"She'd be happy with software developing, that's for sure. That's Brendan's father, isn't it?"

"Yeah. You think Brendan'll be there?" Sofia shot Mina a glance.

"Probably not." Definitely not, unless the list outside the office was wrong. Mina had thought about signing up for Brendan's sixth-period assignment, too, but decided that was a little obvious.

The two girls became aware of someone standing close behind them, and turned as one: Chaco Cabrera, holding up his own Career Day schedule.

He gave Sofia a glance that was oh-so-cool. "Hey, you in software developing for fifth? Me too."

The two girls looked down at him — literally, in the case of Sofia. She was the one who finally replied. "Um, good?"

You'd have thought she slapped him, the way the seventh-grader went dark and shoved past them, stalking away with

340

hunched shoulders.

Sofia watched him go, looking puzzled. "Has he said one word to you all year?"

"No. I figured he hated us. Because of his cousin and all."

"Maybe not so much. He is kind of cute, isn't he?"

"Sofe, you're a foot taller than him!"

"Yeah, well, my mom doesn't wear heels around my dad, either. And it's not like Brendan Atcheson's going to look at *me*."

"I don't know why not — you're the only person in school he doesn't have to bend down to see."

"Oh, like he'd notice me if you were within a mile."

"I wish." *Could that possibly be true?*

"Anyway, boys grow later than girls. Just wait till high school, Chaco Cabrera will be fighting them off with a stick."

Mina looked sideways at her friend. "Unless you claim him first." She gave Sofia a quick hug, and they separated for second period.

The bell rang. Teachers took roll, looked at their notes, and set out to explain the second of the school-wide assignments: the reality that loomed over the dream of first period. Interested in being a cop? Consider salaries, divorce rates, and dangers. Artist? How much does an artist earn, where do they live, what is the cost of rent, food, insurance? Game designer, physical therapist, dental hygienist? Training, student loans, jobs . . .

Cold, hard reality.

CHACO

Chaco opened his notebook and looked at what he'd written about Dream Jobs during period one. His outstretched hand came down on the page, fingers digging in like claws as the cheap paper began to pull, then abruptly tore free. Slowly, he crumpled his words into a tight wad. Math teacher? Yeah, right.

Dreams were shit.

He shouldn't even *talk* to those two putas, not if he was being loyal to Taco. Instead of dissing them — spitting on them, even — there he went, all big-eyed like some pinche kitten. *You going to the same session as me?*

Fuck, he was stupid. Girls were stupid. Just 'cause his birthday was three weeks after the cutoff so he was still in seventh grade and they were in eighth didn't give them the right to treat him like dog shit on their shoes.

Dreams were shit. Reality was one cousin

on trial and another who liked to cut things with knives. Reality was stuck-up bitch girls and a janitor out to twist your arm into doing what he wanted.

Taco was right — and Angel, too. Reality was hitting back, at a school that showed you what you couldn't never have.

LINDA

Linda was going through her speech for a last time when Mrs. Hopkins knocked and stuck her head inside. "Mr. Atcheson on line one."

The neatly permed gray head promptly withdrew before Linda could react. The school secretary was no fool.

Linda sighed, then hit the 1 button.

Thomas Atcheson, already irritated at having to wait for thirty seconds, listened to Linda's first two sentences, cut her off halfway through the third, and after that permitted her nothing but brief phrases. Yes, he had heard some ridiculous and no-doubt criminal rumor about Atcheson Enterprises. In fact, he was delaying a board meeting to reply to her call, which his secretary had imagined was some kind of actual emergency. No, he did not intend to cancel his participation in the school's events, although — as he had told her from the beginning —

he was too busy to come for the luncheon. He would arrive immediately after, for fifth period, as arranged. Yes, he was well acquainted with how pushy reporters could be, but he assumed that the school was at least capable of keeping their guests unmolested on school grounds? Or would he require a bodyguard?

Linda assured him that of course the school grounds were off-limits to the press, but that she could do nothing about the public road just outside, and since the investigation was about to become public knowledge —

Again his voice overrode her, reiterating that he was not in the habit of being bullied into going back on his word. He had said he would be there and so he would, no matter his personal inconvenience.

Before he could hang up, she slipped in her question. "It's just, I was wondering about Brendan."

"What about him?"

"As you know, Mr. Atcheson, I've been concerned. He seems to be going through a difficult patch — typical of his age, yes, and especially after the loss of his mother, but I imagine it will be tough on him to see his father accused of —"

The voice went from hot fury to biting

cold. "Ms. McDonald, my son is not some fragile *child* to be packed in cotton. It's time he understood how cruel the real world can be. Now, if you'll excuse me, I have a board meeting to attend to."

The phone went dead.

Linda carefully laid the handset back in its cradle, and looked at the ceramic apple on her desk. "Oh, yes. That went really well."

NICK: HIS STORY (3)

CLINICAL CASE NOTES AND TRANSCRIPT: NICHOLAS CLARKSON, FEBRUARY 15.

DRH: So, on the Monday morning after you and your friends went into the Weildman House, Bee Cuomo didn't come to school. And she hadn't sent you the pictures she'd taken of the Weildman house. This was late October, right?

NICK: Halloween day. When she wasn't at first period, I got AJ to give me his phone — he didn't want to, 'cause if you're caught, they'll take them away for two weeks. But I just grabbed it and texted her. At lunchtime, I tried calling, but she didn't pick up. I even left a message at her home number. And I went to the office to see if they knew anything, but Mrs. Hopkins said they'd left a home-call message and no one had called back yet.

DrH: What did you do?

NICK: What could I do? I almost went on Bee's bus that afternoon, to see if she was home, but then I thought how stupid I'd feel, stuck clear across town so Mom or Gramps had to come get me, if when I got home I found an email waiting. But there wasn't one. And she didn't answer her phone all afternoon.

When Mom came home, even though she'd had a long day, she didn't argue, just got back in the car and drove me to Bee's house.

DrH: Did you tell her why you were worried?

NICK: No, but she could see I was. Bee wasn't there. Her father came home while Mom and I were talking about what to do, and let us in. We watched him listen to his phone messages, from the school and from his sister, who was flying in from Miami later in the week, and that was all. There were no messages in Bee's room, no notes about going somewhere, nothing.

Nothing but her camera. And I don't know why, but I grabbed it and stuck it in my pocket. Nobody saw me.

I gave Mr. Cuomo the name of some of Bee's friends, and when we left, he was calling around to see if they knew where she was. So on the way home, I told Mom about the Weildman house.

DrH: Everything?

Nick: Not really. Just that we'd been in there, and were doing a project, and stuff.

DrH: What was her reaction?

Nick: She was pissed. And it took her a while to get through to Mr. Cuomo on the phone and tell him.

While she was doing that, I went to my room and figured out how to download Bee's camera into my old desktop. She must've wiped the memory before she came out that day, because the first picture was AJ and me in the garden. Then one of the wood box, and the living room and the library and stuff. AJ and me on the stairs. I went through fast, looking for the one of the guy from the top room. And there was this one picture, you could see the edge of the window and the garden down below. But there wasn't any blond guy with a hat.

DrH: How odd.

Nick: I thought maybe she took some without me noticing, but that was the only picture looking down at the garden, and there was no one in it. No. One.

Later on I called to ask AJ about it, but he started to cry and said he didn't remember, that he'd tripped and fell onto that noisy bed and hadn't seen any man in the garden.

DRH: What happened then?

NICK: Nothing at all! Oh, the police "looked into it." They talked to me and AJ, and Bee's dad. Bee'd left her house on the Monday morning like usual, but she didn't get on the school bus. Two different people saw her riding her bike, somewhere between her house and mine — or, between her house and the Weildman place. The next morning, the cops found her bike in the garden.

When they figured out Bee's password and got her computer open, they found the pictures from the camera, so I didn't have to admit I took it. And they found those things everyone's heard about, what she wrote about her dad. I couldn't believe they didn't arrest him! But they said that some of the stories were science fiction and poems and things, so maybe the ones about her dad were made-up, too.

And they went over every inch of the Weildman house — they were there for days — but they didn't find anything but her bike. No evidence she'd gone back inside. No sign of that blond guy in old-time clothes.

A couple weeks later, some kids broke in

on a dare and lit a fire in the big fireplace to keep warm. The sirens woke me up.

[The recording is silent for a minute.]

DRH: Nick, perhaps you'd like to draw this session to —

NICK: No. I need to finish. It's just . . . hard.

DRH: Bee Cuomo is a friend of yours, it's only —

NICK: It isn't that. I don't mean it's hard to tell it because she was my friend, even though, yeah, she deserved a better one than me. But it's also just hard to tell in a way that makes sense. I *know* what I saw. I know what I *know.* But I understand why everybody thinks I'm hallucinating or something. Delusional.

DRH: Nick, no one thinks you're delusional.

NICK: Sure they do. And maybe they're right. But whenever I start thinking I *do* have some screws loose and I'm imagining things, it makes me feel worse. Disloyal, like.

DRH: Nick, for today, let's just go on with what you remember.

NICK: Right. Well, so, Bee was gone. Everybody was talking about it, there was a TV van parked in front of the school, all these people — "grief counselors" — giving out teddy bears like we were in elementary school or something. But when her . . . when Bee didn't show up anywhere, it was like nobody knew what to do. I mean, kids run away all the time, even though she was awfully young and a good student and stuff. And when you add in a haunted house and a mysterious guy in old-time clothes, it keeps the talk going.

But then it was Christmas vacation. Which was pretty crap, by the way. And when we came back, Bee was like . . . the sore place you have after a bad bruise heals, you know? The Social Studies teacher had put off the field trip to the historical museum — Mom said there was talk about canceling it, but then they decided to move it to the new year. We'd already done the writing part — not about the Weildman house, of course. AJ did a project on the horse-drawn wagons, and mine was on poisonous plants of the Central Coast.

DrH: Really?

NICK: Yeah. Funny, huh? For a while I wondered how I could get one into Mr. Cuomo's dinner.

DrH: Nick, that's troubling to hear.

NICK: I know, but I wouldn't, not really. I was just . . .

DrH: Angry?

NICK: Yeah. Anyway, I almost didn't go on the field trip. All I could think about was Bee taking AJ and me there, back in September. But I didn't want to give people any more reason to talk. And anyway, by then I halfway thought maybe she did run away, join that commune of organic horse-drawn farmers. Plus, Mom was really worried that my grades were slipping and I need to get into the AP classes, and we were getting extra points for the trip. So I went.

And the first part was okay. Some of the rooms were different. The kitchen had a bunch of new gadgets, a couple other rooms were open now. Uh, do you know the place?

DRH: I've been there, but not in years.

NICK: I guess it's supposed to look like everyone just stepped outside — pans on the stove, this half-finished letter with an ink pen in its holder, baby toys on the floor. The museum ladies were wearing these old-time dresses with white aprons and those weird hats — bonnets, I guess. They talked about life in the old days, how much work it was.

It made me a little sick thinking how Bee would've loved it, asking a million questions. I missed her, all the time — still do, but that day it was like a black hole eating up my mind, wondering what happened to her.

Then the lady said something that jerked back my attention.

"This house you're in was once across the field from the Weildman house, and was donated to the historical society. You can see it being moved through town in the pictures in the sitting room, along with photographs of the Weildman family."

It was horrible, and I thought . . . I felt like I was going to cry, so I turned around like I was fascinated by the kitchen tools. The teacher touched my shoulder and said I could take my time. When she took the class off to see the pigs, I went in to look at the photographs.

Sure enough, you could see the place in the background of one picture, along with the Weildman house when the gingerbread was white and all the shingles were straight. The giant rose bush was only as tall as me, and the hedges around the garden came maybe to my waist.

There's a whole row of these really sharp black-and-white pictures, like Bee used to try and make. Mostly the Weildman house and farm — there was even a little shack where Mom and I lived, although it's not the same building. You can see the town and hills in the background.

Then came a photograph that, well, it felt like a kick in the gut.

It showed the inside of the house, that living room with the big fireplace and the chandelier. Only you could see the crystal was sparkling and the wallpaper looked new. It was packed with furniture. And there were people.

Two men and three women, with that stare they had to use then so the film didn't blur, you know? On the left was an old lady with a man standing behind her. On the other side was a little sofa, the kind Grams calls a love seat, with these two ladies in high-necked dresses. The one on the right was turning her head, so her face was blurry. But next to her, perched on the arm of the love seat, was the guy we saw in the Weirdman garden. His hair was shorter, and he looked a little older, and he had on this suit and a shirt with a high collar. But it was the same guy.

DrH: Nick, the man you saw in the garden was probably a descendant of the man in the picture.

NICK: That's what I thought. Until I saw the last picture, and the letter up next to it.

DrH: Tell me what happened.

NICK: Yeah, well. The docent lady found me

sitting on the floor just staring at the picture. She thought I'd had a fit of some kind. A *seizure.* She called an ambulance.

DrH: They took you to the hospital, didn't they?

NICK: I guess they didn't know what else to do. But Grams was on duty, and she found them asking me all kinds of questions while the doctors took my temperature and stuff, but I was just sitting there, nodding and not saying much.

DrH: Why was that?

NICK: I was just thinking, a mile a minute. They wanted to keep me there but Grams decided it was just the shock, the co-incidence of seeing a picture that looked like Bee. So she took me home. I really was okay. After a couple days I went back to school, and that was sorta crap at first, but after a while the kids stopped teasing me about foaming at the mouth and stuff. Things are pretty okay now, I guess.

DrH: Why don't you think it was a seizure?

NICK: I told you, it was me thinking hard. I guess it sort of *was* the shock, too. But I don't think coincidence had much to do with it.

That last picture, on the museum wall? It shows that same man standing in the garden behind a bench. Which is still there — or it was, until the fire. He has his hand on the shoulder of a woman a little younger than him, who's sitting on the bench, with her hair up and earrings and a little necklace. She's looking straight at the camera this time, no blur at all, though I think the baby in her lap was kicking a foot, because the white blanket is kind of smeared-looking.

You want to know what the caption reads? I remember every word.

Marcus Weildman (30), Beatrice Weildman (24), and baby . . . And baby Nicholas. Taken by local photographer Ralph Kurzen, May 20, 1909. Marcus Weildman was killed as a soldier in France during World War One. Beatrice (maiden name Collins) arrived in town as an unclaimed orphan in 1899 and married Marcus Weildman in 1906. Their children were Nicholas (whose plane went down over the English Channel in 1943), Arthur John (who moved to Spokane in the 1930s), and Bonnie. Beatrice Weildman lived in the family home until her disappearance, as mysterious as her arrival, in 1959. She was 72.

DRH: That is indeed . . . intriguing.
NICK: Dr. Henry, we're all there! *Nicholas, Beatrice, AJ* — even *Bonnie,* one of the

Tim twins. And then there's the letter they put beside it. The ink's faded, but you can still read it. I *know* that handwriting. You want to know what it says? I memorized that, too.

My dear "cousin" Amy,
   I send you a studio portrait of your cousin Marcus and his new family, to add to your wall, that you might assure yourself that he is well and happy with his peculiar, rootless wife. I thank you for your friendship, and know that you remain in my affections always.
   The baby's name, I should add, comes from a young boy who befriended me long ago, whose loss I regret, and whose memory I wished to honor.

Your cousin by marriage,
Bea

DRH: Nicholas, I agree this is a striking co-incidence. But do you really feel that your Bee . . . ran away into the past?

NICK: It's the only thing that makes sense. I still really *hate* her father. I hope he goes to prison. And I'm still going to miss Bee, every day.
But last weekend I got Mom to take me back to the museum. To "find closure" —

isn't that what those grief counselors go on about? I stood in front of that picture for a really long time, and I read that letter over and over. And I guess it worked.

DRH: I'm glad to hear that, Nick. But why

—

NICK: Because you know what? In that picture? Bee looks just really, really happy.

GORDON

It wasn't too long ago that a man could vanish merely by stepping away from home. However, as the twenty-first century wore on, the cracks one could slip into grew ever more narrow, and ever less secure.

Gordon found it a full-time job, keeping up with technology.

After the second-period bell, there was a lull in the library. While the sixteen volunteers who'd been fussing around the laden tables took this last opportunity to sit and drink some of their own coffee, Gordon wandered toward the cluster of computers at the back of the room, and settled into the wooden chair.

There was no real reason to use the computers at school — anyone who tracked him to those would soon find his front door. Still, it felt like less of a betrayal to use a public machine rather than Linda's own.

A year ago, his checks had been perfunc-

tory — habit, merely. But after his name appeared on Linda's list, alongside the innocent volunteer mothers and grandparents, he'd renewed his warning bells.

After thirty years, would that police background search make a ping on TaylorCorp's radar? TaylorCorp was big-time now, on a par with Blackwater and Halliburton, only more deeply in the shadows. Would a multinational, billion-dollar security firm give a damn anymore about one Gordon Hugh-Kendrick? Memories faded, records got lost. His name had never been officially linked with the murders of its three employees. And under the name Kendrick, in a part of the world that he'd never visited, married to a person who appeared on no one's record of his time in PNG? He'd come here himself in an almost random accident: an online search of half-remembered names, followed by the whim of a desperate man.

Still, John Taylor had been the founder's son and heir, and Taylor senior had made his name out of being a vicious and unrelenting force. Early on, Gordon had got in the habit of covering his tracks. He'd never spent four years in one place before, never been legally married before — and never

given his name for a police background check.

He nearly left town back in October when he'd learned of the slip. That he stayed was due in part to the cushion of three decades, but mostly because he did not want to cause Linda pain. She'd been distraught when she'd realized her mistake — absently typing his full name onto her volunteers list. Were he to vanish now, she would know she was to blame. And yes, it was her fault, but it was also his.

So he stayed put, and buried his dread under hard runs and grocery shopping and volunteer duties. Weeks went by, months. He began to breathe again — but he also continued to check those distant alarm triggers, each and every day.

Glancing around to make sure no one had followed him to the library's back corner, Gordon went through the cumbersome log-in for his anonymous account, and did his usual quick and methodical run through a decades-long roster of friends and informants.

Only this time, it wasn't so quick. He sat back slowly in the chair, staring at the screen.

Thirty years on, Gordon caught the faint whiff of a predator on his trail.

BRENDAN

The teacher wrote a bunch of figures on the board, the average cost in San Felipe of rent, food, insurance, car payments, all that kind of thing. You were supposed to come up with a list of other stuff related to your "Dream Job" — things like uniforms and special equipment or land (like if you were a farmer) or business (if you were going to run a car repair place).

But jeez, the whole idea of "the practical side of the future" was about a million miles from where Brendan was right now. Might as well be researching tutus and space shuttles.

CHACO

Chaco stared down at the page the teacher had handed out, a long, *long* list of things an adult had to pay for. He knew things like electricity cost money, but fuck — a dollar a day just to *connect* a cellphone? No wonder he couldn't have one of his own.

Still, Chaco really didn't think these were the kind of prices his people paid. His mother couldn't be paying $1,300 a month for the hole they lived in. He heard a brief echo of Tío's voice in his ear (*$11.12 times the 26 hours she worked this week equaled living on the street*) and shook his head to get rid of *that* trap, then read on.

No wonder people sold drugs and held up stores. What choice was there, faced with a list like that?

LINDA

The guest speakers had arrived, most of them. The Parents' Club's coffee was surprisingly good, the croissants plentiful, and the conversation nicely punctuated with exclamations of surprise at the crossing of paths and discoveries of similar taste.

Linda's eyes kept circling back to Gordon. Standing between the firefighter and the architect, he nodded and made the occasional reply, but she could see he was distracted. More than distracted: he looked like a sprinter in the blocks, braced for the gun. The paper cup in his hand might have been a stage prop. What had happened since they'd separated in the parking lot?

"Now, that's a handsome trio."

The voice at her elbow nearly made Linda slosh coffee over her blouse, but she caught herself, showing Olivia a smile she hoped wasn't too strained. "Isn't it, though? Surely there must be *some* firefighters who don't look like gym ads?"

"I think I've seen that one on a calendar. And the guy next to him looks like a model."

"Do you suppose wearing a suit like that changes what you order for lunch? I'd be terrified by anything messier than carrot sticks."

"Guy like him probably lunches on martinis. But your husband's got the better tie. What's the design?"

"Little tiny yellow Jeeps." Linda realized that she'd just given Olivia the opening for a question — or, the opening to move closer to Gordon for a look — and hastened to throw down a distraction. "I talked to Tom Atcheson, for about thirty seconds. And I followed up with an email to say that if he needed to cancel, I would understand."

"The DA hasn't called him yet?"

"Would he do that? I mean, rather than just . . . well, go and arrest him?"

"He'd want as much evidence as he could get first. Once you've done the actual arrest, lawyers come trooping in and throw up fences. There's also the grand jury to consider." Olivia went on, but Linda was no longer listening. Gordon's head had come up, and he was staring intently out the library window. She turned to look.

A shiny blue sedan was parked with one

wheel on the lawn. Its driver, in such a hurry he'd left his door open, was stalking in the direction of the school entrance — then Linda's coffee did slosh, over the table as she slapped the cup down to hurry toward the library's outside door.

Señora Rodriguez happened to be standing at the end of the table, and Linda veered aside just long enough to say, "Could you please start moving our guests toward the gym?" And then she was outside.

"Mr. Cuomo!" she called. "Charlie, good morning, were you looking for me?"

The man, nearly inside the school entrance, immediately reversed direction, storming down the lawn with a handful of papers. Linda came to a halt outside the teachers' lounge (*Please, Lord, let it be empty!*) and tried to hide her alarm at the approaching figure — unshaven, rumpled, and reeking of stale beer.

"Did you *see* these?" He thrust the pages at her face. "Have you done anything about these *goddamn* psycho kids who go to this *fucking* school?"

"Mr. Cuomo! I do not permit language like that in my school."

Her schoolmarm indignation had no effect. "Have you *looked* at these?"

This time she took them: printouts of images she had seen connected to the #speak-forbee tag, crude in all senses, from pornographic to merely childish. Some were even mildly amusing examples of adolescent humor — although she wasn't about to say that to Mr. Charles Cuomo.

When Linda looked up, she found Sergeant Mendez standing on one side, Gordon on the other. She shot a panicked glance over her shoulder, but the library door was closed. No curious guest speakers had spilled out to witness the intrusion.

"Mr. Cuomo, I think you've met Sergeant Mendez. And this is my —"

There was a very fast blur of motion that Linda only deciphered when it was over. The enraged father had started to raise his hand at her — to hit her, or merely thrust a finger under her nose? — but as his arm came up, Gordon stepped forward, twisting the man's wrist away and down.

Before Linda could do more than blink, Cuomo was bent over, with Gordon speaking into his ear. "Sir, I don't think any of us wish to make threats today. Do we?" Cuomo's jerk of protest, instead of throwing Gordon off, resulted in a gasp of pain. He stood very still. "No more threats?" The man's bowed head swung rapidly back and forth. Gordon let go, and the man staggered away, cradling his right wrist. "Jesus, you broke my fucking arm!"

"Not quite."

Olivia tore her astonished gaze away from Gordon and reached for Cuomo's good arm. "Sir, I think you should come with me."

But Linda put out her own hand in alarm. "You aren't going to arrest him?"

"What, you want to invite him to the library for coffee?"

"No! But Olivia, he does have a point. He *is* being harassed. Mr. Cuomo — Charlie, do you think we could talk about this after school? Or first thing tomorrow? When things aren't so terribly busy around here, and you're not quite so . . ."

Olivia offered a word. "Drunk?"

"Upset."

"I'm *not* drunk. And those damn kids are fucking up my life."

"Mr. Cuomo, please, I really do want to talk to you about this." Linda leaned toward him with all the earnestness in her Midwestern soul. "Would you like to come in first thing tomorrow morning? Or anytime, whenever it's convenient for *you*. I'm sure you and I can figure out the best way to approach this —"

If anything, her attempt at placation only

made things worse. He raised his eyes to hers, clearly humiliated now as well as outraged. "This isn't over." He stalked away across the lawn, his shoulder coming a hairsbreadth from thumping into her.

Olivia watched the man's retreat with narrowed eyes, judging his pace with a decade of traffic stops behind her. However, the smell of beer around the man had been far from fresh, and the path he cut across the lawn had no trace of a wobble.

He slammed the car door and started the engine, spinning his tires into the grass as he pulled away. Olivia relaxed the moment she saw him automatically glance over his shoulder at the empty drive, although Linda watched until his car had reached the road.

She blew out a breath. "Thank you. Both."

But Olivia's gaze had returned to Gordon, speculating. "That was a smooth move, Mr. Kendrick."

He gave her a happy grin. "Twenty years of martial arts pop up at the oddest times. Linda, you should get back to the library. Shall I take those to your office?"

"Oh, please." She handed him the unruly sheaf. "Put them in one of my desk drawers, maybe? And let Mrs. Hopkins know what happened. Tell her . . . tell her to keep an eye on the front of the school, in case he comes back."

"Will do."

She touched Olivia's uniformed arm, both to distract her from Gordon and to get them both moving toward the library. "Thanks for not arresting that man. He has just lost his daughter. And some of those pictures must be extremely painful."

Olivia shot a grim glance at the road. "Assuming the accusations are wrong." She opened the door to the library, where they found Señora Rodriguez nipping at the laggards' heels as she drove the guest speakers in the direction of the gymnasium.

Before they stepped into the breezeway, Linda stopped.

"Do you think he'll come back?"

"Tomorrow? I'm afraid so."

"I was thinking . . . You know, if someone wanted to . . . make a stink, the school assembly would be a prime — would be tempting."

Olivia's mind filled in the missing word: *target.* "I think he's gone home to get drunk, and when you see him next, he'll apologize and feel like an idiot. But you're right. Look, you don't really need to introduce me with the other speakers, do you? I could maybe hang around outside, just in case the guy decides to come back and start shouting."

"I'd feel better. I should have hired private security for the event, I can see that."

"No need to. This is my job."

DR. HENRY

". . . she looks just really, really happy."

After Nick left, Cass Henry studied her notes and wondered what she was missing.

As his mother warned her back in January, Nick Clarkson believed that Bee Cuomo had been transported into the past. Sooner or later, either the girl would show up or her body would, and Nick's world would come crashing around him. Cass Henry had to get her wedge under the boy's — yes — delusions before that happened.

But there were things going on with Nick that she couldn't quite figure out.

Nick was a small, dreamy outsider set down in a tough school. He had some of the developmental difficulties associated with fetal alcohol syndrome. His mother dressed him in the wrong clothes and cut his hair herself. His protective grandparents were too visible. He didn't even own a cellphone. In a school like Guadalupe, Nick should have been kicked, tripped, and robbed every day. And yet in the past three weeks — three *weeks*! — she'd watched him go from so shaky he couldn't talk without weeping to a kid who joked about being "looney tunes."

Sudden mood changes set off all kinds of alarms in any psychologist, since a surface happiness is often the mask of a suicide decision. And yet, all her increasingly urgent (and increasingly puzzled) conversations — with the boy, his family, his teachers — uncovered no other warning signs, and nothing to suggest that Nick had linked up with (as had happened at Columbine) an aggressive and violent partner. He just seemed . . . happy.

Last week, she'd spent a couple of lunch hours sitting in her parked car observing the outdoor tables. When Nick came out, she expected to watch him hunch into a corner seat, as desperately unobtrusive as he could get — body language that invariably brought out the worst in tormentors. But instead, he paused by a table of the popular kids, including eighth-graders Mina Santos and Sofia Rivas, and simply talked for a minute before going on to eat lunch with his own sixth-grade friends. Yes: friends.

Her case notes included a sketch page, aimed at tracking Nick's school relationships. After each conversation, she added names and arrows. The page had grown ever more complicated, with arrows running in all directions and a lot of mystifying gaps.

Suddenly she glanced at the clock and stood, shoveling laptop, papers, and voice recorder into her briefcase. She switched off the lights and strode toward the gymnasium, wondering, *What am I missing?*

OLIVIA

The school psychologist trotted by as Olivia was speaking with Tío. They broke off their conversation to exchange polite greetings with the woman, and resumed when she was out of earshot.

"Anyway, Cuomo's a drunk and a bully, and the school's pretty vulnerable today. Let me know if you see him. Do you want my number, so you can text me?"

"I have no telephone. I could whistle — I still have teeth enough for that."

"I guess. And I'll tell Mrs. Hopkins, too. Like I said, I don't think there's a real threat, but it's best to be prepared."

He gave her a polite nod, and went back to his cart. As Olivia continued down toward the office, she pulled out her phone to have Torres and Wong check on Mr. Cuomo's blue sedan with the dealer plates.

Just in case.

■ ■ ■ ■

CAREER DAY

Threads Join

■ ■ ■ ■

LINDA

The racket of feet climbing bleachers died away, although the gymnasium would never be a quiet place, not with nearly a thousand people inside. Linda McDonald stood at the podium under the folded-up basketball hoop, adjusting her notes to let the noise die down some more.

Remember, she told herself, *your purpose is to show how things tie together.* There were eight hundred and some separate individuals here, aged eleven to seventy-three. Eight hundred–odd stories of love and loss, fear and hate, triumph and shame — with no more real chance of pulling them together than there was of controlling her hair on a static-filled day.

Still, that was where she wanted to point them.

The guest speakers were seated behind her, the students up into the bleachers on either side. Teachers — particularly large male teachers — were strategically placed in the heights where the troublemakers tended to collect.

Gordon was in the upper row at the far end. Coach sat almost directly across the gymnasium from him.

Eight hundred souls, brought here to think about potential, and hope, and cherishing the future.

Linda raised her head and put on a smile. "A school is a tapestry of threads," she began.

GORDON

Gordon sat in the farthest reaches of the largest space on campus, and watched his wife prepare to speak. She betrayed no sign of nerves, although he had no doubt that her hands were icy and her heart was racing.

But from the outside, she was nothing but confidence. She stood squarely behind the podium, in control of herself. And when she looked up, expecting silence, she got it. In a firm voice, not relying yet on printed notes, she started with words designed to heal the school and lead it toward the future. "A school is a tapestry of threads," his wife began.

Threads, yes, he mused. Short and long, strong and weak, rough and fine, spun from all corners of the globe.

But even jute could be beautiful. And even silk could weave a noose.

OLIVIA

The doors were open to the gym, and Olivia heard Linda start her speech as she went past. The principal's voice sounded nice and firm, considering she'd privately admitted she was terrified of public speaking. "A school is a tapestry of threads," she stated, and who could argue with that?

Though wasn't a school sometimes more like a sweater than a tapestry? Something with a loose end you could unravel down to a giant blob of kinky yarn? Olivia could remember the awful appeal of pulling and pulling, knowing how much trouble she was going to be in but unable to stop watching the yarn detach, one slow loop at a time, then faster in a delicious little catastrophe . . .

What was it with her, anyway — first taking apart a clock, then unraveling a sweater. Were all children as destructive as little Olivia?

Her phone rang, and she moved away from the open door to take the call.

"Yeah, Torres?"

"Your man's not at home, and we called the dealership. He's not there, either. Want me to issue a BOLO?"

"Not an official one, not yet. Just, uh, keep checking?"

"Will do. And I'll mention it — informally, like — to a coupla CHP buddies. You're sure you don't want us there?"

"No, it's fine. We've got it."

Right, Olivia thought as she put away her phone. *An old man, a white-haired secretary, and one cop: guardians of the galaxy.*

Why was the principal talking about tapestries? "A school is a tapestry of threads." Oh, yeah?

He'd seen tapestries, on that England trip with his mother years and years ago. She'd been like a kid for two whole weeks, all excited over dumb stuff like stone walls and old villages and scones with cream and church bells and rooms crowded with furniture and paintings — and tapestries. With just her and Brendan, she'd actually been having fun.

Until they came home, and the fights started up, and then one day she was gone.

He'd been pretty young, so mostly what he remembered about the trip was stuff like her happiness, and the taste of scones, and the giant Ferris wheel next to the river that you saw in any movie about London. The tapestries he remembered as a kind of dingy wallpaper, not something you'd want to find yourself woven into — old-fashioned, dark, and covered with dust.

Well, yeah, come to think of it. Kind of like school, after all.

MINA

"A school is a tapestry of threads," Ms. Mc-Donald began.

Mina used to have a poster of a unicorn tapestry on her bedroom wall. She'd bought it after seeing the actual tapestry in a museum that looked just like a Medieval castle. When she first saw it hanging there — she'd been in fifth grade when they went to New York — she didn't really like it, since the poor unicorn was not only tied up, it was fenced in. Plus, it had what looked like blood running down its sides. But then Mâmân talked to her about symbols, and pointed out how the "captivity" really wasn't, like the red wasn't blood but juice from the pomegranates overhead — a fruit her mother used a lot.

So she bought the poster.

She liked the principal's idea of a tapestry of lives, how everyone's histories wove together to create a thing of beauty. Or ugliness, sometimes. There was a lot of darkness in the background of that unicorn tapestry, just like there was ugliness all around her. Sofia, losing her sister to a bullet. That sixth-grader Nick over there, risking trouble as he tried to help his friend who'd disappeared. Chaco sometimes came to school with bruises on his face. Brendan, sitting way up high in the bleachers, had a temper that had to come from somewhere.

Mr. Kendrick: well. And even Mrs. Hopkins had a son who died of leukemia last year.

Mâmân, haunted by a homeland she'd left when she was tiny.

"A school is a tapestry of threads," Mrs. McDonald began.

Nick knew a little about weaving. One of the places his mother had moved them to, three or four years ago, was a kind of commune. There were a million chickens. (Who knew that roosters had these huge claws and would attack if you weren't careful? He still had the scar.) And everybody there was into growing and making things.

Anyway, one of the women was a weaver. She'd cut the wool off the commune's mangy-looking sheep (and washed it in the bathtub, which was disgusting and smelled awful) and spun it into lumpy yarn and then wove it on this clanky loom into rugs that when they were new smelled bad, and when they were old skidded across the floor. One of the men fell down one day on a rug and swore at her that she should stop making the things because they could buy better ones at the Kmart for next to nothing, and she'd cried and the whole place had shouted at each other.

Nick and his mom had moved a few days later. And that was all he knew about weaving.

Tío

"A school is a *tapiz,*" the lady principal told the gymnasium.

Tío's wife had been too modern to weave, but his *abuela* did. In the winter, she produced brilliantly colored shawls on a small hand loom that she strung between a ceiling hook on one end and a belt around her waist on the other. In the summers, she worked on larger, more muted pieces on the big wooden frame that her sons set up under the roof behind the house. Many houses in the village had one of his *abuela*'s rugs to warm the floor. Some of them were even sold in the city, for good money.

That was before, of course. She was dead now, along with the rest of the village. The only weaving done under her roof was by the spiders.

CHACO

"A school is a *tapestry*," the principal said. If you'd asked Chaco, he'd have guessed *tapestry* was some kind of pastry, but unless *threads* meant something else, too, it had to do with weaving. And *warp* didn't mean spaceships, and there was something called a *web,* or maybe it was *weft,* but all in all, he was just as glad when Old McDonald moved on to something he understood, about how the guest speakers came from all kinds of places and did all kinds of things, some of them cool although others sounded like crap jobs a judge would sentence you to, that *community service* stuff.

Anyway, it was funny to try and guess what all those people sitting behind her did for a living, and then hear what she said. Some of them had uniforms, so those didn't count — the fireman and the airline pilot and the nurse, even though this nurse was a man. And the woman in the white lab coat could've been the sports doctor or the pharmacist, except she looked pretty much like every CSI on television. But who'd have thought that chubby black kid designed houses? And the big blond woman who taught about Japanese history — but why were people clapping for her?

Chaco leaned over to see if Javi knew who she was.

"I think that's Bee Cuomo's tía," Javi answered.

Busy-Bee's auntie? Didn't look much like her. And she didn't look all sad and stuff, like Chaco thought she should.

He wondered if the auntie knew about Nick Clarkson's hashtag against Bee's dad.

Eleven minutes away from Guadalupe Middle School, a car pulled into a driveway. The driver did not get out, but sat staring at nothing, or perhaps at the house. Several minutes passed before the tightly gripping hands came off the steering wheel, but the car door did not open. Instead, a flash of reflection came off a cellphone as the fingers moved through the rituals of password, text function, then email. Anyone close enough to see through the windshield would have noticed the state of the hands: how they fumbled, then clenched tight, before deliberately unfurling. As if the driver's body was host to some furious internal battle for control.

After a time, the fingers closed down the email. Put away the phone. Pulled out the keys. Opened the car door.

When the driver got out, anyone close enough to see would have been unsurprised to learn that the driver's thoughts were of death.

Not that anyone was close enough to see.

Olivia

When the bell signaled the official end of the assembly, Olivia let out a breath she didn't know she was holding. Cuomo hadn't shown up and made a scene in front of the entire school. Linda's day hadn't been knocked off its rails, nor would Guadalupe's shaky reputation be confirmed by an unfortunate headline in tomorrow's *Clarion*.

On with Career Day!

LINDA

Linda, anticipating a string of minor catastrophes for the first of the Career Day sessions, let the students go a few minutes early, so when the 10:50 bell rang, the gym was already half-empty. But she'd given the guest speakers a five-minute head start, for fear they might be trampled by a stampede of adolescents.

One of the last down from the bleachers was Gordon, looking pleased. "Well done, you."

She flushed. "It seemed to go okay."

"More than okay, it was spot-on. Even the jocks and troublemakers in the top row were paying attention."

"That's almost worrying. Oh, before I forget, could you help out in the cafeteria after lunch? My volunteer for that slot had to go home with a sick kid."

"Sure. I hope the speaker isn't talking about gynecology."

She laughed. "Sports medicine. You should be safe enough."

He nodded solemnly. "I can testify to the evils of shin splints," he said, and they went their separate ways.

LINDA

Linda leaned against the outside wall of room A12, grateful for its solidity. She felt as if she'd spent all morning sprinting circles around the school. Before the last student left the gym, chaos had descended: one speaker neglected to mention that she'd need a television set; another texted his host teacher during the assembly to say he had broken down on the freeway; at least thirty kids claimed that they hadn't received their assigned rooms and where were they supposed to go?

One TV fetched from the equipment shed and generating images; one abandoned teacher delivering a talk about an aunt's job as a UN translator; thirty lost students led to the main notice board, shown their names, and handed late slips — and one principal slumped against the wall, trying not to think how much she wanted a long shower, a strong drink, and a toilet. Not necessarily in that order.

Across A Quad, the Japanese professor seemed to be reciting poetry.

On Linda's left, the visiting nurse, who had started off talking about the importance of immunizations, seemed to have gotten a bit sidetracked into the science of the matter, and how each antibody links up to its specific target and neutralizes it before it spreads. Which was fascinating, but Linda was glad to hear her catch her enthusiasm and come back to earth.

To Linda's right, the blind weaver's raspy voice (from all that pot?) spun an allegory of warp and weft before going on to the texture of sight, the competing scents of raw silk and fresh wool — and then she, too, began to veer aside, into politics, of all things: nineteenth-century Scottish weavers going out on strike over the tiny threads used to bind the main strands together, which mill owners refused to supply since they could not be seen in the final product. Linda found herself turning over the idea of *invisible yet essential; holding it all together* — and then caught herself. The speech was *over*. Also, the weaver's class seemed ominously quiet. She stuck her head around the side of the window, but all the backs were upright rather than slumped or head-down on their desks. Linda peeled herself off the wall and moved on.

This was the first time in weeks — months? — that she didn't have a hundred urgent tasks yammering in her ear. Though she was sure to be ambushed by some disaster the minute she set foot in her office — so instead, she crossed the breezeway to stand in the school entrance and admire its mosaic walls.

They'd have to install a gate around this, Linda thought uneasily. These walls were going to be too tempting for the local vandals — a problem she hadn't anticipated when the restorer began. They'd all assumed he would uncover a well-intended but amateurish effort, of historical and possibly symbolic importance to the school community, but hardly a treasure.

Instead, what came into view was a piece that, in the words of the old hippie they'd hired to restore it, *blew him away.* He had yet to identify this remarkably talented artist, who had worked in a medium of jagged bits and mismatched pieces, but he swore he would.

She'd kept up with the progress of the restoration, but this was her first opportunity to simply stand and look at it. And she had to agree: it was amazing. The oldest bits were some pieces of Chinese porcelain dinnerware that the restorer thought were from the early 1900s. The newest were the 1970s orange of the tile Linda had seen one day when a towel dispenser fell off the wall in one of the girls' restrooms. There were pebbles, similar to those embedded in the school's front walk, and flowers chipped out of the Mexican tiles that used to surround the sink in the art lab. Up at the top, tiny fragments of mirror tossed the light around. An apple tree, under close examination, bore fruit made from a dozen mismatched red buttons; the school's entrance arch was the broken-off handle of a coffee mug. Up in the blue sky flew a tiny jeweled bird — attached, he'd discovered, to a girl's hairpin.

Linda ran her hand over the textures, the smooth and the rough — some of them very rough indeed — and reflected that the mural was like a stone tapestry . . .

At the thought, Linda's hand stopped moving.

The school is a tapestry, yes — but not one woven from malleable fibers. There was nothing soft or fraying about Guadalupe's kids. *Her* kids. And what brought them together had nothing of a loom's deliberation about it.

No: Guadalupe was a tapestry built from

jagged and mismatched pieces that, with care, could find a fit. Unlikely shapes, from a myriad of sources, joined by skilled hands and the eye of a believer. The broken, the lost, and the hidden from view, made into something new . . .

Linda McDonald stood in the entrance-way and laughed aloud. All the hours she'd spent on that damned speech, sifting through words, searching for ways to make the metaphors less clichéd — while all the time, if she'd just stood here and *looked*, her speech would have written itself.

Ah well. There was always next year.

Eleven minutes away from Guadalupe Middle School, a car reversed out of a driveway. Its driver paused to take off a black baseball cap, dropping it onto the lumpy black gym bag that sat on the passenger seat, then shifted into Drive. He drove past the large neighboring homes, streets quiet but for the blower of a gardening service. At the main road, the left-hand turn signal went on. The car joined the light midday traffic, heading away from San Felipe.

___

The session on a cop's life was going well. There were some unexpected faces here — the presence of Chaco Cabrera gave Olivia pause — but either the troublemakers had decided to know their enemy, or they just wanted to stare at a heavily armed woman for fifty minutes. Then again, maybe Linda had assigned them here for reasons of her own.

At least they were paying attention. They laughed more or less where she wanted them to, and their eyes grew big at a couple of the war stories she'd run past Linda to make sure they weren't too graphic. So far, nobody'd fallen asleep or surreptitiously checked an illicit cellphone.

Olivia managed to keep her hand off the butt of her gun, and thought she was striking a decent balance between the romance of the job and the tedium. As for its dangers, well, that was sure to come up during question time. Which would be asked first: *Have you ever shot someone?* Or, *Have you ever been shot?*

In either case, her answer would be the same: No.

But she'd be touching wood when she said it.

At ten minutes before noon, all the threads about to come together at Guadalupe Middle School gave a twitch of motion. The lunch bell sounded. At the far end of the county, Taco Alvarez, sitting beside his lawyer at the defendant's table, looked up at the clock and wondered how his brother, Angel, was getting on. Five miles away, Bee Cuomo's father glanced down at the print-out of the latest #speakforbee outrage, then took his hands off the wheel long enough to tear it to shreds and throw it out the window — although when he later found the two pieces that blew back inside, his rage would flare up all over again. On the other side of town, a framed picture of Mina Santos looked on as her mother wrote a check to the security consultants she used to keep her family safe. On the other side of the world, a man sat in a darkened office and studied the list of names on his computer screen. Closer to home, Thomas Atcheson tried to remember why he had married Brendan's mother.

As all these things were sending vibrations down their respective threads, a car pulled into an industrial lot that was forty-seven minutes' drive from Guadalupe Middle School. The driver, whose face was all but invisible behind the brim of a dark baseball cap, seemed to know where to go. The car pulled through the rows of anonymous white delivery vans and stopped behind the main office building.

BRENDAN

In his rush out the door that morning, Brendan hadn't made a sandwich, and forgot to stick any protein bars in his pack. He had money, of course, but the idea of the lunch line made him feel a little sick. It was less than three hours to the final bell now. The idea of going home to his letter and disc, that unmade bed, and the running faucet and scattered books . . .

He might as well just shoot himself.

But taking the final step was proving harder than he'd anticipated. He couldn't even send Jock a text because he'd have to explain why he hadn't made his move yet. Still, the office was always packed during lunch. It would screw up his timing. Maybe get some air first? Run through everything one last time in his head.

There was a basketball game on — but he wasn't going to join in. And after today, what would it matter? Anyway, he probably shouldn't leave his backpack unattended.

LINDA

The staff lounge was filled with the guest speakers and parent volunteers. Señora Rodriguez thrust a plate in Linda's hand before she could offer to help. Linda politely furnished it with one of the small sandwiches and some carrots, then started working her way around the room to thank the guests.

The three afternoon-only speakers had yet to appear, so she kept an eye on the front drive, to catch them if they arrived — and, equally vital, to guard against a return of poor Mr. Cuomo.

Other than that distant threat, the guest luncheon was going marvelously. Who'd have imagined that a forensic technician and a near-blind weaver would laugh so heartily over a dry remark from a professor of Japanese history? Or that one of the volunteer mothers would prove so fascinated with the work of the organic farmer?

The threads of community, indeed — or rather, disparate pieces, lost and found and brought together.

Nothing was going wrong. Her worries were childish.

"Your wife tells me you knew Bee Cuomo."

Gordon looked around in surprise as the school psychologist dropped into the empty chair beside him. Dr. Henry was one of the school figures he recognized but had barely spoken with, a short, squat, intense woman with wild curls and beautiful milky-coffee skin. She was now peering at him through the bright orange frames of her glasses.

"I beg your pardon?"

"Bee Cuomo. Linda says you knew her."

"I wouldn't say that. I met the child a couple of times, back in September."

"What did you make of her?"

"In what way?" Gordon set his sandwich back down on the plate.

"I'm trying to figure out how the girl became so important to Nick Clarkson in such a short time."

"It doesn't surprise me."

"Why not? And go ahead and eat, you're

obviously needing your lunch."

He obediently took a bite, following it with a swallow of tea before he replied. "I've never had children, and never been in a situation to know a lot of them, so I'm not sure I'm the best judge, but I don't believe I've ever met a child quite like Bee Cuomo. She was . . . fey."

" 'Fey' as in elfin? Or as in otherworldly?"

"Both, I suppose. She'd look at you with this absolutely direct gaze, and at the same time give the impression she was looking somewhere else. Or perhaps listening to something you couldn't hear. If you'd told me she read minds or saw the future, I wouldn't have been entirely astonished. And she was completely fearless. She'd talk to anybody. One day out on the playground, a couple of us were moving toward this pair of eighth-grade boys who were clearly about to go for each other's throats, and out of nowhere, Bee Cuomo walked up and said something. Both boys just froze and looked down at this strange little mite, completely befuddled."

"What happened?"

"Eventually one kid answered. And Bee said something else and their fists came down slowly, and the three of them talked for a minute. When she walked off, they stared at her like they were too stunned to remember what they'd been arguing about. I always wondered what it was she'd said."

"Fey."

"Or brain damaged." She looked up, startled, and he smiled. "As I said, I never knew any kids this age before Linda came here."

Dr. Henry nodded. "She's doing an extraordinary job. A year ago, a lot of adults wouldn't have ventured into the yard during lunchtime."

"She bullied the District into giving her the moon."

"Including my expanded hours here. But it's not just what they gave her. It's what they got. Linda's good. She listens. More than that, she's made sure the teachers are listening, too." She stood up as abruptly as she'd arrived. "Okay, thanks."

The woman hurried away, leaving Gordon to stare at her back . . . then decide that a breath of fresh air might help clear his mind before the afternoon session.

Forty-seven minutes from Guadalupe Middle School, a long white Ford van pulled out of a company lot. As it drove down the busy street, one car after another pulled irritably around it. The driver remained oblivious — either distracted by some internal dialogue, or cautious over the unfamiliar dimensions of the van.

Or perhaps the driver's caution had to do with the contents of the van. Since the only windows were in the front, none of the passersby could tell if there was equipment, or livestock, or something else back there that jostling would endanger.

Had anyone been close enough to see —

No one was. So the van continued on its anonymous, inexorable path.

MINA

People figured Mina Santos for a Mexican-American until they heard her Spanish or saw the lunches her mother fixed. Mina was getting pretty fluent, but *Español* was only her fourth-best language, not as good as her mother's Farsi, her father's Portuguese, or the English they all used at home. Mostly she just let people think she was Hispanic, since saying she was Iranian carried the risk of racist comments or boring conversations about terrorists and head scarves.

The day was almost warm, and Sofia had grabbed a table in the sun. Mina sighed as she took out her insulated lunch bag with the folded paper napkin and the little plastic boxes, wishing for the thousandth time her parents would let her buy lunch. Instead, every day here she was, unpacking her containers of rice and pickles and the flatbread that her friends thought was a really lopsided tortilla.

She guessed that for her mother, it was like the phone-tracking app: safe food to keep her safe.

Putting their only daughter into public school, letting her have a bike and the freedom to use it was probably enough for traditional parents to worry about. Especially after last year. For a while after Gloria's murder — when Mina had helped the witness, hung out with a weird old man, and nearly been murdered herself — Mina lost *all* her freedoms: bike, school, friends. No cellphone, even, until Mâmân realized it was better to have her in touch. Good girls did *not* get involved with murders, ride all over town, or deceive the police — and far worse, her parents. It took months to work her way back from that, months of tears and threats and bargains and obedience. Mina was still in what her father called a *deficit of trust*.

She didn't like to think what they'd do if they found out the things that were going on at school.

If tidy boxes of her mother's cooking was the price to pay, Mina would shut up and eat them. Anyway, she could always find someone willing to trade the kebabs and *pulau* for a bologna sandwich or school-lunch taco.

Today she ate quickly, since she'd spotted the principal's husband walking toward the basketball courts with Tío, and she might be able to get another lesson out of him before the bell rang. Mr. Kendrick was one of the most interesting people she knew. He reminded her of some of her mother's friends, the ones who'd fled Iran when the mullahs came in. When she heard Mr. Kendrick had lived in New Guinea and spoke Pidgin English, she asked him about it, and he promised to teach her. Pidgin wasn't really a language, and it sometimes made her laugh — like when the nut on the end of a bolt was called *mama bilong skru* or sky was *ples bilong klaut,* and my home was *asples bilong me.* (When something broke it went *bagarap* — "bugger" meaning something *so* rude in English-English it made Mr. Kendrick change the subject, which was kind of cute. She'd had to Google it.)

Foreign languages were the baddest thing ever.

She made sure Sofia was okay with her going, then headed toward the courts, where she found Mr. Kendrick holding the ladder so Tío could hook up a new net. They were talking in Spanish — Mr. Kendrick's wasn't nearly as good as hers — and they greeted Mina in that language as she came up. Then Mr. Kendrick shifted to Pidgin — *Tok Pisin* — to ask if she was enjoying her day.

Haltingly, she told him that she liked what the principal had said during the assembly (the *miting bilong olgeta skul*), but was sorry she couldn't hear Sergeant Mendez talk about being a policewoman (*meri bilong polis*). Mr. Kendrick listened. When Tío had finished and carried the ladder away, she and Mr. Kendrick sat at a picnic table to *Tok Pisin.*

Mina might be only thirteen (until next month!) but she knew people thought her pretty. She was also aware — both from boring maternal lectures and uncomfortable personal experiences — what female prettiness did to boys and men. And she was grateful for men like Mr. Kendrick who could treat her like a human being instead of giving off all kinds of creepy hormones.

She trusted him. Sure, he was old enough to be her grandfather, but he was still male. And since another parental crackdown would mean private school for sure, she'd made a point of asking both parents if she could spend time with her principal's husband — in public, out in the open, no closed doors in sight — for the purpose of learning a new language. Naturally, they insisted on coming to school to meet him — like *that* wasn't embarrassing — but Mr. Kendrick was easy about it, and Papa seemed to approve of him and Mâmân ended up treating him like a sort of uncle, so that was fine.

She liked the old fellow. Well, all the girls did, in a giggling sort of way (it was his English accent, mostly), but Mina was learning from him, and not only Pidgin. He had a lot to say about the world and how it worked. And although he had a habit of turning aside any direct questions about his past, something about the way he glanced at her sometimes made Mina suspect she reminded him of someone. Someone whose memory made him sad.

11:59
Coach Gilbert

Coach, being a part-timer, usually came to school just before lunch hour. Not that he was paid for that, but he figured it was useful to have another adult wandering around the playground (they didn't call it a playground, but if these kids weren't playing, what were they doing?). Anyway, it gave him an excuse to keep an eye on Nick.

Today he'd arrived at school first thing, but when the 11:50 bell rang, he gravitated as usual toward the outdoor tables and courts. Not as a coach, although if one of the kids asked him onto the courts he was happy to go. And not as an authority figure, although he could be that, too, when trouble rose up.

No, Coach was just there as part of the background of life at Guadalupe. Sometimes he sat with Nick, although he tried not to make that a habit. More often, he laid out his lunch on the furthest table,

423

reading a book or chatting with whichever teacher had outdoor duty that day, talking with the students only if they approached him first.

But today his usual table had an occupant: Brendan Atcheson.

Coach paused to let his eyes drift over the basketball players while he stood thinking. He didn't want to push the boy. Especially not during lunch, a time Coach firmly believed was meant to provide fifty minutes of school holiday, with a minimum of structure and as much anarchy as the buildings would permit.

However. Brendan might not always be part of the lunch tables' social community, but he was here enough to know where Coach generally sat. Yet there he was, his long arms loosely circling the laden backpack on the table before him.

Claiming the territory, or inviting approach?

In Coach's long experience, as well as in his reading about troubled kids, they'd talk if you gave them an honest chance. And Carol's words came back to him: *You could just ask Brendan himself . . .*

Coach pulled his eyes from the game they hadn't really been focused on and continued across the blacktop. He stopped just short of the table and spoke in his most easygoing voice. "How you doing, Brendan? Hey, I sometimes eat lunch here, but if you want to be alone, son, I'll just head over to one of the other tables."

The boy didn't look up, and his only reply was a shrug, but Coach Gilbert was fluent in the language of adolescent shrugs. This particular one was a surprise, coming from this particular kid. It was virtually a plea to sit.

So Coach sat, his back to the courts, and laid his lunch bag on the table. He took out his sandwich, a packet of corn chips, a can of non-iced tea, and an apple cut in quarters. He opened the tea and took a swallow, unwrapped the sandwich and started in on that, all motions calm, watching kids kick a soccer ball around the field, no suggestion of a glance toward the far end of the table.

When the first half sandwich was gone, he drank some more tea, then picked up the chips. When he got them open, he glanced inside, then made a faint but audible noise and made to drop the packet — then paused, and put it down halfway along the battered wooden surface. "Not sure if you like corn chips? My wife forgets that they stick in my teeth."

Coach packed his own lunches.

He resumed his sandwich, gazing intently into the distance as the boy's hand came out to retrieve the chips.

The two ate beneath an invisible flag of truce. Coach finished the sandwich and opened the bag with the cut apple. He took out one quarter, then nudged the remaining three a little farther along the table. "Like some apple? A little brown, but they taste fine."

To his utter astonishment, the boy scooted down on the bench just enough to reach his offering. What's more, when he had a slice in hand, he didn't pull back to the furthest point from Coach.

What the hell was going on with this kid?

They each ate two quarters of the apple. Coach put the empty baggie into the paper bag, drank the last of the tea, and dropped the can in on top. He then casually swung both legs over the bench to lean back, elbows on the table, facing the same direction as Brendan. As he turned, his eyes caught on the remarkably full backpack.

"You got a lot of stuff today." His disinterested tone indicated that he was just making polite conversation.

"Things I might need."

Coach nodded, and the two sat for a while, watching the activity on the basketball court. A kid smaller than any of the others darted into the traffic under the hoop, snagging the loose ball mid-dribble and getting seriously underfoot as he tried for a lay-up — and almost made it. It failed, but Coach tipped his head. "Any idea who that is?"

"Stevie Garcia. Sixth grade."

Coach hid his surprise at getting a reply. "Well, if I'm coaching next year, he might be worth recruiting."

"He'd be good at the three."

Coach's eyes wavered, but he forced them to stay on the sixth-grader — and after a minute, despite his preoccupation, he could see what Brendan meant. Little Stevie was quick, aggressive, and short enough to get in the way a lot. Players good at getting fouled could rack up the free throws.

Like Brendan.

Coach couldn't stand it any longer. He swung one leg back over the bench to straddle it, looking directly at his star player for the first time. Brendan had his chin on the bulging pack, his arms snug around it. His eyes were on the players.

"Are you okay?" Coach blurted out — then kicked himself. But incredibly, the question didn't send the boy into instant and supercilious retreat. If anything, it . . . good Lord: could that have been the start of a smile? The boy's gaze flickered toward him, then returned to the court.

"I guess."

"Brendan, is there anything I can do?"

The dark eyes snapped back to him, wary now. "What do you mean?"

You could just ask Brendan . . .

Afraid that his words might rupture this faint contact, but knowing he was committed, Coach pressed on. "Couple weeks ago in practice, I noticed this fellow in the stands. That day the kid threw the water bottle onto the court? I thought you looked" — don't use the word *frightened* — "startled. Like maybe you thought he was going to . . . Anyway, who is he?"

Brendan frowned. "You mean Ray? My uncle?"

"Your *uncle*? Why —" Coach couldn't come up with an end to that question, but Brendan gave him an answer anyway.

"Yeah, he's my mom's brother. Why?"

"I was . . ." — not *concerned* — "curious. He seems to watch you, during practice, but I've never seen you talk to him. And he leaves the minute practice is over."

"That's because of the court order. He's not supposed to come near me."

Oh, jeez: I was right. Coach took a moment to be sure his voice was calm before

428

speaking. "Why is that?"

Brendan looked back at the basketball game. "Mostly because my stepfather hates him. When Mom died, Uncle Ray tried to get me to go live with him instead."

Coach could hear the effort it took the boy to sound casual. "I'm sorry, Brendan. About your mother. I didn't know you'd lost her."

The shrug again. "Couple years ago."

"That's hard. My mother died when I was twenty, and it was still hard."

"Yeah, well. They say she committed suicide."

Coach reared back, stunned — but the boy's face warned that too much sympathy would end the session. "I'm very sorry. But your uncle: was wanting you to go live with him enough to get a restraining order?"

"My father convinced the judge that Ray was a bad influence."

"You don't think he is?"

The dark eyes sought Coach out, with some message too deep to read. "No."

"But that day with the water bottle. You seemed to think that he was the one who'd thrown the thing."

"Ray? No! But my father — my *step*father, he . . . has a way of finding things out. Every time Ray shows up, I expect to see Sir —

my stepfather — up behind him in the stands. Stupid, but still." He did give Coach a smile then, but there was queasiness in it. The sort of expression shared by two men who had walked through some deep shit together. The boy was telling the truth — as he saw it, at least.

"Your uncle." Coach retrieved his lunch things from the table. "You think I might meet him, one of these days?"

That funny half smile, again, as the boy's fingers played with a lump in the black nylon. "Yeah. I think you probably will."

"I hope you know that I'm, well, here. If you need to talk."

"Yeah. Sure. Thanks."

"I mean it." But Coach saw that Brendan was drifting away, as surely as if he saw the cut rope floating free. The boy's eyes had focused on the far side of the baseball diamond, where Linda McDonald was finishing up her customary brisk lunchtime walk around the school.

So Coach wasn't surprised when Brendan got to his feet and, with a mumble that passed for a farewell, swung his pack over his shoulder and slouched off. Although if Brendan wasn't careful, his path was going to intersect with that of the principal.

All in all, Coach thought, the conversation

had been a relief. Not only had the boy emerged a fraction from his shell, but the man in the stands did not sound like a pedophile. Good to know that the boy had not been flirting — and yet, Coach still felt obscurely troubled, as he watched his player retreat. He couldn't shake the niggling suspicion that he had missed some vital part of the boy's message.

DR. HENRY

An idea — planted by Gordon Kendrick, in ground fertile by the morning's session with Nick Clarkson — had begun to push at the corner of Cass Henry's mind. The office she usually used had a couple of teachers in it, eating their lunch, so she kept opening doors until she found an empty space to spread out her notes. Elbows on the table, she stared down at her cheat-sheet page of names:

GUADALUPE STAFF:

Linda McDonald — principal, caring, smart. Listens.
(Gordon Kendrick, Linda's husband — school volunteer. British, 70s.)
"Tío" (Jaime Rivera Cruz) — school janitor, hired October. What was he before??

She added a note at the bottom about one of the day's speakers — *Thomas Atcheson*

— Brendan's father, biggest Name in San Felipe: problem for B? — then laid the page aside. The next sheet held a roughly sketched flowchart of circles, arrows, and question marks, mostly describing the holes in her knowledge — visual thinking at its most chaotic. But as she stared down at the scribbles and notes, she felt the beat of an elevated pulse.

Holes.

What if . . . What if those mystifying gaps were in fact a single hole? What if —

She pulled out a blank sheet and redid the flowchart around one central element instead of a lot of smaller ones. It made no sense, and yet it made everything fall into place.

The missing element was Bee Cuomo.

Bee was a child oblivious to social expectations. An eleven-year-old who was extraordinarily — alarmingly — deaf to criticism, blind to the subtle and inexorable cues under which middle school society functioned. She'd dressed like a child, and seemed unaware that there was a wall between the grades. She would start conversations with sixth-grade losers and eighth-grade jocks alike. She'd ask the most popular girl in school where she got her hair cut (and what's more, get an answer). Bee

433

would share her lunch with a kid whose breath could melt plastic.

Eleven months ago, high school student Gloria Rivas had been murdered. Her grieving parents had taken Gloria's younger sister, Sofia, out of school for the remainder of the year, fearing Guadalupe's rivalries and factions. But when classes started up again in late August, Sofia returned to school in the company of her loyal friend and surrogate sister, Mina Santos.

The girls were met by a welcoming committee bullied into place by the brand-new sixth-grade student Bee Cuomo: admiring Sofia's hair, showing her a photo of a new puppy, eating lunch with her.

Grieving Sofia had managed to slip back into Guadalupe with barely a splash. And so far (touch wood) the truce between the Rivas/Alvarez factions was holding.

Convert that flowchart into a Venn diagram, and quirky little Bee Cuomo occupied the shaded area in the middle of various subgroups: sixth-grade outsiders and eighth-grade athletes; English speakers and newly arrived Mexican immigrants; the family of a murder victim and relatives of the accused killer — God knew who else. Bee Cuomo, eleven-year-old Switzerland.

Even more extraordinary: when the child

vanished, the relationship structures built around her did not collapse. The improbable friendship between Nick Clarkson and the Sofia-and-Mina sisterhood was clearly still functioning. Carlos Garcia, friend and supporter of the witness to the murder, walked the halls unscathed. (So far.)

Or was she using the wrong analogy here? Maybe Bee was neither neutral territory on which the factions could meet, nor a bridge for communication. Perhaps the child had been something more along the lines of a catalyst. Something that permanently changed the original.

Nick Clarkson was not the boy he'd been the summer before. Guadalupe itself was not the same school. And although much of that was due to the incredibly hard work of Linda and her staff, wasn't some of it — perhaps just a touch — due to the presence of a fey little girl who didn't realize that she wasn't supposed to walk up to a pair of bristling older boys and ask one of them a question?

Cass Henry had been a family therapist for half her life, and she couldn't remember the last time she'd found herself this puzzled, this challenged, this . . .

Exhilarated.

BRENDAN

You gotta do it, Brendan ordered as he walked across the grounds in the direction the principal was headed. *You said you would. You sent Jock the text. And that letter and disc — sure, you* think *Sir never gets home early, but how do you know? He might go home for lunch every day. And man, you'd be so completely and utterly fucked if you went home and there he was . . .*

Quit screwing around. You've been planning this for weeks — months, really. All you need to do is light the fuse. Just go stand in front of the principal and deliver that little speech you know by heart. Give her what you've got in the pack.

MINA

When Mr. Kendrick left to help set up in the cafeteria, Mina was alone at the picnic table. She'd go back to Sofia in a minute, but it was actually nice to be by herself for two minutes. A bunch of younger boys had started a game under the new net. She glanced around for the teachers, thinking she might sneak out her phone and send Mâmân the noontime text — and who did she see but Brendan, marching across the tarmac straight toward her. Mina's heart gave a little skip. He looked like he had something in mind. Like maybe coming up and grabbing her by the shoulders. Or something.

Then his path began to veer, and she realized he wasn't looking at her — wasn't looking at anything, really. If her pulse hadn't still been thumping — if she'd taken one second to think about it — she'd have shut her mouth and let him march right on by while she sat there hoping nobody noticed how her cheeks were burning.

Instead, she spoke up.

"Hey, Brendan." At her words, he jerked to a halt. "Oh, hey, sorry — you're going somewhere. Never mind."

His eyes came to a focus on her. "Um, yeah — no, that's fine. I just was, you know."

"Busy, yeah. It can wait, don't worry."

He shot a quick glance down in the direction of the road — no, he'd been headed for the principal — but then those dark eyes of his were looking at her, and at the conspicuously empty table where she sat.

She felt the color begin to creep into her face. Brendan looked like a young Jake Gyllenhaal. And really, not all that much younger.

He slung his pack onto the table with a thump. "Nah, no rush. What's up?"

"Um, you know about computers, right?"

"Sure."

"You know Nick Clarkson? How he started that hashtag against Bee Cuomo's father?"

"I've seen it." He climbed onto the bench across from her. Their feet were nearly touching — close enough to give both her parents heart attacks.

"Yeah, I don't know that much about it

either, but I know a couple people who are really into it, and I wondered if maybe they could get into trouble? If they're not careful. I mean, Nick's a nice enough kid and I think he's right that the police can't do anything, but . . ." *Stop blabbering, Mina!* "Anyway, do you know how hard it would be for someone to find out who's posting the things?"

Brendan asked her some questions, most of which Mina couldn't answer, and started talking about IP addresses and anonymity and how difficult it was to hide things from law enforcement, but how there were services that offered anonymity, and —

Actually, he lost her about two minutes in, but she'd have been happy to sit and listen to him all day. Until she realized that people were starting to head back toward the classrooms — there went Coach Gilbert — and if she didn't get a move on, she really would have to risk texting her mother out in the open, to get the midday check-in sent before the bell rang.

Brendan seemed to realize it at the same time, and dropped his hand to the strap of his pack. She hastened to tell him thanks, and that she'd see him around (in the cafeteria in about ten minutes, in fact, although she didn't want him to think she

439

was keeping track or anything). He sort of ducked his head, as adorable as a girl could want, and slung his pack across his shoulder to continue down A Quad in the wake of the principal.

She'd had Brendan Atcheson all to herself for nearly ten minutes. Even if they confiscated her phone for a month, it was worth it.

Olivia was taking another turn along the fence-line. She'd spotted the *Clarion* reporter parked along the side road, eyeing the kids on the playing field — until Sergeant Mendez appeared in all her uniformed glory. The reporter started her car and pulled away in a hurry.

Olivia was walking along the creek, where the chatter of squirrels was nearly as loud as the distant shriek of kids, when she got a call on her cell.

"Hey, Torres. What's up?"

"I just heard back from the dealership. They found the car Cuomo's been driving, parked in their back lot."

"The blue one?"

"Yeah. But he's not there. Nobody's sure where he is, and he's not answering his cell. They're checking to see if there's another car missing, he trades off sometimes without telling anyone, but it means they have to

441

compare the keys to what's on the lot, so it'll be a while. You want us there, at Guadalupe?"

"Not sure it'd do any good until we know what he's driving. He's probably just in a bar somewhere. No, take another pass by, let it go at that. I'm finished with my session so I'm walking the grounds now, and it's quiet. Well, not quiet, but you know what I mean. Any word from the Alvarez trial?"

"The kid's going to be called tomorrow."

"Danny Escobedo? Okay, I'll talk to his mom tonight. Anything else?"

"Nope."

"Okay, bye." Olivia ended the call, and studied the phone in her hand. Cuomo was probably in a bar somewhere, courting a DUI, working himself up to a fistfight. He'd show up with a hangover and a broken nose. Unless he picked on someone who'd been to the same martial arts classes the principal's husband had. (Did a person really pick up that practiced a move in martial arts?)

She sifted through the phone for the list of contacts that Linda had given her, entered Gordon's number into the text function, and sent him a brief message. Then she settled her duty belt and continued on her way.

Nineteen minutes away from Guadalupe Middle School, the air coming through the white van's window ruffled the driver's hair and carried the smell of trees. Douglas fir and pine grew along this section of road, although after a minute the smell changed to horses, and a muck-filled corral came briefly into view.

A blue jay screamed. A few hundred yards later, a squirrel performed its balancing act on the wire crossing the road.

The driver had never felt so alive.

12:30
GORDON

Gordon had felt his phone vibrate against
his leg when he was walking down B Quad,
and checked to see who it was from. Sergeant Mendez. But he'd always felt that using a cellphone in front of the students was
a bit like ordering a beer at an AA dinner,
so he waited until he was inside the cafeteria
to open the phone properly.

Hi Gordon, Olivia Mendez here. Could we
have a talk sometime soon?

A minute went by before Gordon realized
that he was surrounded by the racket of Tío
folding the tables up against the walls and
the speaker banging through the cafeteria's
back doors with armloads of equipment.
He woke up his phone again, and picked
out a reply:

Sure, happy to meet, maybe not today . . .

444

He slipped the phone in his pocket and went to help the physical therapist. And when they'd finished and the PT went to move his car out of the access road, Gordon helped Tío fold the last of the tables.

But all the while he was thinking, *Why the hell didn't I just allow that drunken lout Cuomo to jab his finger under Linda's nose? It's not like Mendez would have let the guy actually hit her.*

LINDA

There'd only been three days that Linda had missed her lunchtime circuit of Guadalupe since school began in August, and today was not one of them. Her brisk ten-minute walk functioned as a reset for body and spirit, clearing her mind and her lungs for the rest of the day.

This time, she'd gone clockwise: up B Quad and past the apple orchard to the creek, then down the roadside fence and across the courts. As she reached the offices, she heard the clatter of folding tables down the breezeway. Today had been an extra load on Tío, but he'd even managed to get the new nets on the basketball hoops. She made a mental note to find some thank-you gift for him, and went through the office door shortly before the end-of-lunch bell.

A dozen or so students crowded around the high counter. Linda raised her eyebrow at Mrs. Hopkins, who first shook her head to indicate she didn't need assistance, then continued with less welcome news. "We're missing two speakers."

"Missing? You mean the afternoon speakers haven't shown up yet?"

"The physical therapist is here — for Sports Medicine — but the other two are not." The secretary looked disapproving but untroubled, and gave a paper to one student, stretched out her hand for the next one's problem, all the while listening to the pleas of the one in front of her — Chaco Cabrera. Mrs. Hopkins put up one finger to pause the young man's flow of words, and addressed herself to Linda. "Dr. Whittaker phoned to say her flight got in late but she'll only be delayed five or ten minutes, so I sent Carmen down to help with her students. The other's Mr. Atcheson. I phoned him ten minutes ago but it went to voicemail, so he may be on the road. I left a message."

Oh Lord, Linda thought. Olivia had said the man was merely being investigated: did they arrest him instead? "What room is it? I'll either take his group or redistribute the kids."

"B18."

"I have my phone." Linda patted her

pocket to be sure. "Text me if you hear from him. Anything else that can't wait?"

"Two messages on your desk, they didn't sound urgent. All right, Chaco: no, I'm sorry, I can't change your session just because a girl is giving you a hard time. Don't sit next to her and you'll be fine — but run along before you need a late slip. Now, Sarah, what have you got into?"

Linda continued through to her office, praying that one of the messages wasn't to say that the world was due to collapse onto Guadalupe Middle School.

NICK

Halfway up A Quad, Nick Clarkson saw Brendan Atcheson walking toward him. Nick kept his head down, but to his astonishment, the big kid stopped and said his name.

Nick could only gape at him. *He knows who I am?*

Brendan took his silence for an answer. "You're doing an online campaign, right? About Bee Cuomo?"

"Uh, yeah. Sort of. I mean, I started it, kind of, but then everyone else —"

"Are you hiding your tracks? Using a proxy server?"

"Um, I'm not sure. I mean, I've heard of it, but . . ."

"You should use one."

"Okay, if you think it's a good idea. Could you maybe show me how?"

Brendan hesitated. "Yeah, but there's loads of other people who could, too. If you

449

ask around. Mina Santos might help you find someone. You know, in case I'm not here, or something."

Nick hastened to reassure the eighth-grader that he wasn't trying to latch onto him. "Oh, sure, I understand. I'll see if I can figure it out. Like in the library, before school tomorrow? Maybe, if you're here early and don't have anything to do, you could stop in and show me. Or not, I'll figure it out."

"You probably would. But yeah, sure. If I'm here in the morning, I'll come by the library."

Nick could tell that the chances of that were less than nothing. "Yeah, okay. Great!"

"See you 'round." Brendan ducked his head and walked off.

Nick watched Brendan continue down the quad toward the office. He'd actually been thinking of getting out of #speakforbee, considering how nasty the stuff was getting. But maybe he'd hang on a little longer.

Even being turned down by someone like Brendan Atcheson felt strangely good.

MINA

Mina came around the far end of B Wing and found Sofia talking with a bunch of other girls. It surprised her. So she kept straight on going toward the restroom at the end of the gym, where she closed herself into a stall.

She heard Sofia come in, heard her "Hey," but Mina just spoke across the dividers. "You go ahead so you're not late, I need to text my mom."

"Man, your mother." Sofia stayed where she was. Mina knew she would be checking her hair in the mirror, waiting — but Mina just stayed behind her door. After a minute, Sofia asked if she was nearly done.

"Don't wait for me."

There was silence, then Sofia made a little sound of annoyance and left. As the door wheezed shut, an ugly little thought snuck into Mina's mind: *Am I jealous?*

Didn't she *want* Sofia to have other friends?

Mina nearly ran after her, but there was the phone in her hand and the mother in her life. So she paused to hit SEND on "All fine here mom thanks for lunch luv M" before shoving the phone away and hurrying out of the bathroom — in time to see Sofia's back vanish into room B18 across the quad.

But standing in the shade of the breezeway, she could see something else as well: Chaco Cabrera, down at the far end of B Quad. Sofia would have had the sun in her eyes, so she hadn't noticed Chaco. Hadn't seen him stop dead; hadn't seen in his face a mix of emotions that even Mina, way down at the end of the gym, could follow: *I should hate you but, oh . . .*

Romeo must have looked at Juliet, the daughter of his family's enemies, with exactly that expression. (Of course, Shakespeare just *had* to kill them both off, but still.) After a moment, the short kid with the scary family and the reputation for sullenness started forward again. Mina began to walk, too. As she went by him, halfway down the quad, she paid Sofia back for that moment of petty rejection by speaking into the air.

"She really likes you, you know."

And walked on toward the cafeteria, grinning in mischief.

Chaco rounded the end of B Wing just in time to see Sofia Rivas, tall and gorgeous, cross the quad and go through the doorway of B18.

She'd been looking straight at him, her last five steps, and ignored him like he was one of the breezeway posts. Puta was going to get what her sister got, if she didn't watch out. Nose in the air bitch. *Haughty* was the word for her, even if it sounded like *hottie.* Though she was that, too.

Oh, Chaco thought as he forced his feet to carry him forward, why couldn't he be Mr. Cool like Brendan Atcheson, all the girls hanging on to him? Like this one coming at him — Mina Santos, short-and-gorgeous friend of tall-and-gorgeous Sofia. Two girls who looked at him like he was something the dog brought home. Well, they wouldn't look down on him once he'd made his name to cousin Taco.

Soon — very soon.

He wasn't surprised when she walked past like she didn't see him. But he was surprised — astonished — when she spoke at him in passing.

"She really likes you, you know."

He stopped dead and stared after her, but Mina never turned around, just walked through the cafeteria's double doors and let them drift shut.

A minute later, when Chaco starting moving again toward room B18, the world was a different place.

LINDA

Linda was hurrying in the direction of B Quad when she heard her name. She turned, walking backward to illustrate her unwillingness to stop fully: the Atcheson boy, shambling under that giant backpack. She'd been aware of him several times that morning, and once or twice she'd thought he was looking in her direction, but he seemed no surlier than usual, suggesting that he hadn't heard any news about his father. She continued moving, but slowly.

"Hi, Brendan, that was a great game last week. Sorry, I'm in a bit of a — Oh, wait." She stopped. "I don't suppose *you* know where your dad is?" Cellphones were banned on campus — the use of them, anyway — but the smart-ass son of a tech millionaire might ignore the rules.

She was braced for his usual vague shrug, but to her surprise, he looked startled. "No, I thought — He said he'd be here."

"Probably stuck in traffic. Look, Brendan, have you —" But before she could decide how to ask *Have you heard any news about your father?* a sound echoed down B Quad: a sudden burst of laughter — the kind that spelled trouble. "Brendan, I really need to take over your . . . to take over one of the classrooms for a few minutes, our speaker's been delayed. Can you wait for me in my office?"

"I have to give you something." The hefty pack swung forward; raucous adolescent voices built in the distance.

"I'll try not to be more than a few minutes, and then you'll have my full attention."

"But I —"

The office door opened behind him, emitting two girls with admit slips. Linda lowered her voice. "I can see this is important to you, Brendan, but if I don't get into that classroom it'll be in pieces. Do you want to wait in my office, or in your assigned room? Where are you, this next period?"

"The cafeteria. Sports Medicine. Yeah, I guess so. It can wait."

The boy slumped, that adolescent declaration that the world had kicked his dreams, yet again. Although maybe that wasn't fair. She should . . .

No, she couldn't: a classroom riot would

not improve anything. And whatever Brendan Atcheson's troubles were, they wouldn't be quickly dealt with.

In any case, it was the boy's father who'd given her the current problem.

She reached out to give the boy's arm a squeeze, and told him to ask Mrs. Hopkins for a late slip. As she hurried toward the sound of impending chaos, she noticed a white van flying down the access road at the far end of the breezeway.

12:41
MINA

When the bell rang, Brendan wasn't there. Mina leaned casually against the stage, fiddling with the Sports Medicine guy's collection of bands and rubber balls, waiting for Brendan to come rushing in.

The clock ticked; twelve other kids; no Brendan.

Mina was *so* glad she hadn't let him know that she would be at his session. Obviously, Brendan Atcheson couldn't care less.

459

The long white van had approached Guadalupe Middle School from the west, waiting in the turn lane while a line of eight cars dawdled behind a farm truck. The ninth car, a Honda that came in from the side road, accelerated to join the queue, but the van swung across the road in front of it. The Honda's driver slammed on her brakes and leaned on the horn in protest.

Mrs. Hopkins glanced out the office window at the sound. She saw the van, pulling too fast into the access road, and shook her head, hoping that whatever piece of equipment the van held wasn't now smashed all over its floor.

BRENDAN

Brendan watched Ms. McDonald hurry down the breezeway, her weird haircut flying in every direction. When she disappeared into B Quad, he turned away, dimly aware of a white van speeding by. *Takes me all morning to get up my nerve, and she puts me off!* He was supposed to go sit in her office, like some kid in a time-out? During the only Career Day session he was even remotely interested in? (And no, not *only* because the list showed Mina Santos would be there.)

Fuck that. The *principal* could wait in her office for *him.*

Maybe he should've given his speech to Coach instead, when he had the chance, and started things there. But Coach was even older than the rest of them, probably too old to get it. Plus that, he already figured Brendan was a loser. No, better to do like he'd rehearsed so many times: stand in front of Principal McDonald — stand,

461

not sit — and give her the speech, watching her eyes grow large before he reached into his pack . . .

Yet another case of the world agreeing that he was a loser who couldn't get anything right. That Brendan Atcheson — didn't deserve the name Connelly — was sure to back out of a thing if it looked a little bit hard. Even his mother gave up on him: didn't that prove that making something of his life was just a fantasy?

But he *couldn't* back out (not now). The disc was made, and he'd *given his word*. Maybe he could, like, push things along a little? Take a small step first, and the rest would follow?

So he did walk down to the office, but instead of just getting an admit slip from Mrs. Hopkins, he handed her the disc that had been burning a hole in his backpack all morning. "This is for Ms. McDonald. She said she'd be here in a few minutes."

Old Hopkins gave it a look that made Brendan wonder if she knew what a computer disc was, but she did take it, and say she'd put it on the principal's desk.

He accepted the late slip and turned away, to be prompted by a disapproving voice. " 'Thank you, Mrs. Hopkins.' "

"Yeah," he called over his shoulder. "Thanks."

12:42
LINDA

Linda waited until she was actually standing in the doorway of the noisy classroom before she hit the phone icon on her cell and lifted it to her ear. A ripple of dismay ran through the students as they noticed her. A trio of eighth-grade boys with embarrassed grins drifted toward the desks. Chaco Cabrera dropped into the farthest-away seat.

Linda just stood there, looking at them as she waited for the call to go through. "Hello, Sergeant Mendez. A white van just went down the access road in a rush. Would you please either go direct them to whatever classroom is expecting them, or come to B18 and watch this class while I go see? Okay, thanks."

She thumbed off the call, silenced the phone as she always did in a classroom, and dropped it into the pocket of her blazer, standing for a moment longer to cow the students into complete silence. Only then did she reach back to shut the door behind her.

OLIVIA

Olivia's phone buzzed twice before she got her shirt pocket undone. "Hi, Linda." As she was listening, the phone made the noise of one incoming text, then immediately another. "Sure, I'll go see what they need."

The texts were from Torres and Mrs. Hopkins.

Cuomo took a bright red convertible down to Big Sur, he's in a bar.

Well, that was a relief, anyway. The text from the school secretary bore a request similar to Linda's: someone driving too fast had gone toward the staff lot and if Olivia saw them, she should remind him that there were children on school grounds.

Olivia was smiling as she put the phone away, and continued down A Quad toward the offices.

The white van braked hard as it went past the first set of double doors at the back of the cafeteria, dangerously close to the sheer wall. An onlooker might have expected it to swing wide into the staff parking lot. Instead it slowed and kept to its path, coming ever closer to the painted concrete blocks. By the second pair of cafeteria doors, it had dropped to a crawl, its side mirror nearly scraping the paint. It continued forward another ten feet to where the kitchen door stood, and there it stopped.

When its engine went quiet, the vehicle was blocking two of the cafeteria's five exit routes.

The driver's door came open. A figure wearing jeans, a leather jacket over a gray sweatshirt, and a black baseball cap walked around the front to check the gap between fender and wall, then circled back along the van's path to the first pair of doors. A shiny metal device dangled from the driver's hand. He threaded it through the doors' two handles, pushing its ends together. Back at the van, he leaned inside the open door and pulled out a heavy ballistic-nylon gym bag.

The man held his right hand deep in the jacket's pocket, as he strode up the empty road, past the high kitchen window, the three sets of gymnasium doors, and the row of vents from the boys' locker room. At the end of the wing, he peered around the corner, then continued, disappearing from sight.

It had begun.

■ ■ ■ ■

CAREER DAY

Lockdown

■ ■ ■ ■

OLIVIA

Olivia came out of the breezeway and there was the white van, parked so close to the cafeteria it was a wonder the mirror wasn't scraped away. She walked forward, expecting a puzzled driver armed with a clipboard to climb down from the open door and ask if she knew where to find room . . .

She had actually gone past the first set of cafeteria doors before her cop's peripheral vision tugged her head around for a glance — and she stood gaping for a moment at the double doors, their matching handles tied together by one of those expensive bike locks that took massive bolt-cutters to get off . . .

Then the alarms started to go off in her head. Her right hand snatched out her sidearm while her left ripped at her shirt pocket for the cellphone. She thumbed it on without taking her eyes from the van, giving a quick glance at the still-open text from Mrs. Hopkins to locate the little phone icon. She tapped it and put the thing to her ear, knees bent and gun out and aimed. Pulse racing, vision narrowed to that open door, Olivia had to wait for three endless rings before Mrs. Hopkins came on the line.

"Hello, Sergeant Mendez, what —"

Olivia overrode her. "There's a van smack up against the back of the cafeteria, blocking one set of doors, and a bike lock through the handles of the others. Do you know anything about that?"

"A bicycle lock? I don't think —"

"Okay, I'm going to go see what's up, but you need to call 911. Tell them I'm going radio silent but I need backup *right now,* tell them to use lights but no sirens, repeat *no sirens.* And I want you standing next to the school alarm switch. If you hear anything at all, hit the lockdown. Got that?"

"Yes, but —"

"I'm gonna send you the license plate. Have the Department find who it belongs to, and text me that information." Let Linda know? The last thing Olivia wanted was hundreds of kids in a screaming panic. "Look, it may be nothing — some speaker's idiotic idea of a cute demonstration — so don't bother Linda yet. I'll let you both know the minute I figure it out." She hung up, snapped a photo of the van's back end, sent it, and pocketed the cell.

Then she switched off the sound on her radio.

Taking another deep breath, Olivia tightened both hands on the gun, and eased along the wall toward the van.

Why would the school's two hottest kids be interested in sports medicine? Nick guessed that Mina Santos made sense, since (underneath how she looked) she was the kind of person who'd want to help people by being a doctor, or at least a physical therapist. (And maybe it was good she wore that kind of clothes — he could imagine that having a really gorgeous doctor could be awkward.) At least her friend Sofia wasn't here. The pair of them always made Nick want to stammer and blush. Funny, though: he'd have thought that of the two, it would be Sofia who was interested in sports medicine, since she'd been a basketball player. Of course, that was before her sister was murdered.

Was basketball the reason Brendan Atcheson signed up for this session? He'd come in late, but went to stand next to Mina, which looked funny because she didn't even come up to his shoulder. Brendan was almost as good-looking a guy as she was a girl. Although until Brendan had stopped to talk with him a few minutes ago, Nick wouldn't have said he was anywhere near as nice as Mina. Maybe he just hid it better.

And what about Nick Clarkson? Well, Nick was there because Mom was a nurse, and so was Grams, and they loved their jobs. The other kids here were a mix, too, a dozen of them, along with the principal's husband, who was probably there to help keep an eye on the pricey equipment. And of course Tío, cleaning up after lunch.

And the PT, who was talking about healing after trauma. Which Nick had forgotten could be a physical thing as well.

OLIVIA

Olivia's blood pounded as she followed her gun along the endless metal side of the white van. *Cálmete,* she ordered herself. *You really don't want to empty your gun into somebody's confused* abuelo.

But she got as far as the open door and nobody's grandfather had stepped out. Olivia braced herself, then whirled around with her gun covering the interior.

Both seats were empty.

So was the rest of the van.

She sagged in relief at the sight of that long expanse of clean floor. No barrels of fertilizer-and-fuel-oil explosives, at least. Could it be that bike lock was innocent? Insanely stupid, illegal as hell — and innocent?

But Mrs. Hopkins knew nothing about it. And Mrs. Hopkins knew everything. *Now* ask Linda?

No, first things first.
Find the damn driver.

Mina realized that she was happy. In the last eleven months she'd been a lot of things, but happy? That word was way too simple for what Mina had been. But today, standing in the near-empty cafeteria while the PT talked about why he liked sports medicine, it occurred to Mina that the world was a better place than it had been for a long time.

It wasn't just that Brendan had come in at last. And it wasn't even because, after handing Mr. Kendrick his late slip, he'd walked around all the others and come to stand *right next to her*! (Looking all preoccupied, maybe, but boys just had to seem cool, didn't they?)

No, Brendan's arrival might have made her aware of her happiness, but it wasn't the cause of it — not the whole cause. She was happy, Mina decided, because of that tapestry thing Ms. McDonald had talked about.

These were the people she was woven in with. Her family. Brendan, sure, but also Mr. Kendrick, quietly ready to lend a hand — to a girl who liked languages, or a guest speaker with equipment, or a janitor with lunch tables to move. Tío himself was a kind of family, the old man folding up all those tables to clean the floors completely, instead of just pushing his mop around their wheels like the old janitor used to. Tío cared about the school, and as far as Mina was concerned, he was more her "uncle" than any of the ones in Rio or Tehran. Even weird Nick Clarkson, next to Mr. Kendrick: she didn't really know Nick, since he was two grades below her, but he was a nice kid, and was risking a lot to stand up for Bee, in spite of all the trouble she'd brought him.

And outside the cafeteria, the rest of her school family: Sofia, of course, who'd spent the past year fighting hard for some scraps of happiness. And in the same room with Sofe, right now, Chaco Cabrera, who didn't know it (yet!) but the girl he scowled at so fiercely was seriously interested in him.

And the further threads — like Sergeant Olivia Mendez. Mina suspected Sergeant Mendez felt this way about the whole town.

And of course Principal McDonald, standing tall at the head of a school that even Mina could see was getting better because of her. And beyond those, at the other end of a text, Mâmân, fragile and strong.

Mina felt like humming with pride.

Brendan

Brendan didn't hear a word the PT was saying. He wondered that the people next to him weren't staring at his chest, where his heart was thumping wildly as it waited for everything to start. Any minute now, the cafeteria door he was staring at was going to come open . . .

OLIVIA

Olivia pressed her ear to the crack between the gym doors, hearing mostly the thuds of her heart. No bike locks here, no van. And a man speaking inside, in a normal voice. No trace of alarm, no panic. Lecturing.

The driver couldn't have passed by more than a minute or two ago. Of course, if that *was* his voice inside, so calm and even, the guy was an outright nut job.

Olivia worked the handle, the door clicked open: not locked. The voice kept on — something about training camp. With the gun at the back of her thigh, she opened the door a couple of inches: Coach Gilbert, forty kids scattered across a patch of bleachers, and the retired baseball player.

Coach saw the door move and started to get up. Olivia forced a smile and shook her head, letting the door drift shut.

If he wasn't here, that left the equipment shed across the drive or the school itself.

She dismissed the shed instantly, because honestly who cared, when there were hundreds of students off to her right?

Gun still tucked against her leg, Olivia reached the end of the gym. She leaned forward to look around the corner: lunch shelter, school yard, outdoor courts, playing fields beyond. Completely empty but for a figure on the far side of the baseball diamond, walking slowly back from the far fence carrying a black bag.

So he must've gone down one of the quads. And though she kept trying to convince herself that there could be an innocent explanation for that damned bike lock (though by God if there was she'd string 'im up), just now she couldn't really believe it. Not when her pounding heart was shouting at her that Guadalupe was running out of time.

LINDA

Linda sat against the edge of the teacher's desk in room B18, back to the door. She was telling the students about her experiences as a young nurse and teacher in Papua New Guinea when she heard the door come open. She figured it was Tom Atcheson — who no doubt had some excellent reason for not bothering to arrive on time — but because he'd irritated her with his high-handed attitude (to say nothing of his lack of concern over Brendan), she decided to make him wait for her to finish what she was saying.

Until twenty-eight bodies went rigid in their seats, twenty-eight faces going taut with shock.

She spun away from the desk, arms outstretched as if to hold the kids back from threat.

All she could see was the black maw of a massive pistol, pointing straight at her.

At the end of the gym, a pair of bathrooms faced the lunch shelter. They should be empty, but as Olivia passed under the girls' room window, she heard a sound. A whisper? Something dragging across the tiles? Where the hell was Torres? It felt like an hour . . .

She flicked a glance down at her watch: two *minutes* since she'd talked to Mrs. Hopkins? Jesus.

The restroom door was set back behind a narrow section of wall that blocked the view from the tables. It was the worst possible layout for a right-handed cop: by the time Olivia's gun cleared the door frame, her whole body would be exposed.

She took hold of the handle (*If this is all some kid's joke, I'll castrate the little bastard!*) then yanked it back and leapt inside, crouching with the gun before her.

The bathroom was empty, but the door's

crash and the noise of her entrance didn't quite cover a quick scuffle and squeak of alarm. One of her knees gave a crack as she squatted to look under the stall dividers: legs, just inside the handicapped stall — four legs, not two, wearing jeans and middle-school shoes. Unless the guy was standing on a toilet . . .

"Girls?"

"Yes?" The voice was high, but naturally so: not that of a terrified child with a gun in her face.

"Is there anyone in here with you?" The door lock clicked. Two girls, wide-eyed, looked out — Esme Gustafson and a friend. "Show me your hands."

Both girls' arms came around: cellphones, with matching pink covers.

"Is anyone else here?"

The friend spoke over Esme's shoulder. "Just us. We needed to —"

"Doesn't matter. Shut this door after me, and lock it. Don't let anyone in until I come and tell you. There's a . . . there's a burglar on the school grounds."

Burglars sounded infinitely less threatening than lunatic terrorists or vengeful drug lords, but the two girls hastened out of the stall. The moment Olivia stepped out of the restroom, she heard the dead bolt turn, fol-

486

lowed by furious whispers.

This would be all over the Internet in ten minutes flat.

Olivia studied the grounds again from behind the narrow section of wall. The figure coming from the fence-line was Señora Rodriguez, she decided — who would *not* be placidly collecting trash if she'd seen something out of place. Olivia came into the open to peer down B Quad. Empty tables. A row of nine closed doors — or at least semi-closed — along the quad's far side. There were three partially open doors, emitting a mix of talking voices.

She came out of the shadows and into the quad, keeping an eye on the right-hand doors leading to the gym and cafeteria. All shut, but no bicycle locks.

Cafeteria first, she decided, then the classrooms. By that time Torres and Wong better damn well be here. And once they knew who the van belonged to, they'd have an idea if they were looking for gang-bangers, drunk fathers, bona-fide terrorists — or some random maniac she'd missed entirely. She could text Mrs. Hopkins and check on Sofia Rivas and Nick Clarkson, since Taco Alvarez was pissed off at one of them and Charles Cuomo at the —

But that was as far as Olivia Mendez got.

Before the thought was finished, before her hand had even started to stretch out for the cafeteria doors, hell broke loose at Guadalupe Middle School.

LINDA

The gun pointed at Linda forever, threatening to swallow her up in its yawning black mouth. She was too terrified to move — not for herself, but because of the children behind her. If one of them started to panic . . .

Her eye, casting about frantically for something that wasn't the end of a gun, caught on the Band-Aid wrapped around one of the man's fingers. For some absurd reason, the banality of the tiny wound changed matters. It freed her to speak — although addressing eight hundred faces in the gymnasium was nothing compared to the effort of summoning words now, in calm, even, comforting tones. "Kids, you know what to do in an emergency, we've drilled this. Just sit quietly for a minute, and we'll figure it out together. Sir, I wonder if we might —"

That was as far as her speech got. She

didn't hear what drew his attention, but when he turned to glance back through the partially open door, whatever was out there set him off. His heavy gym bag dropped with a metallic clatter as his hands came up to the stance seen on a million television shows.

When he started pulling the trigger, the twenty-eight children behind her began to scream.

___

Olivia Mendez was the first to fall.

Even if her sidearm had been up and aimed at the door of B18 — even if she'd been prepared to fire in the direction of the kids hidden behind it — she still wouldn't have had a chance. The first bullet spun her around and threw her police-issue Glock against the cafeteria doors. The second punched through the wood, and then the wall behind her began to explode into pocks — four, five times — before the eighth round plowed up under the edge of her vest. She went still. Blood began to edge down the concrete.

Every student in the school was bolt upright in instant terror. In the Visitors' lot, the *Clarion* reporter, checking her cell for the latest painful insider news of the Alvarez trial, jerked, gaping out the car window. Across the road, the field workers straightened up from their planting, staring open-mouthed at the sprawl of buildings.

Two miles away, a police cruiser finished its U-turn and flicked on its strobing lights, to accelerate up the road from town.

GORDON

Noise hit the cafeteria like a jackhammer. At the first *BLAM,* the PT dropped a dumbbell, Tío jerked upright, the children all stared at each other in confusion — and Gordon spun around to face the quad. An instant later, a second explosion punched a hole through the farther set of quad doors, zipping past Gordon to hit the stage and spray the air with splinters. The kids shrieked, the speaker bolted, Tío cursed, his mop hitting the floor, and Gordon was in motion. At the fourth *BLAM,* Gordon's shoulder slammed into a folded-up table and began to shove. Tío was halfway toward the children. At the ninth, Brendan gave a startled noise as Mina collapsed into his arms.

By then, most of the kids were fleeing after the panicked speaker, who had abandoned the closer set of access-road doors and was racing for the other pair. Tío was gathering the kids who hadn't bolted, shoving them from the line of fire, while Gordon had worked the locks on the farther quad doors and was sprinting toward the others, hauling another folded-up table as he went.

As the fifteenth round slapped the wall, Gordon finished bolting the doors and rammed the table against them, whirling to look at the cafeteria.

One more shot, then a pause. Ringing silence emphasized the sobs of children, the ragged curses of the guest speaker, struggling at the access-road doors, and the wordless noises of comfort from Tío.

The school siren rose up. But in the moment before the wail drowned out all thought, a boy's voice trickled through the cafeteria, strained and thin.

"Mr. Kendrick? I think . . . I think Mina's been shot."

Seconds after the gunfire ended, the lock-down siren began to bellow. It was a known noise, and triggered the automatic response of much-rehearsed drills. Doors were slammed shut. Locks were turned, blinds jerked down, lights slapped off. Guest speakers watched as students leapt from their seats to hunker along the edges of the rooms. Teachers snapped out orders for silence, moved to help the kids with mobility problems, and told the guests what to do. The students in the gym stood up in the bleachers, and after a moment of confusion, Coach ordered them to the boys' locker room — yes, girls, too. In the quad-side window of the girls' bathroom, Esme Gustafson's face came into view. Her eyes went wide at a sight from a video game: a man in a baseball cap, shooting — then Esme jerked backward with a squawk as the bathroom's other occupant remembered the drill and snatched her down.

Three employees did not follow the rules of the drill. For the kitchen ladies, the daily 12:40 bell was their signal to finish loading the dishwashers, roll down the service screens, and (on a nice afternoon like this) go out to sit in the sun for half an hour, their first break since morning. As usual, they took their lunch — and Karen, her pack of cigarettes. Because of the cigarettes, the three ladies kept plastic chairs on the far side of the windowless, concrete-block equipment shed where no one would see them. They were six minutes into their break when the gunfire started. Karen dropped her half-smoked stub, Susanna's coffee flew into the air, and Maria said a phrase her family would not have believed she knew. All three were on their feet, staring wildly at each other as shots smashed through the air. Six, eight — a dozen? Too fast to count, and then . . . silence followed, stretching out . . .

All three squeaked when the siren began to wail.

Maria crossed herself and crept to the corner of the shed, peering down the access road at the back of the school. What she saw confused her. The white van hadn't been there earlier, or they wouldn't have got out the door. The others tugged her back into the safety of the concrete blocks. She crossed herself again with a shaking hand, and told them what she'd seen.

Karen gave a sob. Susanna reached for her cellphone. But when the next volley of shots came, terrifyingly close, the ladies broke and ran for the apple orchard.

Not so the front office. At the first set of shots, Mrs. Hopkins struggled up from her chair to lunge for the panic button. She picked up the phone, snapping orders to her three waiting students as she hit the numbers. They instantly moved to pull the door's shade, turn the lock, and drop the window-blinds, then hunkered down in the lee of the counter. Mrs. Hopkins told the 911 responder that she had to step away for a minute, handing the phone to the most sensible of the three — the girl — while she hurried to the principal's office to do the routine with lock, blinds, and lights. She came back, took the telephone, gave the kids some reassuring words (calling each by name), then lowered herself awkwardly to the floor beside them, putting the receiver to her ear again.

Library; teachers' lounge; computer lab; music center: all the school's rooms were shut and motionless but for the vibrations of terror, the clamor of the siren overriding the whimpers of frightened adolescents.

All the school's rooms, that is, except B18, and across the quad from it, the cafeteria.

GORDON

The world stopped. The Atcheson boy looked up, white-faced, a pietà with Nick and another boy standing behind, while Mina, little Yasmina . . .

She lay in the boy's arms, paint-blackened eyes going wide at the realization of pain — and memory slapped at Gordon, hard and vivid: looking down at the face of another small and bloody woman, dying in his arms. Phrases rattled through his useless brain: *Mina's been shot, shot, minasbeenshot and my god where was linda but minasbeen shot* —

The breath Gordon took was like the jolt of a defibrillator. The world started again — with the blaring awareness that only wooden doors and a folded table stood in the way of the bullets. "Go!" he yelled at the boys, bending to scoop Mina up. "Go go *go!*"

She was so tiny (*Jasmin oh god Jasmin hold on*) and ridiculously light, crooning in pain against his chest now as he wondered (*impossible, surely?*) if he'd brought (*could it be?*) this evil upon innocence, setting a revenge-driven corporate heel onto children.

Halfway across the endless room, his mind began to elbow aside panic and deliver cold analysis: line of fire was door to stage — so a single shooter (so far) at the far end of B Wing. Steel door on Tío's office: accept the trap, or risk breaking cover? Mendez? Even if she's already down, there'll be a SWAT team here in minutes.

(*Linda?!*) He pushed away that thought, too, and barked out orders.

"Everybody in the janitor's room. Clear a space for Mina, find some blankets. Tío, you have a first-aid kit? Somebody call 911, tell them the shooter's on the west side of B Wing, at the upper end. You —" The PT — where was he? Still near the back doors. "Don't open those! There could be a second shooter. You have medical training?"

The man let go of the handles. "Do you —"

Shots hit the quad-side door again, slapping the folded table into the room a few inches every time. The children squealed and pushed inside the office, making it hard to deliver Mina onto the heap of old blankets. She cried out as Gordon laid her

500

down, grabbing his hand. He bent to kiss
her forehead, then shifted to make room for
the reluctant PT.

"I'm not going, Mina, but let the man take
a look. You'll be fine."

Her eyes held his as he gently pulled free,
retreating as far as the door. The little room
was packed, even with four of them still
outside. Until the shooter moved, Nick and
Brendan were safe where they were, just
outside the door. Gordon looked at Tío —
then looked more closely. "You're bleeding."

The old man glanced down at his ragged
left sleeve, stained with blood. "It is nothing. We must get the children to safety."

"Have the PT strap it when he's finished
with Mina. And the kids should be safe
enough — the walls are concrete and your
door's steel. We'll close ourselves inside if
the shooter moves."

Tío had other ideas. "The storage shed,
across the drive —"

The therapist, who had found a pair of
scissors in the first-aid kit, spoke up. "We
can't reach the shed. The doors are locked."

Tío frowned at the obvious. "I have keys."

"From the outside — something's blocking all the back doors. None of them open
more than a few inches."

Above the shots, over the wailing alarm, Gordon heard the breath leave Tío's lungs. The old man swayed, his phlegmatic brown face rigid with horror. *"Ay, Madre."*

Tío: his story

Ellos me llaman «Paleta Man» . . .

They call me "Paleta Man," here in my new country.

Paleta is ice cream, but in San Felipe, the Ice Cream Man has a tall truck covered with bright pictures and signs saying WATCH FOR CHILDREN, with a loudspeaker that plays the same notes over and over, exciting the children and driving their parents mad.

I do not own a truck with loud music. Trucks cost much money, even the old ones, and I am a poor man.

Pero yo soy contento: but I am content. I own a small cart with three wheels and a handle to push it by, with thick insulated sides and a pair of harmonious bells. The children listen for me, and when I turn the corner of their street and play my bells, they run out with their coins to stand looking at my own pictures. They point or they tell me

503

what they want and I reach in and then close the top quickly, taking their money and wishing them a good day. They are polite children, most of them, as the children of poor people tend to be, so they thank me and I walk on, leaving them to their young pleasures of sweet ice. I have been other things in my life, but here, now, I am the paleta man. I sell small measures of happiness in a way that allows me to be out in the open air, and gives me gentle exercise, and keeps me in contact with friendly children. Why would I not be content?

True, it is not much of a job for a man. Certainly it is a job beneath a man who has been to university, who was the headmaster of a village school, in the peaceful days before the soldiers came.

In a better time, another age, I would still be living in that village, writing on the chalkboard and teaching the children history and government and the rules of grammar. I would have a wife, her hair gone gray, who would greet me when I came home and sit with me before the fire in the evenings. I would have grandchildren, perhaps, to read to and to teach. Instead, the war began, and our village was very near to where the revolt boiled up out of discontent and hunger.

Before we thought to worry, there were rebels in the streets, then soldiers. Between the rope sandals of the one and the leather boots of the other, our quiet village was trampled to death.

I was away when my village died, on a mathematics training course. The lecture hall began to buzz with rumor, and I left the city to hitchhike on trucks and motor scooters, and to run in my formal shoes until I reached my village to find smoke and uniforms and television cameras. The tents of the Red Cross were filled with cries.

And my school, my beloved school, center of the village's hopes and dreams? Those men chose the school as the place to end hope. They gathered our children inside. They chained the doors. They smashed the windows and propped their guns on the sills. The child who survived said the men laughed at their shrieks.

My son was still warm when I found him in the Red Cross tent, but he was not breathing.

My wife also died. Not then, but fourteen days later, when she went to the river with her pockets full of stones. I will say no more about her death, because when I do she haunts my dreams, and I am ready to forget. As if that were possible. As if my schoolteacher's hands could forget what they did to the man who ordered the death of my village, once I caught up with him. Blood is so very hot; it shocks the skin when it spills, and the hands never lose that memory. Never.

I am no longer a schoolmaster, no longer a father and husband taking his revenge. My hands are twisted with age as they push their paleta cart up and down the streets of San Felipe where once, I would have been merely one of a dozen kinds of deliverymen. Now only I walk there. Even the newspaper comes from the metal skin of a vehicle.

Because I walk through my *barrio* and do not steer a truck down its streets, my knowledge of the area is close. Intimate. I hear arguments and drug deals and love-making. I see corruption and violence and beauty. I know that a husband has found a job when his children buy real ice creams instead of cheap frozen water. I hear when the teenaged son of a family gets arrested, or when a girl gets in trouble. I know which house is occupied by illegal immigrants and which spreads the plague of the darker drugs. People tell me which *coyote* can be trusted not to abandon his charges in the desert, and I see where a local dealer stores his pills and packets, for fear the police knock down his front door.

One morning, a year or two ago, I heard a gunshot. A large man ran from the back of a shop, pausing to drop something behind a garbage can before he fled in his powerful car. When I went to see, I found a thick roll of $100 bills, six tiny packets of white powder, and a gun. Before I could direct the police toward it (which I have done, once or twice, when I came across wrongdoings), I heard that the man had crashed his car and died. So I kept what I found, lest a child come across it.

Yes, these things and more I know, because I walk the streets and people talk to me, in the neighborhood between the shops of Main Street and the industrial lots behind it.

My own home lies among the fields outside of town, a small trailer whose front supports an enormous rose bush with flowers of palest yellow that become rose hips of dark red — very like the one my young wife planted at our front door in my village in the hills. At the back is an arbor of grape and chayote squash, with a fenced-in garden of tomato and nopal, chilis and marigolds. It makes for a long, dusty walk to town, but it is worth the effort, to be able to spend summer evenings sitting under my arbor with a book from the library, breathing the smell of roses and listening to the silence.

Most of the people who live where I sell my paletas have neither silence nor roses. Trains rumble close to the houses, refrigerated trucks wait with their engines running, wandering dogs are hit by speeding teenagers.

It was just such a thing that got me started on the other side of my work as a paleta man: a dog that was struck, and lay suffering loudly.

I was two streets away when I heard the shriek of the tires and the loud gulping howl of the dog, and I knew at once what it was. The noise did not stop. When I turned the corner past the sweet-smelling *panaderia* and saw the faces of the mothers hurrying their frightened children away from the sound, I knew that it would be up to me to stop the torment.

I knew the dog, of course. Any man who walks the streets discovers which dogs must be watched and which are trustworthy, and this old bitch was a sweet-tempered creature with dry yellow fur. Her boy loved her, and always shared his ice cream with her. But the boy was at school, his parents at work, and the dog lay in the gutter with her hind quarters scarlet with blood.

It was not as if my hands had not done such jobs before. I had been killing chickens for the table since I was a child, and I had put a dog out of its misery before. No need to feel the heat of spilled blood on my hands here, and it would be a mercy — to the creature and to the neighborhood.

I reached into my paleta cart and took out one of the old dog's favorite ice-cream bars. I squatted near her and made something of a show out of unwrapping the bar. She kept howling, but she was also watching my hands. When the treat was free of its paper, I took it by its stick and held it out. After a moment the terrible noise faltered, and her mouth came down greedily on the cold, creamy bar.

As she slobbered her way through it, I stretched out my hand — carefully, since a mortally wounded animal is an unpredictable thing — and stroked her head. Now was the time for gentle hands to remove her from pain.

Except that close up, I could see that the injury was not to her spinal column, but to her leg.

The break was bad. It might even require surgery. And the family was poor. I sat on my heels for a moment, thinking, then looked up at the others — mostly women, but also two young men brought from their houses by the noise. I rejected the one with the bloodshot eyes, and spoke to the other.

"I will go and fetch the veterinarian, if you would keep distracting her with ice creams. There are four, so make them last."

One of the women shook her head. "That doctor won't cross the street unless you hand him money first."

I got to my feet, wincing at the crack from my old knees. "He will come."

I warned the boy to keep his hands clear from danger, and made my way to the animal clinic, three blocks away. The waiting room had several people there with various creatures, but I politely pushed toward the back, and was soon in a room with the doctor. I explained what I needed. He said, "And who will pay me for *that*?"

I had intended to offer him money. I did, after all, have a roll of $100 bills. But as I looked into his eyes, I also remembered what I knew about his business, and I decided that there was a better use for that money. So instead, I smiled, and I said that he would do this for the neighborhood, free of charge. Either that or the police would learn who had been making illegal sales of a drug called ketamine.

The man's bluster froze. He looked at the

open door, then turned to the cabinet and took out his traveling bag.

The dog wore a plaster cast for some weeks, and limps still. The boy now attends the local college, where his tuition is paid by the occasional envelope of $100 bills. The two still happily share ice creams, when they get the chance.

The incident with the dog occurred during my third season behind the paleta cart, but after that day I became everyone's Tío, their helpful uncle. The women refused to let their children buy from the noisy truck when it ventured into my territory, driving him off with their closed purses. They found small jobs for me — repairing a spitting light switch, putting a strong new lock on a door to keep out an angry boyfriend, opening a bedroom window sealed dangerously shut by the paint of years. Once or twice I assisted residents with their newly arrived family members, when *la Migra* came sniffing about. People paid me when they could, gave me vegetables from their gardens, but mostly they bought my paletas, even if the ice cream was a little soft.

I see that I have gone on long with my tale, and yet only now is the story of Tamara Miller beginning. But I do not apologize, because without knowing about the cart and the dog and the little jobs old Tío Jaime the Paleta Man was sometimes called on to perform, my involvement in one woman's problems would surely seem the stuff of an old man's imagination.

But now you know that I am Tío, friend to the *barrio.*

So I knew how the husband of a young woman named Tamara Miller would beat her on two Fridays every month. He would receive his pay, he would cash it at the cashing service next door to the bar on Main Street, he would go into the bar. After some hours, he would go home and hit her. The next day she would not come out of her house. Two or three days later, she would emerge to buy from me one of the ice-cream cups I sell to be eaten with a small flat wooden spoon — a little reward, I think, for surviving another round with her husband's fists, and a tiny gesture of revenge, that his money should be spent on her luxury.

On those days I wanted to refuse her money — but I did not, for fear that she would no longer come out to buy this taste of sweetness for herself. In this matter, her small pride was more important than my own.

She was a nice woman, was Tamara Miller, pretty in that pale way some Anglos have when their hair is too dark to be called blond and too light to be brown. She was tiny, shorter even than my wife, whose head used to rest beneath my chin when I wrapped my arms around her and held her close. Señora Miller's house was the cleanest place in a neighborhood of clean houses — which could not have been easy, since it stood at the end of the busy road with its back on a field, from both of which the dust rose in clouds at every wind. She had a nice garden, too, vegetables and flowers, and when she bought her little cup of chocolate ice cream and peeled off the top to eat it slowly, sometimes we would stand and pass a few words about what she was growing. Two or three times I brought her cuttings from my own garden, so that next to her front door there grew a small rose of palest yellow. I looked at it every time I went past her gate, greeting it as a friend.

Tamara Miller had no real neighbors. On one side of her house lay the yards of a plumbing supply business, on the other rose up the high, blank wall of a warehouse. Across the street was a printer's, and behind her back fence stretched fields. It was a busy place during the day, but everything shut down in the evenings. After dusk the street was deserted.

One morning, three days after the first Friday in the month of May, I sold Tamara Miller a cup of ice cream. She had trouble holding the flat wooden spoon because one of her fingers was in a splint. I said nothing and went about my business, but a short time later I stood with my elbow on the fence of another woman who lived not far from the Miller house.

Señora Rodriguez was a retired cannery worker whose children had grown and whose fingers had itched for grandchildren. She had spent most of her life organizing people, from her husband to the union, and I knew well that nothing would give her greater pleasure than organizing Tamara Miller. I leaned against the fence watching her grandchildren revel in the sugary pleasures she had bought them.

"Do you know Tamara Miller?" I asked her. "In the house near the plumbing supply?"

"Sure. She's very stuck-up."

Actually, what she said was that the Miller girl acted like she had a stick up a part of her body. I said, "It's not the stick up there that troubles her, it's the fist she gets in her face."

"She's not the only one around here," said Señora Rodriguez. She sounded as if she was throwing the problem away, but in truth I knew that she was one of those that women in trouble turned to, and she could be as fierce as a tiger in how she helped them. We often act in ways that conceal our true feelings, especially when those feelings are strong.

"That is true," I said, trying to sound like I was apologizing for all the wrongdoing by all the men who ever lived. "But she is also very young, and without a family. It is too bad she cannot find some way of reaching out for friendship. Maybe she could take a cooking class down at the adult school, if her husband would let her. She was asking me the other day about how to make chiles rellenos. What do I know? Ah well, I must be going. My ice creams will melt in this sun."

As I left, I let my eyes rest on the row of thick, proud chili plants the Señora had along the side of her house. Chiles rellenos, indeed.

That is how Tamara Miller began to make friends in her neighborhood, and learn that there were services in the community to help women like her, things you could divorce a man for that didn't involve calling the police. Over the next few weeks I thought she was going to make it. It seemed to me as if the yellow rose nodded at me in approval, when one third Friday of the month went past and on the Saturday morning there she was, at work in her garden. Señora Rodriguez brought other neighbors to see the pale Anglo woman. The smell of chilis and cumin sometimes overcame the dust smell of the plumbing supply yard next door, and Tamara Miller began to blossom like a neglected plant given water and sun. I told myself what a clever fellow I was, to set such a thing in motion.

Why, why do we never learn?

In truth, though, it should have ended happily. In my village it might have, because the women were strong and in and out of each other's lives all the time, and had brothers and uncles to help them. In this country it is not always that way. It is especially not that way for the poor.

Perhaps if I had not interfered, if I had not arranged for Señora Rodriguez to take Tamara Miller under her wing, then nothing worse would have happened other than a young woman's black eyes and careful walk. I did mean well, but before the month was out, I saw how wrong I was, and I saw where it would end.

One Wednesday, Señor Miller lost his job. That evening his wife came near to losing her life. If one of Señora Rodriguez's friends had not been bringing a paper bag full of tomatillos to Tamara Miller and run to call the police, the husband might have murdered her. Instead, he was jailed for two days until his wife came home from the hospital with plaster on her arm. When she would not press charges, he moved back home. He got another job.

Two months later it happened again.

Six weeks after that, again.

I was no longer content in that neighborhood. The inability of the police to stop a man from beating his wife to death preyed on my mind and visited me with nightmares of my own wife's end. A layer of invisible smoke seemed to lie over the whole area, and the paleta cart became heavier and heavier to push toward it as the cool mornings of autumn came along.

Señora Rodriguez did not give up. She checked on the young woman every day. She brought her food, got her involved in some committee working to ask the city for stop signs. She took her to the doctor to have the plaster removed from her arm, and to the clinic to have stitches taken out, and to the hospital to have her ribs X-rayed, and all the while she talked to Tamara Miller about her options. A divorce, the Women's

Shelter, something called a restraining order. Tamara Miller listened to all the advice, and nodded, and did nothing. She stopped coming out of her house to buy a cup of ice cream from me. Her house ceased to smell of cumin. When I caught glimpses of her, she seemed to me even smaller, stooped over and thin as a broomstick.

When Señora Rodriguez explained to me about restraining orders, I only looked at her. Señor Miller was a powerful young man. He made his living moving heavy objects from trucks to warehouses and back again, and his shoulders were massive. I could not imagine a piece of paper restraining those shoulders. Señora Rodriguez saw the doubt in my eyes, and shrugged. He did not want his wife to leave him; no one in the neighborhood wanted her to stay. The differences in the two points of view were as far apart as those of the government and the rebels in my village. And as likely to lead to bloodshed.

That shrug of Señora Rodriguez's stayed with me all that day and into the night. I sat long in the doorway of my trailer, the last roses drooping off the vine above my head, looking into the soft darkness and hearing the cars go by. If a woman wants to kill herself, the shrug said, what can we do?

The following day I learned that Tamara Miller had been taken to the hospital. This time she would be in for days, even a week. Her husband was already out on bail.

I stood looking at the child who told me this news, my mind gone dark, until the gentle touch of a hand on mine brought me back.

"You okay, Tío?"

"Yes, of course, Thomas. Oh — here is your juice bar. And you, Lupe, what can I get for you today?"

I did not think that Tamara Miller wished to kill herself. I thought that she was trying to become so small that her husband would not notice her. And I thought that if her husband were removed from her life, just for a time, she might be permitted to breathe, and to see that there were other ways to go ahead.

The old dog, it seemed, had taught Tío a new trick: one that would work for other situations than that of an injured leg and a veterinarian selling animal tranquilizers to people.

I walked back to my home that afternoon feeling light for the first time in weeks. After dark, I retrieved the murderer's gun from its hiding place, along with the six packets of drugs and the still-thick roll of illicit money. I separated out half the bills, then cleaned and oiled the weapon, taking care not to touch it with my bare hands. When the roads had fallen quiet, I put on my darkest clothing and made my way back into San Felipe.

Miller's large black pickup truck was not in his driveway. I waited long enough to be certain that I was alone, then crossed the street and went through the gate, up the walk, and took the key from the chipped flowerpot where I had seen Tamara Miller put it.

Inside, after only two days of his wife's absence, the house had begun to stink like the lair of a carrion eater. A light in the kitchen showed debris on every surface. Beer cans surrounded a large stuffed chair, planted ten feet from the huge television screen.

My only regret was that I had no way of adding the man's fingerprints to the gun or the packets. However, I found his hair-brush and sifted its contents down over the items on the sink, working them into the money with my gloved hands. (Is it not amazing, what one can learn from the library?) That would have to do.

I was just in the process of hiding everything on a high shelf in the living room when the windows flared with headlights, and a large motor rumbled up the street. It stopped in front of the house. The lights went out, the truck's door slammed, and a key fumbled at the front door lock.

By then I was inside a room I doubted the man ever set foot in, a tiny space at the back given over to his wife's sewing projects. I stood in the dark listening to his drunken progress through the house: toilet, refrigerator, the snap of a beer can, the thump of his body going onto the chair. I expected the television to go on, but the silence stretched out . . .

After a minute, a faint thump, then a snore.

The snores did not fade as I went silently up the hallway toward the front room. There I saw the explanation of the smaller sound: a near-full can of beer had fallen from his slack hand to soak the carpet.

Tamara Miller had been so proud of that carpet, when they installed it the summer before. She told me it took her three years to save the money.

I stood in the doorway, listening to the creature's snores, and remembered another time I had stood in a doorway, a thousand miles and half a lifetime away.

That door had belonged to a bedroom.

That man had been sprawled on his back across a bed, head tipped, neck exposed: an invitation. That time it had been a knife.

But unlike tonight, there was no hesitation. It had taken me weeks to track him down, and although I would gleefully have chained shut his doors and laughed at his shrieks, the house was filled with servants, and discovery would let him slip away for good. So I delayed only to send a quick prayer to my wife and son, shaping the sign of the cross at my breast, before I slid the sharp point into place, and the hot gush shocked my hands.

Tonight, though, I did hesitate. Drugs, money, and the gun used in a murder, all planted on a shelf for the police to find, following an anonymous telephone call.

Was that enough?

The police themselves had failed Tamara Miller. The court system offered her nothing but holes. Her family was distant, her friends unable to protect her.

If I did not care for her, who would?

Planting the evidence would be far safer — for me: a man known to be a friend of the young wife. A man with no one to say he was home in bed.

But how many more beatings would the safe solution mean for her?

My eyes traveled to the high shelf, then down to the exposed throat. The windows outside showed nothing but silent roadway and the sides of industrial buildings.

With a sigh, I crossed the room and climbed onto the stool to retrieve what I had left there. I pushed the money and the drugs into my coat pocket, and climbed down with the gun.

It took three days before the police came to speak with me about the death of Mr. Miller. They were puzzled, and well on their way to calling it a suicide, but wished to be thorough in their investigation. I gave them what they wanted — a sad agreement that he had not been a nice man — and managed to wake no suspicions on their part.

They left. Tamara Miller came home from the hospital. Life went on.

Then one day last September, Señora Rodriguez came driving along my dirt road, at an hour when the cool sea air was beginning to creep over the fields. With her was Tamara Miller.

The two ladies had spent the day making tamales, a thing women do when they wish to share their kitchen with the world. They brought me a plate piled high. I thanked them both, and sat them under my arbor with glasses of the drink I make from my lemons and the rose hips.

I had seen the Señora any number of times since that night. Once or twice she had seemed on the edge of asking a question, only to withdraw it unspoken. She seemed about to do so now, but glanced at her young companion and changed her mind.

Instead, she looked from the rust-dotted surface of my trailer to the worn state of my boots, and said that if I was interested in a job that was less demanding and more steady than selling paletas, she had heard that a janitor's position was opening up at Guadalupe Middle School.

At the word *school,* my entire body gave a twist of revulsion: children and blackboards; the hopes of a village drowned in blood. I coughed to conceal my reaction, and gave her polite thanks, saying that I would consider it. Not that I had any intention of doing so.

At the door of her car, Señora Rodriguez paused to admire my rose bush, commenting that it would be a glory in the spring. And then she gave me a look, as if to say that our business was not finished, before she and Tamara Miller got into the car and drove away.

As I sat in my doorway and watched the dust settle, three yellow petals drifted down onto my old hand. After a moment, I looked up.

The pale yellow roses are, in truth, very beautiful.

Y yo soy contento.

And I am content.

Gordon seized the old man's arm to keep him from collapsing — but Tío snapped back from wherever he had gone, his eyes focusing on Gordon's.

"*Cada puerto?* Locks? On all?"

The PT answered, "I don't know. But none of them open more than a few inches. There's a car parked in front of the ones on this end. Not sure about that other."

Over his shoulder, Gordon saw Mina's bloodstained orange shirt. "Can you stop the bleeding?"

"No. I've slowed it, but she needs an ambulance."

Tío's office: trap or safety? "Did any of you reach 911?"

Head shakes, all around — God, were these the only students on campus without phones? Gordon jabbed a finger at Tío's land line. "Pick it up," he ordered the teary girl perched on the desk beside it. "Is there

526

a dial tone? Dial 9, then 911. Tell them where you are, say we need an ambulance immediately. You, here —" He dug out his phone and thrust it at the nearest set of young fingers. "Text my wife to tell her what's happening. The rest of you, find a place to sit. We'll be here for a while."

LINDA

The noise of the gun was unbelievable, pounding the enclosed space, a series of explosions from that huge pistol in the man's hand. The students threw themselves against the wall, arms over their heads, weeping in fear. *Do something,* she howled at herself. *Do something, for God's sake, before —*

The shooting stopped, the gun . . . was the thing empty? She could jump up, *now,* tackle the shooter, and scream at the kids to *run* — they could pound on the door to the next room, at least they would —

But before she could get to her feet, the gun spat out a black shape and a full one was slapped in: too late. It began all over again, the BLAM and the *ting* of brass bits being ejected.

He was aiming across the quad at the cafeteria. Shooting at the dozen or more

kids in there, shooting at . . .
  Gordon.

GORDON

Gordon stood in the doorway where Mina could see him, counting the second series of gunshots. He'd gone blank for a moment at the sight of the girl's blood, but he thought there might have been sixteen shots in the first series — a fifteen-cartridge magazine with one carried in the chamber. Illegal, but so was shooting up a school.

This time, Gordon kept better count. (*TEN*) The cafeteria seemed to be the main target. Holes were growing in the nearer set of doors (*ELEVEN; TWELVE*), and the table he'd shoved against it (*THIRTEEN*) was now two feet away. He should have taken another two seconds to lock (*FOURTEEN*) the damn wheels.

(*FIFTEEN*)

Another pause. It went on. Longer . . .

LINDA

The gun went empty again. This time, instead of just slapping in a new cartridge and continuing to fire, the man reached for the gym bag at his feet, coming out with another cartridge. In moments, the gun was loaded — but then he reached down to pull out a second weapon, smaller than the first.

As he stood, he glanced up. For the first time, Linda actually saw his face. "Why?" she blurted out. "Why are you doing this?"

"What choice do I have?" His face was handsome and calm and empty of any emotion except determination. "They took everything. Everything I built, invented, invested in, cared for. Everything that was mine. You can't do that to a man, leave him with nothing, can you? Time someone gets that message across." He shoved the big gun into the back of his belt and turned to lower the silver-and-black pistol at the quad.

GORDON

Just as Gordon was beginning to hope Mendez might have taken the shooter down, the firing started again — different now, nowhere near as loud. With less impact on the door. A smaller-caliber weapon.

But for one of the four males at the doorway to Tío's office, it might have been the start of heavy artillery.

At the second of these new rounds, Brendan's head tipped, as if someone had said his name; at the fourth, he wheeled and bolted toward the shredded door.

Only the table slowed the boy enough for Gordon to catch up, jerking him away from danger.

"Let me go!" The lithe figure fought to get back into the line of fire. But Gordon had fifty years and twenty pounds on the boy, and his arms held tight.

"Stop it! Brendan, stop — ow, Christ, don't make me hurt you, you've got to tell me what —"

In the end, he had to shout directly into the boy's ear. *"What the hell is it?"*

At last the struggles paused. "That's . . ." Brendan's chest heaved against Gordon's arms, and it took a moment before he could get the words out. "I know that gun. I know who's shooting. *It's my father.*"

Tom Atcheson: His Story

If Thomas Atcheson had taken his Glock to the board meeting that morning, not one person in the room would have walked out.

His company — *his own . . . FUCKING . . . company!* — stolen from him, in a dribble of cold legal language. *Criminal* charges? Jesus! Could they possibly imagine they had any right to *his* labors? Mindless idiots who couldn't see that a man with a vision might have his own way of pursuing it. Not one of them could see how stupid they were being. Thomas Atcheson had built this company. He'd shaped it and pushed it and fought for it — and these feeble, parasitic, tiny-minded opportunists . . .

They had no idea how far he would go to protect what was his. Just like his wife, who'd dared to imagine that her ten years of service was worth half his life's work — a woman who'd done nothing more than keep house and host a few parties, a woman whose son he'd welcomed and raised and fathered, a woman stupid enough to believe that *she* could threaten *Thomas Atcheson* with a divorce that split his company down the middle.

And now these imbeciles — headed by another woman, a damned Mexican hired because of quotas (*as if some Chicana could run Atcheson Enterprises!*) — these pinheads imagined that they could do to him what his wife had failed to do?

At least they'd had the sense to look frightened, something she hadn't managed until the very end.

The board meeting had lasted less than half an hour, and then they'd had him escorted from the building. HIM. *Escorted. From the building!* Atcheson Enterprises had shown its *founder* to the street.

Rage pounded through his veins. He'd nearly given way to it on the drive home, his hands twitching with the temptation to obliterate that bicyclist who demanded the right of way, that monkey-brained female in the minivan cutting him off. They'd never know how close they came.

Still, he'd arrived home with fenders intact and no blood on his tires. He managed to put on the brakes and turn the key rather than gunning the big engine forward through the garden and into the front door to see how far he could smash before the place came down around his ears . . . But: no. Control was paramount. He sat in the driveway waiting for his pulse to slow, knowing that if he went straight in, if he tracked that meeting's *shit* into his own home, he'd be so angry he'd wreck the place.

After a minute, he forced his trembling hands to reach for his phone, open it up, check his email and messages.

Nothing — not so much as a text — from any of his so-called colleagues. Men and women he'd hired and carried along, smirking and cowering in the distance. Then to rub salt in the wound, the first email was from that damned woman at Brendan's school, sent just minutes after he'd hung up on her to go into the board meeting.

The call itself had been bad enough — first forced to listen to some fatuous tune, and when the principal finally came on, she had the nerve to yammer about how "sorry" she was to hear about his "troubles" before going and sticking her nose into his private business with Brendan. "Difficult patch," my ass. He'd shut her up fast, by asking if *she* was maybe not capable of doing *her* job of keeping the school secure, and ended the call.

And now she wrote a sniveling "follow-up" message to say that he was welcome to cancel if he needed to.

Which might've only pissed him off a little, except for the two emails that followed hers. Both from that little bitch from the local paper who'd cornered him at some party a while back, and tricked him into giving her his personal address.

So she wanted to ask him about criminal charges, did she?

He came very close to smashing the phone onto the driveway and leaping out to grind it under his heel — but instead managed to keep his hands steady, turn the phone off, put it away in his pocket.

Jesus. If ever a situation called for a drink, it was this one.

Even the door lock fought him. He tried turning the key in the opposite direction — as if he could forget which way his own door unlocked — and to his surprise, heard the dead bolt slide. But only when he turned it back did the door open. Could the stupid boy have forgotten to lock the door? Given Tom's current state, it was probably his own distraction.

At any rate, the damn door was open.

Normally at this point he would lay his briefcase on the table, but his briefcase was still in the office (And oh, the memory of his personal assistant — his *assistant*! — fearfully saying that he had to leave its contents behind!) so he laid his keys there instead. A deep breath. Another.

He could do this.

One drink, then a shower to wash away the filth of the morning, and a thorough brushing of teeth to conceal the smell. After that he'd think about Brendan's school and how to tell a collection of illiterate children — some of whom were sure to be illegals — that they, too, could make a fortune in the tech world.

After all, it wasn't like Thomas Atcheson didn't always have a back door.

The only question was, what to do with the boy?

He stood in the silent office with his Georgian cut-glass tumbler of whisky, musing over the problem of Brendan. Except, he slowly realized, the house was not in fact silent, not completely. There was some tiny noise, nagging over his head, constant and unusual. Almost as if . . .

Up in Brendan's bathroom, Tom Atcheson stared in disbelief at the steaming hot water running straight down the hole. It was well after ten o'clock. Had the tap been running more than *two hours*? And at the top of the sink, dried foam dribbled from the unrinsed bristles of the boy's toothbrush, down the glass, and onto the porcelain, with a nauseating clot of it covering the brush. And beyond the sink — the toilet lid stood up, its contents stinking the air of the entire house. For God's sake, was the boy on drugs?

He turned off the tap and stepped over to flush the toilet, grimacing as he lowered the lid. He walked quickly out and down the hall to the boy's bedroom, half expecting to find Brendan passed out on the floor.

The bed was unmade. Clothing lay strewn about in front of the closet, as if some animal had rooted around inside. All four chest drawers stood ajar. A pair of underwear hung from the side of the laundry hamper. Books and papers lay all over.

Back out in the hallway, Tom made a rapid hunt through the other upstairs rooms. Guest room, laundry, storage closet, even Tom's own bedroom and bath: nothing.

Puzzled, and caught between irritation and disbelief — had the boy been beamed up by aliens, for heaven's sake? — Tom's impulse was to check the garage for Brendan's bicycle, but he pushed the very thought away. The boy knew better than to leave for school with the house in this state, no matter how late he was.

Don't tell me Brendan got himself kidnapped? Tom thought. *Today's not a day to ask me for ransom!* Back at the chaotic bedroom, this time he walked inside, taking care not to step on any of the debris covering the floor. *Please don't tell me I need to watch my home become a crime scene? Today of all days.*

It was all he could do to keep his hands from straightening the books and tugging up the bed cover. Even the chair was a drift of papers. On the boy's desk stood a glass filmed with milk. It took a moment for Tom's eyes to focus on the envelope propped up against it (his personal stationery, taken from his office downstairs). Behind it stood a computer disc in a plastic case. He picked both up, shook his head at the childish name of the game — First Person Shooter — then noticed the small sticky-note attached to its front. It read:

FOR YOU AND THE
SAN FELIPE POLICE
DEPARTMENT

Under the note he could see the disc itself — which bore not a commercial game's label, but three words printed in felt pen.

Brendan's name: his old name.

Frowning, Tom dropped the disc and pulled up the back flap, finding two pages of printout. He unfolded them, and read:

Sir,

I wonder if you know that's how I think of you? Not Dad or even Father, but Sir. You probably think that's only right, that's how a son shows respect, but I'm not your son, I've never been your son, your just the man who married my mother. And then killed her. I know you did it, even though they say she killed herself. If that's true, it was only because you made her life so horrible she couldn't go on.

But I know things. You've always thought of me as too stupid for anything but running down a court and throwing a ball through a hoop, but I'm not. I've figured out all kinds of stuff, like the combination of your safe, and the password on your computer.

This is a copy of the disc I'm giving to the police today. You may not know it yet, depending on how fast they move, but by the time you read these words, your life will be headed down the tubes. You can run, or you can wait till they come for you, it doesn't matter to me either way.

I also want you to know that if you'd let me go live with Uncle Ray back when Mom died, none of this would have happened. I'd have been happy, and you'd have gone on doing what you do.

Instead, you kept on grinding away at me until you made me prove I could outsmart you. When you read this, I'll be with Uncle Ray. He'll pick me up from school, after I've had my talk with Ms. McDonald, and we'll go together to the police.

Oh, and something else. Those texts I get all the time from my school friend Jock? That name makes me laugh every time I see it, because they're actualy from someone who's about the opposite of a jock.

That's right: I've been talking to Uncle Ray, all along.

Have a good life, Sir. Maybe I'll see you at your trial.

Brendan James Connelly

Tom read the letter twice. Ray? The boy would choose that shiftless idiot *Ray*? His eyes lifted from the letter, coming to focus on the litter covering the floor. Brutalized textbooks, abandoned binders, the day's assignments.

Period 5, Sports Medicine, taunted the page at his feet. Another great choice the boy had made: a physiotherapist, not even an MD, talking about how to patch together injuries, instead of Thomas Atcheson pointing out how to make a difference in the world.

Tom made his feet move out of the room. Downstairs, he tapped impatient knuckles against the player until it woke up and accepted the disc. He stepped back so he could see the large wall screen, absently picking up the half-empty tumbler he had abandoned at the sound of a running tap.

The first part of the recording followed the same text as the letter, delivered by the boy's annoying voice, his sneering, two-foot-tall face reciting that list of adolescent grievances, declaring that long-forgotten name.

Then the boy got on (as his smirk made clear) with the meat of the matter: how he'd figured out his stepfather's passwords, broken into his safe. Raided his computer. Copied a series of incriminating documents and emails. Methodically. For months. *Months.*

Tom stopped hearing the words. Long minutes later, he realized he was standing in front of a frozen image. The recording had ended. Some time ago.

He hurled the tumbler at the boy's locked face. Glass flew joyously. Brendan disintegrated into a jagged pattern of intersecting lines. Crystal shards crunched underfoot as Tom leapt across the room to hammer at the EJECT button, snatching the scrap of shiny plastic as it emerged and snapping it across, again and then again. He threw those down and smashed his heel against them, over and over, then stood, panting in front of the broken screen. *The fucking little traitor. All I've done for him!* After a time, Tom became aware of a faraway pain: blood, on his hand. Not only had the damned disc stabbed him in the heart, it had sliced his finger as well.

The house really was silent now. Not that it would be for much longer. Even a small-town police department would know what that disc put in their hands. In no time at all, departments known by their initials — FTC, FBI, SEC, you name it — would be pissing on his shackled form.

Tom was prepared for emergencies, of course he was. But he'd always been aware of a major drawback, depressing as hell: every country without extradition treaties was a moral and social garbage dump. He'd be stuck there, surrounded by people he hated, whose bribes sucked him dry. From the beginning, Tom had known that when it came right down to it, he might actually prefer to put a gun to his head.

If it weren't for the disc, that's what he might have gone ahead and done — what had, in truth, been at the back of his mind when he'd come in the front door. Unlock the gun safe, open the fifty-year-old Macallan he'd paid $11,000 for at that charity auction, and drink his way to putting the Glock under his chin.

He heard a tiny *pat,* and looked down to see a drop of blood on the front of his shoe. He grimaced, and went to the kitchen for a paper towel and a Band-Aid. When he came back to his study — his retreat, his safe place, *violated* by the ungrateful cuckoo-boy, who might as well have taken a crap in the middle of his priceless carpet — he took the Macallan's flawless decanter from its glass cupboard, broke the seal, and filled a second of the cut-crystal tumblers with it.

He savored the first swallow, then went back to his desk. The tray on the corner held papers waiting to be shredded or filed. On the top lay that idiotic principal's inane *Welcome to Career Day* letter, reminders and guidelines to speakers who clearly weren't expected to know what they were doing. But there'd been a second page . . .

He slid a finger under the sheet and lifted, looking at the map below.

Conquering adversity was what Thomas Atcheson did . . .

Tom had dutifully gone to parent conferences at least once a year since Brendan started at Guadalupe — a school for ordinary kids, chosen by his ordinary mother, Tom's then-wife. Tom had even attended two or three basketball games, so he knew how the school was laid out. The cafeteria, the gymnasium. The access road up the side.

The layout of the doors.

Studying the map, a dispassionate corner of his mind remarked on how rage could shift from hot and uncontrollable into cold and deliberate. All it took to restore sanity was a step into decision. Once a man had committed to a course of action, the chatter of rage fell away, and life grew simple.

When there was half an inch of the whisky left in his glass, Tom crunched across the broken crystal to the gun safe. *Did the little prick figure out how to get in there as well?* He couldn't tell. Nothing was missing. But like everything else in his study, it felt unclean.

Leaving the safe open, he went upstairs.

When he came down ten minutes later, his hair was damp from the shower and his $7,000 suit was changed for jeans and a gray sweatshirt. In the black ballistic-cloth bag he carried was a handmade deerskin bomber jacket and Brendan's Career Day assignment. He dropped the bag on the desk, pulled out the page, laid it next to the school map — and smiled.

Give Tom Atcheson a locked door, he'd find another way out. Show him a dead end, he'd chisel a path through it.

And if the locked door was the only one, the dead end his only choice?

He'd just blow the fucking things up.

That's what he wanted to do, of course — literally blow the place up. The Atcheson campus was *his* from its concrete foundations to the trees in its atrium, and he'd love nothing more than to lay charges and level it back to dust and rubble. But he didn't think he had the time, not if the police were coming to call . . .

There was another option. Quicker, louder, more immediate — a lesser target, but one the world might regard as being the greater, since it breathed and moved and screamed rather than quietly holding a man's hopes and dreams.

If he couldn't have it, he'd be damned if

some other man would.

He transferred what he thought he'd need from the gun safe to the nylon bag and started to close it, then paused and took out a smaller weapon. Balancing the Bodyguard in his palm for a moment, he gave it a bitter smile, then loaded it and put it in beside his favorite Glock. The bag across his shoulder, Tom walked over to his trophy wall and took down a black baseball cap awarded to the favored few by one of the software giants. When he pulled it on, the mirrored section of the cabinet assured him that, yes, the brim would keep the security cameras off his face when he drove through the gates of the Atcheson Enterprises loading docks. Just as the sweatshirt would make him invisible to the people working there. Who would think twice about a man confidently taking a van key from the board? And even if they did recognize him, who there would stop Tom Atcheson from driving away in one of his own vans?

Tom dribbled the remaining $9,500 of booze into the drive of his computer, then tipped the last half-inch of the whisky down his throat. He rubbed his thumb over the glass's engraved surface — how appropriate, to think that he'd bought these for his wife — then tossed it into the fireplace, feeling the music of two-hundred-year-old crystal disintegrating against brick.

Never, ever let people screw you into a corner, Tom thought, and went out to claim back a portion of what the world had taken from him.

(*EIGHT*) Gordon wrenched the boy a step further away (*NINE*) from the vulnerable doors (*TEN*). The boy's harsh breaths drowned out the siren, continuing through the next pause — a shorter one, this time. When the slams resumed, they punched at the door then went high to shatter the clerestory windows: the bigger gun now.

"Why d'you think it's your father?"

"Because of the Bodyguard."

"Your father has a *bodyguard*?"

"Stepfather. It's a kind of gun. It's *my* gun."

"The Smith and Wesson 380?"

"Yeah. He keeps it and the Glock in the gun safe at home. The rifle's at the shooting range. Usually."

"What kind of Glock?"

"Um, the 40."

"Fifteen plus one. Ten in the other."

For the first time, Brendan's attention left

the quad doors as he pulled away to look at the face inches from his own. "How do you —"

Gordon traded his wrestler's hold for a hard grasp of the boy's upper arm with one hand and the back of his belt with the other, forcing his captive toward the janitor's office. "Why would your father shoot up the school?"

"I did something to piss him off."

"That's speaking mildly. Brendan, I imagine it's just a gun that sounds like yours."

"Both guns? I tell you, he's fucking *psycho.*"

"Doesn't matter — whoever it is, the police will get him. At least he doesn't have a rifle."

"He might."

"If he did, there wouldn't be any doors left." If he did, Mina would be dead. This time, Brendan let himself be propelled all the way back to the janitor's room.

There was no way Linda could get her arms around all twenty-eight kids, but she tried. They were in the far corner of the room, her back to the shooter, and she was doing her best to shelter them behind her outstretched arms. Each time the gun went off, a shudder ran through all of them, including her.

Sofia was hard against Linda's right knee, huddled behind an overturned desk. Linda could feel the girl quivering. She glanced back at the intent lunatic, then whispered to get her attention. "Sofia? Sofia, look at me, Sofia."

Repetition of her name brought the girl's eyes up, white-rimmed and moments away from cracking — and if one gave way to panic, the others would follow. Linda put on her calmest mask, used her steadiest voice. "Sofia, I need you to listen to me. I need your help, Sofia. Can you do something for me?"

The trembling localized into a nod and a shaky breath. Linda gave her a reassuring smile, trying not to wince at the blow of another round. "My cellphone is in my jacket pocket," she whispered. "Right next to your knee. If I try and use it, he'll see me, but you're behind the desk from him. He won't see you. Can you get it out for me, honey?"

The girl's eyes darted toward the door, but after a few seconds, her hand crept out. Linda shifted to keep the hang of her jacket in the way, and felt the tug as the girl lifted the phone from her pocket.

"Good girl," she whispered. "The sound is off, so don't worry. Turn the phone on. The password's 1987. Got it?" In the corner of her eye, she saw the girl nod. "And kids, don't anyone look at Sofia, okay? Thanks. Honey, open the messages and find Gordon, then type this for me: *Tom Atcheson with two or three guns room B18, nobody hurt here are you all okay?*"

But Sofia's fingers were not moving. Linda's eyes flicked down to see what was wrong.

"There's a text." The girl bent to read it. "From . . ." Her whisper gave way to a ragged intake of breath.

"What?" Linda risked a quick glance over her shoulder. *"What is it?"*

"Mina. He shot Mina!"

TOM

He hadn't expected it to feel so damned *good*. Who'd have thought that blowing the shit out of a concrete wall and reducing some doors to tatters would be so incredibly satisfying? And if he happened to hit some bystanders — who the hell cared?

He emptied the last round of the Bodyguard at the battered door, then tossed the weapon aside. Too light, too small a magazine, he'd only brought it as a message.

The bag at his foot held six loaded 15-round magazines for the Glock and enough boxed bullets to keep him here until dark. But surely even San Felipe's hick police department would know by now that something was going on. Time to get serious. Time to do what he'd come for.

He draped the gym bag's long strap across his chest and stepped into the quad, holding out the Glock. The cop was still, no need to pay any more attention there, so he kept firing at the door, empty brass spitting out with every shot. BLAM (*ting*) and a step. The Glock's punch was an incredible rush — forbidden, visceral, unambiguous. *Fucking orgasmic, you might call it.* He fired merrily at the clerestory windows, giggling with exultation as he pictured the atrium of Atcheson Enterprises disintegrating under the assault. BLAM (*ting*) step. (Glass raining down; employees fleeing.)

BLAM (*ting*) step. (Closing in on the Board Room now, rather than a barren scatter of picnic tables.) BLAM (*ting*) step. (That lawyer, the first to go.) The rhythm was like dancing (BLAM [*ting*] step). Like the waltz he'd done at his wedding to the greedy bitch, only far, (BLAM [*ting*] step), far more satisfying.

BRENDAN

Sir had gone back to the Glock, ripping away at the doors again. The sound was different, though it took Brendan half a dozen shots (*EIGHT;* pause; *NINE*) before he could be sure. Louder.

The Glock (*TEN*) was coming at them.

NICK

Nick had never heard anything like it, never imagined that gunshots could be so incredibly loud and hard and oh god it was *terrifying* — nothing like a TV show, just noise and *make-it-stop* and the stink of scared kids. And blood — no! He couldn't go into that room, he kept thinking it was Bee there so he hung back, just outside the door, keeping everyone between him and Mina, which was cowardly but he'd think about that later.

Only two people seemed anywhere near calm — and Mr. Kendrick wasn't one of them, though Nick would have thought nothing would shake the old guy. Every time he looked at Mina, Nick could feel him sort of shudder, like he was seeing his own kid.

Tío, on the other hand, just stood there like he was waiting for things to finish so he could get out his mop. The other calm one was Brendan. The tall kid was standing just inside the office now, with Mr. Kendrick's arm propped against the door frame, blocking him in. Brendan seemed to have accepted that he was stuck there.

Nick thought the eighth-grader's calmness was a little strange, since he was pretty sure Brendan liked Mina a lot. But Nick could see the side of his face, and it looked more like he was planning a move on the court instead of watching his girlfriend bleed to death. To say nothing of hearing a gun getting louder and louder with every shot, closer and closer.

Then something changed, as if the sound track in a movie shifted — or someone threw open a window in a hot attic. Startled, Nick raised his head, unsure where the change came from — and looked directly into Brendan's eyes. The older boy had turned, just a bit, to look right at him — at *him*, Nick Clarkson, eye to eye like they were equals. Nick blinked, unsure, but there was a world of meaning coming across the short distance, a lengthy conversation in a silent moment. Brendan held Nick's gaze a moment longer, then his eyebrow lifted, a tiny motion with a huge question.

Are you with me?

Six months ago — before Bee, certainly — Nick would've backed away from it. But

Nick had learned from failing Bee, and this new Nick didn't hesitate — didn't even think about it, really. He dipped and raised his chin a fraction. Brendan's gaze went warm, and his quick flick of the eyes sideways at Mr. Kendrick provided the instruction. His hand came up in front of his chest, out of Mr. Kendrick's sight: four fingers, stretched out against his shirt. Four. Three. Two. One —

Brendan dropped and ducked under the Englishman's braced arm, a move he'd done a thousand times on the basketball court. The man whirled, reached out, grabbed — only to have Nick fling himself forward with all his strength, directly into the man's off-balance form, bringing him down in a tangle of clothing and shouts and heavy adult limbs.

LINDA

Catastrophe happened in slow motion. Linda's first warning was the sound of her phone hitting the floor. It landed face up —

Mina shot need ambulance

— but when she blinked, Sofia was already on the move, her young body rising off the ground on those muscular legs, eyes fixed on the door as despair and fury took over: *NO!* Linda reached up but Sofia just stormed through her, knocking her aside (*distant pain*) with the blow of a knee and the texture of denim against Linda's fingertips.

But it was the noise coming from Sofia that roused the others — *nononono,* more a primitive growl than anything resembling words, guttural and compelling and louder with her every step. The cry yanked Chaco Cabrera like a leash. Smaller, younger, farther away from the door — but the boy

561

was in motion before Sofia was halfway across the room.

By the time Linda gained her feet, the room was filled with kids racing for the open door, and all their principal could do was stumble after them, arms outstretched, moaning, "Stay, oh, stay here!"

BRENDAN

Brendan dove behind the folded-up table
(*THIRTEEN*). Heard the struggle behind
him (*FOURTEEN*). Ripped at the lock
mechanism on the doors.

GORDON

Jesus Christ, nervy Nick had panicked — just as Gordon nearly had the older boy — and it was all he could do not to smash the little kid to the floor when their entwined bodies came down, but the frenzied boy whirled and struck out, getting in Gordon's way, almost as if he was *trying* to keep Gordon from

BRENDAN

Brendan (*FIFTEEN*) hit the doors like he was plowing the other team's guard up into the stands. He staggered as their weakened locks gave way, but if his body had learned one automatic response from all those hours on the court, it was that speed outplayed gravity every time. His legs thrust hard to keep him from going down, feet slapping the pavement, accelerating his long body up the quad. At the upper reaches of his vision he saw the Glock's magazine eject, saw it fall through the air, bouncing off the pavement as Sir's hand came out of the gym bag at his side, Sir's head down but he would look up in a second and he would see

Whoever the guy was it wasn't Angel or anyone Chaco knew which yeah surprised him but still it meant there was some pinche loco who thought he could walk in and start shooting up the school, the bullets just *inexorable* — Jesus! — which was nuts enough but then Sofia saw on the principal's cell that Mina Santos was hit and that set *her* off, and a person just couldn't let a girl like Sofia go after a guy with a gun all by herself he just couldn't so Chaco went too, or maybe there was less thinking than that maybe he just got up and went but anyway he was pounding along after those long (*gorgeous*) basketball player legs of hers and he was damned if he'd let a girl stand up for the school on her own especially *Sofia Rivas* so he tucked down his head and ran after her as hard as he could to the door and out it and

SOFIA

The man's back was to her out in the quad and Sofia was aware of *nothing* but the man's shoulders and the strap of gym bag across his leather jacket and the side of his face under the baseball cap as he looked down for something in the bag — but at the same time she was incredibly aware of everything in the universe, some part of her brain slowing down to register the beat of each footstep behind her and the approach of someone from the far side of the leather jacket and Sergeant Mendez on the ground with a stream of thick dark blood and screams coming from all over and a faraway siren and blue sky (— *a bird flying, slow* —) but the man's back was all she really *saw*, those shoulders and the left arm coming up with something from the gym bag like a grenade or a pipe bomb maybe? (*school shooting/pipe bombs*) but he was raising it up to his other hand or maybe to the gun in

that hand so yes it was bullets it was more
bullets and his back was six steps away now
and five and she could see the other person
coming it was Brendan and he was

BRENDAN

Pounding toward him, toward the hands slamming the magazine into the gun and the weapon came up and it would take Sir the time of two steps (*slapslap*) to raise the gun and half a step to pull the trigger and he couldn't *miss,* not at this distance, but Brendan only tucked in and put on more speed because even if he was dead, even if he was already dead when he crashed into Sir it might do some good, might open the Enemy up for his teammates to

GORDON

Go after Brendan, but after two seconds of not-wanting-to-hurt-the-kid Gordon realized that Nick actively *wanted* to get in his way, so he just moved, bellowing a command to "Get 'em into the office!"

The gun started up again as Gordon crashed out into the quad.

For an instant his eyes reported — not a man putting bullets into Brendan Atcheson, but a rugby scrum, a pileup of bodies with more pouring on from both directions.

He didn't stop moving, not even through that split second of confusion, but neither did the shooter, using his gun to bash at a girl who hung leech-like from his shoulder, her teeth bared in fury. A window shattered somewhere and figures converged and a uniformed cop lay on the ground, ten feet away, and Gordon began to shout at the top of his lungs, "Brendan, get them off, clear the way, *BRENDAN!*"

Somehow, his voice got through to the charging boy. At the last instant, Brendan's nimble feet veered a few degrees and those long arms came out, scooping the girl and another kid off the shooter's back and hauling them into the clear area beyond. With the weight off him, the shooter whirled and came upright, the gun swinging around to his son and the tall girl and short boy in Brendan's arms and behind them Linda with blood pouring from her nose —

And Gordon pulled the trigger of Olivia's weapon. Twice.

■ ■ ■ ■

CAREER DAY

After the End

■ ■ ■ ■

GORDON

Gordon and Tío stood in front of the school library watching the mass of uniforms seethe over B Quad. The first ambulance had left fast, four minutes earlier, rushing Mina to surgery. Now the second driver slammed his doors and trotted to the front. Lights began to pulse as it threaded its way through the picnic tables. At the access road, the sirens started up, moving slowly at first until the ambulance cleared the fast-arriving tide of panicking parents.

Instantly, the police closed in on the blood-smeared quad and started dropping evidence markers around the draped body of Tom Atcheson.

The *Clarion* reporter pointed her camera at it all.

Gordon handed Tío back his rag, stained now with the blood he'd got on his hands. He did not realize that he had taken a deep breath until the smaller man spoke.

"You saved the sergeant's life."

"No, her vest did that."

"Yet you did not hesitate to help her. Even though this will make a problem for you. Am I wrong?"

For a moment, Gordon played with the idea that Sergeant Mendez would be so grateful she'd overlook his sins; that her colleagues would set aside their innate suspicions . . . but no. If the *kiap* didn't get him, the news cameras would. "Yes, my friend, life is about to get complicated."

"Señor, I am familiar with the look of people who wish to disappear." He did not add, although Gordon heard it in his voice: *It is a look I have seen in the mirror.*

"Is that so."

"I am also familiar with how one must choose one's time with . . . with alacrity, I believe the word is. Now that the police have done their best for the sergeant, they will raise their heads to look for the man who picked up her gun. It may be that you are happy to speak with them, señor. Or it may be that you fear that speaking with them will limit your movements. That a delay may create further problems."

Gordon had his eyes on Linda, at the far end of the quad with Cass Henry, several students, and a lot of cops. The bridge of

Linda's nose wore a bandage, her bloody jacket lay discarded across a nearby table. She was speaking to a policeman, but most of her attention was on the kids: her right arm anchored a white-faced Brendan Atcheson close against her side, her left lay across the shoulders of Sofia Rivas, whose eyes were smudges of tear-stained mascara. On the bench at her knees sat Nick Clarkson, who had Dr. Henry's hand on one shoulder, and Chaco Cabrera, made a part of the circle by the intensity of her gaze.

But she was not simply comforting the kids: she was admiring them. As he stood there watching, the children had gone from weeping, shuddering figures to young people with straight backs and raised chins. By the time they went home with their rejoicing parents they'd be shaky, but she'd have gotten the first shy, proud smiles out of them.

Linda was going to blame this all on herself: Atcheson, the delay between the white van's arrival and the 911 calls, the blood of Olivia Mendez. And later, the fate of Gordon Hugh-Kendrick, whatever that ended up being.

Had it been a single shot, he might have got away with it. But that second round was his own cold choice, just to be certain. It was that second shot that would tip the balance, ushering him (politely!) into custody until questions could be asked, a more thorough search made, his past permitted to creep in . . .

He did not think they would arrest him, in the end. Hell, he'd probably be declared a bloody hero. But they'd keep him in custody just long enough for his face and name to hit the news, and TaylorCorp would be waiting for him when he walked out.

If that happened, Linda would never be the same.

"Señor." Tío's voice was low, and urgent.

"Sorry?"

"I am trying to tell you, *hermano,* about the field workers across the road. Those who lack documents will have gone by now. Of those who remain to give statements, one drives a small gray Toyota pickup truck. He has been most careless today, *entiende?* The door of his truck is unlocked, and the key is beneath the mat on the driver's side. Were this truck to drive away, it would not be noticed for some hours. Perhaps not even until the morning. However, soon — very soon — the wall around this school will close, making it impossible for a person to slip away."

Gordon stared down at the earnest brown

face. "Tío, you've been standing right here the whole time."

"That is true. But Señora Rodriguez? Ay, there is no controlling that woman — here and away, phone at her ear, busy as always. It is extraordinary what the Señora can achieve, given a few minutes."

Brown eyes held golden ones, and after a moment, Gordon's mouth twitched. He reached out to give the older man's shoulder a squeeze, in lieu of a handshake. But when he turned back toward Linda, he found her looking straight down the length of the quad at him. Framed by uniforms, surrounded by kids, blood on her cheek — and all she saw was him.

Gordon lifted one hand, two fingers raised in a gentle salute of apology and affection and finality.

And then he was gone.

FOUR MONTHS LATER (JUNE 10, GRADUATION DAY, 6:40 P.M.)
LINDA

The sun was low when Linda came through the kitchen door, arms filled with bouquets from the kids, groceries from the market, newspaper from the tube, and rubbish from the mailbox. Junk envelopes and flyers dribbled across the floor, but she reached the counter before the grocery bags followed them.

She left the door standing open, keys dangling, while she put away the frozen dinners and packaged salads, taking out the bottle of white wine in exchange.

This would be a two-glass night. Maybe even three.

The first couple of swallows were large, medicinal gulps. She made herself slow down after the third, resting the half-empty glass against her sunburnt forehead. Empty house, empty life. She should give in to cliché and adopt some cats.

Year one for Linda McDonald, at Guadalupe Middle School.

Graduations were always tough: hug your favorites goodbye, watch your failures walk into their futures. Wonder . . . Mina and Sofia were off to high school, sisters still. Mina was thin from three surgeries, and almost childlike with her face stripped of makeup — especially beside Sofia, who had grown more self-assured with every passing week. Brendan was gone already; he and his uncle were spending the summer in Europe. Nick and Chaco she'd have back in the fall, Carlos and Esme. Tío and Coach.

She was guardedly optimistic about Nick Clarkson. The boy was no longer quite so adamant in his belief that Bee Cuomo had stepped into the past, and the hashtag #speakforbee had gone two weeks with no new offense. Perhaps related to that, Cuomo had stopped harassing her on the phone. Olivia said he'd got sober, at least for the time.

The ache about Bee Cuomo would never go away, but there was a counterweight to the loss of a child now — or rather, two counterweights.

The first was physical: they'd found the artist who created the school's entrance mosaic, and talked him into doing a new one, with a child wearing pigtails and glasses as one of the central images.

The second was in the realm of ideas. Cass Henry was writing a book about the year at Guadalupe: how a school had saved itself. Not that the book would be about Bee Cuomo, exactly — there were sure to be charts and jargon and studies and endless interviews. But basically, the truth might be as simple as it was mysterious: that sometimes the smallest thing could show a community how to heal. How to take its shattered pieces and fit them together again into something new. Linda had given Cass the book's title — insisted on it, really. *Speak for Bee.*

Recently, though, evidence had surfaced to suggest that Bee's disappearance might have been by choice: a seller of antique jewelry (some of it stolen, which explained why the woman hadn't come forward on her own) admitted she'd bought an antique women's Rolex from the girl, two days before Halloween. Bee claimed it was her mother's — confirmed by Mr. Cuomo, who hadn't noticed it was missing — and the dealer had given her $600, along with an old necklace that caught the girl's eye.

When Olivia told her, Linda had very nearly asked if the necklace matched the one around Beatrice Weildman's neck in the historical museum photo — but she caught herself in time. There was nothing to joke about, when it came to Bee Cuomo.

This school year began with a friendship and ended in sacrifice. It was four months since Career Day went off the rails and into death and loss and loneliness. Three months since (following vehement school board debate) Guadalupe had reopened. Eleven weeks since Linda had overseen her school's celebration of the life of Beatrice Cuomo, with the heroes of Career Day given prominent place. And little more than a month since Linda realized Guadalupe had taken on a life of its own.

So it was something of an irony for Linda to look down at the *Clarion*'s headlines on the counter at her elbow:

ALVAREZ SENTENCING PHASE ENDS
Brother Arrested in Courtroom Threats

Olivia had phoned with the news that morning as Linda was dressing for graduation. The sergeant was chafing at not being permitted active duty yet, and began with the ritual question of whether Linda had heard from Gordon. The only faint benefit about the way Gordon had left was that Linda had never been forced to lie — not to

Olivia, nor the investigators, not even to those hard-faced men in suits who had come asking.

All she could tell them was that Gordon was gone, and she never expected to see him again. Even the hard-faced men could see it was only the painful truth.

When the wineglass was empty, she refilled it, sticking one of the frozen dinners in the microwave. The kitchen was going cool with the coastal evening fog, so she moved to collect her dangling keys and shut the door against the night. Walking back, she bent to retrieve the fallen mail. One piece lay just under the table — a postcard, with what she assumed was an ad for a travel agency or car dealership: a bright yellow jeep on a palm tree–lined beach.

The image brought a pained smile to Linda's face: a lanky Englishman in khaki shorts, swerving just such a car across a lonely highlands runway. Before throwing the ad into the recycling bin with the flyers, she flipped it over for an automatic glance at its back — and frowned.

Wouldn't this make a *great* car for a summer holiday?
Are you sure you aren't free the end of June, to join us?

Hope so — you could do with a holiday after the year you had!

Love, Beth

That didn't look like a woman's handwriting — far less that of a woman Linda hadn't heard from in decades. She checked that it was actually addressed to her — yes. Funny. The writing looked almost . . .

The rest of the mail fell to the floor. Two quick steps took Linda to the whatnot drawer, where she dug frantically through the tangle for the magnifying glass. By the last sunlight through the window, the letters of the card's cancellation stamp were remarkably — even suspiciously — crisp and clear.

The card had been posted in a small tourist town on the coast of Mexico, north of Puerto Vallarta.

The handwriting was Gordon's.

ACKNOWLEDGMENTS

Lockdown is a book I have been building for nearly twenty years. At its base are a series of short stories that, when they were first published, had no apparent connection. I, however, always knew these stories were linked. It did take me a while to see exactly how the characters' histories and secrets, strengths and fears fit into each other. But once the pieces came together, the pattern of the novel they were building toward became blazingly clear, and I began to write.

"Coming together" describes more than simply the making of the novel. *Lockdown* is a thriller set in a school under threat, but it is *about* the school's community, its weak points and skills, and the strength it can find when pressed to the brink. A story about how rescue comes from within, and how heroism may rise from the most unexpected direction.

A book, like a school, is built by its community. This one owes much to my friends at Penguin Random House, including two women with the patience of Tibetan lamas, Kate Miciak and Kim Hovey, and Kate's even more long-suffering right hand, Julia Maguire. Then there's Kelly Chian, whose brisk conquest of a manuscript resembling a typesetter's workshop hit by a tornado just boggles my mind. Alex Coumbis and Allison Schuster have the tricky and thankless tasks of nudging LRK across the map, while Carlos Beltrán makes sure what is on the shelf pleases the eye and tantalizes the mind, and Matt Schwartz bends the digital universe to his will. To them and the dozens of others who build books day in and day out, I give my eternal and heartfelt thanks.

As for the words themselves, some of them were given a push in the right direction by my friend, crime writer and basketball magnate S. J. Rozan (whose Bouchercon matches are a high point of that annual conference). Other words, and most of the ideas, were set into play by the hard-working teachers and staff of the various schools my own children attended on California's Central Coast.

Thank you all, for teaching me so much.

ABOUT THE AUTHOR

Laurie R. King is the *New York Times* bestselling author of fourteen Mary Russell mysteries, five contemporary novels featuring Kate Martinelli, the Stuyvesant & Grey novels *Touchstone* and *The Bones of Paris,* and the acclaimed *A Darker Place, Folly, Califia's Daughters* (written under the pen name Leigh Richards), and *Keeping Watch.* She lives in Northern California.

LaurieRKing.com
Facebook.com/LaurieRKing
Twitter: @LaurieRKing